John Preston is the arts editor and television critic of the *Sunday Telegraph*. He is the author of a travel book, *Touching the Moon*, and a novel, *Ghosting*. He lives in London.

Acclaim for *Ink*:

'Preston is not a run-of-the-mill writer and this is not a run-of-the-mill book . . . The obvious label to slap on the novel would be a black comedy, but I am not sure that does justice to its distinctive blend of surrealist slapstick and ingrained melancholy. Perhaps one day the word "Prestonesque" will enter the language and save us all a lot of trouble. For the moment, all one can report is that *Ink* is a delightful, hilarious novel which will make you wonder if anything in life matters'
David Robson, *Sunday Telegraph*

'Readability is not the only virtue that a novel may have; still, it's an important one and *Ink* rates highly on it . . . a teasing, mysterious whowozzit of a tale . . . The combination of readability and intricate plotting recalls Jonathan Coe . . . Preston's style is smooth and efficient and he's good at evoking a sense of place . . . an entertaining, dextrously written novel'
Independent on Sunday

'An excellent thriller lurks beneath the newsprint, and the journalistic setting proves to be a convenient vehicle . . . The plot is complex and captivating . . . a taut thriller'
The Times Literary Supplement

'Part mystery tale, part black comedy, it is a splendid fusion of two genres and lives up to the promise of his fictional début, *Ghosting* . . . A thrilling read, deftly plotted, full of twists and turns. The author has the ability to pull several proverbial rugs at once from under the reader's feet. Preston writes in limpid prose and his observations are sharp and vivid'
Literary Review

'John Preston is a mordantly satirical wit to die for. His second novel, *Ink*, is a lovely Chaplinesque farce set in Old Fleet Street, a daft remake of *Modern Times* for our recent Thatcher-Murdoch times, done both with a lot more jokes and a lot more post-Kafka angst . . . Sharp satire, absurdist relish and the elegiac desire for morality in a sordid world could hardly converge more satisfyingly'
Independent

'Preston provides an illuminating take on the face of news'
Harpers and Queen

'Intriguingly offbeat . . . extracting a good deal of sly humour from his subject'
Christina Koning, *The Times*

'A sharp exposé of the vacuity of television and an impressive evocation of the claustrophobia of its formative days'
Daniel Britten, *Daily Telegraph*

'Poignant and darkly comic . . . a briskly paced, tightly controlled novel, whose images especially of disentegration are deftly employed to reinforce the theme. An enjoyable satire of the world of television, it simultaneously builds into a frightening portrait of the dissolution of a personality, of a man both alienated from others and, more fatally, from himself . . . A funny, sad and disturbing novel'
Kate Hubbard, *The Spectator*

'An existential comedy; comic in the best sense – lugubrious, splenetic, askew, coaxing laughter out of the blackest desolation. Terrific'
Howard Jacobson

'Compelling . . . an astonishing first step as a novelist'
Michael Frayn

'A good novel . . . truly frightening'
Penelope Fitzgerald

'Mixes pathetic hilarity with a disturbing psycho darkness'
Observer

'Frightening, compelling and heart-wrenchingly funny'
Daily Express

'Enjoyable, unexpectedly chilling story of one man's rise to stardom during the early days of the BBC'
Marie Claire

'An extraordinary début, a tragicomedy so perfectly pitched that you knew your eyes were watering, but not why. The hero is a television celebrity painfully conscious of the emotional nullity behind the much-loved, much-imitated voice. His existential crisis is captured with humour and compassion'
Max Davidson, *Daily Telegraph*

Also by John Preston
TOUCHING THE MOON
GHOSTING

INK

John Preston

BLACK SWAN

INK
A BLACK SWAN BOOK : 0 552 99817 6

Originally published in Great Britain by Doubleday,
a division of Transworld Publishers

PRINTING HISTORY
Doubleday edition published 1999
Black Swan edition published 2000

1 3 5 7 9 10 8 6 4 2

Set in 11/12pt Melior by
Phoenix Typesetting, Ilkley, West Yorkshire.

Black Swan Books are published by Transworld Publishers,
61–63 Uxbridge Road, London W5 5SA,
a division of The Random House Group Ltd,
in Australia by Random House Australia (Pty) Ltd,
20 Alfred Street, Milsons Point, Sydney, NSW 2061, Australia,
in New Zealand by Random House New Zealand Ltd,
18 Poland Road, Glenfield, Auckland 10, New Zealand
and in South Africa by Random House (Pty) Ltd,
Endulini, 5a Jubilee Road, Parktown 2193, South Africa.

Reproduced, printed and bound in Great Britain by
Clays Ltd, St Ives plc.

To Maria

'The man must have a rare recipe for melancholy, who can be dull in Fleet Street.'

CHARLES LAMB, 1802

Prologue

A pale froth rose above the rooftops, merging into the darkness. The city lay spread all around – the office blocks wrapped in bands of light, the streets a tangle of deep gulleys glowing orange from the sodium lamps, the tarmac on the roads stained white by the salt that had been spread earlier. Below was the river, a broad, black stain that swept under bridges and between banks crammed with concrete and glass. On its surface the cluster of tall towers stood reflected, all turned on their heads and wavering in the water.

The streets were quite empty. There were no pedestrians about, no cars either. But up here on the roof there were figures. All of them motionless, dusted with frost and turning sightless eyes towards the river. Helmeted warriors riding through the night sky in stone chariots, with heads flung back and spears held aloft; gargoyles with mouths fastened around frozen overflow pipes; heraldic beasts and hunting dogs twisting their necks up into the darkness.

A goods train pulled out of Cannon Street Station, trailing a long smudge of smoke. The sound of the wagons clanking and colliding came across the water. As the noise died away, a man made his way onto the bridge below. He was walking with difficulty; his shoulders were hunched and every few paces he would stagger, almost trip up, then right himself and steady his step. He looked as if he was battling against a buffeting gale which constantly threatened to blow him backwards.

Out on the bridge the wind was even colder. The man walked on, past the stone sentry boxes with their lifebelts hung up inside, until he became aware of a sudden rush of light bursting over his right shoulder. He turned round and there was the dome of St Paul's, vast and stark against the black sky, as if some great white sun was flaring behind it. He shrank from such exposure, such scrutiny, stopping and retracing his steps until the dome sank back out of sight.

Still there was no-one about. He put his hands on the metal balustrade and looked at his fingers, ridged and ink-stained. He felt the metal slowly warm to his touch, and wondered how far on either side of him this warmth extended before it died away completely. The water churned and folded itself around the piles at the foot of the bridge. As he stared out across the river rushing below, he thought how each expanse of water that his eye fixed upon seemed to have a character of its own. Some agitated, ruffled, forever scurrying out of the light. Others more oafish, slowed down by the cold, as thick and black as lumps of tar.

He bent down with his back against the balustrade and undid his shoelaces. First he dropped one shoe over the side, then the other. He turned away, not wanting to watch them disappear, yet waiting for the splash as they hit the surface. But there was nothing. No sound at all. He turned back and gazed down at the water. His shoes had disappeared, been swallowed up in the darkness. He took off his overcoat, then his sweater, and folded them on top of the balustrade.

As he stood there, shoeless, he heard footsteps coming towards him. At first he saw no-one. But then the sound of the steps seemed to hitch themselves to a shape. Another man, not hurrying, but weaving from side to side, dressed in a thin coat that swirled about him, caught by the wind.

A drunk, thought the man on the bridge, relieved. It's only a drunk. The cold coming up through his shoeless feet was intense. It was this as much as anything else that made the man clamber onto the balustrade, pulling himself up with his arms, then swinging his legs over until he was sitting there, swaying, holding on. As he swung himself round, he realized that he must have instinctively leant back, to stop himself from falling. And it was this that made him doubt himself for the first time, question his resolve.

He could see the drunk quite clearly now, head down, blundering about from one side of the road to the other. But as he watched, the man lifted his head and saw him. As he did so, he came abruptly, almost neatly, to a halt. Then he threw up his arms and started to shout. None of his words made any sense. They seemed to disintegrate as soon as they were out of his mouth, dark shredded things flying off into the night.

The man sitting on the balustrade looked down at the water. Although he couldn't say why, he found something extraordinarily comforting about it – enveloping and eradicating. More than anything else he wanted to fall into the darkest depths, to feel the water wrap itself around him. To sink deeper and deeper, down into black alluvial mud and rest there for ever. It seemed as if all the things he most dreaded would vanish there. No fears, no troubles. All alone, with nothing to disturb him. Nothing to cause him pain.

The drunk was rushing forward again, his coat billowing out, arms still extended, hands scraping the air. The man on the balustrade sat and watched him coming closer. But now he saw the drunk was no longer alone. Behind him, reaching back almost to the river bank, was this procession of stone figures. A long, grey line of grotesques. All stained and blackened, they had descended from the rooftops and were stepping out to witness his end. Spilling off the frosted pavements and into the road.

As they shuffled stiffly along, there was this steady

13

scraping sound of stone upon stone. This slow, grinding line of figures. It sounded as if there were horns blaring. Trumpets as well as horns, like some medieval pageant. Streams of air being forced through cracked cheeks. A tremendous din splitting the night air.

The drunk was almost upon him now, still running, his chin jutting forward, this long blaring column stretching behind. And for a moment the drunk seemed about to reach out, to grab onto him and hold him back. But then the man on the balustrade bent forward, and with the smallest of kicks he launched himself out on a slow, elongated glide into the river below.

Part 1

'We enter Fleet Street, which takes its name from the once rapid and clear, but now fearfully polluted, river Fleet, which has its source far away in the breezy heights of Hampstead, and flows through the valley where Faringdon Street now is. Originally, in 1218, it was called the "River of Wells", being fed by the clear springs now known as Sadler's Wells, Bagnigge Wells, and the Clerk's Well or Clerkenwell, and it was navigable for a short distance. The river was ruined as the town extended westwards. In 1765 the stream was arched over, and since then it has sunk to the level of being recognized as the most important sewer – the Cloaca Maxima – of London.'

AUGUSTUS HARE, *WALKS IN LONDON*, 1901

Chapter One

These places the journalists liked to drink in, these pubs and bars, most of them were carefully preserved leftovers from the eighteenth century. The same darkened wood, dim puddles of light, cracked benches and erupting chairs. The same tattered mementos on the shelves, empty bird-cages and heaps of sawdust on the floors. It was true that the bar staff now tended to be Australians, who wore nylon shirts printed with the name of whichever brewery owned the place. The logs in the fires were made of concrete. There were plastic signs hanging above the bar inviting guests to 'Try Our Guest Lagers'. For all that, though, an element of tradition still prevailed.

Groups of tourists came in to study the laminated menus with their quaint spelling and eat the renowned Pepys pies and look on as the journalists talked and drank and showed off. Everyone worked hard to preserve this archaic air. It was in all their interests. The tourists liked to believe they were witnessing a piece of living history, a succession of tableaux vivants being played out before them. Meanwhile, the bars played profitably on their history and their resistance to any but the most pressing forms of change.

Now that the 1980s were almost over, a nostalgia boom was under way. With so much of the past being swept away, people had begun to hanker after it. Places were springing up – ersatz dives and taprooms. They came furnished with carefully assembled bits of old junk, their ceilings already stained with imitation tobacco smoke. But here the junk was real; this was the genuine article. And so, too, the journalists concluded, were they. They took pride in preserving these ancient customs, keeping them alive, seeing themselves as living embodiments of otherwise vanished traditions, even though little, in either their conversation or appearance, gave them any reason to do so.

It was lunchtime. Six journalists were sitting together at a table. Two of them were vying for everyone else's attention. One of them was broadly built with an air of immense self-satisfaction. When he leant forward his trousers stretched across the tops of his thighs and broke into numerous little creases down the seams. He appeared to take pleasure in interrupting the other man, who was dark and anguished-looking, and trying, with difficulty, to maintain his composure. The second man looked uneasily from side to side, as if expecting another interruption, before beginning again.

'Last night Scaife is in the pub. He has a few drinks. Sits by himself reading the paper – nothing unusual. Then he goes back up to the bar, presumably for another drink. All right, Cliff?'

'Fine so far. Please continue.'

'This time, though, something does happen. It seems as though the barman asked him to settle his account before he'd serve him. You know Scaife likes to run up quite a slate – and he's not the most punctual of payers either. Anyway, next thing, Scaife goes berserk. Fists start flying. Glasses shatter. Arms and legs thrash all over the place. It took four of them to get him under control. Finally they managed to carry him outside.'

'And that's it?'

'Hold on.'

'I can't see what all the fuss is about. Can you?'

'But I haven't finished yet.' The anguished-looking man's voice rose indignantly.

'Oh, do excuse me, Julian. I thought you had.'

'I was only taking a breath.'

'Well, is that it, or not?'

'That was it, yes,' Julian said. 'Until the police arrived.'

'Police? What were they doing there?'

'The police were there because of the bomb.'

'Bomb? Bomb?'

The larger man looked around in surprise.

'Exactly. Thank you. Shall I go on?'

'As you wish,' said Cliff.

'The police were there because of the bomb. They came in and said they'd had a call that there was a bomb in the pub. Everyone had to evacuate immediately. Then they searched the place, but they didn't find anything.'

'So what's that got to do with Scaife? Don't tell me . . . No, go on. Tell me.'

'About an hour later Scaife was arrested. They found him in the phone box round the corner. He was lying there on the floor. Passed out with the phone still in his hand.'

'Christ,' said Cliff. 'What is that boy playing at?' He sounded genuinely angry, as if one of his charges had let him down.

'We all have our occasional lapses, Cliff.'

'Telling the police he's planted a bomb? That's hardly an occasional lapse – not in my book anyway. That's a major fucking misdemeanour.'

'I haven't finished yet,' said Julian.

'You mean there's more?'

'There is more, yes. If you'd like to hear it?'

Cliff waved his hand indifferently.

'Right,' said Julian. 'So they arrest him. At least, they try to. But you can't arrest someone if they're unconscious. You've got to wait for them to come round. So they take him off to the station anyway and lock him up for a while with another drunk. When he wakes up the two of them take one look at each other and immediately start fighting again.

'So they separate them and put Scaife in a cell on his

19

own. By this time though he's calmer. All that exercise must have sobered him up. Anyway, he starts waving his press pass about, telling them how it's all been a terrible misunderstanding. Claiming it was all just an exercise to see how alert the police were. The upshot is they let him go.'

'Let him go? That's outrageous. Let him go? But if they let him go, Julian, where is he now?'

'That's what I've been trying to tell you. He's disappeared.'

'Who says he's disappeared?'

'I fucking say so. OK? I fucking say so.'

'All right, Jules. Calm down. I don't know why you always get into such a state.'

'Because you drive me to distraction, Cliff, that's why.'

'You can't explain anything properly. You're always shooting off on tangents, getting yourself all worked up. And then your rhythm goes, and no-one can understand what you're saying.'

'He's not at home,' said Julian, very deliberately. 'I tried earlier. Obviously he didn't turn up for work this morning. I even tried the hospitals. He wasn't there either.'

'Hold on, when did this happen?'

'Friday night.'

'But that's nearly three days ago.'

'Ah, he'll turn up,' said one of the other journalists confidently. His name was Johnny Todd and he was one of the paper's gossip columnists. He wore a tweed suit and looked rather like an effete Home Counties solicitor. Everything about him was carefully calculated, from his breathless manner to his habit of opening his eyes wide with astonishment whenever anyone said anything remotely shocking, as if he was an innocent in such company.

'Of course he'll turn up,' said Cliff. 'He's just attention seeking.'

'Attention seeking, Cliffy? How can he be attention seeking if no-one knows where he is?'

'No,' said Cliff. 'He'll turn up.'

'Poor old Scaife.'

'"Poor old Scaife"? What are you talking about? If you ask me he's brought all this on himself. Yes. No. Excuse me, he has—'

'Be fair, Cliff. He's been through a lot lately. All that stuff with his wife. It can't have been easy, finding them together like that.'

'Who was she with?'

'The man who ran the local off-licence.'

'Ooh,' said Johnny Todd, wincing in an exaggerated sort of way.

'Exactly, I think that's what hurt Scaife the most. After all the business he'd brought him, to go and do something like that, steal a man's wife.'

'And he's been sleeping under his desk,' said Julian.

'Scaife has? I never knew that.'

'He tried to cover it up. I saw this blanket there. When I asked him what it was for, he said it had been so cold he'd had it on his lap.'

'Battersby's been gunning for him too,' said Johnny Todd. 'Apparently he threatened to send him downstairs.'

'What for?'

'To do the Queen Mother.'

'Really? No wonder he lost his rag then.'

'What do you think about Scaife, Bobbie?' asked Cliff.

He turned to his left. Sitting next to him was a small figure with faded red hair and a voice that sounded as if it had been strained through gravel.

'Scaife's a silly fucker,' said Bobbie in a thick Scottish accent.

Cliff nodded. 'Thank you, Bobbie. Succinct as ever.'

Alongside Bobbie was Industrial Gavin. He too was believed to be Scottish, but since he never spoke it was difficult to tell.

'I dare say Gavin wouldn't quibble with that,' said Cliff. 'And how about you, Hugh?

'Hughie? Hello?'

A slim, brown-haired man looked up. So far he had

taken little part in the conversation, apparently being pre-occupied with concerns of his own.

'Perhaps Scaife is a more sensitive man than he appears to be,' he said.

The shock this remark prompted was considerable.

'Sensitive, Hughie? How do you mean?'

'You know, Cliff. Sensitive – it's when you feel things deeply.'

'I know what it fucking means. Scaife's not sensitive.'

'How would you know?'

'What are you implying? I'm sensitive – I bloody am.'

'No, Cliff. Be fair. You're touchy and full of yourself. There's a big difference.'

'Fuck you. Who says I'm touchy? I'm not as touchy as Julian.'

'No-one's as touchy as Julian.'

'That's true enough. Anyway, I'm not touchy – I'm sensitive. There's a difference. It's just that I don't allow myself to give into it. And you know why I don't allow myself to give into it?'

'Because you're a realist, Cliff.'

'Because I'm a realist. Yes, quite right. Shall we go?'

Outside the sun was already starting to go down, sending long, low rays along Fleet Street, across Ludgate Circus and up towards St Paul's. There was an odd, coppery glint to the light, as if candles were burning in all the windows of the surrounding buildings. Hugh thought he had never seen anything so beautiful in his life. To his embarrassment he felt his eyes brimming with tears. A good deal of that was drink, of course. He knew he shouldn't drink at lunchtime. It soothed him, but at the same time it clouded his mind. And afterwards, when the effects had worn off, it left him feeling muddled and more prone to self-pity than usual.

They made their way down the street to a huge black-and-chrome building. On its polished walls were reflected thin, wavering versions of the buildings around, all cast in the same orange glow. Their shadows stretched out before them. Cliff led the way, striding out, shoulders forward, grey thumbs hooked over his jacket pockets. Next came Julian, with his peculiar undulating walk, as if he was forever trying to twist himself into different shapes. He was followed by Hugh, then Johnny Todd, Bobbie and Industrial Gavin.

In the reception area two men in uniform with pieces of braid on their shoulders stood behind a marble-topped counter. On the wall, beaten out in different types of metal, was a mural portraying the triumph of Truth over Falsehood. Truth stood, head back, hair flying, in a long tin tunic, while Falsehood writhed in agony at her feet.

They caught the lift up to the second floor. Outside the lift, lights which were hidden behind chrome conch shells were mounted on walls of biscuit-coloured marble. They might have been in a hotel, or some peculiarly old-fashioned department store. But once beyond a set of double doors to their right, the scene changed dramatically. Here the ceilings were lower, the paint discoloured, the atmosphere far more shabby. Three narrow, darkened corridors stretched out before them in different directions. It had taken Hugh a long time to work out that the right-hand corridor and the central one eventually met up. He had no idea where the left-hand corridor went.

They walked on, past the vending machines and small brown cubby holes where sickly looking men pored over enormous ledgers, following the trail of spilt coffee across the carpet tiles, until at last the corridor opened out into an enormous low-ceilinged room. This was the newspaper office.

Even after all these years, Hugh had difficulty believing that anyone still worked in such conditions. The room was like some mothballed relic from another age. It was packed with row upon row of grey, metal desks where journalists sat, typing away. The noise never abated – the smack of typewriter keys against the thin, carboned leaves of copy paper – a constant roll of snare drums. This was punctuated

23

by a peal of shrill pings, like bicycle bells, whenever a typewriter carriage hit the end of a line.

The view through the windows was so obscured by dirt that even familiar London landmarks took on a strange aspect, their shapes smudged and distorted beneath a vast sooty blanket. Instead, there was a vague jumble of domes, spires and office blocks. Seen from inside, the sky never lightened; it was difficult to work out where the sky ended and the buildings began. Everything blended into the same grey murk. Often Hugh found it hard to get his bearings, to tell which way he was facing.

He could see one of the copy boys, Darren, pushing his trolley, handing round polystyrene cups of tea. Darren was a sour boy with the beginnings of a moustache on his upper lip, who wore his sweater tucked into his trousers. For reasons Hugh couldn't understand, Darren had taken against him. Until recently, he'd brought him tea along with everyone else, but then one day he'd stopped. When Hugh had tried to ask why, Darren just ignored him. Hugh found this baffling, as well as upsetting – to have caused offence without knowing why. He'd examined his behaviour to see if he could recall anything he might have done, any inadvertent remark, but had come up with nothing. Nonetheless, Darren continued to behave as if an apology was due, showing no signs of emerging from this prolonged, brittle sulk.

Hugh pretended not to notice as cups were set down on all the adjoining desks. Two of the secretaries, Joy and Vivien, were standing in one of the aisles that ran between the desks. Joy appeared to be lecturing Vivien; she was leaning forward and talking animatedly, stabbing the air with her finger every so often. Hugh could see the long tendons running up the back of Joy's legs, standing out as she leant forward. Vivien listened, shoulders slumped, responding. A curtain of black hair fell across her face.

When she saw him, Joy broke off and waved. She was always going on about how the three of them should spend an evening together. Hugh liked Joy – as well as having good legs, she was lively and good company – but even so, he wasn't sure about this idea and had made no effort to encourage it. Vivien, too, turned to look at him, but failed to react as usual.

Hugh sat at his desk and contrived to look busy. This entailed more effort than he might have thought, but he was getting used to it. More than three weeks had passed since he'd last written a piece. That had taken him all night to finish – sitting up at home, scrabbling for the words, trying to force them into some sort of comprehensible order. They didn't want to go. Not any more. All the fluency, the ease with which he'd once written, had just slipped away. He seemed to have become physically incapable of putting one word in front of another. They stayed where they were, as heavy and hard to shift as boulders.

It wasn't as though the kind of pieces Hugh wrote required any style. Far from it, the tiniest personal imprint was enough to distinguish them from anyone else's. But even this – this faint, spidery proof of identity – had disappeared. What had gone wrong? He had no idea. All he could be sure of was that various things had given out at around the same time. It felt – and he scarcely dared admit this to himself – as if his system was closing down involuntarily, packing up around him.

His curiosity had been the first to go. He found that he no longer had any interest in finding anything out. Those quests for information that he'd once pursued so keenly, so doggedly, suddenly struck him as futile. Why shouldn't people be allowed to keep their secrets, he asked himself. Free from interference, safe from exposure. Just as he would have been horrified by the idea of anyone prying too closely into his own private life, so he became increasingly loath to root about in anyone else's. Not that he had any shameful secrets; rather it was the absence of them, this dreadful lack of iniquity, that he wanted to conceal. There was, he feared, nothing in his life to excite the interest of the most undemanding gossip.

This unwillingness to pry had already led to a number

25

of awkward scenes. When he was investigating a story, he no longer quizzed anyone about their business dealings, their sexual misdeeds, their general moral turpitude. Instead he found himself apologizing, backing off, assuring them that it wasn't any of his business. Inevitably this prompted astonishment, even affront; they couldn't get over his lack of interest.

It wasn't natural, not for a journalist. Newspapers thrived on mysteries, they pulled them apart and laid them bare. Yet there seemed so little mystery left in the world that Hugh was anxious to hang on to as much as possible. And having got this far, it was a simple step to a much bigger question: What right did the public have to know anything? It certainly didn't seem to do them any good. There were arguments to muster here, he knew that – important questions to do with liberty, accountability and all those sorts of things. But whatever they were, he'd quite forgotten them.

Soon after his curiosity gave out, his confidence followed. It just stole away, deserted him. Surely that's it, he thought. There can't be anything else left. But he was wrong. Last of all his concentration went. For years he'd been oblivious to the clamour around him, but now it seemed to crowd in on him – the roll of the drums, the ping of the carriage bells – invading his thoughts and turning them to pap.

The only thing he could do was try to hide all this for as long as possible. Hide it and hope that he might recover. But the trouble was that people already knew. Of course no-one had said anything. Indeed, they'd all been very decent, that was what gave it away. Unused to behaving so tactfully, their efforts stood out horribly. They steered clear of him as if he was grief-stricken, or suffering from some contagious disease. And perhaps he was. Perhaps that was what they were frightened of. They might come down with it too, and the whole office would be paralysed with indifference.

No-one asked him to do anything any more. Or rather,

the jobs they gave him were as undemanding as possible, jobs that only a few months ago he would have thought of as way beneath him. Hugh wasn't sure how much longer this could continue. Already the attitude of the news editor, Battersby, was changing. Hugh had noticed that he had a new look on his face whenever he addressed him. To begin with he'd thought this might be some new and unfamiliar expression of concern. It had taken him a while to realize it was contempt.

There was a message on Hugh's desk, a piece of paper taped to the top of his typewriter. He'd been sitting there for several minutes before he'd noticed it. The note was from the paper's in-house lawyer, asking him to come to his office as soon as possible. He stared at it, then reluctantly got to his feet. The door of the lawyer's office was open. A man and woman, both elderly, stood with their backs to him. They leant towards one another, their shoulders almost touching.

The lawyer was behind them, facing the door, holding a rolled-up piece of paper. He was a small man with a clipped grey beard and a fawning manner who worked as a conjuror in his spare time. When he saw Hugh he looked relieved and beckoned him in with the roll of paper.

'Mr and Mrs Brand are the winners of our latest competition,' he announced.

'Ah,' said Hugh. 'Congratulations.'

The couple nodded warily at him. The newspaper had a tradition of offering worthless competition prizes. Once these had been keenly contested; people took part for the fun of it and the pleasure of seeing their picture in the paper. But now they couldn't be bothered, and those who did make the effort usually ended up regretting it. The lawyer presented the roll of paper to the woman, giving a little bow as he did so. She took it and turned it over in her hands. It was tied together with ribbon. Several pieces of sealing wax dropped on the floor.

'It gives me great pleasure to invest you with the title of Lord and Lady of the Foreshore,' said the lawyer. 'A courtesy title, as I was just making clear, conferring theoretical domain over a small stretch of the Essex coastline.'

'At low tide,' said the woman.

'Only at low tide, that's quite right. I'm sorry if you found the wording in any way ambiguous.'

The woman shook her head. Her husband blinked and stared at the floor.

'But what are we supposed to do there?' he asked.

'Do there?' The lawyer sounded nonplussed. 'I don't know. Paddle about, in a proprietorial manner, of course. Ha ha. What else do people do on beaches, Hugh?'

Hugh thought. It had been years since he'd been to the seaside.

'Dig for clams?' he said.

'Yes,' said the lawyer doubtfully. 'I suppose you could do that.'

There was a further pause.

The lawyer rubbed his hands. 'Excellent,' he said. Then he showed the couple to the door and called for one of the copy boys to show them back downstairs.

Once they'd gone, he said, 'Sit ye down, Hugh. Sit ye down.'

When they were both seated the lawyer gave a sorrowful smile. 'People expect so much, don't they? They're never satisfied.' He sighed. 'Sometimes it really shakes your faith in human nature.'

Together they sat in silence for a few moments and pondered upon ingratitude. Then they moved on to the matters still outstanding from Hugh's legal case. A couple of months before Hugh had written a piece that had resulted in a libel action. It had only been a minor incident. A very minor incident. Nonetheless, there had been unpleasant consequences.

He'd been asked to write a profile of a man who had just been put in charge of education in one of the larger London boroughs. The education correspondent was away and Hugh had been asked to fill in. Knowing nothing whatsoever about the subject, he'd duly set to, but the pressure of

28

the deadline and his own torpid pace had meant that there had only been time to make a couple of phone calls and to skim through the few library cuttings.

Casting about for details to flesh out the man's unrelentingly colourless life, Hugh had come upon the fact that he'd been arrested several years earlier for disconnecting the brake cable on his wife's car. Gratefully, he stuck it in. The piece, however, turned out to have been misfiled and referred to someone else with the same name. Of course it was an innocent mistake and the fault was not all his, yet there was no doubt he should have checked it first. For a time Hugh wondered if his troubles hadn't perhaps dated from this moment. But the timings didn't work out, he realized. Something had been going on beforehand, the backsliding was already well under way.

The man's lawyers were prepared to settle if they received a printed apology, along with a donation to a charity of the plaintiff's choosing. All these points were discussed without reference to Hugh's culpability. He felt grateful for this, but assumed it had less to do with any wish to spare him embarrassment than with the lawyer's disinterest in allocating blame.

Then the lawyer said, 'Have you seen Scaife?'

'Scaife?'

'Mmm.'

'When?'

'Oh, recently,' said the lawyer. 'Today?'

'Today? I can't remember,' said Hugh.

The lawyer seemed unsure how to proceed. 'You haven't seen him today?' he repeated.

'Not to talk to. Why?'

'Oh, no reason really. Nothing important.'

When Hugh got back to his desk he saw Darren making another round with his trolley. He felt like some tea; he was starting to get a dry mouth. He could have gone to the vending machine, but the tea from there had an odd yellow scum on the surface which looked like sherbet, but tasted of Bovril. There was only one alternative: to go to the canteen. But no-one normally went to the canteen. Every few months it was closed by the hygiene inspectors. Notices were stuck up announcing this, but were soon covered over or torn down.

Recently there had been even more food scares than usual. A number of cases of botulism had broken out around the country, also of salmonella. Now there was talk of banning eggs completely, along with several types of potted meat and fish, until the outbreaks had been controlled.

What complicated matters was the fact that the food scare had coincided with the dog crisis. According to various newspaper reports, dogs had started attacking people with increasing frequency over the past few weeks – children had been bitten, old ladies mauled. Some saw this as evidence of a new brutishness in the national character – the dogs were simply taking after their owners. Others saw it as part of a more general pet uprising.

Determined to act firmly, the government had drafted a bill giving the police powers to seize and destroy any dog deemed to be a menace. Several breeds of dog now had to be muzzled and those whose owners failed to comply faced dire consequences. People out walking their pets found them being snatched away and carried off to be incarcerated with other dogs also deemed to be a danger to the public. The combination of food scare and dog crisis had led to a mood of public jumpiness. People were unsure what was going on; they no longer knew what to eat, or who they should trust.

Hugh was sure he had been to the canteen once, but he had no recollection where it was. Still, that was no reason not to try to find it. At least it would keep him out of the way for a while. He went through the same set of doors that he'd seen Darren come through. Black asphalt steps ran round a stairwell descending into darkness.

Two flights down, he arbitrarily pushed open another pair of double doors. A corridor stretched before him, another low, long featureless tunnel painted in the same cracked cream gloss. No light from outside ever reached here, what illumination there was came from dim bulbs set into the walls.

The corridor was deserted except for two green-carders walking slowly away from him. A strange assortment of stooped, twitching figures, the green-carders were the beneficiaries of some ancient scheme to help the disabled and disadvantaged. They moved about in a veiled world of their own, many of them dressed in the same shapeless dun-coloured cardigans, and they were rumoured to be the only people who knew their way round the building. It wasn't clear what they did. They ran errands and delivered the internal mail, but much of the time they stood around looking guilty, as if waiting to be scolded for some unspecified offence.

Hugh had always felt some tug of kinship with the green-carders. Of course he was in a much better state than they were. Simply to entertain comparisons or any sense of shared hardship was quite wrong. But he did know what it was to overstep himself. His once-athletic exterior had turned against him. Even when sober he'd come to distrust his own behaviour. If he wasn't careful he was apt to become overexcitable. He'd grown used to keeping himself in check. He'd tried to subdue his own impulsiveness, to keep it under wraps, for fear that it might lead him into further trouble.

At the same time he felt as if he was being borne steadily, involuntarily, backwards, into this disengaged seclusion. Swept back on a great tide of water. Withdrawing, all the time withdrawing. Perhaps it was just a way of shielding himself, of keeping himself out of danger. Like the green-carders, he often seemed beset by ungovernable urges, trapped in a body that threatened constantly to let him down and shoot off on some embarrassing tangent of its own.

When he had first come to be interviewed for a job on the paper six years beforehand he had arrived early and visited the lavatory first. As he was standing at one of the

31

urinals, he'd been faintly aware of someone else coming in and lurching unsteadily in his direction. Glancing up, Hugh had seen this flailing figure, apparently about to topple over on him. Jittery enough already, he reared back in alarm, peeing down his leg as he did so. The green-carder, though, had appeared quite oblivious to him. He lurched over to the basin once he had finished, then back out the door.

When he had gone Hugh inspected his trousers. There was a vivid, arcing stain stretching from his thigh down to his calf. Assuming that he'd stand little chance of getting a job if he was thought to be incontinent, he went into one of the cubicles, took down his trousers and wrapped his leg in lavatory paper. He'd tied the ends of the paper together and tucked them into his sock. It had worked better than he'd dared hope, and when he was finally ushered in to see the editor, the stain had all but disappeared.

The editor, a small man with sloping shoulders, was standing looking out of the window. Or rather pretending to look out of the window, since the view was almost entirely obscured. He indicated that Hugh should sit down, then turned away again. His hands were thrust deep into his pockets. When he spoke he had such a faint voice that Hugh had to lean forward to hear him.

'They say that when a man is tired of London, he's tired of life, don't they?'

'Yes,' said Hugh, 'they do.'

'Mmm. Do you know who said that?'

'I believe it was Dr Johnson.'

The editor turned back to face him. 'Do you know, I think you're right. Dr Johnson, yes. He used to live round here, you know. In Gough Square. Of course he'd hardly recognize it now . . .'

He tailed off, then picked up again a few moments later. 'Tell me, do you believe that when a man is tired of London he's tired of life?'

Before Hugh could answer, the editor went on, 'I

suppose that's a bit of a cliché, isn't it? I dare say you disapprove of clichés.'

'No,' said Hugh, 'not necessarily.'

The editor appeared delighted by his response. 'Quite right. A journalist disdains clichés at his peril. The wisdom of the ages distilled into handy phrases. Nothing wrong with that, is there?'

The interview appeared to be going well. Hugh started to relax and crossed his legs. As he did so, he heard a faint ripping sound. At first, he paid it little heed. Then he saw that the lavatory paper had torn and was falling out of the bottom of his trouser leg and onto the floor in a series of long white loops. When he looked up he saw that the editor had noticed it too. He appeared transfixed, a baffled expression on his face.

Hugh had expected to be asked why he wanted to join the paper, asked what had made him imagine that his previous job working on a monthly magazine for the construction trade might fit him for a career on Fleet Street. He had only applied out of desperation, assuming that he stood little or no chance of success. But he wasn't asked anything. Instead, the editor continued to stare at the coils of lavatory paper still emerging from his leg, as if witnessing some ectoplasmic manifestation. After several minutes of this – by now the lavatory paper lay in a white mound by his feet – Hugh was told that he could go. Three days later a letter came saying that the job was his.

Once, when he'd first arrived, he had entertained hopes of making contact with the green-carders. His efforts, though, had come to nothing. The green-carders weren't used to being talked to. He'd wished them good morning and had tried to engage them in conversation, but the merest acknowledgement was usually enough to send them scuttling away in alarm. His fellow journalists, for their part, made it plain that they disapproved of such behaviour. They took no notice of the green-carders, apart from treating them in the most offhand manner. This, it appeared, was part of a more general principle: the paper did not look kindly upon charitable impulses of any kind.

After a while Hugh stopped to see if he could smell food. But there was no smell of anything, except the faint tang of disinfectant. Ahead of him was another set of double doors. Hugh pushed them open and found himself in what looked like a scene of torment from some eighteenth-century engraving. Here the windows were so begrimed that no daylight got through. The noise was far louder than upstairs, the roar and clatter of machinery was broken only by the harsh clink of metal upon metal.

Running down either side of the room, set only a few feet apart, were pieces of incredibly antiquated-looking machinery. At each one sat a man in a brown coat. In front of him was a keyboard and beyond that what appeared to be a small foundry. Whenever the man pressed on the keys, pieces of metal would fly out of the side of the machine, raining down like shrapnel into large wire baskets. Above each machine an elaborate system of belts and pulleys shuddered and whirred.

This, Hugh realized, was where the type was cut and set before being sent to the printers. All the articles from upstairs were sent down to be retyped on the line-composing machines. As the machine operators pressed the keys, the relevant letters would drop down from storage magazines above. Once a line was completed it would be covered with molten metal, which would mould itself to the surface of the letters forming a mirror image of them. These lines of type would be spat out to await collection by figures in leather aprons who collected up the contents of the wire baskets, tipped them into trolleys and wheeled them off to the other end of the room.

He had only been here once before, when he'd first joined the paper and was being shown round. Normally journalists were discouraged from venturing below stairs – the unions didn't like it. Not that they had any interest in doing so. The production of the paper, the process by which it was typeset and printed and distributed, these were things that the journalists didn't bother to concern themselves with. Everyone stayed within their designated patch and took no notice of anything that went on outside.

He walked down between the rattling type machines and the crouched, pounding men. At the far end of the room were a number of long low tables. Here the type was tipped out into huge flat galleys, to be assembled and beaten into shape by men with mallets. These were the compositors. Their lives were spent reading mirror writing. All of them were fluent in it; they could read type that ran backwards as easily as type that ran forwards — much more easily in some cases.

Hugh stood and watched as the trolleys were unloaded, the compositors plucking long shards of sentences out of the pile in front of them, the pages being assembled. It was like being in an underworld where everything had been flopped over, and where time itself seemed to run backwards on this molten tide of metal. Completed galleys were sent off for proofing, ready for the following morning's edition. Carried away on raised arms like huge baking trays. And all the while the belts overhead spun and flapped as grimy, aproned figures strolled about amid the din.

Someone tapped him on the shoulder. Hugh turned round to see a man shouting at him. He indicated that he couldn't hear what he was saying, but the man only grew redder and more angry-looking. Once again Hugh had the depressing feeling that he'd caused offence through no fault of his own. He knew that anyone from upstairs was supposed to ask permission before coming down here. He tried to explain, mutely, that he was lost and couldn't hear; putting his hands over his ears and shrugging at the same time.

It made no difference. The man continued to shout. In the end Hugh turned round and started to make his way back to where he had come from. But the man pulled at his sleeve and pointed him in the opposite direction, towards a small door half hidden behind two stacks of wire baskets. Again Hugh tried to explain that he wanted to go the other way. However, the man simply shook his head and, keeping a firm hold on Hugh's sleeve, pushed him through the indicated door.

Hugh found himself in another stairwell. These stairs seemed more musty, less frequently used than the ones he had come down. There were piles of blackened dust in the angle between the edge of the stairs and the wall. He went down one flight and opened the next door. Nothing looked familiar. Steps led down to a small, enclosed area, bounded on each side by frosted glass partitions. Each partition had a wooden hatch set into it, all of them closed. Through the frosted glass Hugh thought he could see figures, not moving but reclining, apparently prostrate. He tapped on one of the hatches, a hollow, splintered knock. There was no response. He tried another one. Nothing. The hatches stayed shut.

After a while he returned to the stairs and descended another flight. When he opened the door, another corridor bent away before him. Pale grey pipes ran overhead, fixed to the ceiling by metal brackets. There was a whistling sound as water rushed through them. This time he caught a momentary glimpse of movement up ahead and set off in pursuit. By the time he rounded the corner there was no-one to be seen. But at the next corner he caught another flash of movement – an arm and a leg, apparently spinning together in tandem – and a trailing length of dun-coloured material.

The corridor straightened. Ahead of him Hugh could see one of the green-carders, walking with difficulty, tilted over to the left, one shoulder lower than the other. At every step he halted for a moment, almost as if he was having to reassemble himself before venturing on.

Hugh called out, 'Excuse me.'

Momentarily, the man spun round. But before Hugh could say anything else he was off again. Seeking to reassure him, Hugh called out again, 'Excuse me, please.'

The man, however, only quickened his pace. At the end

of the corridor, he careered through a set of double doors which flapped and banged in his wake.

Hugh followed. The doors led onto a metal balcony that ran round three sides of an enormous dimly lit room, like the engine room of some vast ocean-going vessel. Below him he could see pieces of machinery, gleaming and black, with shining silver drums and clusters of levers alongside. Above his head long white ribbons of paper hung in folds from the ceiling. Set into the wall were banks of switches in grey metal casings. There was a smell too. A rich, thick smell, like sump oil. He could see vats of printing ink stacked around the walls, each with a skull and crossbones and a large sticker saying 'Poison!' on the side.

This was where the paper was printed, where rivers of newsprint flowed out to be chopped and folded and bundled into shape. The presses were switched off now, the room apparently deserted and quiet. The building itself seemed to have come to a halt. For the next few moments Hugh lost sight of the green-carder. Then he saw him again – heard him too – running round the balcony, footsteps clattering away. As he watched, the man seemed to duck down, as if he'd stumbled and lost his footing. Hugh wondered if he'd fallen and injured himself. But when he got to where the man had been, there was no sign of him.

He stood there, waiting for the green-carder to reappear. Nothing happened. As he looked about, thoroughly confused, Hugh saw for the first time a small metal door set into the wall on his left, little bigger than a hatchway. He opened the door. There was even less light inside. His eyes took a while to adjust.

A set of steps, no wider than those on a ladder, ran down into the darkness. He could just hear a final clatter from the foot of the steps before the sound of another metal door slamming. He felt about in the darkness for something to hang onto. Slowly, stopping every so often to steady himself, Hugh descended the steps. When he reached the bottom and opened another submarine hatch, daylight rushed in, tugging him out.

Another unfamiliar scene greeted him. He was in a loading bay, around the side of the building. A number of lorries were parked up and huge rolls of paper were being unloaded, winched up by pulleys and swung away on cranes. Men were clambering about on them, fitting chain slings. The rolls of paper were then hoisted into the air, dipping and swaying before disappearing off into the bay.

The green-carder too had disappeared. Hugh walked between the lorries, out onto the street and round to the main entrance. He caught the lift up to the second floor and made his way back to the newsroom. The first person he saw was Joy, standing by herself now, a quizzical expression on her face. She had curly blond hair like spun gold.

She beckoned him over.

'Here,' she said. 'What's all this about Scaife?'

Chapter Two

That evening the same group of people who had met up at lunchtime did so again. Cliff, the thick-set man with grey thumbs, was explaining why he'd forbidden his wife to wear glasses.

'The eye', he said, 'is a muscle. Right?'

There was a slow murmur of assent.

'As you get older,' he went on, 'the lazier it becomes. All this man Mackover is saying is that you have to encourage it to stay in shape.'

'But surely, Cliff, if the optician says she needs glasses—'

'Of course the optician's going to say that, isn't he? But Pauline's not an old woman. She's only thirty-one.'

'So how do you say it works?'

'It's just a matter of her doing these exercises twice a day – once in the morning and once in the evening. I've set up this pendulum in the kitchen, hung it from the dish rack. Pauline sets it swinging. Then she just has to sit there and follow it with her eyes. Sometimes she moves the chair nearer the pendulum, and sometimes she moves it further away. The most important thing, though, is to keep it in focus all the time.'

'And that's it?'

'That's the basis of it, yes. And at night we do these tests to see if there's been any improvement.'

'What tests are those, Cliff?'

'I stand at one end of the kitchen and Pauline stands over

by the hob. And I hold up these cards with very simple mathematical equations written on them and see if she can answer them. You have to do it fast though, otherwise there isn't any point – Mackover's very insistent on that.'

'But what happens if she gets one wrong?'

'Well, I don't send her outside, or anything. We're perfectly civilized about it. No, we just do them over again until she gets it right.'

'I don't know, I'm not sure, Cliffy. It just doesn't seem right somehow.'

'What's not right about that? That's the trouble with all of you, you're not receptive to new ideas. I, however, am receptive to new ideas. Open to all kinds of different stimuli. I dare say this is hard for you to understand.'

'You know your own mind, don't you, Cliff,' said Johnny Todd.

'I believe I do, yes.'

'So is her eyesight any better then?'

'It's still early days yet. But there's already been a dramatic improvement, as Pauline herself is the first to acknowledge. She says she hasn't been able to see this well in years. Not since she was at school.'

'Poor woman. What a fucking life. She'll be blundering about with a white stick soon.'

'Pauline won't be blundering anywhere, Julian. Quite the reverse. Pauline's a doer, not a whiner like you – brooding all the time about being misunderstood, or under-valued, or whatever. Moan, moan, moan. You never stop.'

'I do stop,' said Julian quietly.

'Oh no you don't. Moaning, moaning, all the bloody time. Pauline never moans. And she takes good care of herself. Always beautifully turned out. More than can be said for the women here. My God, the state of some of them. What's that black-haired one called? You know, Joy's friend.'

'Vivien?'

'Yeah, that's the one. What's her problem? She's like a sleepwalker, or something.'

'She's stoned.'

'Stoned? How do you mean?'

'She sits by herself in the churchyard and smokes joints. I've seen her. Almost every night she's there.'

'Taking drugs?' said Cliff. 'Taking drugs? I don't think that's on.'

'It's not as if she's doing it in the office, Cliff.'

'Even so, it's still breaking the law, isn't it? You can't just sit back and let it happen.'

'Why not?'

'Because – because you can't, that's why, Julian. As any sensible person would acknowledge.'

'Maybe she's unhappy.'

'Unhappy?' exclaimed Cliff. He struggled to contain his incredulity. 'What the fuck's that got to do with it?'

But no-one, it seemed, could answer that. In the silence that followed, Julian said to the silent figure on his left, 'You're very quiet again, Hughie. Are you OK?'

'I was just thinking about Scaife.'

'Scaife!' said Cliff bitterly. 'Scaife! Don't get me started on Scaife.'

'He was unhappy too,' said Hugh.

'As I explained at lunchtime, there's no reason whatsoever to be concerned about Scaife. He'll be back. First thing tomorrow morning.'

'I suppose so.'

'Course he will. He's just been too ashamed to show his face. What do you reckon, Bobbie?'

The small, prematurely grizzled figure with tufted yellow hair alongside him was racked by a bout of coughing, recovered, paused in case any further spasms were in store, and then said, 'Scaife's a silly cunt.'

'Yes, well, I can't imagine anyone would want to argue with that,' said Cliff. 'What do you think, Gavin?'

The man sitting alongside didn't say anything, he gave no reaction at all. Far from taking this amiss, though, Cliff nodded approvingly, as if words of extraordinary wisdom had just been uttered.

41

'Exactly,' he said.

'It's your round, Cliff,' said Julian.

'Is that the time?' said Cliff. 'I really must hurry back to Pauline. She gets nervous if I'm late. And she won't want to miss her exercises.'

Hugh walked to the tube station, past the pubs and the shuttered sandwich bars. Rain had started to fall in a thin, icy drizzle. It was colder than it had been in years. People hurried by, swathed in coats and scarves. A bus went by, red and blurred and crowded with faces. At the tube station he bought his ticket and waited for a train. The platform curved away from him, off towards the tunnel entrance. It always reminded him of a beach, this long, pale shoreline with a dark trough beyond, and the bathers all standing about uncertainly, wondering whether to venture in.

But there was hardly anyone on the platform, only a few still figures turned towards the direction board. And when the train arrived Hugh found a seat easily enough in his favourite spot, up against the glass partition. He sat waiting for that lurch in his guts as it moved off again. Everyone sat there, insulated, alone, locked in their private worlds. Quite silent. You got more people talking to themselves than to each other. He loved the ripple of alarm, even panic, that ran through them all whenever anyone raised their voices or threatened to become boisterous, as if they were possessed by this collective shyness, or hatred of any breakdown in decorum. The relief that settled over everyone as silence descended again, and they hurtled on through the black, furred tunnels.

This then was the pattern of his evenings, being borne beneath London, fixing on girls and weaving elaborate, impassioned fantasies around them. Almost every night now he found himself fastening onto some woman on the train. He couldn't help himself. He dreamed of chance encounters and dramatic accidents, of unexpected affinities and shared discoveries. And with who? With anyone. Whoever fell into his line of sight. It hardly even mattered.

In his imagination he followed them as they left the train. Watching as they let themselves into wherever they lived. These open doors and lighted hallways. Then what? He never knew. His imagination never took him beyond their front steps.

He realized he'd been gaping at the girl opposite – a plump, round-faced girl with red patches on her cheeks and heavy, unflattering shoes – and looked down at his paper instead. It was all a matter of finding one's right level, he'd decided. Of lighting on someone whose physical and mental deficiencies roughly matched his own. Aim too high – at those impossible strutting beauties – and he was sure to be disappointed. His mere gaze landed on them like a pestilence. Aim too low, though, and he might be selling himself short. Where did he belong? What had he been equipped for? How were you supposed to tell?

All that was needed was some fortuitous intervention. Every evening he sat and waited for fate to do its work. And every evening nothing happened. He knew this had to stop, that it was doing him no good. But it was getting harder and harder to pull himself down to earth. He didn't like what he found there, not any more.

When Hugh looked up he saw that the girl with red cheeks had gone. In her place was a man with flat black hair who gripped the armrests with both hands and gazed back at him with a sharp, affronted stare.

The carriage had filled up. All the seats were taken and there were people standing around him. All swaying about in their thick winter coats as the train drew in and out of the stations. There was a woman standing with her back to him. An Asian woman, as far as he could tell, with the palm of her hand pressed up against the glass partition at his eye level. He could see the creases running across the joints of her fingers and the soft mound below her thumb. It sat beside his ear, pulsing away like a small brown heart.

*   *   *

43

That night, as he did two, sometimes even three, times a week, Hugh went to the Sri Lankan takeaway around the corner from his flat. It had opened a couple of months earlier with pots of African violets along the counter and leaflets distributed to all the houses near by offering introductory deals. But no-one went. Hugh had begun to think he must be their only customer. He went there now as much out of a sense of duty as anything else.

Every time he asked if they had the cuttlefish curry, listed on the menu as a speciality of the house. At first there had been apologies and explanations – the difficulties of getting hold of cuttlefish, a delivery that had failed to arrive. Then Hugh found his request being greeted in an amused, yet faintly reproving way, as if he had made some off-colour remark. Latterly, it prompted only despairing shrugs.

And the young couple who ran the takeaway no longer seemed pleased to see him; they simply looked embarrassed, as if he was a witness to their shame. They had misread the mood of the public. The place was sinking. The violets had gone, the menu was becoming smaller and smaller. All they ever seemed to have now were thick, tasteless pancakes stuffed with yellow potatoes mixed with tiny black seeds that got stuck in his teeth. Hugh bought one and ate it, walking home. The lorries thundered along the Harrow Road, bigger and somehow more solid-looking than any of the buildings. The tarmac was stained white by the salt that had been laid earlier in anticipation of the expected freeze.

Two hours later, when Hugh went up to bed, the pancake still lay in his stomach like a log. Swollen with indigestion, he lay there, twisting about, trying to read. He'd found an old guide book to London in a shop on St Bride's Lane. Published in 1901, it was like the guide to a lost city. Most of the buildings it referred to had been demolished, the street names had changed, the landmarks been swallowed up. But occasionally familiar sights still showed through, like steeples in the mist.

Every night he'd take a stroll through these deep, dark thoroughfares before sleep came. Down stone canyons blackened with soot, past the remains of the great palaces on the Strand, through courts and churchyards, rows and rookeries . . .

The area where he worked had once been known as Alsatia – the abode of the rogues. After the dissolution of the monasteries, Alsatia retained 'the privilege of sanctuary' – anyone within its boundaries was effectively beyond the reach of the law. It quickly became a refuge for vagabonds and bad characters of every description. Brothels and gambling dens flourished there. So too did theatres, including Duke's Theatre, designed by Christopher Wren, which faced the river and had a façade resting on open arches, enabling theatregoers to come and go by boat. Dryden described it as being like 'Nero's palace, all shining with gold'.

The area was dominated by Bridewell Prison, built on the site of Henry VIII's Bridewell Palace. Here Henry had summoned his lords of court to inform them that he was greatly taken with Anne Boleyn and intended to dissolve his marriage to Catherine of Aragon. And here, a hundred years later, prisoners – women as well as men – were flogged on the bare back in front of the prison's president, Sir Robert Clayton; the flogging only stopping when he banged his gavel on the block before him. Alsatia, it was said, resounded to their cries. 'Oh good Sir Robert, knock!' they would be heard to beg. 'Pray, Sir Robert, knock!'

'An artist, after a time,' wrote the author proudly, 'will find London more interesting than any other place. Nowhere else are there such atmospheric effects on fine days, and nowhere is the enormous power of blue more felt in the picture; while the soot, which puts all the stones into mourning, makes everything look old.'

London's detractors, he noted, 'tended to lay their strongest emphasis upon its fogs', before quoting Nathaniel Hawthorne on a visit to London in 1869: 'More like a distillation of mud than anything else; the ghost of

45

mud – the spiritualized medium of departed mud, through which the dead citizens of London probably tread, in the Hades whither they are translated.'

The dead citizens of London – a good many of them anyway – lay just down the road, in Kensal Green Cemetery. Hugh walked there sometimes, along the avenues of crumbled, vandalized graves. Hardly anyone went to the cemetery any more, only a few disconsolate teenage girls pushing their children around in prams and the occasional junkie looking for refuge.

Once it had been a popular place for family outings. They came to picnic and to commune with the souls of their relatives. But all that had changed. The lines of communication had been cut. Such things were considered morbid now. People were more frightened of death. They had no confidence about what came next, no wish to be in any kind of proximity to it. All those heartbreaking sentiments: the longing to be reunited, the pain of being abandoned. No-one could bear it.

Sometimes when Hugh woke in the middle of the night, as he did with increasing frequency these days, he imagined that he could hear the dead calling to him from down the road. This soft, plaintive crooning that came to him at night from out of the frozen graves. To begin with he found this oddly comforting, as if he was being sung back to sleep by a choir of skeletal Swingle Singers. Latterly, though, it had begun to trouble him more and more.

And now, as he lay there, with the yellow pancake still lodged in his insides and the nightly chorus yet to start, he felt a sense of desperation wash over him like some odourless gas.

Chapter Three

The body rose and fell on the tide. Face down, arms outstretched, legs dangling. It had lain on the bottom of the river for four days, crouched down in the mud, while the great current of grey water flowed overhead. Then, as if an anchor line had been cut, it floated back to the surface. No-one witnessed its reappearance. Soon, leaves and other river rubbish gathered between its outstretched arms, obscuring its outline. At high tide it drifted out into the middle of the river, swinging about in the wash of the few passing boats and riding upon the waves. And at low tide it floated in towards the shore, hanging there in the shallows.

Then one night it snagged on a mooring post. When the tide went out, the body remained wrapped around the post. The next morning some children playing on the foreshore saw it suspended there, several feet out of the water, like a sailor halfway up a mast, searching for land. They saw the blackened eyes turned towards them, and the swollen tongue pushed between perforated lips.

The children ran away and called the police, who sent a launch out from Wapping. Two men with hooked poles tried to pull the body off the mooring post and into the boat, but there was more of a swell than usual and the policeman driving the launch had difficulty manoeuvring it alongside.

Then the body turned out to be stuck fast, the hands

clasped around the post, one foot snagged on a length of rope. They managed to hook it around the thigh and the neck, but still it wouldn't move. Several further attempts were made – the launch bobbing about, the men in the back flailing around with their poles. One of the hands was pulled free and for a moment it looked as if that might do it, but the body stayed where it was, the other hand still gamely clinging on.

Finally, one of the policemen climbed out of the launch and began to shin up the mooring post. It was hard for him to get any purchase and he kept slipping down, his feet scrambling about, his chest streaked with slime. Gulls wheeled and screeched overhead. At last he managed to reach the body, freeing the legs and tugging at what was left of the clothing. With a long tearing sound it fell back into the water, almost taking the policeman with it. His colleagues in the boat rushed to pull it out, leaving the policeman still halfway up the pole, struggling to keep his grip and calling for help.

The body was recovered and left to drain in a metal tray on the bottom of the boat. A preliminary examination was made. It was noted that the body was male. The skin was bloated and discoloured. The nose appeared dented. It was also noted that the ends of the fingers were missing. There were no other obvious signs of injury. Some of the hair had fallen out, only stray hanks still adhering to the sides of the scalp. Given the length of immersion and the extent of the decomposition, no attempt was made at this stage to guess the dead man's age or race.

Chapter Four

When Hugh arrived at work, the office was stirring into life. People were arriving, hanging up their coats, complaining about their journeys. A number of the journalists slept under their desks, no longer having homes of their own to go to. They could be seen first thing in the morning still huddled on the floor, fully dressed. Upon being woken, they would get up, sit down and immediately begin typing, as if this was some automatic response they had no control over.

There was no sign of Scaife. Hugh had only been sitting at his desk for a few minutes when Cliff came and sat beside him. While neither fat nor particularly muscular, he still looked as if his frame was covered with shifting plates of flesh. As he leant forward, they seemed to rise up his chest and sit on his shoulders. Paddling his chair forward with his feet, he said, 'I think we should all stay quiet about Scaife for the time being.'

'Wouldn't it be more sensible to tell someone?'

Cliff shook his head and a few smaller plates of flesh shifted with it. 'No point causing difficulties. He'll be back soon enough.'

It was clear that Cliff was taking Scaife's non-appearance as a personal affront. Hugh marvelled at how Cliff seemed to exist in this state of perpetual indignation, bristling with desire for confrontation of any kind. He'd never come across anyone so free of doubts before, so sure of himself. Cliff's view of the world was as starkly black and white as a tiled floor. Although Hugh didn't agree with any of the views Cliff expressed – he was often appalled, even disgusted, by them – he couldn't help but find something comforting about this great mass of certainties, battening onto them as a way of trying to resolve his own confusion.

In the last few months Cliff had become even more full of himself than before. This dated from the time when he'd been given his own column to write. A concentration of Middle English prejudices, shot through with a tone of whimsical bigotry, it had proved to be an enormous success. Now he was regarded as one of the two leading candidates to take over the editorship if the present editor – currently in hospital – did what he was confidently expected to do and died. The other candidate was the news editor, Battersby.

'But what if he doesn't turn up?' said Hugh. 'How long can we leave it?'

Cliff folded his thick fingers across his stomach. 'Certainly a few more days.' He got up to go. 'So that's agreed then.'

He walked off without waiting for a reply. Hugh looked around, reluctant to start pretending to work. The office had filled up. All around him people were typing furiously. Once it had seemed to him as though the world blew in here, in all its richness and diversity. Yet far from enriching anyone it swept over, it seemed instead to leave them even more impoverished, more pedantic than before.

And now the world was changing. A new age was dawning. Less rich and corrupt than before. Harsher, blander, more desiccated. Fleet Street was coming to an end. The exodus was already under way. In a few weeks' time the paper would be moving to one of those newly built glass towers in Docklands with air-conditioning and lifts lined with carpet. Whether Hugh moved with it looked increasingly less certain. And then what? He had no idea. Journalists who lost their jobs seldom prospered at anything else. Careers spent recording the foibles of the world hardly prepared them for living in it. Mostly they drank themselves to death, or went into public relations, or bought themselves little teashops on the south coast.

Opposite Hugh sat Stanley, hidden behind his visor. Believed to be the oldest journalist on the paper, he was a peevish man who was too vain to wear glasses. Instead, he'd had a special magnifying visor made which he held over his face while he read. For years he had been the senior parliamentary correspondent, based in the House of Commons, from where he would phone in his copy every day. Recently he had been moved back to Fleet Street. Hugh could see Stanley's features now, massively enlarged and distorted, swimming about before him like some sea creature viewed through a glass-bottomed boat.

As expected, Darren brought round cups of tea for everyone except Hugh. Rather than try to find the canteen again, Hugh went to buy a cup of coffee from the vending machine. The machine shuddered and hosed a stream of thin brown liquid into a plastic cup. When he got back he saw Julian sitting in the same chair Cliff had recently vacated. Julian looked even more agitated than usual.

'Has Cliff been to see you?' he asked.

Hugh nodded.

'What do you think?'

Julian scrutinized him through dark, deep-set eyes. Hugh liked Julian, but he could be a trial. He was inordinately prickly, quick to take offence and inclined to profound sulks, constantly running former conversations back and forth through his mind, examining them for veiled insults that he might have missed at the time.

His sense of grievance, of being 'got at', spilled over into everything. Julian did have a sense of humour, but it only extended so far before defensiveness and suspicion took over. This, combined with a belief that others didn't take him sufficiently seriously, meant there were a number of occasions when it gave out altogether. His private life was in an almost constant state of crisis. He lived with a

French girl who worked in a restaurant. Their relationship lurched from one public row to another, largely, Hugh gathered, as a result of Julian's suspicious nature.

Not long before, Hugh had watched them arguing at a party. He'd heard Julian's voice arcing steadily upwards with indignation and seen his girlfriend sitting opposite, looking upset. It took him a few moments to realize that she wasn't saying anything. Maddened by this lack of response, Julian was effectively arguing against himself, doing both parts. He'd ended up by storming out of the room in a fury. These rows tended to be succeeded by concerted efforts on his part to ingratiate himself with her again. In his spare time he did carpentry and was currently engaged in building a porch for his house.

'I don't see how we can conceal Scaife's absence for long,' said Hugh. 'Anyway, won't his wife report him missing?'

'She'll probably be delighted to see the back of him,' said Julian. 'Puts us all in a very difficult position though.'

'Cliff seems very sure he'll be back soon. Do you think he knows something we don't?'

Julian looked at him, his brow furrowing. 'Cliff knows nothing,' he said. 'Nothing.'

Relations between Cliff and Julian had been deteriorating for some time. In part this was due to jealousy on Julian's part; the success of others always serving to remind him of his own perceived misfortune and prompting a fresh outbreak of brooding.

Cliff, too, could never resist goading Julian, while he, in turn, was seldom able to resist rising to the bait. Nonetheless, they seemed, in some curious way, to be locked together — almost as though they relished their constant sparring — if only because each remained certain that he would eventually get the better of the other. A short while ago Julian had apparently referred to Cliff as a 'pro', a remark that was taken to imply some measure of grudging respect on his part.

'Can't you two be quiet,' said Stanley.

He had put down his visor. His face, restored to normal size, looked shrunken and puny. Julian glared at Stanley. When he'd finished he turned back towards Hugh, catching sight of the plastic cup on his desk as he did so.

'What do you drink that shit for?' he asked in astonishment.

'Actually I rather like it,' said Hugh, trying to sound convincing.

He became aware of someone standing beside him. It was Darren, his sweater tucked into his trousers, his moustache looking even more defiantly unconvincing than usual. Darren's gaze also flickered down towards the coffee cup, then back up again.

'Battersby wants to see you,' he said with relish.

Having delivered this information, he spun round as if he was practising drill and walked off.

'What's that about?' asked Julian.

'I don't know.'

'Well, what do you think it might be about?'

Hugh shook his head. 'I don't know that either.'

He got up and walked down one of the aisles between the desks to Battersby's office. It was a small glass-partitioned box without a roof, like a makeshift enclosure where animals might be kept before a livestock auction. Battersby was sitting staring out through the grime-coated window at the blurred buildings beyond. Hugh knocked on the glass partition and was told to come in. The office was piled high with old newspapers. They covered every available surface, including the floor.

Battersby wore his hair brushed forward in a Nero style that made him look as if he was backing into a breeze. A jagged fringe hung down over his forehead. He had an abrupt manner and was apt to shout at people without warning. It wasn't clear if this was a way of trying to impose his authority, or some neurological complaint he was unable to control.

'Now tell me,' he said, 'what's the matter with you?'

'How do you mean?' said Hugh.

'You haven't come up with a decent story in weeks. Maybe months. What's happening?'

As he struggled to think of a suitable reply, Hugh was aware of the ringing of the typewriter bells outside in the newsroom and the crackle of the strip lighting overhead.

'I don't know,' he said.

'You don't know?'

'No.'

Battersby prided himself on knowing exactly what was going on in the office. But at the same time there was an edge of uncertainty to him, an awareness that at any moment his knowledge might be outstripped by events. His career had been hampered by his gullibility; he was unable to resist a good story, no matter how implausible. Twice, he was convinced he had found Lord Lucan. There had also been several apparent sightings of Hitler's former deputy, Martin Bormann.

'You already stand to lose the paper a great deal of money through an act of complete carelessness,' he said, 'and now you're not writing anything at all. I'm not sure which is worse.'

'No,' said Hugh sadly, 'nor am I.'

An expression of considerable distaste came over Battersby's face. He lowered his voice.

'Is it something personal?'

'In a way.'

Any uncertainty in Battersby's manner abruptly resolved itself. 'Well, you can't go bringing your personal problems into the office. It's not professional. You come here to work, then you go home. That's where your problems belong. This isn't some sort of sanatorium.'

'I can't write any more,' said Hugh.

'Writing?' said Battersby, surprised. 'Writing? What's writing got to do with it?'

'I'm finding it very difficult to write,' he said again.

Battersby, he saw, was peering at his hands, inspecting them for signs of damage.

'I can't get the words to come out properly,' said Hugh.

'How do they come out then?'

'Not . . . not in the right order somehow.'

'Backwards?' asked Battersby, his voice now no more than a whisper.

'Not backwards,' said Hugh. 'It's difficult to explain.'

Battersby stared at him. 'You can't have writer's block,' he said. 'You're not a writer. This is journalism. It doesn't matter if a few words are the wrong way round.'

'You don't think so?'

'Of course not. You can't go worrying about things like that. As long as they're roughly in the right order that's as much as anyone can hope for.'

'I seem to have lost a lot of confidence.'

'I don't want to hear that,' said Battersby. 'Don't tell me things like that. You can't carry on like this. In just a few weeks we'll be out of here.' He waved his hand at the glass partition and the rows of typing figures beyond. 'When we move into the new office things will be very different, believe me. There'll be no room for any passengers. You understand?'

'Yes.'

Battersby sat and groomed the top of his head with his hands, as if he was inspecting himself for nits.

'I've got a mind to send you downstairs,' he said eventually.

'No,' said Hugh. 'Please. Not that.'

Battersby looked up. 'It's got to be done sometime, you know. She won't go on for ever. Still,' he said, 'I can hardly bear to think of life without her.'

Hugh stood in silence as Battersby collected himself.

'All right then.' He picked up a piece of paper and threw it across the desk to Hugh. 'You say you can't write. Well, this shouldn't tax you too much.'

Hugh turned the piece of paper round. A man's face stared up at him. It was a photofit, made up from various components: eyes, chin, forehead, hair, cheekbones. All of them looked as though they might fly apart at any moment. The chin was as broad as a wedge, the hair looked like a bathing cap, and the mouth drooped on one side, giving the face a strangely apologetic, resigned expression.

'The police pulled him out of the river a couple of days ago,' said Battersby. 'They asked if we can run the picture, see if anyone comes forward to identify him. Here, there's another sheet that came with it.' This was headlined THAMES IDENTIFICATION DIVISION and consisted of three lines of closely typed text giving the time the body was recovered and the name of the officer responsible for the case.

'Go and see them,' he said. 'There must be something more you can add to this.'

Both of them knew that this was the sort of work normally given to the most junior reporters, even to schoolchildren on work experience. An exercise in showing willing, nothing more. Hugh couldn't be sure if this was an attempt to humiliate him or an act of charity. He suspected Battersby hadn't made up his mind either. He started to walk out of the office, but before he got to the door Battersby called him back.

'Hold on. I haven't finished with you yet. Have you seen Scaife around?'

'Scaife?'

'Yes, that's right. Scaife.'

'I think I saw him earlier,' said Hugh.

'Did you?'

'I believe so, yes.'

'Where?'

'He was just going out. He said he felt bad. He thought he was coming down with flu.'

'Not another one,' muttered Battersby. 'Well, he never bloody told me.'

Back at his desk Hugh sat for a while watching everyone around him. Most of his colleagues were men, but there were a few women. Traditionally women in Fleet Street had done their best to look and behave as much like men as possible. They had the same lousy teeth, leathery skins and wheezy laughs. But that too was changing. A new breed of women had arrived. They were younger, brisker and more industrious. They also didn't drink very much, so they were more alert. Their presence made the men feel drab, moribund and insecure. As a result they were regarded with a good deal of suspicion, if not outright fear. Mostly they kept to themselves, moving about in packs, with their padded shoulders and lacquered hair.

He called the police station in Wapping and asked to be put through to the Thames Identification Division. The phone went dead for several minutes. He was about to try again when a man's voice came on the line. Hugh explained who he was and asked if it might be convenient for him to come round.

'Come whenever you like,' said the man.

'I could come now.'

'All right then. Come now.'

On his way out Hugh went to tell Joy that he wouldn't be back for a while, in case anyone happened to be interested. But she wasn't at her desk and he couldn't face talking to Vivien, who sat frowning away at nothing in particular. Ahead of him in the corridor, one of the green-carders was walking along, kicking out each foot in front of him and then swinging himself round into every step. Reluctant to overtake, Hugh hung back until the man had veered off through an open door into another glass-partitioned office with rows of figures sitting motionless inside.

Chapter Five

Wapping High Street stretched ahead of him, a deep brick canyon with warehouses rising up on either side and thin metal bridges running between them. Some of the warehouses were still used to store spices. Despite the cold, the air was heavy with the smell of nutmeg and cloves. There was frost on the railings and ice on the puddles. Every so often Hugh caught a glimpse of the river between the buildings, patches of grey water and looping lines of foam.

He sat on a bench on a thin strip of grass and looked across at the far shore. Everything around him was being demolished or redeveloped. The warehouses were being turned into flats for young City overlords, or else torn down and replaced with squat glass towers, each with the same idiotic porticos stuck on top like little rainhats. An entire landscape was being levelled. He could see the long arms of the cranes swinging about and hear the smack and echo of the piledrivers. Along the river, at Limehouse, there was nothing left of the docks at all.

It was starting to rain. The clouds were the same colour as the water. They both seemed to blur together into one soft grey mass that folded him between them. On the other side of the river Hugh could see a single house still standing with patches of waste ground on either side of it. A tall, thin black house with a steep gabled roof, shuttered up as far as he could tell. It looked like a leftover from another world – a world of wharves and lightermen, barges and steamboats. The riverbanks teeming with people and packed with buildings, sheds and boathouses, spilling over one another at the water's edge. Hugh stayed there for some time as the rain spattered on the surface of the river, turning it into a vast bouncing mass of spouts and whirls.

At the police station he gave his name at the counter and was asked to take a seat. He'd hardly sat down when the door swung open and a man in shirtsleeves with pale ginger hair clipped very short at the sides advanced towards him, hand already extended. When he shook the man's hand, Hugh noticed that the backs of his fingers were covered in tufts of the same pale ginger hair.

'Peter Long,' said the man. 'Why don't we go upstairs?'

Hugh followed him up a staircase and into a narrow room lined with filing cabinets. There was a desk and a window that overlooked the river. Through a break in the clouds, the light hit the surface of the water and seemed to sweep it away, off towards the sea. Two boats were travelling along the river in opposite directions. The water split and shredded behind them as if great zips were being drawn down it.

There was an air of clenched containment about Long. He moved with precise, fussy little gestures, as if he might burst with excitement if he wasn't careful. They sat down. Hugh asked if there was anything he could add to the information they had already sent in. Long thought for a moment. He shook his head in anxious swipes before he spoke, as if to clear it of anything irrelevant.

'We pulled him out three days ago. Not far from here. No identification. No note, although that could have rotted away, of course. Aged in his late fifties, perhaps early sixties. Small – only five foot five. Didn't weigh much either – no more than eight stone. White. Quite a few fillings, but he'd still got his own teeth. That's really about all I can tell you.'

'How long had he been in the river?'

'Not always easy to tell.' He spoke with admiration in his voice, as if matched against some endlessly cunning adversary. 'You see, if you jump in the river, chances are that you'll be knocked unconscious by the impact. People who aren't knocked unconscious often try to swim for it; they change their minds, decide that life isn't so bad after all. But it's too late by then. Your muscles seize up with the cold – you'd be lucky to last more than a couple of minutes. The odd one makes it to the side, but not often.

'The next thing that happens is you drown. And then you sink to the bottom. Now, how long you stay there depends upon a number of different factors. If you're a woman you'll come back to the surface more quickly than if you're a man, because women decompose faster. If you've eaten a large meal before you throw yourself in, then you'll also float up more quickly because your stomach will fill with gas. Some people like to wrap up warm. That can make a difference, the weight of the clothes. Sometimes they weigh themselves down specially. We had one man last year with a sandbag stuffed down his trousers.'

On the desk in front of him Long's ginger hands had begun to dance independently, each fired up with excitement.

'It can take them a few days to come up again. It could be weeks. Judging by the condition of this chap's body I'd say he'd been in about four or five days. But as I say, it's difficult to tell. We had a report from a man who said he'd seen someone taking a leap off Hungerford Bridge late last Friday night. He called the police and the launch was sent out. But by the time they got there he must have sunk. It could be the same chap. The trouble is the man who called the police said he couldn't come and identify him and the description he gave was next to useless.'

Long passed Hugh a clear plastic file. Inside were two sheets of paper stapled together. Hugh read the statement. It sounded as if the man was recounting a dream. He claimed to have seen someone jumping from the bridge, but said he had no idea what time it was, or what the person had looked like.

'Rather unsavoury character,' said Long. 'He'd been in

trouble with us before. Hardly falling over himself to help.'

Hugh made a note of the man's name and address and handed back the file.

'I understand that the body's fingers were missing,' he said.

'Ah yes. But there's nothing unusual about that. The fingers and hands are often the first to go, along with the lips and the ears. The nose too, of course,' he added.

'What happens to them?'

'Eaten away. People talk a lot about how polluted the river is, how there aren't any fish in it any more. But there's plenty in there, believe me. Shrimps and the like, marine life. All sorts of things willing to have a nibble. And with the hands we also get what we call the "degloving" effect. First the skin turns all wrinkly, then it lifts off altogether. Nails, fingertips – it's just like stripping off a glove. This chap here had lost most of one hand and the other was starting to go. There's nothing unusual about that, but it does make it very difficult as far as identification goes.

'That's the big problem, you see,' he laughed. 'One of them anyway. There's no shortage of others. You take someone out of the water, they turn black within twelve hours.'

Long paused and looked down at his hands which, as if suddenly chastened, came to a halt. 'That can make it very tricky,' he said. 'Especially for the relatives.'

'So there's no telling who this man may have been?'

'Not really. There's no record of anyone of his age and build in the missing persons file. There's nothing unusual about his socks or his underwear. He doesn't appear to have been wearing any shoes. Nothing distinctive about his trousers either, or his blood group. He had a few fillings, but you can't contact all the dentists in the country, it's just not practical. There's nothing much else to go on, I'm afraid.'

Hugh looked at the grey band of water moving behind Long's head. He had the impression that the river had been

61

briefly diverted from its normal course and was flowing through the police station, up the stairs, along the corridor, into Long's office and out through his mouth.

'You see, we don't even know if he's from London,' he was saying. 'People come from all over the place to throw themselves in the Thames. And the ones we fish out alive, when we ask them why they chose the river, they can't answer. They don't seem to know themselves. It's just this magnetic attraction. Waterloo Bridge is the most popular. I suppose because it's the most romantic and you get the best views, but Hungerford always has a few. The extraordinary thing, though, is that every year we get almost exactly the same number of people drowning – between forty-five and fifty. Never changes.'

Long leant forward. 'When I retire that's what I want to do,' he said. 'Go round all the capitals of Europe – the ones that are on rivers, of course – and compile a study of their jumping statistics. No-one's ever done that before.'

Hugh put his notebook back inside his case. 'Well,' he said, 'this all seems fairly straightforward, at least from my point of view.'

'Aren't you going to come and see him?' asked Long.

'See him?' said Hugh. 'Whatever for?'

'I think you'd better. The photofit's no good. They never are. We're supposed to have a full set of features downstairs, but people keep walking off with them. There are only a couple of sets of ears left. I did this one myself. I'm afraid it's mainly guesswork. You ought to see for yourself what he looks like.'

'I ought to get back.' Hugh felt a sudden need for the comfort of the office.

'He's only down the road. We could go now.'

'No, it's all right. I wouldn't want to put you out.'

Long sounded touched. 'Don't worry about that. I could do with a break. Stretch my legs.'

'I really ought—' began Hugh again. But Long was already on his feet, putting on his jacket. Hugh followed him back downstairs and out to his car. Long got in and reached across to pull up the lock on the passenger door.

They drove along Wapping High Street and joined the highway heading east. At the traffic lights a group of Asian women were waiting to cross the road. They wore grey anoraks over their saris with the collars turned up and the sleeves pulled down over their hands; they stood uncertainly on the kerb, hanging back, before finally launching themselves across the road in a long loping line, clouds of breath streaming out behind them.

Long sat bolt upright, gripping the steering wheel with both hands as he swung the car through the corners. After ten minutes they turned off onto a slip road that wound its way down a long slope with low grass mounds on either side, like bunkers on a golf course. They followed the signs to the hospital car park. Long drove into the car park and round to a special reserved area with names posted proprietorially above the parking spaces.

The hospital was a vast, dark building with row upon row of steel-framed windows and walls stained with rainwater. In places the walls appeared pitted, as if chunks of concrete had been scooped out. They walked past the main entrance and round the corner to another door. It had a large notice alongside warning unauthorized visitors to keep out.

Long pressed the intercom and announced himself. The door swung open. There seemed to be no-one around, no sign of life at all. They walked down a long corridor and into a large white-tiled room. Here the windows were all made of frosted glass and the light was a diffuse, milky colour. Hugh felt as if he was moving through some strange, thickened atmosphere.

Two men were sitting in the corner reading newspapers. When Long introduced Hugh, they got to their feet and nodded shyly, as if they weren't used to seeing strangers. All around were what looked to be shallow porcelain baths set up on plinths at about hip height. They looked as though they were floating in the milky light, bobbing about on some indoor boating lake. Beneath each one was a tap and a plughole, like the bottom of a urinal. This, Hugh realized, was where the dead were laid out, to be plundered and pulled apart. And here was the paraphernalia of death – the hacksaws, the knives, the pliers – all scattered about on stainless-steel trolleys. Buckets and stacked tupperware boxes. On the walls long green aprons were hanging next to coiled lengths of hosepipe.

He looked down. At his feet were several pairs of wellington boots. Beside them was a bucket. At first Hugh registered nothing, except that there was something inside. Then he saw that it was a head with the top sawn off and the brain removed. He could see the inside of the skull, a curved yellow surface with ridges and grooves, like the inside of a cave. And on the outside, the nose sloped away and the eyes were shut, the eyelashes pressed together, as if in prayer. He felt the sudden lurch of seasickness.

'Shall we go through?' said Long.

There was a set of doors that led into another room. It was about the same size as the one they'd been in before, but this room was almost bare except for a few trolleys. One wall was made up of huge steel doors that stretched from floor to ceiling. There were small pieces of paper stuck on the doors, what appeared to be scrawled and torn reminders that fluttered briefly as they walked in. The two men opened one of the doors. A faint chill blew into the room, a sudden sea breeze. Inside, the fridge was like a giant filing cabinet, deep drawers with metal handles stacked on top of one another.

They pulled out one of the drawers. A body lay there in a cream-coloured plastic bag. Hugh could see the bump of its head and the twin points of its feet with the plastic stretched between. One of the men unzipped the bag. The zip made a sound – a sharp, resentful whinny. Afterwards, Hugh asked himself what he had been expecting. Not this, at any rate. This was nothing like the sound of the dead that came to him at night – that soft, lamenting croon, drifting up the road. Instead, it was as if a sharp blast of anger had rushed out of the bag and filled the room.

The body was naked. It lay twisted slightly, the head turned to one side. The skin was black and dusty-looking, like a fig. Everything seemed distended, swollen with rage. The tongue, yellowed and wrinkled, still protruded from between the lips, although they themselves were oddly tattered, as if someone had been snipping at them with pinking shears. Inside, the gums were a pale mustard colour. The eyelids too had been eaten away and the eyes were open wide, staring up, the whites of the eyes covered in a thin blue film. While one of the hands had gone – neatly unhinged at the wrist – the other lay turned upwards, the bones of the fingers tapering like claws.

All this Hugh tried to take in, doing his best to appear as calm and detached as possible. But all the while he found himself filled not so much with revulsion as sadness. Sorrow at the pity of it. Here was where people gave up whatever composure they'd summoned to face death. Not so much gave it up as had it wrenched away from them.

'You can see what I mean about guesswork,' said Long.

They stood in silence and stared at the body for a while longer, at this angry, inflamed thing before them.

'The injuries are all consistent with a fall,' said Long, and he pointed with the tip of a pencil at various shallow depressions in the skin. 'I can let you see the post-mortem report if you like, but there's nothing unusual there.'

He nodded at one of the men, who zipped up the bag, pushed the drawer back in and closed the fridge door. Out in the car park Hugh thought that he might fall over. To his relief he managed to make it to Long's car and sat gratefully in the passenger seat. They drove back to the police station at the same rigid crawl as before.

'Is there anything else you need?'

They were standing by the car. Long squatted down to look at his reflection in the wing mirror and tugged at the knot of his tie.

Hugh shook his head.

65

'Well, call me if you think of anything.'

Long straightened his legs. 'It wouldn't surprise me if we had snow later,' he said.

The first person Hugh saw when he got back to the office was Joy. She was standing by the window filing her nails, turning her hands to catch what light came through the glass. Joy always took good care of her nails, Hugh had noticed. Her toenails too. At the first sign of warm weather she would be wearing open-toed sandals, her long toes painted some brilliant colour, often orange or pink.

'There you are,' she said. 'What's the matter? You look terrible.'

For a moment Hugh was tempted to tell her what had happened. Joy, he knew, would be sympathetic. But her sympathy could be oppressive; she never knew when to let up. He decided he couldn't face it, so he said something about getting caught in the rain and left it at that. Joy looked at him, her chin jutting forward in her characteristically inquisitorial way.

'You should get out more,' she said. 'Not at work. I mean, socially.'

Hugh knew what was coming.

'Why don't you come out with me and Vivien one evening? We could all have a laugh together.'

'All right,' he said.

'You always say that, but when it comes to fixing anything up, you get all stand-offish and make an excuse.'

'No I don't.'

'Yes you do. Every time. Right then, let's fix up something now. What about tomorrow night?'

'Tomorrow . . . ?'

'See, you're doing it again.'

'Tomorrow would be fine,' said Hugh.

Joy nodded and smiled. 'I'll have to check with Vivien, but I'm sure it'll be all right. She won't be doing anything else.'

They could see Vivien from where they were. She was

standing in the middle of one of the aisles, her shoulders slumped, her curtain of black hair hanging forward.

'She could do with cheering up,' said Joy.

Hugh was on his way out of the office when he saw Julian standing by the lifts.

'Hello, Hughie. Fancy a drink?'

It was, thought Hugh, the last thing he felt like doing. But on the other hand, he had no wish to be on his own, to see that naked body on the slab rise up before him once again. Any distraction was welcome. Besides, he knew that Julian would only sulk if he refused.

'All right,' he said.

They walked down the biscuit-coloured stairs and round the corner. Hugh sat down while Julian bought the drinks. It was a pub they seldom visited and had more modern facilities than the ones they were used to. The games machines were close to where Hugh was sitting. The air was thick with the sound of electronic whooping and squalls of static. Various people stood hunched over the machines, guiding frail white craft through swarms of alien invaders, or tubby hermaphrodites through narrow portcullises, jabbing buttons with their fingers, their expressions showing neither pleasure nor pain, only blank glares of concentration.

Julian sat down beside him.

'I can't stand it any longer,' he cried.

'Stand what?'

'Everything: journalism, life. For years I've been trying to get away. Get a posting abroad somewhere, but every time they come up with some pathetic excuse. I don't know. I never expected it to be like this.'

'What did you expect it to be like?'

'Oh,' said Julian, smiling with unexpected wistfulness, 'different somehow. I often thought . . .'

'What?'

'You'll only laugh at me, Hughie.'

'No I won't.'

'I often thought I might make a rather good editor. I've got some very bold ideas, you know. It's just that no-one asks me for them. You want to do something, though, don't you? Something to prove that you've been here. That's why I'm building this porch. It's not much. I know that . . .'

It struck Hugh that Julian too was a romantic – at least he had the desire to take things at face value, even if his nature seldom permitted it.

'How about you, Hughie?' he said. 'Any secret ambitions?'

The answer, of course, was that Hugh heaved with them. So much so that it was like having a perpetual form of indigestion. A great impacted cluster of yearnings that sat there on his chest. They slowed him up, got in his way. And at times – lying awake at night, say – they even seemed to mash together with the voices of the dead into this clamorous chorus. The worst thing of all, though, was that he couldn't even be sure of what was there. He had the yearnings, all right. But while they multiplied inside him, they seemed to grow ever more indistinct and elusive.

'I once thought I'd like to be a—' he said.

The machine nearest to them gave a loud, trilling squawk.

'A waiter, Hughie?' said Julian. He sounded surprised. 'I would have thought you would have set your sights a bit higher than that.'

'No,' said Hugh, 'a writer.'

'Ah.'

Julian's reaction suggested this was an equally unusual ambition.

'I suppose I'd like to do at least one thing I can be proud of,' said Hugh.

Julian laughed. 'Hardly in the right profession for that, are we?'

'No,' Hugh agreed.

'Do you ever dream of getting a really big story?'

'I used to. Not so much any more. But then I can't even seem to write a little one.'

'Mmm. Have you wondered how far you would go in pursuit of a story, Hughie?'

'How do you mean?'

'Well,' said Julian, 'for instance, would you betray a friendship for a story?'

'I hope not.'

But as he said it Hugh found himself wondering if there was anyone's friendship he valued that highly.

'What? Not even if you were really desperate?'

'If I was really desperate, I might,' Hugh conceded. 'I don't know. Let's hope it never comes to that.'

'It might do,' said Julian gloomily.

'What about you?'

'My life is made up of betrayals,' said Julian. 'Another one or two isn't going to make any difference.'

The machines were all going now, jabbering and moaning, angrily trying to outdo one another. Julian pushed his empty glass out in front of him.

'Aren't you going to get me another drink, Hughie?'

Chapter Six

Hugh walked to the tube station. The rain had stopped but a thin mist hung in the air, strings of droplets that brushed against his face. Crossing the road he walked down the passageway along the side of St Bride's churchyard. He could see a figure sitting on one of the benches at the far end of the churchyard and the glowing end of a cigarette. Presumably this was Vivien – not that he had any desire to find out.

As he hurried on through the mist, Hugh imagined he could see Bridewell Palace rising up before him, like an inflatable castle with towers and battlements and pennants streaming. The cries of the prisoners shrivelling unheard in the damp air. 'Oh good Sir Robert, knock! Pray Sir Robert, knock!'

On the tube he scanned the passengers sitting opposite to see who he could fasten onto tonight, whose face would tide him over on the journey home. But there was no-one. Just a row of unremarkable people, heads bowed over newspapers, or staring up at the advertisements with knotted, baffled expressions.

With no-one else to engage his attention, Hugh fell to thinking about himself. He found he could no longer trust his own reactions to things. His judgement had gone. That, of course, wasn't all. He'd suspected for some time that he was becoming clumsier, both mentally and physically. Vital connections – those that had once given him some measure of finesse – had been disconnected, and so he seemed to flail about in this purposeless haze.

Outside the station a man passed him with a small black dog on a lead. The dog was muzzled. It sniffled and snorted and ran its nose along the pavement. As Hugh walked home, he looked in through the narrow lace-curtained windows as he went by. There were families sitting round talking and watching television, their voices muted by the steel-framed double-glazing that all these houses now seemed to have. When he'd first moved to Kensal Green, Hugh had assumed that it would only be a matter of time before the area came up in the world. After all, it was close to fashionable areas such as Notting Hill and Ladbroke Grove. But, as he'd discovered, there were certain parts of London that remained immune to any form of gentrification. Kensal Green was one of them; it seemed to have fallen off the property map altogether.

The only signs of improvement were the double-glazing and stone-cladding with which an increasing number of residents were covering their houses – knobbly blocks of reconstituted stone that stuck onto the brickwork and were supposed to give their houses an imposing, manorial air. Instead, they ended up looking like little khaki igloos. When he told people where he lived they always looked at him oddly, their lips instinctively beginning to frame the single word, Why?

At the Sri Lankan takeaway Hugh thought he'd spare everyone's embarrassment by not ordering the cuttlefish curry. Instead, he asked for a yellow pancake. But even this produced anxious whispering from the couple behind the counter. The man went off into the kitchen behind the counter. Eventually the pancake was ready and the woman handed it over with the same downcast, yet faintly reproachful air.

In the street outside his flat, boys were riding up and down on their bicycles, pointing their TV remote controls through the windows. He could hear the bellows of annoyance from his neighbours, who had forgotten to draw their

71

curtains and found their televisions unexpectedly hopping about from one channel to another.

When he got inside and unwrapped the foil packaging, he saw that the pancake filling was more yellow than usual. Brilliantly so, like daffodils. They must have overdone one of the spices. He tested it to see if it tasted any different. At first it was too hot to tell and he waited for it to cool down before taking another bite. It seemed just as tasteless as usual.

There was a postcard from his mother on the doorstep and one message on the answerphone. His mother was on a cruise in the South Seas. She'd been gone for a week and had another three weeks to go. 'Other passengers very considerate,' she had written. 'Plenty of invitations to join them at mealtimes. Very hot. Being very lazy. Next stop Jakarta. Yesterday we saw a porpoise. Much love, Mum.'

He could tell who it was as he rewound the message. Other people's voices squeaked and warbled as the tape sped back. But with Noel it was more like a harsh, metallic rattle. Slowed down and going in the right direction, his voice sounded even more disapproving. Hugh wasn't sure if he could be bothered to call him back.

Almost all his other friends had married or paired off. He seldom saw them any more. He found himself envying their happiness so much that it was easier for him to stay away. They in turn seemed to regard him as a relic of their pasts that they could now manage quite well without. Only Noel had remained single, similarly afflicted by absurdly high hopes and diminishing expectations. It was what kept them together.

And there were other reasons why he no longer socialized as much as he had once done. In the past, he'd been embarrassed to invite people back to where he lived because it was too much of a mess. But now he was embarrassed because it was too tidy. A terrible kind of pernicketiness had come over him lately, a desire to ensure that everything was as carefully ordered as possible.

Only a few weeks before, he had read of a woman up the road in Harlesden who had been found sitting in her bedroom with all her possessions neatly bundled into rubbish bags around her. When the bags were opened they found her three children inside, also neatly chopped and bundled up. She had become convinced that, if she sat there for long enough, a giant hoover in the sky was going to suck them up to heaven. So for weeks she'd been sitting and waiting, all tidied and sorted, while the outside world raged incomprehensibly outside.

As a result of all these things, Hugh spent more and more time with people from work. They weren't friends exactly, but he enjoyed their company and they seemed in no more of a hurry to get home than he was.

He sat and watched a football match on television. For a long time nothing of any consequence happened, but whenever he left the room for any reason he came back to find one or other side had scored. After a while it seemed churlish of him to hold up the game by continuing to watch. Despite the cold the boys were still riding their bikes outside, skidding and spinning and giving shrill whoops of delight. He tried to read, but somehow his imagination wasn't up to it. The streets of old London lay flat and inert around him.

As he'd done earlier in the pub, Hugh felt a great impacted mass of desires shift within him – larger and more indigestible than the yellow pancake. He felt choked by this sense of unfulfilment, by these dreadful romantic yearnings, by this need to prove himself. But his life offered no opportunities to satisfy any of these things. Even if it had, he wasn't sure if he would have taken them. He was operating on such diminished resources now that he doubted there was anything left over for experimentation.

When he went up to the bathroom later to remove the

73

black seeds from his teeth, Hugh looked in the mirror and saw that his lips were stained yellow. Inside his mouth it was even worse. He tilted his head about, staring at his reflection, looking at the way his gums and tongue had this jaundiced tinge to them. It took him a while to realize that the inside of his mouth was the same colour as the corpse's he had seen that afternoon.

Chapter Seven

The next morning Hugh asked Darren to see if there were any cuttings in the library on the witness who'd reported seeing a man jumping off Hungerford Bridge. Darren looked at him, his face quite impassive. It was impossible to tell if he intended taking any notice.

Then Hugh sat down to write his piece. It hardly involved writing at all, most of the information was already in the press release Battersby had given him. All he could do was try to build some fluency into these abrupt, bullet-like sentences and make them more easily digestible. Mainly it was just a matter of fiddling with the punctuation – yet even this he found heavy going. Part of him longed to describe the body, describe the piteousness of it, along with his own feelings of sorrow and shock. But that, of course, would have been inappropriate, as well as, he suspected, being quite beyond him.

When he'd finished, he took the piece to Battersby who looked at it without interest, then tossed it into a tray.

'Where the bloody hell's Scaife?' he asked.

'I don't know.'

'When did you say you'd seen him?'

'I'm not sure. Yesterday, I think.'

'Well, was it yesterday, or not?'

'Yes,' said Hugh. 'I think so.'

The phone began to ring. Battersby answered it, his attitude changing rapidly from annoyance to servility. 'No, no,' he said. 'Naturally I wasn't expecting to be able to speak to the Home Secretary in person. I merely wondered if he might consider writing a leader-page article for us. Yes. About dogs, that's right.'

With his spare hand Battersby waved Hugh away. On his way back to his desk Hugh went to the lavatory. These old porcelain urinals had been designed for men with plenty of urine to discharge. They were the size of pulpits and the colour of horses' teeth. There were also a great many of them, stretching down one side of a long room, as if they'd been designed for all the journalists on the paper to empty their bladders simultaneously.

The smell of disinfectant was so strong it made his eyes smart. Some distance away he could see Industrial Gavin, staring fixedly ahead as he peed. All Hugh knew about Gavin was that he went climbing on his holidays and came back with scabs on his forehead where pieces of shale had become embedded. He couldn't remember how he knew this – certainly not from Gavin himself. Once, a long time ago, he thought he'd heard Gavin speak. But thinking about it now, he became less sure. It was a mystery to him why Gavin and Cliff were such close friends. But Cliff was always bringing him for a drink and would treat him with great fondness, even respect. Gavin reminded Hugh of one of those mice or birds that convicts kept in their cells, mute creatures trained to feed from the hand, who they could claim as their own.

As Hugh was standing at the urinal the lawyer came and stood next to him. The top of the urinal came above his shoulders, with only his head visible, and the sweep of the porcelain gave his voice an odd, echoey quality.

'What's happened to the doors?' he asked.

'I'm sorry?'

'The cubicle doors. Someone stole them all during the night.'

Hugh zipped himself up and looked around. He saw that the doors to the cubicles had indeed been removed. There were patches of bare wood on each of the lintels where the hinges had been.

'Who do you think would want to do a thing like that?' asked the lawyer.

'I've no idea.'

'Well, it's very inconvenient,' he said. 'Surely they can't have started demolishing the place quite yet. I suppose you've heard the news?'

'What news?'

'The editor. He's taken a turn for the worse, I'm afraid.'

While Hugh had seldom seen the editor since his job interview, and could barely remember what he looked like, this news made him feel surprisingly sad. Even when in good health the editor was an indistinct figure – removed, shrouded, almost like an oracle. Occasionally Hugh would hear reports of his apoplectic rages, of men being reduced to tears by the sharpness of his tongue. People would emerge from the daily editorial conference, quaking and complaining that the editor had been in a particularly foul mood that day. But all this went on behind closed doors, far beyond Hugh's small sphere. There was no doubt, though, that the editor's absence had contributed greatly to the general mood of uncertainty. This lack of any clear leadership, along with the move to new offices, served to make people even more jumpy than usual.

Together Hugh and the lawyer went over to the basins. Gavin nodded at Hugh, then pulled down a fresh length of roller towel and made his way out.

'Very sad,' said the lawyer. He shook the excess water off his hands before touching the towel. 'It can't be long now.'

All day no mention was made of the fact that Hugh was due to spend the evening with Joy and Vivien. He'd allowed himself to hope that Joy had forgotten about it. But then, at six o'clock, he saw her walk up to Vivien and steer her by the elbow towards the Ladies.

They emerged fifteen minutes later. Joy, he saw, had tousled her hair and applied some more lipstick. As far as he could tell, Vivien looked exactly the same as before. Then, as she walked away from the door, still half steered by Joy, but now pulling her arm away in annoyance, he noticed that she had put on different shoes. They were light emerald green in colour. She looked as if she was wearing a pair of luminous snowshoes. There was a bag hooked over her shoulder and Hugh could see the scuffed heels of her other shoes poking out of the top. They began to make their way towards his desk. Before they got there Darren came by. He had a brown envelope in his hand.

'What's this?' asked Hugh.

An expression of irritation came over Darren's face. 'It's the cuttings file you asked me for this morning,' he said. 'If you don't want it then I'll take it away again.'

'No, that's fine. Thank you.'

He took the envelope, but before he could look inside Joy said, 'All set then?'

'Do you want to go now?'

'Why not?'

'All right,' said Hugh.

He put the envelope in his top drawer. They caught the lift downstairs, pushed through the front doors and stood on the pavement outside.

'Brr,' said Joy. 'I hate this cold, don't you?' She was hugging herself. The traffic heading in both directions was almost at a standstill.

'What shall we do first then?' she said.

Joy was smiling, looking from Vivien to Hugh. Vivien said nothing.

'What did you have in mind?' asked Hugh.

'I didn't have anything in mind, that's why I'm asking.'

'We could go for a drink.'

'We could do that. What do you reckon, Viv?'

It was like trying to raise someone from a trance.

'All right,' said Vivien. 'But not here,' she added with sudden vehemence. 'Let's go somewhere else.'

They ended up catching a bus down the Strand and getting off at Trafalgar Square. There were groups of tourists sitting on the rim of the fountains, feeding the pigeons and having their photographs taken. The water had been turned off in case it froze, but still the pigeons and the tourists came. Hugh remembered how his parents had brought him here as a child. He too had been given some birdseed to hold out. Instantly, the pigeons had descended on his hand, the air had been thick with the beating of their wings. He remembered that mingled sense of exhilaration and nausea as they pecked away at his palm, brushing his fingers with their claws. There had been an odd wormy, metallic smell about them, and he remembered the sense of relief when the seed was finished and they'd flown off to perch on someone else.

Vivien, he saw, had also stopped and was staring at the pigeons. He wondered if she was stoned. Certainly Joy had to cajole her into moving once more. Even then she hardly lifted her feet as they began to walk up Charing Cross Road. This could be a long evening, thought Hugh, and he felt something of Vivien's slothfulness overcome him.

They hadn't gone far when Joy asked, 'Where do you fancy?'

'I don't really mind,' said Hugh.

'Well, that's helpful. Vivien?'

'What?'

'Where do you want to have a drink?'

'Not fussed.'

'My God,' said Joy, pursing her lips. 'You two.'

She began to walk more briskly. They both followed her, turning left into Leicester Square and then left again. There was a pub on the corner with banners hanging from the windows advertising a new brand of beer. They'd stiffened and curled in the cold. Inside they found a spare table in an alcove, but there was only one stool. Hugh bought the drinks, then he and Joy went off to find some more stools,

Hugh having first told Vivien that she should keep the table for them.

Seeing what sort of a state she was in, he spoke more loudly than he might otherwise have done.

She stared back at him. 'All right. Don't shout.'

They found two stools and carried them over. For some time Vivien seemed offended by Hugh's behaviour, refusing to look at him or else scowling. She seemed to veer between torpor and sudden bursts of aggression with no warning whatsoever. The trick, in so far as there was one, was to try to catch her in one of the brief lulls in between.

'Anyway, I never liked him,' Joy was saying. 'He really gave me the creeps. What do you think, Viv? Don't you hope that Scaife never comes back?'

'He made a pass at me once,' said Vivien. She spoke in the same dreamy, disengaged way as before.

'Did he?' said Joy. 'Where?'

'In the Ladies. I couldn't see who it was at first. He was standing by the window. I thought it was one of the cleaners. Then he asked me if I'd like to go into one of the cubicles with him.'

'He never!'

'What did you say?' asked Hugh.

Vivien turned towards him. 'I said I didn't want to go back into one of the cubicles, I'd only just come out.'

'Quite right,' said Joy. 'Anyway, what was he doing in the Ladies in the first place?'

'I asked him that.'

'And?'

'He just said he preferred it in there.'

'That's no excuse. You've never told me that before,' said Joy. 'Never.'

Vivien shrugged. 'I'd forgotten all about it.'

'How can you forget about something like that?'

'I just put it out of my mind. Then, I don't know . . . something must have reminded me.'

To Hugh's alarm, he saw that Vivien was looking at him

again. He took another drink. So much of human behaviour was a mystery to him, he realized. You thought you'd formed some idea of how most people conducted themselves; there were certain loose parameters they stayed within, or seldom strayed outside. Then it turned out it wasn't like that at all. They ventured much further than you'd ever imagined possible. Did things that defied belief. Things he would never have dreamed of doing.

Often Hugh found himself making excuses for people, trying to squeeze their behaviour back within comprehensible boundaries. It wasn't so much a matter of wanting to think the best of them – although that came into it – as a reluctance to admit the extent of his ignorance.

Of all the people he knew, Scaife was the least governed by any code of acceptable behaviour. There was nothing remotely unusual about his appearance – clipped brown hair, the same grey suit and unironed shirts – yet he had something wild and reckless about him, a determination to push things a good deal further than they would normally go. Indeed, Hugh had noticed that Scaife only seemed to enjoy life when it was in as great a state of flux as possible. Chaos was his element. Outbreaks of tranquillity only bored him.

'Someone stole all the cubicle doors in the Gents last night,' Hugh said.

'Did they?' said Vivien, more animatedly than he might have expected. 'Whatever for?'

'I don't know. It's a strange thing to do, though, isn't it?'

'He asked me out once,' said Joy.

'Who did?'

'Scaife.'

'What happened?'

'He asked me out to dinner. I thought . . . anyway, I went. He'd booked a restaurant. It was a perfectly nice place. We started eating – I can even remember what we had. Then, halfway through the main course . . . he made a suggestion.'

'What sort of suggestion?'

'A disgusting suggestion,' said Joy.

'How disgusting?' asked Hugh, intrigued.

'I'd rather not go into it.'

'C—can't you give us some idea?' he said.

'She said she didn't want to,' said Vivien. 'All right?'

'He asked me if he could do something,' said Joy. 'Something that I found – well, I'm pretty broad-minded. But this . . . I said I wasn't interested, thank you. Scaife didn't seem in the least fussed. He took it in his stride and we carried on eating. *He* did anyway. I found my appetite had gone. I couldn't touch another thing. But we carried on chatting, and at the end of the meal he called for the bill. When it arrived he started looking for his wallet, patting his jacket and so on, and looking more and more worried. Then he said, "I'm terribly sorry, Joy, but I appear to have left my money behind. This is very embarrassing, but would you mind paying the bill and I'll reimburse you in the morning."'

'What happened?'

'Well, I paid it, didn't I?'

'And did he pay you back?'

She shook her head.

'He never offered, and I never asked.'

'Why ever not?' asked Hugh.

'Because she's got her pride, that's why,' said Vivien.

They stayed at the pub for another hour or so. Hugh was surprised by how relaxed he began to feel. A great deal of that was down to Joy. She had a natural gift for putting people at their ease, for drawing them out. On the few occasions when conversation threatened to flag, she always managed to think of something else to say, undaunted by his awkwardness or Vivien's swings of mood. He began to find himself thinking what an attractive person Joy was. He'd felt like this before, but the feeling always faded pretty quickly. This time though it lingered. He reproached himself for ever finding her overpowering or a nuisance. And while he couldn't be sure – he didn't trust himself to read the signals properly – he got the impression that she was looking upon him with a similar quickening interest.

They decided to go for a Chinese meal and walked across Leicester Square towards Gerrard Street. Hugh was aware of walking with more of a spring in his step than usual. They went into the first restaurant they came to. Even Vivien seemed more vivacious than before; her shoes weren't slowing her down at all now. She took off her jacket and hung it over the back of her chair. When she leant forward to take a light for her cigarette, Hugh could see the skin bunching between her breasts.

'Shall we have the set dinner?' he suggested.

'Suits me,' said Vivien.

At the table alongside was a group of Chinese people. All of them were adults, except for a small girl wearing a pale-blue dress. In order to try to get their attention, or else simply to relieve her boredom, the girl rocked from side to side like a metronome, her eyes open, her neck taut. Instead of taking any notice, one of the adults beside her would simply stretch out a hand and hold her in place while they carried on with their conversation. Whenever they released her, she'd wait a few seconds before starting up again, rocking away, until another hand reached out to hold her still.

The set meal arrived. By the time they'd finished the tablecloth was stained and dotted with small heaps of discarded food.

'We could go on somewhere else,' said Joy.

'We could go dancing,' said Vivien.

'What do you think about dancing, Hugh?'

'All right.'

They called for the bill and split it three ways. Outside the streets were busier. People were walking down the middle of the road paying no attention to the oncoming traffic. Vivien crossed over to look in some shop windows.

'You're a funny man,' said Joy.

'Am I?' said Hugh.

'It doesn't matter, though.'

'Doesn't it?'

'No.'

He took her hand and they continued walking down the street.

Afterwards, he tried to work out just where it had all started to go wrong. As far as he could tell, there hadn't been any one turning point, more like an accumulation of things to which he hadn't paid sufficient heed. By the time he became aware of what was going on, they'd developed this terrible momentum of their own. That, at least, was how he tried to explain it to himself. But then, as he couldn't help but acknowledge, it was so much easier to see himself being swept along by circumstances, rather than to acknowledge any active role in what had happened.

He and Joy followed Vivien up Charing Cross Road to a doorway where a piece of rope was strung between two metal barriers. There was a queue of people standing behind the rope. They joined the queue, shuffling forward every few minutes. Eventually they reached a doorway where a man stood with his arms folded beneath a lime-green light. Hugh noticed that a number of people were speaking Spanish.

'What is this place?' he asked.

'This is a salsa club.'

'But I don't know how to salsa.'

'That doesn't matter. Anyway, Vivien can teach you. She's had lessons.'

They each paid five pounds to get in. The man held open the door and ushered them through. A set of stairs led down into the basement. At the bottom of the stairs was a hatch where you could check in coats and bags. Beyond it was a bar, and beyond that a dance floor packed with spinning couples.

The barman paid them no attention, until Vivien banged her fist on the counter and shouted at him. Then, to Hugh's surprise, he ignored the couple whose orders he was taking and came over and served them instead. They stood with their drinks and watched the couples dancing. There was barely enough room for everyone to fit on the dance floor. Joy nudged Hugh in the ribs and winked at him. He felt an enormous sense of excitement – the music, the atmosphere, the people pressing in on every side, swaying and bending like trees in a storm. He tried to manoeuvre his arm round Joy's waist, but she moved away before he could make contact.

Vivien asked Hugh if he'd like to dance. He turned to Joy, hoping she might raise an objection. But instead she yelled, 'You two carry on. Don't mind me.'

They made their way onto the dance floor. Hugh tried to tell Vivien that he didn't know the steps, but she took no notice. There was so little room that all he had to do was stand still and wobble his hips about in faint approximation to the beat. They continued like this for the first few dances. Then Hugh became aware that people around them were moving back, out of the way.

To begin with he assumed this was due to his own clumsiness. Then, looking up, his saw to his alarm that Vivien was moving with increasing abandon. For fear of getting hurt, the other dancers shrank away and a large space soon opened up around them. Now Hugh was far more exposed than before. He looked to Vivien for guidance, but she was oblivious to everything. Shaking violently, her hair tossing, her breasts swinging about in some peculiar counter-rhythm of their own, slapping her green shoes down on the floor. His only choice was to thrash about and do his best to ape her movements.

When the music stopped for a moment, Hugh tried to make it clear that he'd had enough, but she took no notice. In the end he walked off and left her on her own.

He went back to find Joy. There was no sign of her. It was only after pushing his way through more knots of people that he saw her standing on the other side of the dance floor. She was talking to a man, their heads bent close together. When he reached them, Joy introduced him.

'This is Jesus,' she said. 'He's Guatemalan.'

They shook hands. Jesus had a weather-beaten face and jet-black hair.

'Do you want to dance?' Hugh asked her.

'Not now,' she said.

'Well, when then?'

'When I feel like it. Why don't you go and have another dance with Vivien?'

Instead, Hugh went off for another drink. By the time he was served Joy and Jesus were dancing, moving about the floor in tight, syncopated steps. Jesus had one arm wrapped around her bottom and a hand flat against the small of Joy's back, holding her against him. Hugh stood by himself for a while, then Vivien came up to join him. She was breathless and there was a ring of sweat around the top of her blouse.

'Where did you get to?' she asked.

Hugh didn't answer. Instead, he tried to get the barman's attention, but failed. Once again, Vivien had to bang the counter and shout before he came over. Hugh bought her a drink.

'Who's Joy with?' she asked.

'He's called Jesus.'

'Where did he come from?'

'Guatemala.'

Vivien finished her drink. 'I'm going outside,' she said.

'What for?'

'Have a smoke.'

'Are you?'

'Why shouldn't I?'

Vivien's hair was damp and she had to push it out of her eyes, hooking it back over her ear.

'No,' said Hugh. 'No reason.'

'Come if you want.'

Hugh looked at the dance floor. He could see Joy and Jesus, still entwined, flexing back and forth.

'All right,' he said.

They made their way back up the stairs. The man on the

door stamped their hands so that they could get back in. An alleyway ran down the side of the building. Vivien ducked into it and Hugh followed, squeezing his way past several tall rubbish bins.

She took out a joint and lit it, inhaling so deeply that almost half had gone by the time she passed it to Hugh. He sucked as hard as he could. The tip glowed between his fingers and the smoke had a sweet composty taste which mingled with the smell from the bins. He handed it back to Vivien. She took another drag, then handed it back to him.

At first he felt nothing. Then it was as if a slow tide of pleasure passed up his body from his feet to his head. He could hardly see Vivien standing beside him, but all at once he was peculiarly aware of her movements – that heavy sway as she shifted about, the scrape of her shoes on the ground. High above them there was a narrow rectangle of sky. By tilting his head back he could see the clouds drifting by, pale shreds scudding past.

For some time now Hugh had been nervous about taking drugs. He loved the sense of being taken out of himself, yet at the same time he was fearful of abdicating what control he had. A few months before he had been invited to a New Year's Eve party where guests were asked to come in fancy dress. Hugh didn't know the people giving the party well and was appalled by the idea of having to dress up, but no other invitations had been forthcoming and eventually he'd decided to go. However, when he went to hire a costume he'd found there weren't many left to choose from. He'd ended up going dressed as a Roman legionnaire, with thonged sandals, plastic helmet, breastplate and a plastic sword stuck in his belt. Feeling especially self-conscious given the skimpiness of his tunic – it only just covered his bottom – he'd gratefully accepted a joint when it was handed to him. Another one soon followed, then another. By this time Hugh's head had started to swim. He decided to go upstairs to try to collect himself, but instead he'd fallen asleep beside a pile of coats.

When he'd woken up almost everyone had gone, including the people who had promised to give him a lift home. Barely aware of what he was doing, he'd stumbled down the stairs and out of the house before realizing that he was still in his legionnaire's costume. For a moment he had stood there, frozen in horror, like a prisoner caught in a searchlight. There was nothing for it but to walk down the Finchley Road with his plastic helmet under his arm, the wind miserably cold on his bare legs. People had waved and hooted as they drove by. Hugh had shaken his sword at them, endeavouring to look as casual as possible. Nonetheless, the incident had scarred him, made him more wary than ever.

'What are you looking at?' asked Vivien.

'Clouds,' said Hugh.

Vivien too leant back. She put her hand against one of the bins to steady herself.

'Not much to see, is there?'

'No.'

'You could get dizzy if you stand like this for long.'

'I thought I could see some stars.'

'Where?'

'I'm not sure. Perhaps they were planes.'

Vivien sighed. She had moved again and was standing in a thin patch of light.

Hugh could see that she still had her head tilted back. 'The stars in the bright sky,' she said.

She stopped, and then went on: 'Looked down where he lay.'

'Who?'

Vivien was smiling to herself. 'The Little Lord Jesus . . .'

'Oh.'

'. . . Asleep on the hay.'

Vivien began to sing. She sang softly, as if she was singing to herself. But still the sound of her voice seemed to spread out and fill the alleyway.

'The cattle are lowing,' she sang, 'the baby awakes. But Little Lord Jesus no crying he makes. I love thee, Lord Jesus;

look down from the sky. And stay by my bedside till morning is nigh.'

'That's lovely,' said Hugh when she'd finished.

'It just came back to me. I used to sing it as a child.'

'So did I,' said Hugh.

They made their way back past the steel bins and out of the alley. At the door they held up their hands so the doorman could see their stamps.

Joy and Jesus were still dancing, they hardly seemed to have moved their feet. But each shifted their hands about constantly, so as to get a better purchase on the other. At one point between dances Joy broke away. She patted Jesus on his outstretched palms and headed off towards the lavatory. Hugh followed her.

'All right then?' she asked when she saw him.

'I suppose so,' he said.

They were standing by the door to the Ladies. There were women pushing past to get in and out.

'It's just . . .'

'What?'

'Well, I hoped – you and me,' said Hugh.

Joy pinched him loosely on the cheek.

'It's only a bit of fun,' she said. 'He's nice, Jesus, as far as I can tell. Of course, it's not easy.'

'Why not?'

'He doesn't speak any English.'

'What, none?'

'No,' said Joy, laughing and tossing her head. 'Not a bloody word.'

When Hugh got back to Vivien he said, 'I think I'll be off.'

'Where are you going?'

'Home.'

'I might go home, too,' said Vivien. 'I don't much feel like dancing any more. Shall we say goodbye to Joy?'

'No point disturbing her.'

It had begun to rain again and there was a thin, charred sort of smell in the air. They stood in the doorway and watched the rain blowing about in front of them. The tube had shut down and so they walked to the bus stop. No buses came by. After they'd been there a while Vivien suggested they catch a taxi. But there were no empty cabs either. It continued raining. They waited for another ten minutes.

Hugh was wondering what to do when he saw Vivien step out into the road in front of an unlit cab, her arms outstretched. The driver swerved to avoid her, skidded, then stopped. He wound down the window and shouted, 'You could get killed doing that.'

Vivien seemed quite unconcerned. Hugh saw there was no-one in the back of the cab. The driver turned out to be on his way home. He was heading west and eventually agreed to take them as far as he was going. Vivien sprawled on the back seat, her feet stuck out in front of her. Hugh saw that her shoes had darkened in the rain.

The windows in the taxi soon misted up. Whenever the engine idled or the taxi went over a bump, the whole chassis shook. Hugh lay back, feeling as if they were being bowled through the empty streets in an opaque, rattling bubble.

Chapter Eight

The driver dropped them off close to where Vivien lived. Hugh hoped to find another taxi to take him on, but still there were none about. They ended up walking to Vivien's flat in a Victorian house near Warwick Avenue. She said he could come up and call a minicab. The door-closer hissed behind them. There was a patch of worn lino in the hallway and envelopes scattered across the doormat.

They climbed the stairs. He followed Vivien into a sitting room hung with scarves and other pieces of material. Hugh sat on the sofa and called various minicab firms. Most of them were engaged. One said they could send a cab round, but it would take at least half an hour. He ordered it anyway.

He'd begun to feel awkward again. Vivien stood by the window smoking. She handed him the joint without saying anything. Hugh took it, hoping that it might make him feel less awkward. And it did, just as, in the alleyway, he found himself floating slowly upwards like an un-tethered balloon, a sense of bliss seeping through him.

The next time he looked, Vivien was crouched on the floor, her feet planted squarely beneath her thighs, her hair loose. Her face scrunched up as she inhaled. When she had finished she swayed slightly.

'What is it?'

'I didn't say anything,' she said.

'Oh. How are you feeling?'

'All right. How about you?'

Hugh didn't like to say. At the same time he wasn't sure if he could help himself. As he tried to cope with this, he felt the room rocking in sympathy. He remembered being back in the Chinese restaurant and watching the little girl in the blue dress rocking from side to side. He was reminded, too, of his thoughts of the unknowability of people; how they could react to things in entirely unforeseen ways.

'Vivien,' he said.

'Yes, what?'

'Nothing.'

She shrugged and reached over to hand him the joint. He took a drag and his resolve momentarily hardened. He held it out for her.

'Vivien?'

She looked up, still crouched in front of him, her skirt hanging between her knees.

'Yes?'

'Would you do something for me?'

'What?'

There were arc lights inside his head that seemed to flare and leave his eyes dazzled. When they cleared he could see Vivien still looking up at him.

'Would you show me your breasts?' he asked.

She lowered her head and her hair fell back over her face. She looked sunk in thought. Her shoulders rose fractionally and then fell.

'Why should I?'

'I just want you to.'

At first Hugh thought she intended to do nothing. He hadn't really expected her to. But at least he'd asked – that was the important part. Or so he hoped to convince himself. Then, to his surprise, she sat up and started to undo the buttons of her blouse. When she reached the bottom she had to twist round and tug the material out of her skirt. As she did so, Hugh thought there was something

92

almost leonine about her features that he hadn't noticed before.

She took off her blouse, and then reached behind her to undo her bra. Leaning forward, she held one hand cupped across her chest while with the other she pushed her hair back.

She looked up at him. Then she took her hand away and the bra came with it. Her breasts swung and settled, as large and dark and altogether dramatic as he had imagined they might be. The joint had gone out. She relit it and inhaled, before raising herself up on her haunches, stretching lazily and holding it out for him. There wasn't much left, hardly more than a twist of burning paper. It stung his lips as he inhaled. Hugh shut his eyes just for the pleasure of opening them again.

Somehow it seemed particularly important to him that he should keep this brittle divide between them. But here again he had nothing to worry about. Even when he reached out and touched Vivien's breast with his fingertips, she stayed quite impassive, neither pulling away nor offering any encouragement. He ran his fingers around one breast, and then the other. And when he sank down onto the floor and licked her nipple, feeling its tight knottiness of skin against his tongue and between his lips, she bent back slightly. Nothing more.

When he drew away he could see his tongue-trails running over her breasts. Vivien continued to regard him in the same detached, slightly disdainful way. But Hugh was sure he could detect something more languid than ever about her movements now. The two of them seemed to be floating in soup. It was, he thought, one of the most delightful sensations he'd ever had.

Vivien reached for her bra.

'What are you doing?' he asked.

'You asked to see my breasts. Now you've seen them.'

'I know. But . . .'

'But what?'

93

She held the bra to her chest. 'You hardly bother to acknowledge me in the office. It's as much as you can do to say hello. Now you expect me to display myself in front of you.'

She got to her feet and stood over him. Then, with a sideways flick, she threw the bra in his lap and walked out, pulling the door behind her.

There was a shriek as the intercom went off on the wall behind him. Hugh got up and pressed the button.

A voice said, 'Minicab.'

He closed his eyes again and hoped the room would stabilize.

'Minicab,' repeated the voice insistently, strained through the speaker.

'I'm sorry,' said Hugh. He shook his head as he spoke for added emphasis. 'You must have the wrong flat.'

He picked up the bra and followed Vivien through the door. There was a narrow corridor with a door on the left and another door ahead of him.

'Vivien?' he called out. 'Vivien?'

She came out of the door on the left. Her breasts were still bare. So too were her legs, and her skirt had ridden up her thighs. They stood facing each other in the corridor.

Hugh made as if to touch her breast again. Vivien swatted his hand away. Then she had another mood swing.

'All right,' she said. 'If that's what you want.'

She took hold of her skirt and pulled it up over her hips. Leaning against the wall, she sank down slightly. Her legs bowed, her feet splayed. She was naked underneath.

Hugh pulled off his shirt, his trousers, his socks and his pants, jigging about from one foot to another. When he was naked he ran his hands up her thighs and took hold of her by the hips. He felt her drop her weight onto him as he pushed himself inside her.

He had, he realized, never felt this sexually confident before. Had never been anywhere quite so moist, so accommodating. Had never felt this thoroughly erect, or

94

such a feeling of abandonment. He looked down and saw the glistening shapes sliding back and forth, and he felt thrilled to be a fully-fledged participant in all this.

As Vivien sank down on him, and they rose and fell together, it was as if she was both engaged and disengaged. Abandoning herself, yet at the same time holding herself back, keeping part of herself quite hidden. They seemed both joined and entirely separate. And somehow this served to elevate Hugh's pleasure even more.

He took hold of her wrists and held them up against the wall, so she seemed to hang suspended against him, falling forward. He pushed into her, hearing his skin slap against hers. The ooze and stick, dark, estuarine noises. And the sound of their breaths, quickening and rasping. Swarming upwards, hand over hand.

She wrapped her arms around his neck and hung onto him. While he buried himself in her, head between her breasts. Hands clasping her buttocks, bending and straightening his legs. He could feel himself starting to come, that long giddying thread starting to be drawn out of him. He could feel Vivien arcing herself backwards, labouring and scrambling, hoisting herself up and down, tugging at his balls.

Then a cry emerged, unstoppered, from both their throats. It seemed to him as though they collapsed into one another in this sudden folding motion. He felt a long series of spasms as he came inside her. Over and over, for longer than he thought possible. Eager to expend every last drop inside her.

And when at last they were done, they slid, still locked together, to the floor.

Part 2

'Those who make researches into Antiquity may be said to pass often through many dark lobbies and dusky places, before they come to the *Aula lucis*, the great hall of light; they must repair to old archives, and peruse many moulded and moth-eaten records, and so bring light as it were out of darkness, to inform the present world what the former did, and make us see truth through our ancestors' eyes.'

J. HOWELL, *LONDINOPOLIS*, 1657

Chapter Nine

'What's that thing you've got there, Cliff?'

'What thing?'

'There. That thing in your hand.'

Cliff was carrying a black box. It had a special carrying handle on the top.

'This?' he said. 'This is my new portable phone.'

'What do you mean, portable?'

'Well, you carry it about with you.'

'Who does?'

'I do.'

'By yourself, Cliff? I'm surprised you can manage it.'

'On the contrary, it's very portable. It's already transformed my life.'

'How much does it weigh?'

'Oh, not much. It probably looks heavier than it is.'

'But you're all sweaty, Cliff. And your ears have turned red.'

'I tell you it's not heavy.'

'Why don't you put it down anyway? Give yourself a rest.'

'I'm quite happy carrying it, thank you.'

Cliff stood there, holding on to the box, trying to look relaxed. 'You wait,' he said. 'You may be laughing now, all of you – except Gavin. But you won't be laughing for long.'

'Why not, Cliff?'

Cliff drew himself up. 'Because I am the future,' he said.

Several incidents the next morning had combined to unsettle Hugh. He arrived in the office to find that brown envelopes had been put on top of all the neighbouring typewriters apart from his own. He watched as Stanley tore open his envelope and read the contents.

'What is it?'

Stanley lowered his visor. 'It's just some memo about computer training. Haven't you got one yet?'

'No,' said Hugh. 'I haven't. Not yet.'

A few weeks before a notice had gone up on the board saying that everyone would have to attend a day's computer training. At the new offices everything was going to be computerized. Instead of a typewriter, each journalist would have his own screen and keyboard. Opinions differed on the usefulness of computers. Some saw them simply as abominations, proof that an older, more exuberant era was passing and a drier, automated one coming in its stead. Those journalists who'd already attended training, however, spoke with disbelief about the different things a computer enabled one to do. Chief among these was deleting one's mistakes – an idea so novel, so entirely at odds with what anyone had been taught, that it needed explaining a number of times before it sank in.

Watching Darren making his way round with the tea trolley, and unable to face another cup of coffee from the machine, Hugh decided that he'd make another attempt to find the canteen. Not wanting to draw attention to the fact that he had been left off the tea roster, he didn't ask directions from anyone in the office. Instead, he went down one flight of stairs – he was sure this at least was right – intending to stop the first person he saw. But there was no-one to ask.

Two doors led off the stairwell. Hugh pushed open the left-hand door and walked down the long corridor that stretched ahead. At the end of the corridor he came to a T-junction. Only hesitating briefly, he took the left-hand corridor. But he hadn't gone far when any optimism he'd initially had gave out, and once again he was forced to admit that he had no idea where he was. He stopped and began to think about retracing his steps.

At that moment a set of double doors opened further down the corridor and a group of green-carders came out. They had their arms linked together and were moving with more difficulty than usual. Hugh saw they were carrying something between them – a large piece of machinery by the look of it, all packaged up. He started, tentatively, to make his way towards them, unsure of what their reaction was likely to be.

It was even worse than he could have anticipated. As soon as they saw him, the green-carders spun around, almost dropping whatever they were carrying. Immediately, they began to make their way in the opposite direction, still linked together, struggling with their load. One of them, however, detached himself and stood in the corridor while the others hurried away. As Hugh made his way towards him, he saw that the man appeared determined not to allow him to pass. He had his arms folded and his legs braced and his dun-coloured cardigan trailed behind him.

When they were about fifteen feet apart Hugh stopped. He wasn't sure what to do. He had a familiar sense of being misunderstood, only this time the scale of the misunderstanding had reached new and more disturbing heights. Whenever he made a move forward the man tensed up, as if ready to meet any sudden charge. The two of them stood and stared at each other, until the man, having checked over his shoulder that his companions had gone, simply turned and walked away. Again, Hugh abandoned any thought of trying to find the canteen and made his way back upstairs. He felt more shaken by this than he liked to admit.

On his way upstairs he saw Vivien. He turned a corner

in the corridor and there she was, coming towards him. She was still some way off, talking to another of the green-carders, her head bent, hair forward, slowing her pace to match his. Despite this, there seemed to be a fixity of purpose about her, an alertness he hadn't seen before. Hugh kept his own head down and hoped she wouldn't notice him. But as they passed, he felt her eyes lock momentarily onto him, then shift away.

He felt – he didn't know what he felt. He didn't want to analyse his feelings. He knew he was shocked by his own behaviour and that he'd made a terrible mistake – one that he had no intention of repeating. It was extraordinary how you could be consumed with desire for someone one moment, then equally hell-bent on getting away from them the next.

He hadn't stayed the night at Vivien's. She hadn't invited him to, and even if she had he doubted if he would have accepted. Instead he'd left and walked home. It only took him about an hour, but the rain hadn't let up the whole way. In so far as it was possible, he had decided it would be better to pretend the whole thing had never happened.

When the first editions of the paper were handed out Hugh looked for his story. He found it at the back of the news section, just before the television listings and the horoscopes. Battersby, he saw, had left off his name, presumably on the grounds that the piece was too unimportant to deserve a byline. He sat and looked at the photofit of the man's face, the heap of planes and angles, bearing no resemblance to what he had seen the day before. He folded the paper and put it in the bin.

At lunchtime they went for a drink and Cliff explained why he had forbidden his wife to feed the birds.

'I've told her she shouldn't, but I can't seem to get through to her.'

'But, Cliff, I mean, in this weather, they're freezing to their perches.'

'Because there's an issue of principle involved here. If

102

Pauline feeds them now, she might think she's doing them a favour, but she isn't. Because what happens when it warms up again? They will have got used to being fed, won't they? They'll have lost the will to forage.'

'Surely, though, she's just helping them stay alive.'

'I simply said to her this morning – they were all there, standing in line on the bloody windowsill – and I merely pointed out that what she thought was an act of kindness was in fact sapping their initiative.'

'"Lost the will to forage" – Jesus. You really are mad.'

'I'm not mad, Julian. I'm a realist, that's all. Nature must be allowed to take its course.'

'But what about the dog crisis, Cliff,' said Johnny Todd. 'I see there was another attack last night, in Stevenage. And it now turns out they've impounded the regimental mascot of the Royal Fusiliers.'

'I don't want to talk about the dog crisis,' said Cliff. 'If people invite these brutes into their homes they deserve what's coming to them.'

Generally, though, he was in an expansive mood.

'How are you getting on with building your porch, Julian?' he asked.

'All right,' said Julian suspiciously. 'Why?'

'I just wondered. Natural curiosity, if you will.'

'I've done the drawings,' said Julian.

His suspicion hadn't disappeared completely, but carpentry was the one subject he was apt to get carried away talking about.

'I can't get properly started though until the weather improves. I'm only planning to use old timbers.'

'Sounds very nice,' said Cliff. 'Cottage style?'

'In a manner of speaking.'

'Lovely.'

'Yes,' said Cliff, almost to himself. 'I thought you'd be using old timbers.'

'What's that supposed to mean?'

'Nothing. Nothing. It's just that Battersby asked me where I thought the lavatory doors might have got to.'

'And what did you tell him?'

'Well, we talked of various possible explanations, and I happened to mention in passing that you were building a porch.'

'You did what?' said Julian.

'It was only a casual remark.'

'But now he's going to think that I stole the fucking doors.'

'Oh, I wouldn't have thought so,' said Cliff. 'No, surely not. As I said, it was only a joke.'

'You fucker,' said Julian.

'It was only a joke, Julian,' said Cliff.

'You know how gullible Battersby is. He'll believe anything he's told. Jesus.'

Hugh noticed that Julian was actually wringing his hands in anguish.

'Tum, tum, tum,' said Cliff. 'I see change and decay all around me.'

'Have you seen Vivien today?' asked Bobbie.

'Vivien? Who's she? Oh, I know, the drug-addled one. What about her?'

'I don't know. She's changed, that's all.'

'In what way?'

'She just looks different somehow.'

'Yeah. Almost radiant.'

'She wouldn't be a bad-looking woman if she took more care of herself.'

'Can't say I've noticed. Have you noticed anything, Hughie?'

'Noticed what?'

'Have you noticed anything different about Vivien?'

'No. Why should I?'

'No reason particularly. Just wondered.'

'How should I know?'

'All right, Hughie. Calm down. What's the matter with you today? Bit touchy, or what?'

'It's been almost a week now,' said Hugh.

'What has?'

'Since Scaife disappeared.'

'Oh,' said Cliff. 'Scaife.'

'You said he'd be back on Tuesday morning.'

'Did I? It's possible that I may have been a little over-optimistic, but the theory still stands. He'll be back. He's obviously having difficulties in his life and he's embarrassed to show his face again until he's worked them out. Perfectly understandable. Give it another couple of days. If he's not back by then we should start to get worried.'

'God, you're full of crap,' said Julian bitterly.

'You sure you're OK, Hughie?' said Johnny Todd. 'You look a bit green to me.'

'Maybe he's coming down with the flu.'

'Could very well be. There's plenty of it about. You poor thing, Hughie.'

'No,' said Hugh. 'I'm all right.'

After lunch Hugh sat back and tried to let himself relax amid the clatter of other people's endeavours. He could hear Cliff from three desks away on the phone bribing one of the old frauds who huffed and puffed to order on the leader pages. Cliff was trying hard to be ingratiating, but this only served to emphasize his natural belligerence.

There was a set procedure on such occasions: you called up someone and asked them to fulminate on some topical subject. Most were MPs – passed-over windbags and professional nuisances whose names still carried a little clout. At first they refused, saying that in normal circumstances they'd be delighted to. Alas, though, on this particular occasion they had to go to some vital function, usually involving their children. You then expressed sadness, emphasizing that this was a subject on which a particularly high degree of expertise was called for.

Still they said no. Much as they would have liked to have accepted, they simply couldn't. It was at this point that money would be mentioned for the first time, dropped like a stray sock into the conversation. A further refusal ensued. The sum was then doubled. This had to be done carefully, so as not to give offence. No-one liked to think of themselves as bribable, rather as hard negotiators with inflammatory opinions to match.

Again they refused. There would be further pleasantries. After which the sum was raised again, this time by around 30 per cent. By now the cracks were beginning to appear. In all but the toughest cases another small increase would suffice. Thus the paper beat its contributors into submission with bundles of money.

Cliff sounded as if he was still around stage three, although his patience was clearly failing. 'Of course you'll make it to the last race,' he was saying, his voice thickening. 'Besides, the little lad will be running his heart out. He'll never have time to look around and see who's there.'

It was only at this point that Hugh remembered the cuttings file that Darren had brought him the evening before. He took the envelope out of his desk. There were three pieces of paper folded inside. He spread them out on his desk. The first was headlined ACADEMIC IS SEX PEST. He read how Andrew Gardner, a history lecturer at the University of Surrey, had been arrested for importuning women on trains. In one incident he'd asked a woman if she'd like to become the mother of a master race. When she'd refused he'd called her frigid, then thrown a drink in her face. The other two cuttings referred to similar incidents, both of them involving threatening approaches to women. In the most recent of these Gardner was referred to as unemployed.

Something – he wasn't sure what – made Hugh look up. He saw Vivien walking down the aisle towards him. She was still some way off, but she had the same purposeful look as she'd had earlier. He noticed that she also seemed to be standing more upright than usual. Her hair bounced on her shoulders.

Turning around, he saw Darren bearing down on him from the opposite direction.

Darren got there first.

He said, 'Battersby wants to see you.'

'What about?'

'How should I know?'

Hugh half got to his feet. And as he did so, Vivien arrived.

She said, 'I want a word with you.'

'Now?'

'Yes, now.'

Hugh looked from one to the other.

'I'm afraid that won't be possible,' he said. 'I have to go out.'

And as they watched, he stuffed the cuttings file into his case, picked up his coat and hurried past them towards the lifts.

Chapter Ten

Hugh sat on the top of the bus as it made its way down through Camberwell and Dulwich, through Beckenham and Bromley, and out towards Croydon. South London always made him feel as if he were stuck beneath an enormous iron bell. The clouds were greyer on this side of the river, the air staler. The people seemed even more doltish and depressed, as if the clanging in the sky hurt their heads.

The houses spread everywhere, crawling over the hillsides in endless shabby lines. Dark Edwardian terraces with overhanging eaves. Brown brick bungalows with diamond-pane windows and bottle-green shrubs by the door. Baptist chapels with signs outside assuring people that they were being watched over, that they hadn't been forgotten. The few daubs of colour – petrol stations, shop signs – only served to highlight the general drabness of it all.

Despite the modern blocks of flats and pedestrian precincts, it always struck him as oddly old-fashioned. Everything still looked covered in wartime grime. The shops still sold the same piles of ironmongery and bric-à-brac as they would have done in the Forties or Fifties. Fifty years before that, thought Hugh, there would have been fields here instead of houses. His guide book to old London stopped at Lambeth, dismissed as 'a labyrinth of featureless streets and poverty-stricken courts'. Beyond that was open country – trees, hedgerows, villages. Now it was impossible to imagine anything less rural. Everything had been tarmacked over and absorbed into the same ashen sprawl.

The bus conductor tapped Hugh on the shoulder and told him that this was where he should get off. The light was already starting to go and the street lamps were coming on. Clutching his A–Z, he started walking along the main road and turned off right up a narrower road that climbed a hill in a series of irregular bumpy terraces. The pavement was iced over in places. There were houses on either side of the road. They all exuded the same fierce spruceness, like men with short, sticky hair.

The road rose up, levelled off, then rose again. Ahead of him Hugh could see a house that even from some way off looked different to its neighbours. There was a low wall – more like a parapet – separating the small patch of front garden from the pavement. Part of this had collapsed. As he got nearer, he saw that the garden too appeared to have fallen back on itself, to have grown up and then caved in under its own weight. There was an undulating layer of dry vegetation, like sponge, that threatened to spill over the path and was only held in place by the tangle of stems below. This too was still covered in frost from the night before.

He checked the number and made his way up the path. A pane of glass in the porch was cracked, the window frames looked soft and sodden. He rang the bell. It gave out a flat, thumping ting. There was no reply. He tried again, pressing the bell for longer. Still there was no sound of anything moving within. He made his way around the side of the house, the vegetation springy under his feet, and tried to peer in the windows. In most of them he could see nothing but his own reflection. He did the same on the other side of the porch. The tangle of vegetation was at a lower level here, as if it had collapsed into a trench, and he had to stretch to get his chin over the window ledge. With his sleeve he rubbed at the glass.

Inside he could see two figures: a man and a woman sitting in armchairs, several feet apart. Otherwise, the room appeared empty of furniture. Between them the floor was covered with newspapers. Hugh's first thought was that they were dead. They sat there in their chairs, facing one another, not moving. Then, in response to his tapping on the window, they each turned to look at him in the same unhurried way. And for some time they continued to stare.

Hugh climbed out of the trench and went back to the front door. He rang the bell once more and waited. He was about to go back and see if either of them had moved when the door opened.

The man stood in front of him. He was tall and desiccated-looking and his feet appeared to be wrapped in scarves.

'Andrew Gardner?' Hugh asked.

The man shifted about on his turbaned feet, rocking back slightly.

'Who is it?' came a woman's voice from within.

Hugh introduced himself.

'Who is it?' came the woman's voice again.

The man said, 'This is private property.'

He turned and shouted over his shoulder, 'It's a journalist.'

Shortly afterwards the woman appeared. There was a dim light at the end of the hallway and Hugh could see her coming towards the door. Her shoulders were broad and her neck thick, but the rest of her body seemed to taper away beneath her. She swung her arms and hurled herself from door frame to door frame. Her feet trailed along behind her, barely scratching the floor, as if she was flinging herself along a set of wall bars.

By the time she got to the door she was breathless. 'Why can't you leave my son alone?'

She had a small, shrill voice, and when she spoke she made a series of lifting motions with her chin.

Hugh explained that he was doing a story on the man who had been found drowned in the river.

'I wondered if there was anything further Mr Gardner

110

could add to the statement he gave to the police,' he said.

'What's all this then?' said the woman.

She pushed her finger into the man's stomach. He groaned softly. 'You didn't tell me anything about this,' she said.

'If perhaps you'd remembered anything else?' said Hugh. 'Any other details?'

Gardner said nothing. They stood there in this little frozen tableau for a while longer.

'Even if I did know anything, I don't see why I should tell you,' he said petulantly.

There was an air of both donnish abstraction and extreme slipperiness about him, as if his actions were none of his concern, yet at the same time carefully calculated. He spoke with a note of indignation and a rumbling sense of discontent. Life, he implied, had dealt him a bad hand, for which he could take no responsibility.

After another pause he started up again. 'I told the police everything I knew. I was perfectly helpful about it. I did what I was supposed to do. I was crossing Hungerford Bridge and I saw this man sitting on the wall. At first I thought he was just looking at the view. Then, as I got closer, I saw that he had his feet over the parapet. I ran towards him. I even shouted. But before I could get to him, he jumped. I looked over into the water, but there was no sign of him. He seemed to have disappeared.'

'And that's it?'

He had half turned away from Hugh as he was telling this story. Now he turned back to face him.

'That's it.'

'Why didn't you tell me this?' said his mother.

'He doesn't tell me things,' she said to Hugh. 'Look at him. I can't even make him get dressed properly any more. How's he ever going to meet people if he doesn't get dressed? He says he's got nothing to wear. He came back with some new clothes recently, but they were much too small. Didn't fit him at all. What did you go and get those for?'

Again Gardner didn't answer, merely lifting one of his hands in a gesture of annoyance. Hugh put his notebook back in his case.

'Will you be writing anything then?' she asked.

Hugh gazed out over the spongy overgrown garden and the brown neglected house. Above the glow of the street lights the sky was a sharp petrol-blue.

'No,' he said. 'I wouldn't have thought so.'

He wished them goodbye. From the bottom of the path he looked back and saw that they were still in the doorway, Gardner half crouched, his mother wedged in beside him. From the way they were standing, they looked as though they were holding the place up.

Chapter Eleven

Noel was already in the restaurant when Hugh arrived that evening. He was sitting pretending to study the menu, a short, dark man with twists of hair that stuck up behind each ear like wings on a helmet and small, stubby teeth like a child's. They met about once a month, always in a restaurant of Noel's choosing. That way Hugh found it easier to shirk responsibility for the whole thing.

They had more in common than either cared to admit. Both of them single; both heaving with unfulfilled yearnings; both starting to see themselves as increasing social liabilities; and each seeing in the other's plight some consolation for his own. But whereas Hugh had long grown used to holding himself in, keeping himself in check, Noel had learned no such lesson. Never before had Hugh come across anyone with such disregard for his own welfare. Constantly beaten back by unsuitable, unappreciative women, Noel took each disappointment as if it was his first, and launched himself at further setbacks with the same blind zeal. The more he was hurt, the more determined he was to try again. He dusted himself down and plunged back into the fray. A victim of his own ridiculous nature.

At times Noel spoke apologetically, dazedly, of his own behaviour. It was a burden to him, he conceded, albeit one that he was powerless to do anything about. Good advice, appeals to be prudent – he was as incapable of heeding them as he was of reining himself in. Any tiny, stunted instincts for self-preservation that he had once possessed had, it seemed, disappeared long ago.

Hugh marvelled at this. At the brimming eagerness that drove Noel on. He'd always wondered if one day it might finally give out and Noel would become as wary and watchful as he was. For a long time there'd been no sign of it. But latterly the strain had been getting to him. He'd begun smiling at things that weren't funny – or rather baring his teeth in a mirthless flicker that split his face for an instant and then was gone.

And there were other, less obvious, changes, ones that had been forced on him by circumstance. He'd run out of targets to launch himself at. They'd all disappeared, got paired off. With no-one left to aim for, there had become something almost wizened about him. And his attitude to things had changed and become increasingly reproving. Whether this was some sort of self-reproach that had become translated into a more general air of sternness, or mere anger, Hugh didn't know.

Noel's choice of restaurants was like his taste in women. He had an unerring instinct for rooting out places that served the filthiest food in London. The waiter brought Hugh another menu and they ordered a bottle of wine. It was only a bottle of house wine, but when it arrived Noel made an elaborate show of tasting it, sucking in his cheeks and swilling it round his teeth.

'Excellent,' said Noel eventually. 'What do you think?'

'It's all right, I suppose.'

'Very good,' he said to the waiter.

'So how are things with you, Hughie?' he asked.

'Oh, not too bad,' said Hugh.

'And work? How are things going there?'

If he hadn't been so practised at equivocating, thought Hugh, he might have become flustered. As it was he made a few non-committal noises which Noel didn't pursue. They had become used to treating each other with tact, and if this was sometimes indistinguishable from indifference,

114

well, so be it. There were worse things to put up with in a friend.

During all the years they'd known one another there had been times when one of them had had a girlfriend. Then the strain on their friendship was almost more than it could stand. But no such liaison ever lasted long – a few weeks, months at the most. And when it was over they simply took up where they'd left off, older and more battered, their mutual dependence coloured equally by resentment and gratitude.

Hugh asked Noel about his work. In all the time they'd known one another, he'd never quite been able to work out what Noel did. Something to do with exhibition stands, he knew that. But while Noel wasn't actively evasive about his job, he was never forthcoming either. Hugh couldn't be sure if this was a deliberate attempt to cloak himself in mystery, or something else. Another symptom of his thwarted romanticism, as if the details of his life meant nothing to him and he was constantly gearing up for a new, more exciting existence, one that had unaccountably failed to materialize. Here again their lives overlapped to a greater degree than Hugh chose to acknowledge.

'How's Sue?' he asked.

For some time now Noel had been in love with a woman who Hugh had never been allowed to meet. His conviction that his feelings were reciprocated had persisted, despite numerous signs to the contrary, including her marriage to someone else.

A troubled look came into Noel's eyes.

'She's not happy. Who can blame her? I don't think that marriage will last. She used to call me up to tell me how stupid her husband is. She's always saying what a good listener I am. But she hasn't called much lately. She used to drop round a lot, too. Of course, it's difficult for her to get out much any more.'

'Why? Is she sick?'

'No,' said Noel, 'she's pregnant. I thought I'd told you.'

There were only a few other people in the restaurant.

The ceiling was hung with netting and the walls were painted with portholes. The waiter came to ask what they wanted to eat. Noel took a long time to make up his mind. Hugh, by contrast, asked for the first thing his eye lit upon. He ordered fish stew, and saw the waiter pause momentarily, his pen above the paper, before writing this down.

Their food arrived almost immediately. Hugh's stew turned out to be a kind of brine porridge.

He took a mouthful and grimaced.

'Jesus,' he said.

'You expect too much,' said Noel, 'that's your trouble.'

'What do you mean?'

Noel flashed one of his lightning mirthless smiles. 'You expect too much.'

'We both expect too much, don't we,' said Hugh. 'That's why we're here.' He spoke without thinking, almost to himself.

Hugh looked up and saw Noel staring at him in surprise. 'We have unrealistic expectations,' he went on. 'They never used to seem unrealistic, but they do now. That's age, probably. Age and desperation.'

'Steady on, Hughie,' said Noel quietly.

But Hugh found he couldn't help himself. He was as taken aback by this outburst of honesty as Noel, yet somehow it was as if a line had snapped and was uncoiling inside him.

'No, but it's true, isn't it?' he said. 'I used to think there was someone out there just for me. That we were intended for one another and all I had to do was find her. Where is she? I wondered. Where's she hiding? Behind a bush? Stuck in the wainscotting?

'A certain amount of coyness can be very attractive, of course,' he continued. 'I mean, you don't want it all to be too easy. So you stay patient and imagine that one day the clouds will part, and there she'll be. But what if they don't? What if nothing happens? What then?

'I mean, at least you're lovelorn,' he said. 'That's something. It's practically a vocation with you.'

Hugh stopped.

'I'm sorry . . .'

But Noel shook his head, then busied himself with finishing his food. Neither of them said anything. Hugh waved for the waiter and asked for another bottle of wine. When it came the waiter also cleared away their plates.

'Excellent,' said Noel. 'Thank you.'

An expression of disbelief passed quickly across the waiter's features. The evening had lurched off course. Their meetings often tended to be doleful occasions. This, though, was worse than usual. Neither of them was used to frankness, but now they were stuck with it, a stranger at their table. They sat and stared at one another disapprovingly, each seeing in the other things they had no wish to recognize in themselves.

'You must be careful about giving in to self-pity,' said Noel. 'In my experience women find that sort of thing very off-putting.'

Hugh took another drink. The wine had gone straight to his head.

'In your experience?' he said.

'That's right.'

'I see.'

'You can't spend the rest of your life wondering if your future wife is stuck inside every passing shrub, Hughie. It's not practical.'

'I know,' he said, 'I know.'

'Your problem is that you don't just want to meet a woman, you think you've got to rescue her first. But a lot of girls today, they don't want to be rescued. They're not the maidenly kind.'

'It's true that I have this tendency to idealize women,' Hugh conceded.

'You do them a disservice,' said Noel. 'And I don't think you do yourself any favours either.'

'How do you work that out?'

'Well, I think it's apt to make you a bit of a prig sometimes.'

117

Hugh looked up.

'A prig?' He laughed uncertainly. 'Don't you mean a libertine?'

'No, I do not,' said Noel. 'It's about time you got used to life as it is.'

Hurt as he was, Hugh could see the sense in this. But still he couldn't quell this urge for things to be different; it sat there inside him like a jumping nerve or a chilblain, throbbing away.

'Besides,' said Noel, 'you're not the type.'

'The type for what?'

'For chivalry or adventure or whatever. You're not the type. You wouldn't have any aptitude for it.'

'You don't think so?'

Noel shook his head. 'I know so,' he said.

Soon afterwards they asked for the bill and divided it. Noel went to the lavatory while Hugh, still sunk in thought, backed into the coat the waiter was holding up for him.

When Noel came back he said, 'Why are you wearing my coat?'

Hugh looked down. The sleeves ended some way above his wrists.

'So I am.'

He took it off and put on his own coat.

Outside, the gritting lorries had been out again. Their feet scrunched as they crossed the road to the tube.

'My God, it's getting even colder,' said Hugh.

'Very nice place, I thought,' said Noel. 'Extremely reasonable. I wouldn't mind going back there.'

When Hugh got home there was another postcard from his mother on his mat. It was dated three days after the last one, but had taken less time to arrive. 'Everything fine,' she'd written. 'Jakarta great fun. A nice fellow passenger called Mr Glim, a lone traveller like myself, offered to show me round. He's a widower with five children! All grown-up. He knows this part of the world well – very

118

charming and a great fount of useful knowledge. Writing this just before we set off again. Onward to Surabaya then!'

That night Hugh was unable to sleep. He read some more of his old guide book and listened out for the crooning of the dead from down the road. But everything was quiet. Something was nagging him. He tried to work out what it could be. He worked backwards over his evening with Noel, and then further back over the day, but nothing revealed itself. And when he did eventually fall asleep, it was with this unspoken question still lying there beside him.

He woke at three in the morning with the sensation that he was trapped. As if his arms were pinioned to his sides. As he struggled to free himself from the bedclothes, he realized what had been bothering him. It came at him with a little ting, like a typewriter bell. The realization kept him awake for the rest of the night.

Chapter Twelve

Hugh made his way up the path to the front door and rang the bell once more. There was no response and so he went round the side of the house. The ground gave way beneath him as he sank back down into the trench below the living-room window. His fingerprints were still on the glass from the day before. Inside, Mrs Gardner and her son were sitting just as they had been then, facing one another in their armchairs, quite motionless.

He tapped on the glass. Once again they came to, turning towards him in the same unhurried way. He went back to the front door and waited. When the door opened Mrs Gardner was standing there squinting angrily up at him.

'What do you want?'

'I wonder if I might see your son for a moment,' Hugh asked.

'What for?'

'There's just one other thing I need to ask him.'

'I won't have him disturbed again. He's very sensitive.'

Behind her in the hallway he could see Andrew Gardner emerge from the living room, gazing abstractedly about him. Slowly, he came towards them.

'There was something else I meant to ask you,' said Hugh. 'You told the police that the man you saw jumping into the river had left a pair of shoes on the balustrade.'

Gardner's eyes flickered and settled on him. 'So?'

'I wondered if he'd left anything else there.'

'What do you mean?'

'What is this?' asked his mother. 'What are you talking about?'

'I wondered if there might have been some clothes there, too,' said Hugh.

'Clothes?' said Mrs Gardner; her chin had started going up and down again. 'Why should there have been?'

'You mentioned before that your son had come back recently with some clothes that didn't fit him. I wondered where he had got them from.'

Together they looked at Gardner, who shifted about under their scrutiny. 'What are you accusing me of?' he asked.

'I'm not accusing you of anything,' said Hugh. 'I don't mind if you took the clothes or not. It's just that, if you did, I'd like to look at them.'

Mrs Gardner prodded him again and he gave out a low whistling moan. 'You told me you got those clothes at a jumble sale,' she said. 'You never said you'd stolen them.'

'I didn't steal them,' he protested. 'They were just there, I couldn't see any harm in it. I should have known they wouldn't fit.'

'And where are they now?' asked Hugh.

Gardner's face tilted forward impassively onto his chest. 'They're upstairs,' he said. 'Up in my room.'

'Could I have a look?'

'What for?' asked Mrs Gardner.

'If you let me look, I promise I won't come back.'

Mrs Gardner and her son stepped back into the hallway to talk to one another. He bent towards her while she craned up towards him, whispering. Hugh couldn't make out what they were saying.

When they'd finished, Mrs Gardner turned and said, 'You won't come back?'

Hugh nodded.

'All right then.'

He followed them down the hallway. Mrs Gardner swung herself along from handhold to handhold. There was a smell he couldn't recognize, or rather a series of different smells that seemed to be packed down in layers, one on top of the other. The light was so dim that it was hard to see where they were going.

They climbed the stairs to Gardner's bedroom. The room proved to be surprisingly tidy. Indeed, thought Hugh unhappily, there was a familiar air of pernicketiness about it – the bed made, books neatly stacked, shoes set in line under a chair. He wouldn't have been so out of place here himself. He recognized that sense of holding onto something; erecting this brittle stockade against the world outside. It was as if the elements that had already invaded downstairs hadn't yet penetrated this far.

Gardner went over to the cupboard, reached up and brought down a bundle of clothes. He laid them on the chair beside the bed. There was a sweater, a pair of trousers and an overcoat. Hugh began to go through the pockets. They were all empty.

'There was no money either,' said Gardner.

'And nothing else?'

Gardner stood, leaning to his left, breathing hard.

'Andrew . . .' said his mother.

'There wasn't any money,' he repeated.

'What else was there?' asked Hugh.

Gardner went over to the bedside table and lifted up a blue glass jar.

'Only this,' he said.

He took what was inside and handed it to Hugh.

It was a slim, ragged, canvas-bound booklet with Seaman's Discharge Book printed on the outside. The booklet was made out in the name of Malcolm Field. Inside was what appeared to be a record of employment. There were the names of various ships down the left-hand column and a corresponding column of dates running down the right. On the inside back cover was a photograph of a man of 50 or so. He had a pale, watery face and a cluster of small dimples on his chin.

'Is this what you were looking for?' asked Mrs Gardner. She was peering over his shoulder.

'I don't know,' said Hugh.

'Poor Andrew . . . Now you can leave us alone like you promised.'

It wasn't until Hugh was on board the bus that he took out the booklet and examined it more carefully. Opposite the photograph on the inside back page there was a space marked for dependants and next of kin. Beneath it several lines had been crossed out in thick black ink. Beneath these were two more lines. These hadn't been crossed out, but they were still illegible. The writing was so small that he couldn't make it out.

Back in the office he once again tried to read what was written in the booklet. Still he couldn't decipher it. Julian came by and asked if he was coming for a drink. Cliff was already waiting in the aisle, with Gavin standing several feet behind him, like a longstop.

'I think I'll stay here,' said Hugh. 'I've some things to do.'

'Still feeling off-colour, Hughie?'

'Just a bit.'

Eventually Stanley raised himself from the desk opposite. Once he'd gone, Hugh reached over and picked up his magnifying visor. He held the visor in his left hand and the Seaman's Discharge Book in his right. There was a technique to this, he discovered. If you held the visor too close to your face, it misted over. But as the condensation cleared, he saw the letters, swollen to several times their original size, swim up before him. On the first line was a signature, Malcolm Field. And written below, in the same tiny handwriting, the words, 'In the care of Missions to Seamen, Tilbury.'

He turned over the pages. Right at the end of the booklet, he saw that four numbers – 1785 – had been written on one of the blank pages, cutting across the bottom right-hand corner of the paper. There was no indication what the numbers referred to.

*   *   *

As Hugh was leaving that evening he saw Joy standing by
her desk, throwing envelopes into the wire post baskets.
The tendons in her calves were particularly prominent.
There was no sign of Vivien. Hugh hadn't talked to Joy
since their evening out – at least not properly. He was
uneasy about doing so, assuming that Vivien would have
told her that they had spent the night together. But there
had been nothing unusual about her behaviour towards
him since. It was hard to believe she would have been able
to restrain herself if she knew.

She grinned when she saw him and beckoned him over.
When she'd finished sorting the envelopes she took hold
of his arm.

'What have you been up to?' she asked.

'Out on a story.'

'Really? That's not like you.'

Hugh looked down at Joy's fingers. She was wearing
orange nail varnish.

'Do you want to come for a drink?'

'Oh, I can't I'm afraid,' she said. 'Not tonight. I've got to
go somewhere.'

'Where are you going?'

'I'm meeting someone.'

'Who?'

'Don't be so nosy.'

'Is it Jesus?'

She let his arm go.

'What did you say?'

'That man you were dancing with the other night.'

Joy laughed uproariously. 'What would I want to meet
him for? He couldn't even speak English.'

'No. I just thought—'

'I'm meeting a friend of mine. That's all you need to
know. And I really should be going. Did you enjoy our
evening out?'

'On the whole,' said Hugh.

'You looked as if you were having a good time. We

124

should do it again sometime. Vivien liked it, too. At least I think she did. It's not always easy to tell with her.'

Joy put on her coat.

'Night then,' she said. 'Have a good weekend.'

After she'd gone Hugh sat at his desk for a while, loath to leave. Eventually he got up and walked down the corridor, past the vending machine. By the doors onto the stairwell he saw what he thought at first was a sack of mail on the floor. As he got nearer, he saw it was a man lying face down. He could see a crown of white hair on the back of his head and his arms splayed out on either side of him.

Hugh ran over to help. The man was trying to lift himself onto his knees and elbows. Scattered around him were a number of large books. Hugh helped him to his feet, holding on to one of his arms. He saw that it was one of the green-carders.

'Are you all right?'

'I must have tripped,' he said.

The man was tall, but very thin. Unnaturally so, with long arms and legs and a long, tapering torso. His hair was shaved above his ears, making his head look even more narrow than it actually was. When it was clear that the man could stand unaided, Hugh went and picked up the books. There must have been about twenty of them, all the same size, as big as old church bibles. Some had fallen open and Hugh could see neat columns of figures in red and black ink running down the pages.

'Thank you.'

'Can I give you a hand?' asked Hugh.

The man was about to refuse, but he was still unsteady on his feet and reluctantly he allowed Hugh to carry the books for him, along the corridor and down the stairs. The man moved gingerly down the stairs, kicking each foot from one step, then almost toppling down onto the next.

To begin with Hugh assumed this was because of the fall. But as they reached the corridor below, he saw that the man raised himself up on his toes as he walked. He seemed unable to put his heels on the floor. His whole frame was like this frail, wavering, extruded form, with each bone balanced on top of another.

They walked down the corridor and came to a doorway. The man reached into his pocket for a key and unlocked the door. The room was no bigger than a broom cupboard. There was no window, only a table, a chair and a set of shelves laden with more ledgers. On the wall behind the chair was a row of hooks with keys hanging off them.

Hugh put the books on the table, aware as he did so that the man was watching him closely. He had dry, cornflower-blue eyes.

'You're very kind,' he said.

The man's voice was much stronger than Hugh had expected.

'We don't know one another. My name is Walter Eames.'

'Hugh Byrne.'

They shook hands. Hugh felt as if he was sliding his hand into a long, dry glove. He went back upstairs and out to the lifts. Outside it was a little warmer. He crossed over Fleet Street. As he walked past the churchyard, he kept his head down and didn't glance in its direction.

Chapter Thirteen

Hugh drove east, past the carpet warehouses, the tyre stores and the rows of small, stained curtained houses that faced the road. Some of the houses were a dark cream colour and the others a dim pink, like lipsalve. He seldom used his car any more and it felt stiff and unfamiliar to drive, drifting out into the middle of the road if he took his hands off the wheel. As he went on, he had this sense of passing through cloud that parted reluctantly before him. Eventually the buildings began to thin out and he could see occasional strips of marshland on either side, moss-green fields scarred with drainage ditches and lines of dry, stumpy trees. There weren't many cars about, only lorries that swayed and ground their gears as they went by.

After an hour the road curved round the side of a hill and then shelved away sharply to his left. Ahead of him were the docks. Hugh had never been out this way before and he couldn't believe their size and scale. A huge open-ended valley lay before him, choked with ironmongery. The horizon bristled with cranes, their arms jutting up into a sky alight with this bright magnesium glare.

He drove up to the main gate expecting to be stopped and questioned, but the booth by the gate was empty, and so, after a moment or two's hesitation, he carried on through. There were warehouses on either side of the road, their doors open and yellow light spilling out. He slowed down and tried to see if there was anyone inside, but they too appeared to be deserted. It was dusk and the air seemed to have turned as grey as the sky had been when he'd set out. He drove on, past mounds of gravel the size of slag heaps and blue cranes like stiff-backed nursery chairs. He came to the first of the docks. The water looked as hard and flat as glass. There were no ships to be seen, only a few sailing dinghies tethered together and sitting quite still. On the other side of the dock was another warehouse, taller than the others and more modern, little more than a corrugated-iron shed. Here too the doors were open and the lights were on inside. Hugh stopped the car and went in through the doors.

Stretching away as far as he could see were enormous cylinders wrapped in brown paper and stacked one on top of the other from floor to ceiling. He realized that these were the rolls of newsprint he saw being unloaded every day outside the newspaper offices. They rose high above his head in huge tapering columns. It was like being on the edge of a densely packed forest. But the trees had all been cut down, pulped and re-erected here in much cleaner, more ordered lines than before. He touched one of the rolls. It was warm. He could even smell the resin. Hugh was standing there, both hands resting against the curved surface in front of him, when a man appeared from behind one of the columns. His coat was the same colour as the brown paper wrapping.

'What are you doing here?'

Hugh asked if he knew the way to the Seaman's Mission. The man tore off a piece of brown paper and drew him a map. Back in the car Hugh followed his directions, taking the ring road around the docks. There were piles of scrap metal behind sagging chain fences and warehouses with cracked and broken windows. Rounding a corner he saw the river for the first time, between a flour mill and another cluster of cranes. He'd expected it to be much wider here, already spreading out towards the sea. But if anything it looked narrower than in central London. On the far bank was a cement works, a huge grey landscape of chutes and

128

towers and tanks and winding narrow-gauge tracks. He stopped for a while, looking out over the water drifting by under the searchlights. Down river he could see flames flickering on top of the oil refinery chimneys.

The road took him round to another of the docks' entrances. Ahead of him was a tall, red-bricked Victorian building, like a hospital or a school, with steep-pitched roofs and narrow windows set in stone. It stood on its own in a patch of wasteground. A low wall had been erected outside to form a car park. Hugh parked his car and climbed the steps to the front door. Set above the door was a piece of stained glass with the words 'For Friendship' picked out in leaded letters. A man was standing halfway up the steps holding on to the railing with both hands.

The door was locked. Hugh rang the bell. Inside he could see a lobby with several men standing round or sitting on benches. One of them came over and opened the door. At the far end of the lobby was a counter and behind it rows of pigeon-holes, most of them empty. There was a bored-looking boy in a white shirt on the other side of the counter chewing a pencil. Hugh asked if he could see whoever was in charge.

'You want to see the chaplain?'

'If that's possible.'

The boy disappeared into a back room. From inside Hugh could hear a man saying, 'Who wants to know?' in a put-upon sort of voice and the sound of a chair being pushed back.

The boy came back followed by a grey-haired man with a doughy face, pressed into shape by the sides of his steel spectacles. There were crumbs at the corner of his mouth and he brushed them aside with a paper napkin.

'Yes? Can I help you?'

Hugh told him that he was trying to trace someone who he believed had stayed in the mission. 'Are you a relative?' the chaplain asked.

'No,' said Hugh, 'I'm a journalist.'

'And what makes you think this person might have stayed here?'

Hugh took out the Seaman's Discharge Book from his pocket and put it on the counter. The chaplain picked it up and held it between his thumb and forefinger, then he turned to show it to the boy who was standing behind.

'Where did you get this?'

Hugh explained how the man had been found drowned in the river three weeks earlier. The Seaman's Discharge Book, he said, had been among his things. 'I wondered if you recognized the picture.'

'Oh,' said the chaplain sighing. 'We recognize him, don't we, Eamonn?'

The boy shuffled and grinned.

'Eamonn's our receptionist,' said the chaplain.

'And organist,' said the boy.

'Never mind that now. Yes, we recognize him. He'd been with us for about five years. At least that. We informed the police he'd gone missing, of course, but I can't say they were very interested.'

'Can you tell me anything about him?'

'Well, let me see. He was very –'

The chaplain raised his hands and spread his fingers expressively.

'– Quiet.'

'Thank you, Eamonn. He was very quiet. Very withdrawn. I didn't even know what nationality he was. For the first few months he was here he never said a word. I wondered if he might have had some sort of breakdown. He would spend the day in his room and only come down for his meals, or to go to the library. Sometimes he'd sit by himself in the billiards room and read. And then, almost every evening, he'd come to our chapel service.

'Of course, you get a lot of very lonely people in a place like this. They find it difficult to make friends or to relate to anyone else. But some of them just want to be left on their own. I'd noticed that all the other men steered clear of him. I tried to get him to talk about himself, about his

130

background. He'd written that he had no next of kin when he registered. They often say that, though, if they've lost touch or had a row. But it was hopeless, you couldn't get anywhere at all.'

The chaplain shook his head, as if such behaviour would have tried anyone's patience.

'Then one Christmas about two or three years ago I was halfway up a stepladder in the hall hanging some decorations when I saw him coming out of the restaurant. Without thinking, I said, "Good morning, Mr Field," just as I must have done hundreds of times before. To my astonishment he looked up and said good morning back to me. I was so surprised I thought I must have imagined it.

'So I did the same thing the next day. Again, he wished me a good morning, only this time I had the impression that he was smiling to himself as he spoke. That evening I invited him into my office. He followed me in and stood on the other side of the desk. I asked him if he'd mind letting me have a few more details about himself. We're supposed to keep these reports for the social services, you see, on anyone who stays here longer than a year. About their health and general state of mind, in case anything should happen.

'And again he smiled and looked at me and didn't say a word. He just stood there until I told him he could go. I didn't try again after that. I thought, well, if that's how he wants to be, then good luck to him.'

The chaplain smiled, to play down any suggestion of pique.

'Can you remember when you last saw him?'

'It's not easy to say,' he said. 'You see, a lot of people come and go as they choose. Of course, we don't have anything like as many men staying here as there were a few years ago. The ships don't come any more. The docks are all being closed down – now they're building newspaper offices there instead. Even so, we still have about seventy men staying at any one time. It's not easy to keep track. Some of them get a pension cheque or disability benefit and pay for a couple of months in advance. Then they go away for a week or two, sometimes longer. Others say they're going to come back and never do. It's one of the principles of this place that we never enquire too closely what they're up to.'

'Is there a register of some sort?' asked Hugh.

'There is, but I don't know if it would be much help. Still, I suppose we could have a look. Go and get it, will you, Eamonn.'

But the boy made no move, and the chaplain had to ask again, more impatiently this time, but with a note of playfulness in his voice, as if this was a regular routine they went through. A few minutes later the boy came back with a book, which he put down on the counter and opened.

'In theory, everyone who's staying here has to sign in and out,' said the chaplain. 'But as you can see, not everyone takes it that seriously.'

Indeed, it was almost impossible to make out any of the names – some had been crossed out altogether. Others had comments or doodles added to them in different-coloured inks. Whole pages had been defaced and looked as if they'd been immersed in liquid. They were as stiff as vellum. They searched for Field's name, but found nothing.

'What about the payments book?' suggested Eamonn.

Without waiting for the chaplain to say anything, he went back into the inner office and fetched another, much smaller book. This was in better condition. Beside each man's name and room number was a record of how much money he'd paid and when. Field, they saw, had paid for his room a month in advance and still had another four days to go before he fell into arrears.

'Did he ever get any letters?'

'No,' said the chaplain. 'I don't believe so.'

'One every three months,' said Eamonn. 'Always in the same brown envelope.'

'You don't know who it was from?'

He shook his head.

'And what about friends? Was there anyone he talked to?'

'There were the Somalis.'

'Yes, Eamonn. I was coming to the Somalis,' said the chaplain. 'A couple of years ago, a number of Somali gentlemen came to stay here. They'd all been on British tankers and they didn't want to go home because of the war. Besides, I think they liked it here. It's nice and warm and I treated them as equals. They respected me for that. They were all Muslims, of course, very devout. But one man was keen to improve his English and he spent a lot of time in the library. We call it a library, but actually the bookshelves are in the back of the chapel. Anyone can go in there and read. One day he asked me if he could sit in on one of our services, just to see what went on. I said naturally he'd be welcome. So that evening he came and sat at the back, and the next day he was there again.

'I think that's how he and Mr Field became friends. They began to have their meals together. You'd see them, wouldn't you, Eamonn? Not actually saying anything, not as far as one could tell. But sitting there, enjoying each other's company.'

'Is this man still staying here?' asked Hugh.

'Mr Adad? Oh, he's still here. Most of the other Somalis left eventually. But he stayed on.'

'Do you think I might have a word with him?'

'Well . . . I don't see why not. It's a question of finding him. I've got to take evensong soon, so he may turn up to that. Not to worship, you understand, just to look. But we can go and see if he's around.'

The three of them walked across the lobby, through a swing door and down a corridor. There was pale-blue anaglypta paper on the walls and a carpet dotted with crimson blooms. On the noticeboard a poster had been stuck up warning of the dangers of leg ulcers, along with appeals for missing relatives and a newsletter entitled 'Shelter from the Storm'.

They looked into the billiard room. A number of men

were sitting in silence looking at hands of cards. The lights were switched on over the billiard tables, but no-one was playing. Then they looked in the television rooms. There was a different room for each channel. The sets were mounted on brackets high on the walls and armchairs were dotted about; in the gloom it was just possible to make out several figures leaning back, staring up at the wall.

'No sign of him here,' said the chaplain. 'I suppose he might be upstairs.'

They climbed a set of asphalt steps. The smell of disinfectant was almost as strong here as it was in the lavatories at work. On each half-landing there was a square porcelain basin set into an alcove at the top of the stairs, and beneath it a foot bath. The chaplain knocked at a door. On the other side of the corridor one of the doors was open. Hugh could see a man inside, lying on his bed reading. At the foot of the bed was a wardrobe with a chest of drawers at right angles to it.

There was no reply to the chaplain's knock. He tried again, then twisted the handle. It was locked.

Back in the stairwell the chaplain listened unhappily to Hugh's request.

'I don't know,' he said. 'We give people our word that we won't look inside their rooms. It's the only privacy some of them have.'

'Surely in these circumstances, though. When it looks as if he might have died. Surely you could make an exception?'

But the chaplain was unable to decide, and so Eamonn went and got the pass keys. They climbed up another floor to Field's room. Eamonn offered the key to the chaplain, but he looked away.

The room was empty. Empty, that is, of everything apart from furniture. There was a bed, a bedside table, a chest of drawers, a wardrobe and a basin tucked in a corner. The only thing on the wall was a set of instructions regarding fire drill. Hugh looked in the drawers, inside the wardrobe, even under the bed, but there was nothing. No imprint of any human habitation at all.

'Looks as though he cleared out,' said Eamonn.

Downstairs Hugh asked if he might come to evensong.

'I suppose so,' said the chaplain. 'If you want.'

Four men were already sitting in the chapel. They stared as Hugh came in. There was an electric organ, a short length of communion rail and a red ensign draped over a chair next to the altar. Above the hymn board two angels had been painted on the wall, lunging towards one another like trapeze artists. At the back of the room were the bookshelves, rising from floor to ceiling. Several of the shelves were completely empty. Others had only a few books on them, and these looked to be falling to pieces, with shredded dust jackets and torn spines hanging down.

The chaplain made his entrance, followed by Eamonn, who sat at the organ. After the benediction there were prayers, with the chaplain kneeling on the step by the communion rail. Hugh looked about at the other men kneeling down. He found himself regarding them with envy as they dropped into their mumbled responses and lost themselves in prayer.

Everyone recited Psalm 107 – 'Others went to sea in ships'. Then they rose and Eamonn began to play the organ more slowly than Hugh would have believed possible. They struggled through 'Sunset and Evening Star', with the chaplain periodically jerking his elbow to try to hurry Eamonn along.

'Twilight and evening bell,' they sang raggedly together.

'And after that the dark!

And may there be no sadness of farewell,

When I embark:

For though from out our bourne of time and place

The flood may bear me far,

I hope to see my Pilot face to face

When I have crossed the bar.'

They were gathering themselves for the final verse when the door at the back opened and another man came in. He

135

slipped into his seat so quietly that Hugh was hardly aware of his having done so. It was only the faint awareness of some new presence that made him turn. An elderly man was sitting two rows back staring straight ahead of him with one hand cupped over his cheek. His skin was dark and crinkled. When they got to the end of the hymn he didn't move. Once again the chaplain pronounced the benediction, and then filed out with Eamonn a few paces behind.

Everyone rose to their feet and started to leave. All except for the elderly man, who stayed where he was, one hand still held over his face, as if troubled by some memory of toothache.

'Mr Adad?'

The man looked up. 'Yes?'

Hugh asked if he might have a word. The man stood reluctantly. When they were in the corridor, Hugh introduced himself and explained how he was trying to trace Mr Field.

'What has happened?'

Hugh told him how a man had been found drowned in the river three weeks ago who he believed was Mr Field. He'd expected some reaction to this, some expression of dismay or disbelief. Instead Mr Adad simply started to walk away. But when he stopped at the foot of the stairs, Hugh saw that he was shaking.

'Please,' he said. 'I do not wish to talk here.'

He began to climb the stairs. Outside his door he took out his key and fumbled as he tried to fit it in the lock. His room was exactly the same as Field's, except that a suitcase had been wedged into the gap between the top of the wardrobe and the ceiling, and there were two framed photographs on the bedside table.

Mr Adad sat on the bed. He took out a handkerchief and dabbed at his forehead.

'I have been awaiting his return', he said, 'for some time now. He is my friend, you see.'

'Did he say anything about going away?'

He shook his head.

'You didn't think he might go off and kill himself?'

Mr Adad shut his eyes.

'No, no,' he said. 'Never.'

'And no-one ever came to see him here?'

He shook his head. 'Nobody came.'

'What did you talk about?'

'We talked about many things – yes. A great deal.'

'What sort of things?'

'We talked about the sea. He asked me if I missed it.'

'What did you say?'

'Sometimes I say I do. I miss coming to a port in the night-time, when you look out and you start to see movement in the darkness and hear dogs bark. I miss that.'

There was a pause during which Mr Adad continued to dab at his forehead with his handkerchief. 'Yes,' he said again quietly.

'Did he give you anything before he left?'

Mr Adad looked up. 'He gave me something.'

'What was that?'

'He gave me time. He helped me with my English. We read books together from the library. The same sentences over and over, until I was right. Until I understand all the words.'

'What sort of books?' asked Hugh.

'Improving books. Poetry.'

Mr Adad got up from the bed, went to the cupboard and took a book from the shelf inside. He opened the book, leafed through the pages and then began to read. He had a fierce declamatory way of reading, as if he was addressing a large audience. Standing there beside the bed, his voice filled the room and bounced back off the walls. At first he sounded unsure of himself, landing heavily on each new syllable. But as he went on, his voice settled and deepened and his accent almost fell away.

'I fear thee, ancient Mariner!
I fear thy skinny hand!

137

And thou art long, and lank, and brown,
As is the ribbed sea-sand.'

He stopped, shut his eyes for a moment or two, and then began again.

'I fear thee and thy glittering eye,
And thy skinny hand, so brown.'—
Fear not, fear not, thou wedding-guest!
This body dropt not down.

Hugh tried to visualize the two of them together – Mr Adad reading, and Field alongside, correcting any mistakes. He took Field's pale watery face from his photograph and attempted to set it on a body, to give it some movement, some approximation to life. As Hugh looked, he seemed to see him there momentarily, taking shape. But the illusion only lasted a moment before the figure faded and slipped from sight. Mr Adad continued:

Alone, alone, all, all alone,
Alone on a wide wide sea!
And never a saint took pity on
My soul in agony.

He finished reading. As his voice died away the room felt strangely empty. He shut the book and put it back in the cupboard.

'That is what we read,' he said.

Hugh stood up.

'I do hope he has come to no harm,' said Mr Adad.

Outside, Hugh made his way down the asphalt steps and back to the lobby. Four men were sitting wedged together on a bench by the front door, staring straight ahead, not talking to one another. There was no sign of Eamonn or the chaplain.

Chapter Fourteen

Climbing the stairs to the office the following morning, Hugh passed a number of men, taking measurements and noting them down on clipboards. They moved aside to let him go by. Soon after he'd sat at his desk Darren appeared beside him. It was time, Hugh decided, that he took a different attitude towards Darren, time he stopped behaving as if he'd done anything wrong. After all, he now had enough to feel guilty about without any further distractions.

'Yes,' he said, wheeling round in his chair. 'What is it?'

Darren's face was even more immobile than usual. The little pelt of hair above his mouth didn't stir.

'The police want to see you,' he said.

'The police?' said Hugh. 'Whatever for?'

'I was just told to fetch you as soon as you got in. They've been waiting for you.'

Hugh got up and followed Darren down to the lawyer's office. Also in the room were Battersby and two uniformed policemen. Everyone was sitting down. There was, Hugh saw, no chair for him.

The lawyer introduced the policemen.

'These gentlemen thought you might be able to help them in their investigations,' he said.

The policemen looked at him. They each had the same peculiar sheen to their faces and hands.

'I understand you saw Leslie Scaife on the evening of

February the seventeenth,' said the first policeman.

'Did I?' said Hugh.

'This was the evening when Mr Scaife, having been evicted from the pub for causing a disturbance, then telephoned from a call box around the corner to say that a bomb had been planted there.'

'Yes,' said Hugh. 'Yes, I believe I did see him earlier that evening. Briefly.'

'And when did you next see him?'

'I can't remember exactly,' he said.

'Well, was it the next day? The day after? The day after that?'

'The day after, I think.'

He checked his notes. 'In fact, you told Mr Battersby that you'd seen him on February the twentieth.'

'Yes,' he said.

'You're quite sure about that?'

'I think so.'

'Good. So you saw Leslie Scaife in this office on the morning of February the twentieth. Tell me, did you notice anything unusual about him?'

'In what way?'

'His clothes, for instance. Were they torn or blood-stained?'

'What's this about?' said Hugh.

'Just answer the question,' said the first policeman. 'Did you see Leslie Scaife on the morning of February the twentieth?'

The room was very still.

'I'm not sure,' said Hugh.

'You're not sure? Why not?'

It was shocking, thought Hugh, how all circumstances seemed to conspire against him. One little lie – a favour to a colleague – and look where it had got him. Trying to keep Scaife out of trouble, he'd merely succeeded in dropping himself in it.

'No,' he said.

'No?'

140

Hugh shook his head.

'Are you saying that you didn't see him at all?'

'Yes.'

'Why did you tell Mr Battersby that you had?'

'I was trying to cover up for him.'

'You lied in other words.'

'Yes . . . Why?' he said. 'What's happened?'

Eventually the lawyer spoke. 'I'm afraid Leslie is now being sought on a very serious charge.'

The second policeman exhaled thoughtfully through his nose. 'Three nights ago,' he said, 'a Mr Thomas Beale, who lives in King's Lynn, was subject to a particularly savage attack by a man who broke into his house in the early hours of the morning. He was beaten about the head and groin area with what's believed to have been a spade, and he is still in a coma.'

'What's he got to do with Scaife?'

'We understand that Mr Beale had formed a relationship with Mrs Ann Scaife, the wife of Leslie Scaife. Nothing was stolen in the break-in, and the description that Mr Beale has been able to give us of the assailant matches that of Mr Scaife. We're therefore looking for Mr Scaife, with a view to eliminating him from our inquiries.'

'Or charging him,' said the first policeman.

'Naturally we were interested to hear that you claimed to have seen Mr Scaife on the morning after the assault. As it turns out, you've wasted a good deal of our time.'

After a while the two policemen stood up. Battersby and the lawyer stayed sitting down.

'If Mr Scaife should get in touch, you will let us know, won't you?' said the first policeman. He handed him a card with his name and telephone number on it.

When he returned to his desk, Hugh tried to distract himself by looking through the first edition of the paper. Cliff, he saw, had devoted most of his column to the dog crisis. 'Give a dog a bad name?' he had written. 'I'll say so. That's because they deserve it. You give them a home, feed them, take them for walks. And how do they repay you?

141

They try to bite your bloody arm off, that's how. Man's best friend? Killers in the kennel more like. These filthy brutes, defiling our public places, sinking their incisors into our loved ones. It's the stinking hypocrisy that makes me vomit. We live in dangerous times. The enemy isn't without, it's right there lying on the hearth, slavering away.'

There was a good deal more of this. Cliff went on to pour scorn on the government's plans to muzzle certain breeds, calling instead for a widespread programme of mass slaughter. Hugh forced himself to read on, so as to keep his mind clear of anything else. He was nearing the end when he saw that Darren had reappeared by his side.

'Battersby wants to see you.'

Battersby was back in his office.

'Close the door,' he said.

Hugh looked around.

'There isn't one.'

'It's a sliding panel,' shouted Battersby. 'Pull it across.'

Hugh did so. When it was shut Battersby said, 'Do you have any idea how foolish you made me look in there?'

Hugh had noticed before how, at moments of extreme anger, the skin seemed to pull back from Battersby's teeth, giving his face a sharper, more feral look.

'I'm sorry.'

Battersby shook his head dismissively, as if attempts had been made to fool him this way before. 'Sorry's not good enough. Tell me, how do you see your future on this paper?' Before Hugh could reply, Battersby pressed on, 'Bleak would be a good word, I think. But for the time being there's something I'd like you to do.

'Yes,' he said, 'I want you to go downstairs. Do you know what that means?'

'I think so,' said Hugh.

'Well, just so there's no confusion, let me make it clear. I want you to go down to the library and read through everything that's ever been written on the Queen Mother. I mean everything, and rewrite her entire obituary. Not just

142

buff up what's already there. Rewrite the whole thing. You've got three days, and I don't want to see you up in this office until you've finished. Understood?'

'Yes.'

'Now bugger off,' said Battersby.

The library was one floor below the newspaper offices. The door was stiff and Hugh had to push hard against it before it opened. He found himself in a large, dark room lined with metal shelves. It was bitterly cold. The shelves reached down to the floor and disappeared off into the darkness somewhere up near the ceiling. They even covered the windows, so that what light there was filtered through this tracery of shelving.

Each of the shelves was crammed with buff-coloured envelopes – thousands upon thousands of them, all crammed with press cuttings. To enable people to orientate themselves letters of the alphabet had been painted in white letters on pieces of board that jutted out from the shelves at regular intervals. There was a smell of worn, fingered paper. Down the middle of the room was a row of desks and above it strip lights suspended on long chains.

Hugh found the light switches and turned them on. If anything, the room became even gloomier than before. Over by one wall was a set of library steps with a slatted platform on top like a tennis umpire's chair. He pushed the steps across the floor, climbed up to the top and began to search for files on the Queen Mother. There was nothing, at least nothing he could find.

'Who are you looking for?'

The voice came from the foot of the steps. Due to the dust and the darkness he couldn't be sure who was speaking. He dismounted the steps. When he reached the bottom he saw Walter Eames standing there with that same brittle, watchful air. Walter's head was extended on his long, stalklike neck. There was something raw, almost moist, about his telescoped features.

'The Queen Mother,' said Hugh.

'You won't find her there. She's got a separate section to herself. There are miles of envelopes. Is there anything in particular you're after?'

'Everything,' said Hugh.

Walter whistled. 'You'll need a truck then. What have you done to deserve that?' He stooped and looked at Hugh with unexpected sympathy. Hugh felt a sudden stab of gratitude for his concern.

'Oh,' he said, 'it's a long story.'

Hugh followed him to the other end of the room. He noticed again how Walter walked up on the balls of his feet. It gave his movements a feline quality and made him look oddly stealthy.

There was a special alcove, like a loading bay, devoted to the royal family. The Queen was at the end, with the Queen Mother on the left. Her press cuttings took up an entire wall, then spilled over onto another set of shelves that had been erected alongside. Next to this were the obituaries. In theory, everyone with any kind of public reputation had an obituary on file, ready to be published when they died. In practice, though, many of them had never been written in the first place, while others hadn't been updated in years.

Once the paper had had a full-time team of obituary writers, who checked discreetly on people's state of health and went to work at the first sign of infirmity. But they'd all been laid off several months beforehand after a market-research survey revealed that readers found it depressing to read about dead people, no matter how distinguished. In future, only those who had died in particularly embarrassing circumstances were considered worthy of an obituary, along with members of the royal family.

Hugh stood and looked at the wall of envelopes.

'Where are you going to start?' Walter asked.

'At the beginning, I suppose.'

'You'll find they're probably not in the right order. Things haven't been filed properly down here for some time.'

Walter went away. Several minutes later he came back pushing a luggage trolley.

'Here,' he said, 'this might help.'

'Thank you.'

Hugh spent the rest of the morning taking the envelopes down from the shelves and arranging them in chronological piles on the tables. At lunchtime he went upstairs to see if anyone wanted a drink. But it turned out they had already gone to the pub. It wasn't until he emerged into the light that he noticed he was covered in dust. It had turned his hair grey, streaked his clothes and even filled his pockets. He brushed himself off as best he could.

In the pub there were more people than usual sitting around a table.

'Hello, Hughie,' said Julian. 'You look like death.'

'No,' said Hugh. 'It's only dust.'

He told everyone what had happened with Battersby. Although there was a certain amount of sympathy for him, conversation, inevitably, was dominated by the news about Scaife.

'Extraordinary,' Johnny Todd was saying. 'I never imagined he'd do anything like this. Something stupid, all right, but attempted murder – wow!'

Todd was wearing an even more boldly chequered suit than usual. There was a handkerchief sticking out of his breast pocket, made from the same material as his tie. His socks, Hugh noticed, were a bright lime-green colour, and there were buckles on top of his shoes. While he was inured to most forms of depravity, and far too contrived a figure to give in to genuine astonishment, his manner suggested that he was having some difficulty coming to terms with the scale of Scaife's misdeeds.

'He tried to kill the man with a shovel.'

'It doesn't look good.'

'It could hardly look worse, could it? Well, he might have actually killed him. I suppose that would have been worse.'

'Still,' said Julian. 'It's not all bad news.'

'How do you work that out?'

'Now we know that he's still alive. Before we thought he might be dead.'

'I never thought he was dead,' said Cliff.

'No, you thought he'd be back the next morning,' said Julian. 'If it wasn't for you, poor Hughie wouldn't be stuck downstairs with the fucking Queen Mother.'

Cliff raised his thick fingers, then let them fall. 'Scaife always had a temper,' he said. 'Remember that time he bit the actress.'

'He did what?'

'Scaife. He was sent to interview some actress or other and, halfway through the interview, he launched himself at her and bit her.'

'What did he do that for?'

'There wasn't a reason, Julian. He just did it. That's my point. He's not a rational person. Apparently the doctor had to give her a rabies shot.'

'Scaife has rabies?' said Johnny Todd.

'It was only a precaution. Still, it's not what you expect, is it? You turn up for an interview thinking you're going to be talking about how you've always wanted to play opposite Bertie Block, or whoever, and the next thing this lunatic is sinking his teeth into your arm. It's not on. That sort of thing gives us all a bad name.'

Hugh remembered Julian's approving reference to Cliff as 'a pro' and wondered if he might take a similarly dim view of such unprofessional behaviour. Julian, however, seemed quite unmoved.

'So, what's Scaife going to do now?' someone asked.

'He'll have to go abroad, won't he? Do a runner, like Lucan.'

'Don't mention Lucan to Battersby. He'll be after him like a shot again.'

'But Scaife hasn't got his passport. The police said he'd left it behind.'

'That's it then. He's had it.'

'I know what I'd do,' said Julian. 'I'd look to my friends to help me.'

'Mmm, sadly I don't know who Scaife's friends are,' said Cliff.

'We are.'

'What?'

'We're his friends.'

'But he must have some closer friends than us.'

'He's never mentioned anyone.'

'Never?'

'Not so I remember.'

'So, what happens if he tries to get in touch?'

'I think you should all remember that attempted murder is a very serious crime,' said Cliff with a managerial air.

'What do you mean?'

'I'm just making the point that if you should help Scaife, then you lay yourselves open to being charged as accessories.'

'But what about loyalty?' said someone else.

'Loyalty? Loyalty? I believe in loyalty,' said Cliff. 'Of course I do. But I think you've got to weigh up the pros and cons of something like this, that's all. I'm simply being a realist here.'

By the end of the afternoon Hugh had finally arranged all the envelopes in chronological order. He'd begun ploughing through the earliest cuttings on the Queen Mother's birth and christening. Here, at least, there was gratifyingly little material. What few cuttings there were crumbled to dust in his hands, the newspaper was so old and fragile. The rubber bands that once held them together had long since perished. At one stage he was aware of Walter coming back in and watching him from the far end of the room.

Hugh found it even more depressing than he'd expected. His heart sunk lower and lower with each piece of paper he unfolded, each wretched little snippet of information he read. The hunting parties, the coming-out balls. Between the larger piles of envelopes he arranged smaller piles of cuttings. They stretched all the way down the table and fluttered off like pieces of tissue whenever he made any sudden movement.

At six o'clock he went back upstairs to collect his things. Again he was covered in dust. It was in his ears, his nose, even in his eyes. All he wanted to do was go home. However, his day wasn't over yet.

He was bending over his desk when Vivien said, 'We need to talk.'

'Please,' said Hugh, 'not now.'

But when he looked up he saw that once again Vivien was looking disturbingly resolute. She seemed to be standing more squarely, more upright than usual. In certain lights, he noticed, her eyes were almost black. While there had once been something almost leonine about her, now she had a strangely majestic bearing, like some big crested bird.

'Yes,' she said. 'Now.'

'Here?'

'No. Not here.'

He followed her down the corridor to the vending machine, where she stopped and pushed back her hair.

'I don't like the way you've been avoiding me,' she said.

He started to protest, but she took no notice.

'Yes you have, and I find it insulting.'

'I've just had other things on my mind,' he said.

Hugh was quite unprepared for what happened next. Vivien bent forward and shook her head slowly from side to side, while at the same time keeping her eyes fixed on his. The languor in her eyes as she swung her head about made this fixity more penetrating than anything she might have said. And while there was some truth in what he had said, this sense of being seen through – not momentarily, but utterly – left him feeling as if he had been winded.

'I never intended to insult you,' he said humbly.

'There's no need to scuttle away every time you see me,' she said. 'It's pathetic. You seem to think that I'm pursuing you, that I'm harbouring some grand, unrequited passion.'

Now Vivien laughed, her deep, throaty laugh, full of unnecessary gusto. 'That I really find insulting. My God, who do you think you are?'

Here we go, thought Hugh, and he lowered his head in readiness. But even this, despite its note of scorn and calculated hurtful implications, was delivered in tones that suggested Vivien didn't think the matter was worth getting that worked up about.

'I admit I was taken aback by your behaviour,' she said. 'It's not what I was expecting. But then, if we hadn't smoked those joints I can't imagine it would ever have happened.'

'Quite,' agreed Hugh.

'Not that it's any of your business, but this isn't something I make a habit of doing.'

'No, I'm sure.'

'At least not with people like you. Anyway,' she said, 'let that be an end of it.'

Hugh waited until Vivien had turned the corner before moving. He saw that she was wearing a pair of shoes he hadn't seen before. Just before she disappeared a memory came to him of her heels slipping out of her green shoes as she walked up Charing Cross Road.

On the tube back home Hugh lifted his hand to his nose. For some reason his hand smelled of vinegar. The smell was so strong it made him flinch. The other hand was just as bad. What was it, he wondered? He must be secreting some sort of chemical – the opposite of musk – some all-purpose repellent. He imagined it seeping out of his glands and soaking his clothes.

He glanced at the people around him. For some reason they appeared not to have noticed. Perhaps they were just locked in their own separate spheres of stink, immune to everyone else's. But somehow he doubted it – at any rate, he doubted that they could ever match his own terrible secretions. He saw himself being swept along beneath

149

London, down great brick tunnels, through sluices and sewers, damp and discredited, with a long, sour vapour-trail streaming out behind him.

When he went to the Sri Lankan takeaway he found that the door was locked and there was no light on inside. There was a handwritten note stuck on the inside of the window where the menu had been. It read, 'Restaurant closed until further notice.'

Chapter Fifteen

The next morning there had been two reported sightings of Scaife in northern France and another in Belgium. In the first he had been spotted buying a train ticket, in the second he had been seen in an art gallery. Given Scaife's character, rather more credence was being attached to the first than the second. Hugh stood by his desk looking at the life of the office around him, then he went down to the cuttings library to resume where he had left off the day before.

The task facing him seemed even more daunting than it had been. The wall of envelopes looked bigger, the mounds of paper on the tables more mountainous. As he went through each envelope, Hugh read through the cuttings and made notes. Slowly, jerkily, the Queen Mother grew from girlhood to adulthood in front of him. He saw her broad, pasty features take on definition and her hair shrink up into a bun.

She had been born in an age of deference. The hierarchy set, the patterns unchanging. Now all that was coming to an end. A new age of scorn was dawning. People were less respectful, less servile. Now they were preoccupied with their own self-advancement. They wanted a slice for themselves, and they'd begun calling for it in loud, indignant voices. Once Hugh might have imagined that an age of scorn would have suited him perfectly, but now he wasn't so sure. Fear of the future was making him look with increasing fondness on the past.

He'd been there for three hours when he saw the door at the end of the room open and Walter come in. He looked like a figure materializing out of the mist, teetering along as if he'd been goosed from behind. Yet there was something peculiarly resilient about him, as if he might be blown off balance at any moment, but would be able to right himself easily enough.

'How are you getting on?' he asked.

'Pretty slowly,' admitted Hugh.

'How long have they given you?'

'Two more days after today.'

'What happens if you don't finish in time?'

'I expect I'll be sacked. But then, I'll probably be sacked even if I do.'

Walter smiled. 'I know the feeling. We're all being chucked out when the paper moves. They say they don't have the facilities for us any more.'

'What will you do?'

'Who knows?' he said. 'We're trying to make plans. Anyway, if you could let me have the trolley back later. You know where my room is.'

For the rest of the day Hugh worked away, only emerging briefly at lunchtime to buy a sandwich. There were times when he was so bored that he found himself falling asleep; he'd nod off and then come to seconds later, wondering where he was, lost in this dark underground chamber with the faint metallic gleam of the shelves rising all round him.

But as he went on, he started to see a pattern establish itself in the Queen Mother's life. The same faces began to recur. Not just other members of the royal family, but a host of previously unfamiliar faces – the courtiers and sycophants. There they were, year after year, these massed deferential presences standing two or three paces back. Smiling away, yet appropriately cowed, hoping that the force of her benevolence might be turned upon them for an instant.

152

Dispensing all this goodwill could take it out of you, but the Queen Mother never seemed to falter, or indeed to register anything other than glazed imperturbability as she snipped ribbons, awarded prizes and went about her unceasing round of public functions. Year in, year out, as the world erupted and settled back around her.

On she went, through courtship and marriage to the shy, stuttering Duke of York. The marriage had taken place at Westminster Abbey. Plans to broadcast it to the nation had been abandoned after the Abbey Chapter voiced fears that men might listen to the sacrament in public houses with their hats on. The ceremony was delayed when a clergyman in the bride's procession fainted – during the pause the bride left her father's side and placed her bouquet of white roses and heather on the tomb of the Unknown Soldier.

And so on, through motherhood – with the Home Secretary in attendance at the birth of her daughter Elizabeth to ensure there was no inadvertent baby-swapping – and married life. The duchess persuaded her husband to visit the speech therapist Lionel Logue in Harley Street to try to correct his stutter. There the two of them would sit for hours intoning 'Let's go gathering healthy heather with the gay brigade of grand dragoons' over and over again.

By the end of the day she had celebrated her twenty-fifth wedding anniversary, renounced the title of Empress of India and nursed her husband through his last fatal illness. On the night of 5 February 1952 the King had retired to his bedroom at Sandringham at ten thirty, while the Queen and a number of friends had stayed up to watch a film in the ballroom. At around midnight the nightwatchman had seen the King fasten the catch of his bedroom window. The next morning the King's second valet, James Macdonald, had found him dead in bed. He was fifty-six.

Hugh found himself feeling more affected by this than he cared to admit. It took him some time to compose himself. He dusted himself down and wheeled the luggage trolley back to Walter's room. The door was locked, but the one next to it was half open. He could hear the sound of conversation within. He knocked. Immediately, the talking stopped.

Leaving the trolley outside, he pushed the door open. A number of green-carders were sitting behind a table, including Walter. In front of them on the table were several narrow wooden boxes. And on the other side of the table was a queue of men reaching back to the door. The men drew back to let Hugh in.

As far as he could tell – he wasn't in the room long enough to form much of an impression – the green-carders were in the process of handing out small packets to each of the men. None of them looked familiar. Several were dressed in very old, shabby clothes. The ones at the front of the queue shambled patiently forward for their packets.

When the green-carders saw Hugh they froze. None of them moved, except for one man, who looked around and then rose to his feet. Hugh saw that he was the same man who had blocked his way in the corridor three days before. Now he didn't say anything, but simply stood with his hand raised, pointing towards the door.

'I'm sorry,' Hugh began. But he couldn't go on. He didn't try to explain what he was doing. Instead, he backed out of the room, shut the door behind him and took the trolley back to the library.

For the next two days Hugh laboured over the Queen Mother's obituary. While he still had difficulty writing, he found that he was able to stick together sentences from different articles and thereby assemble something which resembled a fresh piece of prose, but was in fact a collage of other people's work. There were inevitable jarring, juddering variations in style and tone between paragraphs, indeed from one sentence to the next. However, he decided not to worry about this, but rather to plough ahead as best he could.

Slowly the cuttings grew less yellowed, less fragile. The

Queen Mother swanned blithely on. Only on one occasion, as far as Hugh could discover, had she ever been visibly knocked off her stride. On a state visit to Cape Town in 1947, a 'giant Zulu' had broken through the police cordon and charged at the royal party. The Queen Mother began to beat him about the head with her umbrella before realizing the man was trying to offer Princess Elizabeth a ten-shilling note as a birthday present.

Hugh began to recognize the names of the journalists who had written the original articles. The Fifties passed and he moved on through the Sixties – tour of Fiji, appendicitis operation, duet with Noel Coward . . .

He heard the door open at the far end of the room and looked up to see Walter once again making his way towards him. For a while he stood beside him, not saying anything but watching him type away. Hugh finished cramming two utterly dissonant sentences together and pushed his chair back. Still Walter didn't say anything and Hugh began to grow uneasy. To break the silence he said, 'I came looking for you last night.'

'Yes,' said Walter. 'I know you did.'

He put his hand on Hugh's shoulder. It lay there, long and bony.

'Can I trust you?' he asked.

'Trust me?' said Hugh. 'I believe so. Why?'

At this Walter simply shook his head. He patted him on the shoulder, then turned and walked away down the length of tables towards the door. Hugh could only sit and watch in confusion as the dust swallowed him up.

He worked on, aware that time was running out, skimming through the cuttings, searching for any relevant snippets of information. Half the time, he realized, he was hardly taking in anything, and he had to force himself to slow down and concentrate. He was growing slapdash.

He'd finished going through the contents of one envelope and was about to start on another when he saw that there was one more cutting stuck in the bottom of the envelope. He took out the crumpled, concertinaed piece of paper and unfolded it, pressing it flat on the table with his hand. It was a photograph of the Queen Mother at a function shaking hands with a man. They were leaning forward with arms extended and hands clasped, as if each was trying to pull the other off balance. The two of them were surrounded by a mass of blurred, peering faces.

There was, Hugh realized, something familiar about the man, although he was at a loss to say what it was. He was only aware of the faintest, unfocused glimmer of recognition. But his head felt so overloaded by the weight of information he'd absorbed that he couldn't take anything else in. Instead, he put the cutting back in the envelope and pushed it to the back of his mind.

By the afternoon of the second day the obituary lay before him like some huge patchwork quilt, each paragraph typed on a different sheet of copy paper. Hugh made some final alterations and then gathered all the pieces of paper together. When he'd finished, he carried the obituary upstairs for Battersby to read.

Battersby was sitting in his office with his feet on a chair in front of him, looking at the afternoon edition of the paper. Holding the obituary cradled in both arms, Hugh managed to knock on the glass. Battersby glanced up, then beckoned him in.

'What the hell's that?' he asked.

'The Queen Mother's obituary,' said Hugh. 'I thought you'd want to see it.'

As always, it took Battersby a few moments to adjust to the possible implications of this new piece of information. His eyes skidded about then settled. 'Ah yes. Well, you'd better put it down.'

Hugh did so, dividing the obituary into two piles, each roughly the same height. Battersby looked at them both without enthusiasm. 'The last thing I want in here is more mess,' he said.

Nonetheless, he sat down and began to read. Every so often he paused to stare at Hugh, and then continued reading. Something had happened to Battersby's hair,

Hugh noticed. Instead of being combed forward in its usual Nero style, he had tried to insert a parting. But after so long being styled one way it was not easily re-groomed. On one side of the parting it still fell obstinately forward, on the other it stayed swept back. Depending on which way he turned, Battersby now appeared to be wearing two different heads of hair.

It took him ten minutes to finish. When he was through he sat in silence.

'More awe,' he said.

'What do you mean?'

'More awe,' said Battersby again. 'There's not enough awe. It's not reverential enough. Where's the great figure-head of our nation? The beacon in times of sorrow?'

He shook his head. 'It's just not here. I'm looking for it, but I can't find it. And another thing, it tails off towards the end. You can't have that. I want people to have a lump in their throat when they're reading this, to break down on the tube, sobbing on street corners. You make it sound as though her death will come as a big relief all round.'

'What do you want me to do?' asked Hugh.

'Do it again, of course. But this time I want a tear in my eye when I've finished.'

'What do you think of the style?'

'Style?' said Battersby, momentarily thrown again. 'What do you mean style?'

'The way it's written.'

'It's all right, I suppose. Makes sense if that's what you mean. Anyway, I don't want style. I want awe.'

The telephone rang. Battersby picked it up, his expression rapidly changing to one of surprise, even wonder.

'Home Secretary,' he said, 'how very kind of you to call. You got my message? A piece, that's right. Yes, about the dog question. Laying out the government's line and your own thoughts on this whole vexed matter. Of course I understand how busy you are. No, next week would be fine.'

Battersby held his spare hand over the receiver and

157

looked up at Hugh. 'What are you hanging around for?' he asked.

On the way back to the library Hugh stopped at his desk. He wondered if he might have received any notification of computer training. As far as he could tell, everyone else had done so. But there was nothing. On the left of his type-writer, however, stood a cup of tea with a sachet of sugar and a plastic stirrer beside it. His first thought was that one of his neighbours must have got it for him. The only person around was Stanley, hidden behind his visor. But Stanley had never offered to get him tea before and there seemed no reason why he should start now.

Then Hugh wondered if some other tea boy was on duty, one who hadn't been properly briefed on the importance of shunning him. But he could see Darren over by the news desk, handing out papers. The only other explanation was that Darren himself had dispensed the tea. This, however, seemed so far-fetched as to be inconceivable. Hugh picked up the cup and took a sip. Apart from being cold it tasted normal enough.

'I believe I mentioned Mr Glim before,' his mother had written. 'I can't tell you how attentive he has been. But not in a nuisance way. He never outstays his welcome. He made me a special cocktail today – it quite knocked me out! I thought I might be rather lonely on a cruise by myself, but I needn't have worried. Will post this in Pekalongan. Stopping briefly this p.m. We're off to have a look round.'

That night Hugh had a dream. He dreamed that he was standing on the banks of a great river. A ferry – or rather a rowing boat – was carrying people from one side of the river to the other. It was dusk and there were few passengers about. But waiting on the far bank was a solitary figure, pacing about impatiently.

The boat made its way across the dark sweep of water towards him. He climbed on board and the boat set off back across the river. Hugh could see two men rowing, struggling against the current to keep the boat on course. Another man was steering while a fourth stood in the bow shouting instructions. The passenger sat by himself behind the rowers, swathed in some sort of cloak.

As the boat came closer, Hugh realized that the crew were all green-carders. He could see their dun-coloured cardigans flying about in the wind. The man in the bow, he saw, was the same man who had blocked his way in the corridor, and as far as he could tell the man steering was Walter, or at least some nocturnal variation of him. But however hard he tried, he was unable to make out the face of the passenger who sat wrapped in his cloak, head obscured, as the green-carders ferried him across from one bank to the other.

Chapter Sixteen

In the library the next morning Hugh set about trying to shoehorn some more feeling into what he had already assembled. Into the cracks between the sentences he crammed any craven little gobbets, any lickspittling senti-ments he could think of. He worked without shame now, possessed by a dull, barely suppressed loathing for what he was doing.

After he'd been working for two hours he felt his brain starting to fog again. He had to force himself to concen-trate. When the fog in his head cleared he saw that he was holding the same photograph he'd found the day before – the Queen Mother leaning forward to shake the man's hand, with a sea of swimming faces pressing in around them. Now he looked at it again, shifting his chair under one of the strip lights so that he could see more clearly. This time he read the caption: 'The Queen Mother wishing lone yachtsman Tom Kingman good luck as he sets off on his attempt to become the fastest man to circumnavigate the globe.'

Hugh stared at it for some time, then he fetched his brief-case. He took out Field's Seaman's Discharge Book, turned to the photograph at the back and held it in front of him with one hand while with the other he held up the news-paper cutting. As he studied Field's photograph, he noticed a number of things that he'd not spotted before:

the puckering around the chin; the narrow, meandering nose; the swollen cheeks.

Then he looked again at the photograph of the yachtsman. It had been taken from a different angle, so it was difficult to make any direct comparison. Nonetheless, he shut his eyes and endeavoured to pass the two faces through some prism in his imagination, laying one on top of the other. Slowly they inched together. When he opened his eyes and looked at the two faces again the resemblance between them struck him even more forcibly than before.

He got up and pushed the library steps over to the letter K. Then he climbed the steps and looked through the envelopes, through masses of Kings, a cluster of Kingleys, and then on to Kingman. There were only five of them. One was an under-secretary at the Ministry of Defence, two were gardeners, the fourth was a doctor and the fifth a headmistress. None of them was called Tom. Hugh was trying to puzzle this out when he saw that Walter had come in again and was standing at the foot of the steps looking up at him.

'What are you after now?' asked Walter.

Hugh told him.

'Is he still alive?'

'I don't know.'

'If he's dead he won't be up there.'

Hugh came down the steps.

'Where will he be then?'

'If he's dead he'll be next door.'

Hugh followed Walter past the bay in which members of the royal family were kept and into the furthest recesses of the library, where he had never ventured before. At the far end was another set of double doors. Walter opened the doors, then felt about for a light switch.

Ahead of him was a narrow passageway lined with books. These, Hugh saw, were bound copies of old editions of the paper. The oldest ones were bound in calf. Their creamy spines had now turned stiff and translucent, like greaseproof paper. The more recent ones were bound in white canvas. They were stacked up from floor to ceiling on either side. In the gloom they stood out like rows of bones.

The passageway opened out into another room. There were the same strip lights, hanging on chains from the ceiling. The lights came on in sequence, one after the other, disappearing into the distance. This room was several times the size of the one they'd just left; it was as big as an aircraft hangar. In here there was no daylight at all, only what appeared to be miles of shelving, reaching from floor to ceiling. An endless series of nooks and alcoves stretching away as far as he could see. It was also even colder than next door. There was the same smell of worn, fingered paper, only much stronger and yet somehow flatter.

Both the room and the smell reminded Hugh of somewhere he'd been recently. At the time he couldn't think where. It was only later that he realized it was the warehouse at the docks, with the brown rolls of newsprint stacked up in columns, reaching towards the roof.

'What is this place?' he asked.

'This is where we keep the dead,' said Walter. 'If you're alive you're back there, once you're dead you get put in here.'

They made their way down to the letter K. Instead of steps, these shelves had long metal ladders that hooked onto them and could be slid from one section to the next. Hugh climbed one of the ladders. The dead seemed to spill out all around him, crammed together, spilling from their envelopes. He found two entire shelves full of Kingmans and pulled himself along through the alphabet of Christian names.

There was only one Tom Kingman. On the outside of the envelope his dates had been written in black felt pen: 'Yachtsman. 1926–1969.' There was a question mark after the last date.

'Have you found what you wanted?' asked Walter.

'I'm not sure,' Hugh replied.

He dismounted the ladder and took the envelope over to one of the tables. He tipped out the contents and picked a cutting from the top of the pile. The cutting was headlined KINGMAN GOES SLOW. With it was another photograph. This one had been taken from head-on and Hugh found himself feeling less confident about any resemblance – the man's face looked sleeker, more confident than Field's. He stared at the photograph for a while longer.

'Actually,' he said, 'I don't think this can be what I was looking for, after all.'

Walter shrugged. Hugh folded up the cutting and put it back in the envelope, along with the others. Then he replaced the envelope on the shelves. Together they went back down the passageway into the other room.

For the rest of the day Hugh worked on. When he'd finished rewriting the obituary, he took it back upstairs. Battersby read it more slowly this time. At one stage, about halfway through, he gave a little moan. When he got to the end he took out his handkerchief.

'You think it's better this time?' asked Hugh.

'It's a bit better,' Battersby allowed reluctantly. 'Mind you, a life as rich as that almost tells itself. As long as petty prejudice isn't allowed to get in the way. Yes, it is better. At least it'll do for the time being. Now leave me,' he said. 'I have more important things to attend to.'

Hugh left the office and sat at his desk. Darren was pushing his trolley down the aisle towards him. As he drew level, he poured out a cup of tea and set it down beside Hugh. It was followed by a bun wrapped in a paper napkin – an old-fashioned, sugar-encrusted thing studded with burned raisins. Hugh grunted his thanks, but didn't look up, not wanting to draw attention to his rehabilitation. The sugar crystals on top of the bun were as big as shards of glass. He wrapped it in the napkin and put it in his top drawer. He drank the tea, trying as he did so to work out what could have prompted this change of heart.

The same people Hugh had seen taking measurements

on the stairs were now doing the same in the office. He watched as a group of them stopped near by Cliff's desk. Cliff was talking on the phone, leaning forward, straining out of his jacket, and seemed not to notice at first as one of the men trailed his tape measure over his desk. The tape measure was removed and extended again – this time running upwards from the floor to the ceiling.

Hugh saw Cliff's eyes flicker to his left, as if in vague, barely conscious acknowledgement of what was going on. Then the tape measure toppled and fell onto him, a long wavering strip of metal crumpling across his shoulders. Cliff finished his phone call – he didn't seem in any hurry – got to his feet, took hold of the man and began to wrap the tape measure around his chest, pinning his arms to his side.

At first his colleagues seemed about to rush forward and rescue him. But then their nerve deserted them and they hung back as Cliff frogmarched his captive down the aisle towards one of the exit doors. He pushed him through the door, and held it open for the others to follow. They all did so meekly, shrinking away from him as they left. When the last one had gone Cliff strode back, holding out his arms in front of him and brushing his hands together in an exaggerated sort of way.

Hugh waited at his desk. He took out Field's Seaman's Discharge Book and sat staring at it for some time. At six o'clock he went back downstairs to the library. He turned on the lights and walked down the length of the room, through the passageway and into the second library where the files of the dead were kept. It was like being in a mausoleum – the cold, the darkness, the residue of count-less lives rustling around him. He climbed the ladder and took out the Kingman files – there were four of them.

'You're working late,' said Walter.

He was standing at the foot of the ladder, this frail, extruded figure looking up at him.

Hugh had the files in his hand. He climbed down the rungs and put them on the table alongside Field's Discharge

Book. He saw Walter looking at the files. Then he picked up the Discharge Book.

'Where did you get this?'

'It . . . it came into my possession,' said Hugh.

Walter began to leaf through the pages. When he came to the photograph of Field he stopped.

'Does he look familiar?' asked Hugh.

'Why should he?'

'No,' said Hugh. 'No reason.'

Again, he felt himself under scrutiny. And although it wasn't quite as disconcerting as being seen through by Vivien, he still found himself feeling unaccountably guilty.

'Just some research,' he said.

Walter continued to look at him.

'You'll be sure to shut up after you,' he said.

Hugh nodded. Then he stood and watched as Walter teetered away into the gloom.

Chapter Seventeen

The weather had turned cold again. There was a dry brittleness in the air, an absence of any sort of moisture. Despite the cold, the boys were still riding their bicycles up and down the street when Hugh returned home. As he came closer, he could hear their wheels rasping on the grit as they practised their skid turns. And from inside the houses came the exasperated cries of his neighbours as their televisions hopped about wildly from channel to channel.

When he was inside his flat, Hugh took the envelopes from his briefcase and emptied the contents onto his living-room carpet. He put Field's Seaman's Discharge Book alongside the cuttings. Then he picked up the piece with the photograph of Kingman that he'd seen earlier. It had been taken on the quay in Dartmouth, prior to his embarking on the first single-handed, round-the-world yacht race. Kingman was standing in his waterproof gear, his arms outstretched, grinning hugely. He had one of those broad, ripe melon faces and looked to be the picture of heartiness.

Once again, Hugh compared the two photographs – Field's and Kingman's – shutting his eyes and endeavouring to lay one on top of the other.

Next to the photo in the paper was an account of Kingman's progress from Dartmouth to the Bay of Biscay. 'Despite a leaking hatch and suffering from seasickness,' the piece reported, 'he remains in good spirits and is confident of catching up with the race leaders.' Kingman had spoken to his wife on the radio, slept well and made himself a meal of ham curry.

The next two pieces he read were accounts of Kingman's departure from Dartmouth. The quayside had been lined with cheering well-wishers, and a small flotilla had followed him to the mouth of the estuary. Both journalists had expressed admiration for his bravery, while drawing attention to Kingman's comparative inexperience as a yachtsman, his age – at forty, he was some years older than the other competitors – and the size of his yacht, which was a good deal smaller than anyone else's.

Kingman himself, however, appeared quite untroubled by doubts, and had been scornful of anyone who questioned his preparation. His last act before leaving land had been to kiss the mayoress on both cheeks and then lead the local sea scouts in a chorus of 'A life on the ocean wave'. One of the pieces had a photograph of a small, dark-haired woman waving at an empty seascape. 'Mr Kingman's wife, Margaret, bids her lone mariner husband a tearful farewell,' ran the caption.

Hugh set about arranging the cuttings in chronological order. When this was done he started at the top of the pile and worked his way down. The early articles were all about Kingman's preparation for the voyage. An electrical engineer from Bristol, he had left his job and cashed in his life savings in order to raise money for a yacht that he had designed himself. Of the four other yachtsmen attempting to become the fastest man to circumnavigate the globe, Kingman was the last to embark.

His early progress down the coast of Spain and across towards the Canaries had been a lot slower than expected. It had taken him two weeks to complete a leg of the journey that had taken his fastest rival only eight days. There had also been a series of accidents – water had got into his food compartment and his self-steering mechanism had been unable to cope with the heavy swell.

Kingman, though, remained characteristically undaunted. He managed to repair his self-steerer, and his food stocks were not as badly affected as he'd first feared. Much of it was in tins and the labels had simply come off – for the rest of his voyage Kingman never knew what he was going to eat whenever he cooked himself a meal. None of this mattered, though. He had spent the whole of his life preparing for just such a testing endeavour and a few mishaps along the way were only to be expected.

For the next two weeks Kingman continued to head south down the west coast of Africa, towards Cape Town. The plan was that he would round the Cape of Good Hope and then set off across the Indian Ocean towards Australia. But still he continued to make slow progress. At this rate he stood no chance of catching up with any of his competitors, let alone making the fastest circumnavigation. His messages, however, continued to be full of optimism. He was confident that he would be able to go faster once he got used to the way his boat handled. If his small back-up team in Dartmouth were starting to have their doubts they kept them to themselves. In the absence of anything worth reporting, press coverage dwindled away to almost nothing.

Then, remarkably, Kingman put on a sudden burst of speed. Having averaged only fifty nautical miles a day over the preceding month, he more than doubled this over the next four weeks. The tone of the newspaper reports changed rapidly. Having been written off as a hopeless case, even something of an embarrassment, Kingman was now staging a dramatic recovery.

Coming from behind, lacking the sophisticated equipment of the other competitors, he was showing a refusal to bow to the odds which could hardly fail to excite admiration. It didn't matter that, by this stage, no-one gave him any chance of winning. Far from it – his efforts seemed all the more admirable as a result.

There were articles outlining what a great sacrifice he'd had to make to buy his boat, as well as various attempts made to analyse his character. Here there was comparatively little to go on. Friends and colleagues paid tribute to his stoicism, as well as to his sense of determination, then seemed stuck for anything else to say. Not that this mattered, either. As well as being brave and steadfast, Kingman, the articles all noted with delight, was 'refreshingly down to earth'.

And still his speed increased. His daily average over the next four weeks was a remarkable 170 nautical miles. If he continued at this rate he would start to overtake his rivals, one of whom was now having serious mechanical difficulties of his own. Another of the yachtsmen, a Frenchman, had complicated matters by announcing that, even if he reached the finishing line, he had no intention of stopping there, but intended to carry on until he became bored or ran out of food. The organizers seemed unsure whether this constituted unsportsmanlike behaviour.

Kingman was also having problems – with further leaks, with the self-steering gear, and now with his radio. Owing to a faulty transmitter he was having to make most of his communications using Morse Code. Yet the tone of his messages remained relentlessly upbeat. By now he was in the middle of the Indian Ocean, almost 1,000 miles from land, an estimated three weeks away from the southern shore of Australia.

It was at this point that all communications with Kingman ceased. This in itself was not unusual. Other competitors had gone for several days without being heard from. Besides, he'd already reported having problems with his radio. To begin with, therefore, no-one was particularly worried. After a week, though, people began to get concerned. But it was difficult to know what to do. No-one had any accurate idea where Kingman was and it was impracticable to scour vast areas of the Indian Ocean searching for him.

In the end there was little choice but to sit and wait and hope that he would get in touch. Another two weeks went by. Only Mrs Kingman, it seemed, remained unconcerned.

'He'll turn up,' she said. 'I know my husband.'

Hugh picked up another cutting. This was headlined, KINGMAN MYSTERY DEEPENS. It reported that nothing had been heard of the lone yachtsman for more than ten days. A number of theories were advanced for this: he might have had an accident, he could have become becalmed in a part of the ocean where the atmospheric conditions interfered with his radio transmission, or his radio itself might have broken down. There was another photograph of Margaret Kingman. 'I'm sure there's nothing to worry about,' she was quoted as saying.

She was right. Kingman did turn up. Twenty-three days after his last message, Wellington Radio in New Zealand picked up a weak signal from him. Everything was fine, he said. He was still having problems with the radio and a jib pole had broken in a storm, but otherwise he was continuing to make excellent progress.

Unfortunately it was impossible to pinpoint his position as his signal disappeared before he was able to give his latitude and longitude. He had, however, said that he expected to round Cape Horn within the next ten days. If he was right it would mean that Kingman hadn't simply kept up his previous daily average, but had once again managed to improve on it. Presumably without being aware of it, he had also overtaken his nearest rival. And this wasn't all – if he maintained his present rate he stood a good chance of winning the prize for the fastest time.

All this, of course, caused even more excitement. It was, everyone agreed, an astonishing feat of seamanship. The only frustration was that no-one was able to plot Kingman's course with any degree of accuracy. People were keen to know just where he was and when he was going to round Cape Horn. But in the absence of any real information all they had to go on was a series of increasingly speculative newspaper reports.

Another nine days elapsed before his next communication, this time sent by Morse Code and picked up in Brazil. Afterwards there were accusations that the Brazilians had failed to read his message properly, or else had missed out vital parts of it, all of which they angrily denied. Kingman, it appeared from his message, had already rounded Cape Horn and was now somewhere south-west of the Falkland Islands.

Just where, though, was the problem. The Brazilian radio operator insisted that Kingman had once again not given his latitude and longitude. The British, naturally, refused to believe this. Kingman was far too skilled a sailor to have made such an elementary mistake. The row went on, with no-one in Britain, at least, in any doubt who was to blame.

Fortunately it was curtailed by another message from Kingman, this time giving his exact position. He was, he said, north of the Falklands and heading up the coast of Brazil towards the West Indies. His radio was still out of action, but in this latest communication he sounded more relaxed, less clipped than he had been before: 'Calm seas. Setting sun like a mighty brass ball. Perfect peace and pleasure. Learning to love the operator.'

There was speculation as to what this last sentence meant. Some thought it was a reference to his self-steering gear. Others assumed that it was simply an error in transmission. In the gap between these last two messages, the French yachtsman had announced that he no longer wished to be involved in the race, having decided that such competitions were childish and undignified.

Meanwhile another yacht had sustained heavy damage going round the Horn and was unlikely to be able to continue. This meant that Kingman was now one of only two sailors left in the race. His rival, another Englishman, was still some way ahead of him. But his yacht had also suffered damage rounding the Horn and his speed had been falling as a result. Everything therefore was left to play for. Two further messages from Kingman followed in quick succession. In both he gave his position and asked for news of his rival.

Then he disappeared again. A week went by. This time

171

no-one expressed concern. His silence, people thought, might even be a ploy to conceal his whereabouts, thereby retaining the element of surprise in the final stages of the race.

It was five days later – twelve days in all since Kingman's last message – when a tanker north of the Azores reported seeing a yacht apparently drifting aimlessly about with only one small sail raised. Concerned that whoever was sailing the yacht might be in difficulties, the captain of the tanker decided to investigate. A launch was lowered. When they were alongside the yacht the captain shouted a greeting and asked if he might come on board. There was no reply.

The captain and one crew member then climbed onto the yacht. They called out a second time and descended the steps into the cabin. It didn't take them long to see that the cabin was deserted. The captain reported later that it was in a state of chaos. There were clothes and charts strewn everywhere and the sink was piled high with dirty dishes. Several tins of food – spaghetti, corned beef and peaches – had been opened and left, half-eaten, next to the stove.

The two men came out on deck and checked there. This took even less time. They noted that the boat appeared to be in good order. There was no sign of any accident, and yet it was clear they were the only people on board. They looked for a logbook, but were unable to find one. The dinghy too was missing. A line was thrown across to the launch which then towed the yacht over to the tanker. There it was hoisted onto the deck. The captain radioed the tanker's owners in London for advice.

It was only at this stage that anyone made any connection with Kingman. The captain of the tanker was told to search the surrounding area and see if there was any sign of him. The Navy and Air Force were informed and after a gap of three hours an air search was under way. No-one found anything. As darkness fell the search was called off for the night. The next morning it recommenced, although by now there was no real hope that he would be found alive. In such conditions no-one was expected to survive more than four or five hours in the water. At the end of the second day the search was abandoned and Kingman presumed drowned.

The news of his disappearance caused a sensation. The discovery of a deserted yacht drifting about in the middle of the ocean would be mysterious enough in any circumstances. In this case the circumstances could hardly have been more dramatic. There was nothing on board the yacht to suggest that Kingman had been in any difficulty.

In the absence of any real evidence, theories abounded. It was possible that Kingman had been swept overboard. However, the condition of the yacht didn't lend much weight to this: the cabin may have been in a mess, but the tins of half-eaten food were still by the stove, apparently where he'd left them. Any wave large enough to have swept a man overboard would surely have caused more disruption inside the yacht. But if Kingman hadn't suffered some sort of accident, what had happened to him?

The other possibility – one which no-one cared to entertain – was that Kingman had taken his own life. In many ways this was the most likely explanation. Having spent so long on his own, could Kingman have simply cracked up? Had the pressure and the loneliness been too much for him? The trouble with this theory was that, again, there was nothing to back it up, no suggestion that he was depressed, unstable, or anything other than his usual optimistic self.

Much attention was paid not only to the state of the cabin, but also to its contents. As the captain of the tanker had noted, Kingman still had adequate supplies of food and fresh water on board and nothing significant appeared to be missing. A list was made of what had been found and this was published next to Kingman's own inventory of his supplies, compiled just before he set sail. Hugh looked down the two lists to see if anything struck him as odd, but there was nothing. Whatever problems Kingman had been having with his radio he appeared to have solved them before he disappeared, for it was found to be in perfect working order.

Mrs Kingman said nothing, despite all manner of inducements, but she had to put up with hundreds of reporters and cameramen camping out on her lawn. After the speculation came a general sense of resentment that Kingman had failed to turn up; it was almost as if he had taken advantage of everyone's good nature by playing so shamelessly with their emotions. Once every plausible angle had been exhausted the papers couldn't wait to get rid of him. Kingman was despatched back into obscurity and life settled down again.

It wasn't until ten years later that he was officially declared dead. The news scarcely rated a mention, although there were a couple of short pieces on what had happened to Margaret Kingman. Since her husband had sold all his assets to raise money for the voyage, she had been left with almost no money. The little that was left went on death duties – the situation having been made worse by the fact that Kingman had died intestate. She had sold their house, but the money raised had all gone to clear his debts.

Despite all this she didn't appear in any way bitter; she accepted what had happened with the same equanimity as she had accepted everything else. Even so, it was embarrassing to see the widow of a national hero brought so low, and understandably no-one wished to dwell on her troubles for too long. In the final cutting she was asked if she had any regrets. The question clearly surprised her. 'None whatsoever,' she said. 'My husband died doing something he believed in. How many of us can say that we have known similar fulfilment?'

The question was left hanging at the end of the piece, as if, thought Hugh, the journalist had tried but failed to come up with an effective rejoinder. He looked at the byline and saw to his surprise that the piece had been written by Stanley.

There were four envelopes full of cuttings. According to the labels stuck on the outside, though, there should have been five. Hugh sat back on the carpet. He must have overlooked one of the envelopes. Either that or it was missing.

Chapter Eighteen

With the impending move, the atmosphere in the office was changing. Every time Hugh looked up he seemed to see Battersby walking up and down the aisles, as if he was on an endless tour of inspection, peering over people's shoulders to see what they were doing. Fortunately, he never seemed to get up as far as Hugh's desk – something else always caught his attention first. A memo had been circulated that morning saying that all journalists who intended to be away from the office for more than an hour had to get written permission from him. This had been greeted with general disbelief; plainly no-one intended to take any notice. Even so, it was reckoned to be an unwelcome sign of things to come.

Battersby's attempts to keep tabs on everyone were complicated by a number of factors – it wasn't clear who had a genuine reason for being absent, who had simply not bothered to turn up for work and who was off having computer training. Almost everybody in the office had now received notification of their computer training. Hugh suspected he was the only one who hadn't, and for this reason he'd decided to stop asking.

Instigating conversation with Stanley proved more awkward than he had anticipated. In all the time they'd sat opposite one another they had hardly exchanged more than a few words. At first Stanley took no notice of him. Then, on the second attempt, there was at least a reaction.

From the other side of the visor he saw the soft green mass of Stanley's head lift momentarily from whatever he was doing, then drop down again.

The third time, the visor was lowered, his head came up again and turned round in more familiar directions before his gaze settled on Hugh.

'I was looking at the cuts on the yachtsman Tom Kingman yesterday,' said Hugh.

There was no reaction. Nothing that Hugh could identify as either encouragement or rebuff.

'Yes,' he continued, 'I read your piece with great interest. Perhaps I could talk to you about it sometime.'

'Why?' said Stanley.

'Well, it's a fascinating story. Also, I wondered if you might still have a contact number for his widow.'

The visor was replaced. 'What do you want that for?'

'I happened to notice that it was almost twenty years ago since he went missing. I thought we might do some sort of anniversary piece.'

'If anyone is going to do an anniversary piece then it should be me.'

'Of course. But if you like I could make myself useful doing some groundwork first.'

'Make yourself useful?' Stanley spoke incredulously.

'I could try to trace some of the relevant people. Assuming they're still alive. But it's so long ago you probably haven't got the numbers any more.'

Again, the visor came down. 'I've got every telephone number I've ever been given,' said Stanley.

'Have you really?'

'Of course, they're all here. All properly collated.'

'Where?' said Hugh.

'Here. By my desk.'

Stanley picked up one of his address books and held it open like a hymnal.

'May I have a look at them?'

'No,' he said, 'you may not. A journalist stands or falls on his contacts,' he added.

'Oh yes,' said Hugh. 'Quite.'

'An organized mind. That's the key.'

When Darren came round with his trolley, Hugh noticed that he appeared to have been crying. Apart from the puffy state of his eyes there was a general air of moistness about him, even the beginnings of his moustache appeared unusually damp. Again, a cup of tea and a bun was set down without comment. Given the improving state of their relations, Hugh was tempted to ask him what the matter was, but in the end the opportunity didn't present itself.

There was no sign of Walter downstairs, either in his room, or in the library of the living. Nonetheless, Hugh made his way as quietly as possible through to the library of the dead. He climbed the ladder once again and searched through the cuttings. There was no sign of any further file on Kingman. Of course, it was possible that the file had simply been lost, or misfiled. He searched through the envelopes on the adjoining shelves, but found nothing. After a while, he gave up. He turned off the lights, then shut the library doors behind him.

When Stanley left for the day, Hugh went back round to his side of the desk. In all the time Hugh had been at the paper, he realized, he had never crossed this divide before. Everything looked different from here. He gazed across the low barrier of books that divided them to where he'd just been sitting, and his absence from his own desk gave him an unpleasant shock. He imagined the life of the paper rolling on quite effortlessly without him and someone else slipping into his place.

Stanley's address books were kept in a special metal shelf, like a trough, that butted onto the side of his desk. There was a separate book for every letter of the alphabet. He took out the volume marked K and found Margaret Kingman's number without any difficulty.

He dialled the Bristol number and a woman's voice answered.

'Is that Mrs Kingman?'

'Who?'

'Could I speak to Mrs Kingman please.'

The woman giggled nervously. 'No-one by that name here, I'm afraid.'

'She used to live there. Do you have any idea where she moved to?'

'Hold on.'

After a while another woman came on the line. She sounded older. Hugh explained that he was trying to find Margaret Kingman and wondered if she could help. The woman said that she and her husband had bought the house from Mrs Kingman, but that was more than fifteen years ago and they had no idea where she was now. 'She did say something about moving to London,' said the woman. 'I have a feeling she had family there. I don't know if she ever did, though.'

Hugh thanked her and rang off. He put Stanley's address book back on its shelf. The cleaners were already making their rounds, emptying the waste-paper baskets and making futile attempts to vacuum the carpet tiles. The hoover sucked them right off the floor so they blocked the air intake, then the motor would start to scream in protest and the cleaner would have to stop and peel the carpet tile off the nozzle. The man that Cliff had frogmarched out of the office the day before was back with his colleagues, measuring up again.

Hugh found everyone in the pub, where Bobbie was telling a filthy story.

'How filthy is this story?' said Cliff. 'I'm not sure if it sounds like my sort of thing.'

'Don't be such a bloody hypocrite,' said Julian.

In the last few weeks Cliff had been getting increasingly pompous. Although the editor had not yet died, there seemed every reason to suppose that he would soon do so. While Battersby remained the front-runner to become the next editor, Cliff was thought to be only a short way behind.

'Bobbie's quite a connoisseur of filth, aren't you?' said Johnny Todd.

'Why, thank you.' Bobbie appeared genuinely touched.

Hugh had never been able to work Bobbie out. This zest for telling filthy stories was well known. But while there was no lack of enthusiasm to hear them, the general feeling was that Bobbie tended to overdo things, to tip over the line from mere obscenity to something else, something more numbingly foul. Perhaps this was just something to do with being Scottish, but at times Hugh wondered if it was a matter of miscalculation, whether this eagerness to be one of the boys made Bobbie take things a little bit too far.

'Everyone comfy?'

'Just get on with it,' said Cliff.

'Right,' said Bobbie. 'There's this chap out at Heathrow.'

'A chap?' said Julian mockingly.

'All right then. A fellow,' said Bobbie. 'You know, a man. He smuggles in porno videos from Holland, then he flogs them on to his mates. Every week he gets a new consignment, and every week he sits down to watch them, to find out what he's got. On Wednesday evenings his wife goes out to keep-fit classes with her girlfriends. So every Wednesday he puts the kids to bed, sits down in the living room and watches the tapes. But because he doesn't want the noise to wake the kids, he plugs in the headphones.

'Week in, week out; he's been doing it for years,' continued Bobbie. 'Never any problems. By the time his wife gets back, he's finished and has put everything away. She's very prim, doesn't know anything about it. Not her sort of thing at all.

'So this Wednesday night, everything happens quite normally. Wife gets changed into her tracksuit, goes out to keep-fit. He puts the kids to bed, settles down, headphones plugged in and off he goes. But this week it turns out the keep-fit instructress has got flu. Class has been cancelled. So the wife comes back with her friends. Naturally they're a bit disappointed, feeling kind of low. She tells them to

180

go and get comfortable in the living room while she makes the coffees, so the friends go through into the living room. Of course, the husband hasn't heard them come back. He's sitting there, quite oblivious, trousers round his knees, knob out, slamming away. Bang, bang, bang.'

There was a muffled intake of breath. Hugh wasn't sure from whom. Bobbie, however, ignored it.

'Wife comes in, carrying a tray full of cups. Can't work out what's going on. All her friends are up one end of the living room, facing the wall. Not saying anything. Not knowing where to put themselves. And at the other end is her husband. Still clueless. Still giving it some of that.'

'What did she do then?' asked Julian, quietly.

'Well, there was a bit of a scene, as you might imagine. First thing next day she filed for divorce. I've been writing the court report this morning. So what do you think of that?'

Bobbie was wheezing away by now, red tufted hair rocking back and forth, plainly expecting accompanying bursts of laughter. But there was nothing. It was as if they'd all readied themselves to laugh, but had been unable to follow through with it. The laughs had got stuck in their throats. Instead, an air of stupefied silence seemed to settle on everyone present.

Cliff was looking at Gavin in a concerned sort of way, as if he wanted to clap his hands over his ears and protect him from such depravity, but it was too late for that. Gavin, for his part, appeared quite impassive. Julian was looking disapproving. Hugh had noticed before how Julian, though not prudish in any normal sense, liked to set his own agenda of tastelessness and tended to be censorious of anyone who stepped outside it. Even Johnny Todd looked thoughtful, waiting for some cue as to how he should react.

Hugh also kept quiet. The subject of masturbation was touchy enough – the idea of being caught doing it too appalling to contemplate. He wondered if everyone else felt the same way. Perhaps it was this that explained their

181

silence. Bobbie continued to look round, baffled by their reaction.

'You're right,' said Cliff at last. 'That is an absolutely disgusting story.'

He was still looking worriedly at Gavin, in case there might be some delayed adverse reaction. After another period of silence, conversation slowly started up again. Hugh found himself less willing, or able, to join in than usual. He felt oddly disengaged from everything around him. Vaguely, as if coming from some way away, he was aware of voices rising and falling. Or rather clustering together, then pulling back, like figures in a dance rushing headlong towards one another, then retreating, re-grouping, ready to try again.

He was roused from his reverie by someone saying, 'Well, Hughie certainly ought to know.'

He looked up. People were looking at him with expectant expressions. His first thought was that they were still talking about masturbation.

'How would I know?' he said defensively.

'Well, you ought to know more than anyone else.'

'No I don't.'

'You must know all about her by now, Hughie.'

One kind of panic was succeeded by another. Hugh struggled to adjust.

'I don't know anything about her,' he said.

'Come now, Hughie. You must do.'

'Why should I?'

'There's no need to be coy about it. From what I've heard you're quite an authority.'

Abruptly, a number of things fell into place. He realized that Vivien must have told Joy about them having had sex together. Joy, in turn, must have passed it on. Hugh felt caught, found out. But while he had no particular desire to come clean, he couldn't see any reason to be apologetic either.

'You're asking me why she's so moody?' he said. 'Is that

182

it? How should I know? I suppose it's something to do with all the drugs she takes.'

People's expressions, he saw, had begun to change – presumably in response to his attitude.

'If you're so interested why don't you ask her yourself?' he said. 'Anyway, so what if she does go and smoke joints in the churchyard? Surely that's no business but hers.'

Still they continued to stare at him.

'Look,' said Hugh. 'I only fucked her once, OK? It was no big deal for either of us.'

Once again there was a stunned sort of silence. Cliff, in particular, was looking even more disconcerted than before. When he spoke his voice was quite hollow.

'The Queen Mother, Hughie?'

Slowly he shook his head.

'My God, things must be even worse than I thought.'

Hugh left the pub, crossed Fleet Street and headed down St Bride's Passage towards the tube. He'd only gone a few paces when he stopped. The entrance to the churchyard was up a couple of steps to his right. He climbed up the steps into the churchyard. There were benches around the outside. Above his head the spire rose into the sky, tapering in tiers. He stood still for a moment, looking round for a burning cigarette end. All the benches on this side of the churchyard appeared to be deserted. He walked through the gravestones to the other side, once again standing still, trying to conceal himself behind a particularly large stone. But this side of the churchyard was quite empty.

After a while he walked across the graveyard, back down the steps and into St Bride's Passage. People went by, still tightly wrapped up against the cold. As he always did whenever he came down here, he thought of Bridewell Palace materializing before him. Its ghostly outline, like Brigadoon, rising above the rooftops. The streets teeming with troops of bad characters of every description.

He had read recently how, in 1783, a visitor had come to Bridewell Prison – 'a house of correction for idle, vagrant, loose and disorderly persons' – to see what conditions were like. The visitor asked how often the straw in the prisoners' cells was changed. On being told that it was once a month he protested, only to be informed that this was the only London prison where either straw or bedding was allowed.

Walking along, Hugh once again tried to conjure this apparition, to kick his imagination into life. But it was no good. The incident in the pub had disturbed him more than he cared to admit; he felt more stuck in the present than usual, less able to scuttle back into the past. These watery spectres barely took shape before they vanished into the air. There was nothing here except a few pubs and shuttered sandwich bars.

St Bride's Passage ran parallel with the side of the churchyard for about thirty yards, then turned left into a covered section with shops on either side. Hugh had only gone a few yards down the covered section of the passage when he thought he saw someone he recognized in front of him. The shock made him slow down, almost to a halt. The man had his back to Hugh, so that he couldn't be sure. Yet there seemed to be something familiar about the way he was walking, about the shape of his head, the back of his neck.

He quickened his pace to try to catch up, but the man was already turning right into New Bridge Street. When Hugh got there he saw that the pavement was crowded with people going home from work. It was difficult to make much headway. He lost sight of the man, then spotted him again, still walking along briskly, looking neither left nor right, his face never coming into profile. He watched him disappear into a knot of pedestrians, then re-emerge on the other side.

There was a clear stretch of pavement ahead. Hugh broke into a run, swerving into the road to avoid anyone coming towards him. He saw the man stride into another cluster of pedestrians, all of them walking much more slowly, and he waited for him to emerge again. Hugh was running alongside now, trying to get a good look. Buses swerved and taxis hooted as they went by.

There was no sign of him. Hugh slowed down, thinking perhaps he'd been going too fast, that he might have over-shot. He turned round, scanning the faces of people as they passed him. Then he pushed through to the other side of the pavement, wondering if the man might have stopped to look in a shop window.

Hugh gazed about, wondering if he might have crossed the road or ducked down another alleyway. He waited for several minutes, in case the man reappeared. But it was no good, he was nowhere to be seen.

Chapter Nineteen

There were twenty-three Kingmans in the London telephone directory. Hugh started to work his way through
them. He had to speak softly so as not to attract Stanley's
attention. He'd spoken to five, all without success, when
Darren came by with the tea trolley. Again, thought Hugh,
he looked upset. Not so obviously tearful as the day before,
but still shaken, out of sorts. He put down the tea and bun
and moved away, manoeuvring his trolley across the
ripples and scuffs in the carpet tiles.

Hugh was sitting looking at the phone directory when a
pair of hands were placed over his eyes.

'Hello, stranger.'

'Hello, Joy.'

'How are you doing then?'

He turned round.

'Not too bad.'

Joy leant over his chair. Once Hugh had taken this as a
sign of possible intimacy. But now he realized that it
meant nothing. She was just one of those people who got
too close, who never knew when to back off. He noticed
for the first time that there were a number of tiny vertical
lines above her upper lip.

'We should go out again sometime,' she said. 'I'll ask
Vivien. See what she's up to.'

'If you like,' said Hugh.

186

'She's been a bit funny lately. I don't know if you've noticed.'

'No,' said Hugh, 'I haven't noticed anything. How do you mean?'

'I don't know,' said Joy. 'Not herself. Preoccupied.'

For the rest of the day Hugh continued phoning. He kept one eye out for Battersby as he marched up and down the aisles and only half a mind on what he was doing. He tried another twelve numbers, all without success. By now he was nearing the end of the list and wondering what he was going to do when he had finished.

'Thank you,' he said, and put down the receiver. Then he picked it up again and dialled. There was a ringing tone on the other end of the line, then a click.

'Hello?'

The routine came easily to him now. 'I'm sorry to bother you, but I'm trying to get hold of a Mrs Margaret Kingman.'

'Yes.'

'Are you Margaret Kingman?'

'Yes.'

'Were you once married to a man called Tom Kingman?'

'Who is this?'

Hugh explained that he was a journalist. 'I wonder if I could come and talk to you about your husband,' he said. He looked down at the phone. There was a round plastic grille over the mouthpiece and crescents of dirt around the little holes, like dark deposits left by his words as they squeezed themselves down the wire.

Another woman's voice came on the line.

'What do you want?'

Before Hugh could say anything the second woman said, 'She can't help you.'

'I'm sorry—'

'She can't help you. Do you understand? Goodbye.'

And she put down the phone.

*   *   *

187

Towards the end of the afternoon Joy came back to see him. She looked thoughtful, less sure of herself than usual.

'I've spoken to Vivien,' she said.

'Oh yes.'

She frowned. 'Is there something going on between you two?'

'I don't think so. Why?'

She shook her head. 'Doesn't matter.'

'What did she say?'

'She said no.'

'Oh,' said Hugh. 'Did she say why?'

'That was the weird thing,' said Joy, sounding thoroughly perplexed. 'She just said no.'

The flats had been built in a long concrete shelf, five storeys high, with beech hedges dividing one staircase from another and pathways running down between narrow strips of grass. The pathways had been sprinkled with sand. When Hugh rang the bell there was no reply at first. Then the intercom roared, as if a blast of air had just escaped from it, and a voice called out, 'Who's there?'

He recognized the second woman's voice from the phone. He said nothing.

Again she asked, 'Is that Meals on Wheels?'

Hugh moved from the front door and stood behind one of the hedges. A few stiff, brown leaves still hung from the branches and shook whenever the air stirred. He looked up at the windows. They were all blank except for one. On the second floor he could see a face pressed against the glass, trying to peer down at the porch. Behind it there seemed to be another face, paler, less distinct. After a while they both moved away. Hugh stayed where he was.

He waited there for an hour. The sun appeared briefly through a grey wash of cloud, but it wasn't enough to melt the frost that made the grass stand up in tufts. Then a van arrived and a man took two large white polystyrene boxes from the back and walked up to the front door. He had one box stacked on top of the other, and he walked up the gritted pathway, taking care to put each foot down flat. Hugh couldn't see which bell he rang, but the door swung open and the man went inside. A few minutes later he came back down empty-handed. He drove the van along a few yards, stopped, got out again and carried two more polystyrene boxes up to the next front door. There were six doorways in all, and it took him more than half an hour to do the lot. When he'd finished he drove away.

By then Hugh didn't know how much longer he could last. His toes were numb and the tips of his fingers had turned yellow. It wasn't just the physical discomfort either; he felt self-conscious standing there by the hedge. Almost as if he was naked, with only a few leaves for cover. He kept looking around to see if anyone had noticed him, but no-one seemed to have done. A man in an anorak walked past holding three dogs on leads. All three were muzzled. They jerked their heads up and down as they walked, and thin plumes of condensation streamed out behind them and hung in the air.

He was wondering whether to go when the front door opened and a woman came out carrying a string bag. She took a few paces down the path, and then turned and waved, swinging her free hand in a wide arc. Up at the window above Hugh could just make out another hand moving back and forth behind the glass. The woman got into a car and drove away. He waited until the car had disappeared and then went and rang the bell again.

There was an even longer pause this time. Then another voice said, 'Yes?'

Hugh put his mouth to the intercom. The shame made him shut his eyes.

'Meals on Wheels,' he said.

'Already?' asked the voice, sounding surprised.

Hugh started to apologize, but the buzzer was already buzzing and the electric bolt had jumped back in the lock. The polystyrene boxes had been left just inside the door. He made his way up the stairs. There was a half-landing with houseplants climbing round the window and

189

a smell of broiled food that rose from the carpet.

At the top of the next flight of stairs, a door already stood half open. He knocked on it. A voice from inside called to him to come in. Hugh pushed open the door. It opened straight on to a dining room. There was a round table in front of him with several chairs around it, all pushed in except one. Beyond it was another doorway.

'You're early. I'm still clearing up,' he heard the woman say.

He could see her through the doorway, standing at the sink with her back towards him. On the draining board beside her were three aluminium lids used to keep food warm. Once she'd finished washing up, she paid special attention to the aluminium lids, bending over and fitting them inside one another. They clanked dully as they knocked together. One was dented and wouldn't fit to her satisfaction.

Hugh watched and found that he too was becoming pre-occupied with the aluminium lids, with these meals that came in bell jars – the same scoops of molten vegetables, puddles of gravy and strips of limp meat. He wished he hadn't come.

The woman in the kitchen dried up her lunch things, stacked them up, then came back into the dining room and set them down on the table. Only at this point did she look up.

'Who are you?'

Her head lifted as her weight slid forward onto her elbows. She was a thin, fragile-looking woman with grey hair twisted back in a bun. Hugh found he couldn't speak. He recalled the photographs of Margaret Kingman he'd seen in the papers. It wasn't difficult to make out the same features in the woman before him, but it was as if they'd all been pared down and whittled away. There was something dried up and forlorn about her. She looked like some drastically eroded version of her former self. In the photographs in the paper she'd had an air of jollity and fortitude about her. Now only the fortitude remained.

190

She stayed where she was, head up, half crouched over the table.

'You won't find anything of value here,' she said.

There was no fear in her voice, only a dry matter-of-factness. Some of these old women were like veterans of urban warfare, used to being knocked down and robbed. No longer surprised by these casual swipes of brutality and greed, but toughened, resigned.

'No,' said Hugh, shocked. 'I haven't come to rob you. I called yesterday. I'm the journalist.'

She straightened up. 'You had no right to come,' she said.

'I know.'

She raised her eyebrows, very slightly.

As she gazed at him, she passed her hands back and forth around the edge of the table, as if she was measuring lengths of material.

'What do you want?'

'I wanted to ask you about your husband.'

'I've got nothing to say,' she said.

Hugh's unsuitability for this sort of thing struck him with renewed force. He was rubbing his hands together to restore some circulation, at the same time trying to disguise his nervousness.

'I only wanted to ask a few questions,' he said. 'Then I'll go away. I won't bother you again.'

There was a threat here, of course, barely buried, but there for them both to see. But it only prompted the same expression of mildly amused scorn.

'I'm sorry,' said Hugh. 'I shouldn't have come.'

'What's your name?'

After he had told her she said nothing for a while.

'All right,' she said. 'Since you're here you'd better come through.'

He followed her down a short flight of steps into the living room. Two matching armchairs sat squarely facing each other with a standard lamp beside one and a table between them. It was hotter down here, comfortingly so after the cold outside. On the walls were squares of embroidered material, mounted on long vertical strips like Christmas cards. They were very brightly coloured, these runnels of blues and greens and reds that seemed to ripple down the walls and flow into one another. The heat must have been coming from some sort of wall vent. In the currents of hot air the embroidered squares floated and flapped about like stamp hinges.

The table was covered with a cloth which had tassels reaching down to the ground. On the table were a number of ornaments – some small pottery figures, a silver box, a glass vase in the shape of a hollowed-out heart. Mrs Kingman sat in one of the chairs, pointed to the other one, then folded her hands together.

'Well?'

'I wanted to ask you if you had any idea what happened to your husband,' said Hugh.

'If you mean, do I have any information that I've withheld, or kept to myself all these years, then the answer is no. In that sense, I expect you probably have as much idea of what happened to him as I do. If you're asking me, do I think he committed suicide, my answer is, I don't know. For a long time, I refused even to consider the possibility.

'We were married for twelve years. In that time we were very happy together. Much happier than I ever expected to be.' She unfolded her hands and smoothed down the material on her skirt. 'But I had to accept that my husband did not feel the same way. There was something missing in his life which I couldn't fill. He had this yearning to prove himself, to do something that would lend shape and meaning to his life. Sometimes I've even wondered if he was trying in some way to make himself worthy of me, or to make himself worthy of happiness. I don't know.'

She was tilted forward, not so much towards him as away from the chair, out into the room, palms pressed on her thighs. For a while Hugh thought she had finished, but then she went on, 'Perhaps I had my husband wrong. Certainly, to meet him, he seemed to be the most straight-

192

forward man I'd ever met. That's what appealed to me. If you are troubled by uncertainties, as I've always been, then you often gravitate to someone who seems untroubled by doubts. Does that make any sense to you?'

'Yes,' said Hugh. 'Yes, it does.'

'Perhaps, looking back, he wasn't quite as straightforward as I liked to imagine. I suppose he was rather buttoned-up, although I liked to think of him as self-contained. He wasn't one to talk about his feelings.

'I don't think he liked the modern world much. He felt ground down by things, by people he believed in. He'd invest his faith in them and then get very upset when they fell short of his expectations. I used to wonder what would happen when he came back. Would he be happy at last? Would he have got this yearning out of his system? Or would there be something else? Some other receding horizon?

'So,' she said, 'to answer your question by a very roundabout route, I don't know what happened to him. And I don't want to know any more. People say you always want to know what's happened to someone you love, but to me there's comfort in not knowing. When my husband was away I used to lie awake and listen to the shipping forecast on the radio and try to imagine where he might be. Sometimes I still do.

'When someone dies you think you'll have some idea when it happens, or if they're in trouble. Some warning. A message even, if the bond between you is strong enough. But it's not like that at all. There's nothing.'

The hot air coursed up the walls. The flaps of embroidery lifted and settled.

'Have you ever lost anyone you loved?' said Mrs Kingman.

'My father died,' said Hugh.

'When was that?'

'Almost twenty years ago now.'

'How old were you?'

'Sixteen.'

'Were you very close?'

'In a way.'

'And now?' she said. 'Do you feel close to him now?'

Again Hugh found that he wasn't able to answer.

Mrs Kingman smiled. 'You see. You start to wonder if you ever really knew them at all. They're gone, and everything that's left becomes clouded by doubt. More and more so as time goes on. Until all that's left is this little shred that hangs in your thoughts and won't go away.'

Hugh got up. He walked over to the window. There was a set of bookshelves on one side of the window and below it a table with some bits and pieces on it. Photographs mainly, along with an old ink well and stand.

'My husband's things,' said Mrs Kingman. 'I had to sell everything I could to pay off the debts, but I managed to save one or two reminders.'

The buzzer sounded. Mrs Kingman got up to answer it. Hugh took out one of the books from the shelf. Inside the front cover Kingman had written his name in ink, a tiny, crabbed signature trailing off into nothing. He stared at the writing.

The book fell open in his hand. A narrow column of print ran down the centre of the page. It took him a moment or two to realize that this was a book of poetry. He looked again at the spine and saw that it was an old anthology of the Romantics. The book fell open at the same page as before. He looked down.

'I fear thee, ancient Mariner!
I fear thy skinny hand!
And thou art long, and lank, and brown,
As is the ribbed sea-sand.'

A couple of pages on, a passage had been underlined, this time in pencil.

Like one, that on a lonesome road
Doth walk in fear and dread,

And having once turned round walks on,
And turns no more his head;
Because he knows, a frightful fiend
Doth close behind him tread.

Behind him he heard the sound of bags being set down on the dining table, the soft exhale of polythene. He turned round. The woman he'd seen earlier was standing at the top of the steps. To Hugh's surprise she stamped her foot when she saw him.

'Who are you?' she demanded.

'It's all right, Ellen,' said Mrs Kingman.

In no way reassured, the woman came down the stairs, keeping her eye on Hugh all the time.

'This is Mr Byrne who called earlier,' said Mrs Kingman. 'The journalist.'

The woman stopped in her tracks. 'I thought I told you to go away.'

'I'm afraid he didn't take any notice.'

'You leave her alone!' cried the woman. 'Do you hear?'

'Don't worry, Ellen. There's no need to be concerned. Mr Byrne is just leaving.'

Hugh put the book back on the shelf. He'd reached the landing when he heard the door to Mrs Kingman's flat close. Outside, he saw the man from Meals on Wheels moving from pathway to pathway, collecting up the polystyrene boxes and taking them back to the van. The man moved much less cautiously than he'd done before, walking briskly along, so that the white boxes bounced up and down in his arms.

Chapter Twenty

'What's the matter with you?' said Noel.

'What do you mean?'

'You seem in a very strange mood, if I may say so.'

'You may say so,' said Hugh. 'If you wish.'

He screwed up his eyes and squinted at the menu, imagining that his eyelids were gummed together. 'In what way strange?'

'Are you drunk?'

'Maybe a bit.'

'I thought so. I could smell it on your breath when you came in.'

'Why did you ask then?'

'I was trying to ascertain why you were so jumpy.'

They were sitting in another of Noel's restaurants. This time he'd excelled himself. There was no-one else in the place, as far as Hugh could tell. It wasn't easy to see. Either in an effort to create atmosphere, or else to save on electricity, the lights were so low they barely cast any illumination at all. For some reason they had been put in the middle of the room rather than round the side, where Hugh would have felt less conspicuous. Since there was no-one else there he supposed it didn't matter. Off in the distance, a huge symmetrical lump of meat the size of a man's torso revolved on a vertical spit.

'Who's jumpy?' Hugh asked.

'You are.'

Noel sat opposite him, once again moving too fast for his own good. The swirls of hair that stuck up behind his ears looked especially prominent tonight, like corkscrew wings, as if he'd just spiralled down to earth.

'Tell me,' he said, 'are you drinking a lot at the moment?'

Hugh gave this some thought. 'I wouldn't say so. No more than usual.'

'You never used to be a big drinker. You can't take it. Do you drink when you're on your own?'

'If you don't drink alone then there's no point in drinking at all,' said Hugh.

As soon as he'd said this he wasn't sure what he meant. It wasn't even true; he never drank that much at home. He suspected he was just repeating what someone else had said because it sounded clever. Nonetheless, he set his jaw defiantly, so as to give his words some weight.

'Presumably you drink a good deal at work. Journalists always seem to think it makes them more interesting. They could hardly be more wrong. In my opinion anyway.'

'My God, I don't know how you had the nerve to call me priggish,' said Hugh. 'Just listen to yourself.'

'I'm simply expressing concern for your welfare. I can't imagine anyone else would.'

'They might do,' said Hugh after a while.

The food came without his being aware of having ordered it. Some time later the empty plate was removed without his having been aware of eating it. Between these two things happening Noel said, 'I've got something to tell you, if you're sober enough to take it in.'

He stopped and sawed away at his food, then took a mouthful, chewing it with his flimsy teeth.

'Well, go on.'

The corner of Noel's mouth jumped into a little rictus. He gave one of his mirthless smiles.

'I've seen someone.'

When Hugh didn't react, he said it again, 'I've seen someone.'

'Yes?' said Hugh impatiently. 'What sort of someone?'

'Someone,' said Noel, 'at Embankment tube station. I got into a train and there was this girl sitting opposite. I looked at her, and she looked back at me.'

'Oh. Then what happened?'

'Nothing happened,' said Noel. 'The train filled up and people got in the way. Then she got off at Gloucester Road.'

Hugh felt a sense of great relief.

'That was it?'

'You don't understand,' said Noel. 'It wasn't as if we just looked at one another. There was much more to it than that. I felt . . . I don't know, I felt as if we could see into one another. And I'm sure she felt the same.'

'So what are you going to do?'

'I don't know. I thought . . .'

'What?'

'You know, you hear those things on the radio sometimes. People who've spotted one another and haven't had a chance to talk. One of them broadcasts a message asking the other one to get in touch. Do you think they ever do?'

'I wouldn't have thought so. I mean, the chances must be tiny. Less than tiny.'

'I know,' said Noel. 'I know. I thought I might try, though. There can't be any harm in it.'

'I suppose not. If you're that desperate.'

'It's not desperation. It's just that sometimes you feel that things are meant to happen. Haven't you ever felt that?'

'All the—' Hugh stopped himself. 'Just because you think things are meant to happen doesn't mean they do.'

'No. But sometimes they must.'

'I don't want to spoil your fun, but I have to say to you, quite truthfully, that I don't like the sound of this girl.'

'You've never met her,' said Noel.

'No, obviously. But nor have you. What's she doing sitting on trains winking at people?'

'She didn't wink.'

'All right. Giving you the eye then. Probably does it all the time. She could be a hooker for all you know.'

'She's not a hooker,' said Noel. A hurt look had come into his eyes. However phoney his flashes of merriment may have appeared, his hurt seemed real enough.

'I just don't want you to make a fool of yourself again, that's all.'

'I'm only thinking of broadcasting a message. Where's the harm in that?'

'Waste of time,' said Hugh. 'In my opinion,' he added.

'Why do you always have to ascribe the worst possible motives to everyone? You take the most innocent encounter and twist it into something horrible.'

'I wouldn't say that.'

'I would,' said Noel.

The waiter came to refill their glasses. A couple came into the restaurant, looked around and then left.

'You're just jealous.'

Hugh laughed at the absurdity of this. He did so quite heartily and without amusement. 'You're my friend,' he said. He corrected himself. 'One of my oldest friends. Naturally, I want whatever's best for you.'

'Yes?' said Noel. He looked doubtful. And for all Hugh's efforts, his resolution still held. 'Anyway, I'm going to try. Whatever you say.' Once again he prepared to saddle up and ride out, to launch himself forward, blind to the consequences.

'Well,' said Hugh, tapping the table top several times very regularly, like a metronome, 'you must do whatever you think is best.'

'Just within the site of Temple Bar, on the right of Fleet Street,' Hugh read, 'is Child's Bank, which deserves notice as the oldest banking house in England, where Francis Child, an industrious apprentice of Charles I's time, married the rich daughter of his master, William Wheeler the goldsmith, and founded the great banking family.

'Lord Westmoreland, dining here with Robert Child in 1782, asked what Child would do if he was in love with a girl and her father would not allow their marriage. "Run away with her, of course," the banker cried imprudently, and Lord Westmoreland forthwith eloped with his daughter, Mary Anne.

'The father pursued them, and had nearly caught them, when Lord Westmoreland, kneeling on the seat of his carriage, shot dead the leading horse of his pursuers. Mr Child would not forgive them, but, dying in a few months, left all his fortune to their eldest child, called Sarah.

'To protect themselves, the Westmorelands christened all their children Sarah, even their son; but the property remained with the eldest daughter, who married Lord Jersey. A fine old gothic crypt under this bank was destroyed when the old house was pulled down, 1877–78.'

Hugh put down the book and turned off the light. There had been another postcard from his mother when he got home. 'Last minute change of plan,' she had written. 'Mr Glim, who I believe I mentioned before, has asked if I would like to visit an extinct volcano three days trek away in the Javanese interior. Bearers and provisions provided. Setting off this afternoon. We will rejoin the boat in Port Moresby.'

He was deeply shocked by his mother's impulsiveness. That night he couldn't sleep. There was no clamour of voices rolling up the road like some dark tide. No cyclists outside his window. No anguished bellyaching from within. Nothing. But still he couldn't sleep. He lay there, motionless, as the darkness thickened and eventually lightened around him. Then he got up and went to work.

Chapter Twenty-One

Hugh found Battersby sitting in his glass box staring out of
the window. The building opposite, another newspaper
office, was due for demolition. Everything but the façade
was going to be felled and carried away. Then a new back
with smart new innards would be added. Already men in
yellow helmets were standing around in groups on the
roof, and two large blue cranes were being erected alongside. Something similar was supposed to happen to their
offices as soon as they moved out.

'Could I have a word?' asked Hugh.

Battersby looked uneasy.

'What about?'

'I think I might be on to something.'

'On to something?' he asked. 'What's that supposed to
mean?'

'It's about that man who was pulled out of the river.'

Battersby said nothing, and so Hugh started to tell him
about Field, the Seaman's Discharge Book and Kingman's
widow. It was a complicated story, involving some awkward
leaps in time and space. What links there were now struck
him as more tenuous than he cared to admit. Nonetheless,
he struggled to make it as comprehensible as possible.
And, despite lack of sleep and certain implausibilities here
and there, it seemed to him once he'd finished that he'd
done a rather better job than he'd expected.

Battersby sat in silence, digesting this.

Then he said, in a surprisingly reasonable tone of voice, 'What do you think I am?'

Before Hugh could say anything, Battersby said, 'No.'

'No?'

'Don't answer that. You see, I know what you think I am.'

Hugh had no idea what he was talking about.

Battersby nodded. 'Oh, I know what people say about me. That I'm far too gullible for my own good.' He had the pitying air of one who has been constantly underestimated in life. 'Well,' he conceded, 'maybe I have let my enthusiasm run away with me at times.'

'And now', he said, leaning forward, 'you expect me to believe *this*?' Momentarily his voice cracked. With an effort he steadied himself, brought himself back down to earth.

'Tell me,' he said, 'do you ever read the paper?'

'I'm sorry?'

In the same slow, unhurried manner Battersby said, 'Do you ever read the fucking paper?'

Hugh felt himself flushing. Battersby took a copy of the previous day's paper from his desk, turned over several pages, found what he was looking for and thrust it at him.

'Down the bottom,' he said. 'News in Brief. Go on, read it.'

Hugh started to do so.

'No,' said Battersby. 'Read it aloud.'

'Police confirmed today that the man who was found in the Thames ten days ago has been identified as William Hollis, aged sixty-three. Mr Hollis was identified by his family after an appeal for information was published in this paper. There are understood to be no suspicious circumstances regarding his death.'

'Do you want to carry on?'

'No,' said Hugh.

'Good,' said Battersby. 'That, at least, is a relief.'

Any further conversation was prevented by Battersby's secretary, who knocked on one of the walls of his glass-sided pen. She was a large, timid woman who had been with him for a number of years and had become increasingly worn down as a result.

'Can't you see I'm busy,' he shouted.

There was a pause and then the woman began to knock again. Battersby sprang up from his chair and went to remonstrate with her. His audience was over.

Back at his desk, Hugh phoned the police station in Wapping and talked to PC Long about the report in the paper. Long confirmed it.

'I don't suppose there's any possibility of a mistake,' Hugh asked.

'A mistake?' said Long. 'Why should there have been a mistake? He's been identified by his family, the dental records match. Oh no, there's no possibility of any mistake.'

Long sounded delighted. Hugh thought of his pale freckled fingers jumping up and down as he talked. He put down the phone. In contrast to the day before the office was unusually quiet. An air of stillness had descended. In the new offices, Hugh had heard, special sensors had been fitted to the lights so they'd turn off automatically if there was no movement below. He imagined people lying motionless at their desks, drunk or simply exhausted, with the room gradually returning to darkness around them.

There was no sign of Darren. No-one else came round with the tea trolley. Hugh went to get himself something to drink from the vending machine.

Vivien was standing there, inserting some change. He found himself looking at her in a surprisingly dispassionate way: not nervous or wary as he'd been before, but oddly settled and self-possessed. He stood and waited while she stuck in the coins, then pressed the buttons to make her choice. Nothing happened. She pressed the refund button, but the machine failed to return her money.

Hugh held out some change.

'Here,' he said, 'do you want to try with this?'

Rather to his surprise she took the money. He could

smell a faint smokehouse sort of smell on her breath, although he supposed it might be coming from the machine.

'Have you seen Darren today?' she asked.

'I don't think he's in.'

Hugh heard the coins tumble into the depths of the machine.

Vivien pushed the buttons.

Again nothing happened.

'Oh, for Christ's sake,' she muttered.

The gap between torpor and fury in Vivien may have been wider than he'd first thought. Nonetheless, it didn't take much to tip her from one to the other. Balling her hand into a fist she struck the machine very sharply, just to the left of the hatchway where cups and drinks were dispensed.

To begin with, this too had no effect. Then the machine gave out an odd noise. An infinitely wearied sigh of dejection, with some feeble, almost buried note of protest. It reminded Hugh of the noise a pack animal might make at the moment when a particularly heavy load is lowered onto its back. Shortly afterwards, the machine started to dispense a mixture of coffee, tea, Bovril and oxtail soup. A boiling brown stream shot out of the hatchway and hit Vivien in her stomach.

She gave a cry of pain, tried to hop out of the way, then caught her heel in between the carpet tiles and fell over. There was a new, much stronger, more acrid smell, like burned gravy. Meanwhile the machine shook and bellowed as the liquid gushed forth.

Vivien was struggling to get to her feet. But, as she did so, she slipped. Hugh managed to grab her under her arms and tried to pull her off to one side of the corridor. However, the relentless hot brown stream soon surrounded them, spreading out in all directions, like a muddy river in full spate. He splashed about, aware all the time that his trousers were growing hotter. Vivien had her arm round his neck and was trying to get her footing. She was still doubled over, clutching herself. Hugh was unable to believe that the machine had such a volume of liquid inside it.

The eddies encircled them and surged away down the corridor towards the newsroom. From there a few stray cries of alarm could now be heard. These were soon followed by sounds of a more concerted panic. People looked up to see a tide of hot sludge bearing down on them. Somewhere a fire alarm was ringing.

Then, all at once, the machine gave out one last despairing bellow and the flow stopped. Cut off like a sluice. Hugh still had hold of Vivien. She was hanging there, bent over his arm.

'Are you all right?' he asked.

'I think so,' she said.

But when she tried to stand up on her own, she winced with pain and doubled over again.

'I'll take you to the nurse,' said Hugh. 'Would you like me to carry you?'

She shook her head. They made their way down the corridor to the nurse's office. Hugh banged on the door. Through the window he could see a stout woman in a white uniform sitting on a chair, legs stuck out in front of her. He banged again and she came to with a start. He helped Vivien into the room. There were two narrow collapsible beds, one on either side of the room. The nurse erected a screen down the centre of the room and told them both to get undressed. Hugh put his clothes over the radiator. He was given a cotton gown to wear and told to lie down on the bed.

The nurse attended to Vivien first. Through the screen he could see her outline, standing with arms above her head and the tops of her fingers sticking up over the screen. And he could hear Vivien's voice, oddly muted, answering the nurse's questions.

When the nurse came to see him she asked him to hold the gown open. Around his stomach and down his thighs his skin had turned red, as if he'd been wearing a burning garter belt. She applied cream to the inflamed areas. Then he was told to wait on the bed.

The next thing he was aware of was the nurse leaning over him asking him how he felt.

'I don't know.'

'You've been asleep,' she said.

'What time is it?'

It turned out to be soon after two in the afternoon. He raised himself up onto his elbows and looked through the screen, but he couldn't see anyone there.

'What happened to Vivien?'

'Oh, she went home some time ago. Her friend came and took her.'

'What friend?'

'Joy.'

Hugh swung his legs down off the bed.

'Your clothes are dry,' said the nurse. 'But I'm afraid they're a bit stiff.'

The combination of the dust from the library and the liquid from the vending machine meant that his suit had set almost solid. He could barely get it on. His trousers cracked and chafed when he tried to bend his legs. He found he could only walk with difficulty. He took a few exploratory steps beside the bed.

'Are you sure you're all right?' asked the nurse. She sounded concerned.

When Hugh went back down the corridor he saw that much of it, along with one end of the newsroom, now resembled a tropical delta. Long crinkling bands of steam rose from the ground and settled at around waist height. Deposits of silt had been left along the walls, while carpet tiles floated about like lily pads. The air was strangely humid. His own desk was unaffected, but others, including Cliff's, were now cut off by a small lake, at whose shores the tea, coffee, Bovril and oxtail soup mix lapped away.

Clearing up was under way. Journalists and other members of staff attempted to sweep the sludge into buckets, dustpans and any other containers they could find. For a while Hugh joined in, but found his movements were so impeded by the state of his clothes that there was little he could contribute.

It wasn't until the middle of the afternoon that the clearing-up was completed. By then something of a carnival atmosphere had taken over, with people reluctant to settle back down to work, and Battersby trying vainly to restore order. The gravy smell grew more intense as everything dried out. For several days afterwards there were fears that rats might find their way up from the canteen and start eating people's notebooks.

At five o'clock Darren came by with the tea trolley. Although some of the newsroom was now impassable owing to the flooding, he parked the trolley on the nearest dry patch and carried cups down to the waiting journalists. Hugh saw that, instead of his usual sweater tucked into his trousers, Darren was dressed in a black suit. This was all the more noticeable on account of the suit's cut: the jacket was a wide, boxlike affair with large buttons, such as you might find on a pierrot's costume, while the trousers tapered violently below the knees like jodhpurs.

As a cup of tea and a bun were set down on his desk, Hugh felt he should make some effort to talk to Darren.

'That's a very smart suit you're wearing.'

'I've been to a funeral,' said Darren.

'Ah,' he said, 'I'm very sorry to hear that.'

Before he could say anything else, Darren continued on his round.

That evening Hugh couldn't face going for a drink. On his way out he saw a number of green-carders walking down the corridor. Owing to the state of his clothes, he moved almost as slowly as they did. Hugh saw that they were also dressed in black. They appeared even more glum and preoccupied than usual – presumably they'd been to the funeral too. At the far end of the corridor they stood aside to let him go through, not saying anything. Hugh walked stiffly by.

*　　*　　*

The following morning two men in overalls were stripping down the vending machine. Plastic containers full of different-coloured powders – one red, two brown and one jet-black like carbon dust – were scattered around them. There were still several wet patches on the floor, but on the whole it had dried out surprisingly well.

Despite the smell, the dampness in the air and the stickiness underfoot, the whole office seemed brighter than it had been for a long time. It took Hugh a while to realize that it really was brighter. The building next door had been knocked down. He couldn't believe they had achieved so much so quickly. Now there was nothing left but the façade, a single wall held in place with wooden buttresses. Behind it was a pile of rubble and a large hole in the ground. Several men stood on the side of the hole peering into it. Light now streamed into the office, impeded only by the layers of grime on the windows.

He saw Cliff and Industrial Gavin sitting together at Cliff's desk, apparently deep in conversation. Every so often Cliff raised his hand, as if to interrupt, then dropped it down deferentially. Over in one corner of the office, another disappointed-looking pair of competition winners was shaking hands with the lawyer, prior to being ushered down the back stairs by one of the copy boys. Vivien, he saw, was sitting with her back towards him and talking on the phone. He was about to go and ask her how she was when he saw Battersby advancing up the aisle towards him. He walked with his neck almost horizontal, his two haircuts lowered and his arms swinging from side to side, as if sweeping all obstacles from his path.

'There you are,' he said. 'You're never around when I'm looking for you.' He stared at him. 'Just look at the state of you. Look at your clothes.'

Hugh had tried sponging down his only suit at home the previous night, but had only met with limited success. He started to explain about the accident with the vending machine.

'So that was you, was it?' said Battersby. 'I might have guessed.' He sighed noisily. 'Come with me. I've got something I want you to do.'

Hugh followed him back out into the corridor. They stopped outside a doorway. Battersby opened the door and turned on the light. They were in a small room with no windows, piled high with boxes. Several of the boxes had saucepans spilling out of them. Printed on the sides of the boxes in large red letters were the words, 'First-class Fondue Sets'.

'What are all these?' Hugh asked.

'Probably unclaimed prizes from some competition. Don't worry about those. No, it's this lot I want you to deal with.'

In front of them were more boxes. These were full of papers.

'Readers' letters,' said Battersby. 'As you can see we're a bit behind with the replies. Scaife was doing some before he disappeared, but it doesn't look as if he got very far. Still,' he said, 'it shouldn't take you too long. Not if you get a move on. I want them all answered.'

Hugh carried the top box back to his desk. He began opening the envelopes, reading the contents and then arranging them into two piles. One pile consisted of letters from people who appeared relatively sane, albeit consumed by rampaging pedantry, the other of letters from the obviously deranged. The first pile was quickly dwarfed by the second.

'Dear Sir,' Hugh read. 'I wish to draw your attention to the sloppy pronunciation of newsreaders. A good many of them sound as if they have stones in their mouths. I cannot help noticing that a number are evidently not of British descent.'

Before long, he found that the same reply would suffice for a number of letters, with only minor variations. Thus he would write, 'Dear—, Thank you for your letter. While the paper cannot agree with your proposal to hunt stray dogs with crossbows/circulate stale air on the underground by means of fitting huge propellers to the fronts of trains/harness criminals to specially adapted sleds and lease them out to haulage contractors, we welcome all correspondence from readers and expressions of their views, however diverse.'

A number of letters turned out to be from the same people. On these Hugh wrote, at the end, 'It is with regret that the letters editor must declare this subject now closed.' This made little difference. Undaunted, they simply switched to something else, some other means of fanning their fury back to life.

Hugh found it disturbing to be surrounded by so much ill-will. Such undiluted loathing. There were depths of hatred here he'd never dreamed of. Some of the correspondents could barely write they were so angry; their letters looked as if they'd been pecked at by large birds. Throughout the morning his estimate of human nature dropped steadily.

He went to the lavatory as much to get away from all this loathing as anything else. As he was standing at one of the urinals, he became aware of strange sounds coming from one of the cubicles. A man appeared to be talking in a low, yet angry-sounding voice. Every so often he would pause, as if awaiting a reply, then start again.

Hugh looked around. No-one else was there. The long line of streaked, wrap-around urinals was deserted. He couldn't work out what was being said. Moving as quietly as possible, he walked towards the cubicle door. Still the words weren't clear.

Then, all at once, he heard a voice say, 'I am Alpha and Omega. The Beginning and the End.'

Hugh stopped in his tracks. The phrase was repeated. It was followed by some more indistinct mumbling, then another burst of clarity.

'And there came unto me one of the seven angels,' said the voice, perfectly audible now, 'which had the seven vials full of the seven last plagues, and talked with me, saying, "Come hither, I will show thee the bride. The Lamb's wife."'

There was something familiar about the voice. In particular, the way in which the sentences had been broken up into a series of much shorter sentences and were being spat out with enormous venom. Hugh had begun to move away from the cubicle door, off towards the wash basins. But he hadn't gone far when he heard the chain being pulled. The lavatory flushed and the door opened.

Cliff came out. He was carrying a book. As soon as he saw Hugh, he tried to hide the book behind his back. Cliff didn't say anything, he simply stood by the open entrance to the cubicle. It was hard to work out which of them was more shocked.

'Hugh,' he said.

'Hello, Cliff.'

'Have you been in here long?'

'Not that long,' said Hugh.

After a moment or two's indecision, Cliff slowly brought his arm round from behind his back. The book was still in his hand. He turned the spine towards Hugh.

'I've been reading the Bible,' he said.

'Have you, Cliff?'

'I expect you think that's odd.'

'Not necessarily,' said Hugh.

'I've been practising for the editor's funeral. I'm only telling you this to avoid any misunderstandings.'

'I see. Don't you think that's rather premature?'

'In what way?'

'Well, he hasn't died yet.'

'That's true,' conceded Cliff reluctantly. 'But it's as well to be prepared for these things. After all, everyone knows it won't be long.'

'What do you think will happen then?'

Cliff had recovered himself now. His small eyes were quite steady.

'Big changes,' he said. 'Very big changes. Does that alarm you?'

'It does rather, yes.'

'Do you read the Bible, Hughie?'

211

'Er, no. Not often, Cliff.'

'You should do. I commend it to you. There's a great deal of interest in it, a great deal of relevance to our troubled times.'

'I'm sure there is.'

'God is nothing like as merciful as he's cracked up to be, you know,' said Cliff. 'Far from it.'

At tea-time Darren came by with his trolley. Hugh saw that he was wearing his usual outfit today: sweater tucked into high-hitched trousers.

'What are you doing?' Darren asked.

'Reader relations,' said Hugh.

Darren raised his eyebrows. 'I wouldn't want to have relations with any of our readers.'

'No,' said Hugh. 'I know what you mean.'

He remembered there was something he'd been meaning to ask Darren about. 'I notice that everyone else seems to have got notification of their computer training,' he said, 'but I haven't had anything yet. I just wondered if it might possibly have got lost in the internal mail.'

Darren gave what might have been the glimmer of a smile. 'It wouldn't surprise me,' he said. 'It's complete chaos down there now.'

'Is it really?'

'Oh yes. Things getting lost all over the place.'

'I see.'

'No-one cares any more. You can't blame them. They're all getting slung out in a couple of weeks, so why should they bother? The other day they found a pile of mail that had been there for over three months.'

From outside there came the sound of something collapsing. A soft, subterranean crump, followed by the long cascade of bricks falling. Another building was being demolished.

'What did you say?' asked Hugh.

Darren looked at him. 'I said, the other day they found a pile of mail downstairs that had been there for over three months.'

'That's what I thought you said.'

'There was nothing for you there,' he said.

'No,' said Hugh distractedly.

There was something at the corner of his mind, scratching away again. He couldn't work out what it was. Darren was still standing by him; he seemed to be expecting Hugh to say something, but Hugh couldn't think of anything to say.

'I'm feeling more cheerful today,' said Darren.

'Are you?' said Hugh. 'Ah, that's good.'

'Yes, I went to a funeral yesterday. That was pretty upsetting.'

Again Hugh was aware of Darren's desire to prolong their conversation, although he had no idea why. He wished he would go away, so that he could concentrate on whatever it was that was nagging away at him.

'Was it someone close?' he asked.

'In a way. An old boy who worked downstairs.'

'Had he been ill for long?'

'He wasn't ill at all as far as I know,' said Darren.

'Was it an accident?'

'I wouldn't say that. He jumped in the river.'

'What do you mean?'

Darren lowered his voice.

'He drowned himself.'

'When?' asked Hugh.

'A week or so ago. But they only identified him the other day.'

'Was he called William Hollis?'

'Did you know him?'

'No,' said Hugh. 'Not exactly. Do you know why he ... ?'

'Despair, I imagine,' said Darren. He spoke confidently, as if this was a state he was not unfamiliar with himself. 'His whole life was here. Poor old dear. He hadn't got anywhere else to go.'

Hugh looked down. He was holding an envelope in his hands. He turned it over and saw from the postmark that it had been posted several weeks earlier. Abruptly,

213

he realized what had been scratching away at him.

He got to his feet.

'Where are you going?' said Darren.

'To collect my car,' said Hugh.

'What for?'

Hugh didn't reply. He grabbed his coat and his case and pushed his chair in. Darren stood and watched him go, the surprise on his face giving way to affront.

Chapter Twenty-Two

Hugh drove east through the evening traffic, a slow nose-to-tail conga that shuddered and bumped its way out of London. The stained pink houses bordering the road struck him as even bleaker than before. The clouds too seemed lower; it was as if they were all making their way into the narrow fold between the earth and sky.

He sat in his car, grateful for this sense of insulation, for being able to look out and see a landscape held out-stretched beyond his windscreen. The clouds were so low that they covered the docks. The valley, which had been choked with cranes and dockyard machinery when he'd last come here, now looked as if it had been swept by an avalanche with only a few broken spars to be seen. Hugh took the same road as before that encircled the docks. He passed the warehouse where he'd stopped to ask directions. Through the open doors he could see the brown columns of paper stacked up and stretching off into the distance.

There were no ships anywhere, only a few rowing boats tied up to the quay. On the other side of the river he saw the cement works. Everything looked flat and grey under the arc lights. A miniature engine pulling a number of wagons was making its way round the base of a large grey hill. The river itself appeared almost motionless, as if the cold had turned it to treacle.

The mission building was stuck on its own behind the

chain-link fencing that separated one section of empty tarmac from another. Hugh parked his car and went up the steps. If anything, his clothes had become even stiffer in the cold. It was like wearing armour. In the hallway several men sat on a bench not saying anything; the ones on either end were having to brace their legs to make sure they didn't fall off. Hugh found the same boy, Eamonn, behind the reception counter. He was leaning forward reading a magazine, so engrossed that it took him some time to realize there was anyone there.

'Oh hello,' he said. 'Back again?'

Hugh asked for the chaplain.

'He's at prayer, I'm afraid. But he won't be long.'

It was only a few minutes before the chaplain reappeared. Once again he was wiping crumbs from his mouth. He looked at Hugh blankly, then without enthusiasm as he was reminded who he was.

'Oh yes, of course. What can I do for you?' he asked.

Hugh asked if he'd heard anything about Field. Behind his glasses the chaplain made appropriate adjustments to his expression.

'Alas, no. Nothing at all.'

'You mentioned last time that Field received a letter every three months.'

'Did I?'

'I wondered if anything had turned up for him.'

'Eamonn handles the post, don't you?' said the chaplain. 'He'd know all about that.'

But at this the boy grew aggrieved. He turned aside and in a low voice said, 'I told you.'

The chaplain beamed brightly at Hugh. 'I wonder if you'd excuse us for a second.'

They withdrew into the back office, from where there came sounds of a hushed squabble.

'I beg your pardon,' said the chaplain when he returned. 'It would appear that a letter did come. Eamonn quite rightly told me, but I appear to have let it slip my mind.'

'Would it be possible to let me see it?'

216

Eamonn went to one of the pigeon-holes, took out an envelope and slapped it down on the counter. It was addressed simply to Mr Field. Hugh was about to pick up the envelope when he saw the chaplain's gleaming hand hovering above his.

'What are you doing?'

'Can't I open it?' asked Hugh.

'Open it? I don't know about that. What if he comes back and wants his mail?'

'If we open it then we might find out why he hasn't come back.'

Still the chaplain was undecided.

'I don't know,' he said.

Eventually Eamonn took the initiative and produced a paper knife, handed it to Hugh and watched as he sliced the envelope open and took out the single sheet of paper within.

It was an invoice from a storage company in Wembley saying that payment was outstanding and should be settled immediately.

The chaplain was looking over his shoulder.

'Is that any help?' he asked.

'I don't know,' said Hugh. 'It's hard to say.'

Chapter Twenty-Three

The road followed the curved wall of the stadium and headed off up a slope away from the Empire Pool and the conference centre. There was frost on the stadium roof, running along the ridges of the corrugated tiles. It was a strange, forgotten area here behind the stands and the coach parks, still full of leftovers from the Olympic Games forty years earlier. Triumphal avenues lined with squat, pillared buildings, now crumbling and empty, and colonnades half-buried below street level. Now they'd been turned into garages, or knocked down and replaced with light industrial units. Several of the bigger blocks had been gutted and taken over by storage companies.

Hugh found the place he was looking for easily enough. A blue banner hung above the entrance advertising prices per square foot, and a line of removal vans was parked outside. Various employees were milling about in the reception area. Some were shivering, hunched forward. All wore white nylon uniforms with zips up the front and the name of the company written across the backs of their shoulders.

He presented the invoice and was directed to the accounts department down the corridor. The bill came to almost £50. He didn't have enough cash on him to pay it and so he wrote out a cheque. The woman who took it didn't seem to notice that the name on his cheque didn't match the name on the invoice. Either that, or she didn't care.

When she'd filed his cheque away, she stamped the invoice, directed him to the lifts and told him to go up to the fifth floor.

The lift was large and cold and the walls were lined with dimpled steel that spread his reflection into a mass of grey pockmarked parts. When it stopped at the fifth floor, Hugh pulled open the shutters.

The room he found himself in looked like a replica of some ancient settlement, a life-sized archaeological model built to advance understanding of our remote ancestors. It was divided up into hundreds of brick cells. The cells were of different sizes, but all had walls about six feet high with chicken wire stretched over the top instead of roofs. There was a series of avenues running down the length of the room with smaller, narrower passages leading off them.

Hugh checked the invoice and set off down one of the avenues. The room was even colder than the lift. Through the chicken wire he could see pieces of furniture, chairs, tables, cupboards and mattresses. Some were simply piled on top of one another. Others had been fitted together like wooden puzzles with no inch of space wasted.

As he walked along, Hugh thought of all the disrupted lives they represented. Aspirations dashed, or put on hold, or awaiting fulfilment. The overseas posting, the sudden change of heart. Such a weight of expectation, or disappointment, crammed into these makeshift cells. And yet, for all this evidence of transition, they reminded him more than anything else of tombs, with the deceased buried somewhere within, surrounded by personal possessions to ease their journey from this world to the next.

He found the unit he was looking for near the end of one of the subsidiary passages. The unit was scarcely bigger than a cupboard. The door was locked with a large padlock.

'Of course it's locked,' said the white-suited man he found near the lift. 'These are secure units. Haven't you got the key?'

Hugh explained that he'd lost it, showed him the

stamped invoice and asked if he couldn't just saw the lock off.

'You could if you had a hacksaw,' said the man. 'But you're not supposed to. It's against the rules.'

On Empire Way Hugh found a hardware shop and bought a hacksaw and a torch. It took him fifteen minutes to saw through the padlock. By the time he'd finished the lock was so hot that he burnt his hand trying to twist it open. He'd never had any aptitude for anything practical, and along with the frustration and the pain he couldn't help feeling surprised that he'd got this far without any greater mishap.

Still the lock wouldn't budge, and so he had to cut through the other side as well. The hacksaw blade rasped and screeched as he drew it back and forth across the metal. He kept stopping to see if anyone was coming. But the man he'd spoken to earlier had disappeared and there was no-one else around.

Eventually the padlock fell at his feet. Hugh switched on the torch and pushed open the door. The room appeared to be empty. His torch-beam played over the walls and bare floor. Then he saw there were two tin trunks stacked one on top of another in the far corner. Dust lay on the floor around them and cushioned his footsteps. The top trunk was unlocked. It was as dusty as the floor.

He lifted the lid. The trunk was full of men's clothes. There were shirts and sweaters and jackets, all neatly folded away, all smelling faintly of mothballs. But moths had got in regardless. Great patches of the clothes had been eaten away. He held up a sweater and saw white pupae hanging from the ragged holes around the chest.

Hugh's first impression on opening the second trunk was that this too was empty. There was a shallow tray that fitted into the top. The tray contained nothing. When he took it out, Hugh saw that the trunk was full of what he took to be maps. Unlike the first trunk, it had not been packed neatly, rather the maps had been roughly rolled and stuffed inside. Hugh began unrolling the pieces of paper, trying to anchor them at either end.

As he did so, he saw that they were not maps, but nautical charts. The light was too dim to see them clearly. Some of the figures and comments were written in pencil and the marks had faded almost to the point of invisibility. But he could still see enough to recognize the same tiny constricted hand he'd seen in the anthology of poetry at Mrs Kingman's and in Field's Seaman's Discharge Book.

At first he thought there was nothing else in the trunk, then he saw that there were two books lying in the bottom, both bound in dark material. They'd almost been swallowed up in the darkness. The first book contained what appeared to be rough notes, most of them written in ink. Passages had been crossed out, corrected and repeated. There were more calculations, columns of figures and navigational details.

Again, the writing was so small that Hugh found it hard to decipher. Also, the pages were crinkled and stiff and some were stuck together. In places the ink had run. On several pages the writing seemed to make no effort to follow the lines running across the page, as if it was mirroring the action of a boat, rising and falling.

The second logbook was neater, at least to begin with. For the most part this too was taken up with navigational details, all meticulously recorded. But there were also what appeared to be more personal comments. In the light from the torch-beam Hugh could only make out occasional brusque phrases: 'Lights all out.' 'Electrics up the spout.' 'Port forward hatch leaking again.'

The book fell open some two thirds of the way through, at a point where several pages had been torn out. In the later passages there were fewer details and more comments. As in the first book, the writing grew steadily more untidy and less legible. 'I snatch the air,' Hugh read on one page. Beneath it was written, 'Streaming through my hands.'

He heard footsteps outside. He switched off the torch and waited. Through the chicken wire he saw the ceiling divided into a grid of hard diamond shapes. The footsteps faded away. He began putting the clothes back into the first trunk, folding them as neatly as the holes would allow. The charts too he rolled up and put into the second trunk. Then he took the two logbooks and tucked them in his jacket. He pulled the door shut behind him and went out to the lift.

At work Hugh put the two logbooks in his desk drawer. He'd promised himself that he wouldn't read them until that evening. Instead, he tried to lose himself in the now familiar torrent of abuse and resentment from the paper's readers. They obligingly frothed up into fury around him. After a couple of hours he pulled open his desk drawer and looked at the logbooks inside, but resisted the temptation to start reading them.

Alongside them, in the drawer, he saw the library files on Kingman. Partly in order to give himself some breathing space, he decided to take them back downstairs. The library doors were shut. He pushed them open and felt about for the switch. The strip lights came on in sequence, one after the other down the length of the room, as if they were leading their way into a child's grotto.

There was the same smell, the same grey glint from the shelves. Hugh could never quite believe that he was alone here. He always half expected some lost stowaway to emerge blinking from one of the alcoves. He walked down the length of the room and pushed open the door at the other end, once again feeling about for the switch. The passageway stretched ahead of him, lined with the bound volumes of old editions, their milky spines casting a thin pallor onto the floor, like a rumpled layer of gauze.

In the farther library the temperature was colder than ever, the atmosphere more sepulchral. Hugh gazed about him at the crammed shelves and spilling brown envelopes. He thought of all these past lives, now all but forgotten, packaged up and filed away. For a moment he imagined them bursting back to life, like birds suddenly released from their cages, swooping down around him, then returning to roost on their shelves.

He was shutting the library doors behind him when he saw Walter coming out of his room. Walter was carrying a tray. On it, to Hugh's surprise, were what appeared to be the same sort of aluminium lids for keeping food warm that he'd seen at Mrs Kingman's. When he greeted him, Walter looked unusually embarrassed. After a moment or two's indecision, he took the tray back into his room and set it down.

'What are you doing?' he asked. 'I thought you'd finished.'

Hugh explained that he had one or two things to put back. Walter nodded, then tilted his long, grave face to one side, almost resting it on his chest in the way that birds do when they fall asleep.

'I heard about Mr Hollis,' said Hugh.

'Yes, a great sadness,' said Walter. 'He loved it down here, in the library. It was his domain. He had a little room of his own there.'

'I saw him,' said Hugh hesitantly.

'What do you mean?'

'I saw his body in the morgue.'

Walter raised his head from his chest. A ripple seemed to run up his frame.

'I don't understand.'

Hugh told him about being sent down to see the river police and then about being taken to see Hollis's body. Confusion as much as anything else made him keen to unburden himself. Yet something made him hang back and not mention Kingman or the Seaman's Mission.

When he had finished Walter didn't stir.

'Who knows about this?' he said.

'I tried to tell Battersby, but I don't think he took any of it in.'

'You haven't told anyone else?'

'No.'

A familiar lowering sense came back to Hugh – he hadn't

had it for some time – of generating disapproval without being sure why.

'Is there something wrong?' he asked.

Walter wouldn't answer. He remained motionless, one long hand holding on to the edge of the table. It seemed as if, for whatever reason, the thin bond of trust that existed between them had been abruptly broken.

That afternoon, as he came to the end of one pile of letters and prepared to divide another one up according to degrees of lunacy, Hugh looked up to see Vivien standing beside his desk. She had her arms folded. Her hair hung forward, but didn't obscure her face.

'I wanted to thank you for helping me yesterday,' she said. 'I was going to say something when I left the nurse's room but you were asleep.'

'I must have just dropped off,' said Hugh. 'I haven't been sleeping too well. How are you feeling?'

'I'm . . . slightly sore,' said Vivien. 'How about you?'

He looked at her.

'Lately I seem to have lost all my mirth,' he said. 'Quite a lot of it at any rate.'

He expected to see something in her eyes, pity perhaps, or something harsher, more judgemental, but they were so black as to be unreadable.

'Why do you think that is?'

'I'm not sure.'

She nodded at the piles of letters. 'You're selling yourself short.'

'What makes you say that?'

'Perhaps I see you more clearly than you do yourself,' she said.

Hugh remembered the time when Vivien had put her head close to his, and stared into his eyes, and for a moment at least it had felt as if all his thoughts and feelings, even his organs, hung dangling before her gaze. It was the same now. Yet far from trying to shield himself, as he would normally have done, he found he was only too happy to allow her to roam round his insides, unearthing what she could.

In this respect, he reflected, any traffic between them still only moved one way; she remained as much of a mystery to him as she'd always been.

'Anyway,' she said, as if their conversation had strayed further than she'd intended it to. 'I just came by to say thank you. That's all.'

Chapter Twenty-Four

That night, at home, Hugh sat down to read the logbooks. To begin with, the first log consisted mainly of notes and calculations. These all appeared to relate to Kingman's position and progress. There were also notes in the margins – little reminders and admonishments Kingman had written to himself. Several were underlined: 'Too fast', 'Try again', 'Won't wash'.

At the back of the book were lists of stores and beside them records of what had been consumed and when. These too came with comments attached: 'Eating too much!' and 'Not enough bloody coffee!' Against several entries was the single word, 'waterlogged'. There was a separate section in the log recording radio and Morse messages, and another in which he kept notes of any medical problems he had. With one exception these looked to be very minor: boils, bruises and several bouts of seasickness.

It was clear that the log, at least the first half of it, had been kept meticulously. Everything was itemized in Kingman's minute handwriting. Even the crossings-out had been made with a ruler. But as it went on, the entries grew steadily more haphazard, messier, less organized. A number of them had been repeated several times, albeit with small adjustments. Tables of figures had lines roughly scrawled through them. Not all the entries were dated.

Hugh tried to work out what was going on. He turned over the crinkled pages, reading the same repeated passages and the increasingly frustrated asides. Kingman appeared to be losing patience with himself. The tone of his comments grew less breezy and more reproachful as the log went on. 'You can't say that', 'Sheer ineptitude'. And several times the single word 'FOOL' written in capital letters.

He turned back to the beginning. The first substantial entry was dated 8 November, three days after Kingman had set sail from Dartmouth.

'It is pointless to pretend that everything has functioned as it should,' he had written. 'If I am being perfectly honest I must admit that just about everything that could go wrong has already done so. I have managed to stem the leaks and dry out most of the cabin, but the pump is almost useless, so I ended up using towels instead. Sadly, this is almost the least of my problems. The generator is playing up, the sails don't fit properly and the self-steerer can't be relied upon at all. At this rate I'll have barely got to the Pacific by the time the others have finished.

'Still, there are compensations – however few and far between. Sat on deck last night as the sun was going down, and for a few minutes at least I forgot my troubles. Empty sea all around me and the stars lighting up overhead. Great feeling of peace and relief. So this is why I'm here, I thought. So this is why I'm here. And then I got up, tripped over the tiller and banged my head on the boom.'

The following three entries gave only his position, the weather, the wind direction and the miles he had covered. The next entry of any note was dated 12 November. It suggested that neither Kingman's mood nor his speed had improved. 'More leaks. Every time I repair one of the hatches another starts letting in water. And the faster I go, the more they leak. Woke up this morning with the bedding soaked. Made myself a cup of tea and found that the teabags were also wringing wet. Miserable way to start a day.'

227

Another four abrupt entries later and Kingman was writing, 'Finally repaired generator today and spoke to Margaret on the radio. She asked how it was going and I said fine, but I think she could tell that I didn't mean it. Really? she kept saying. Really? Really? Yes, I said. Really.

'Afterwards I wished I'd been honest. I'm not being fair to her, pretending it's all going fine when it isn't. Somehow I couldn't bring myself to, though. If I'd said how things really were I'd only have depressed her. And me.'

But by 21 November his spirits had improved. 'Finally beginning to pick up speed. Not much of an improvement so far, but at least nothing's bust or blown up lately. Porpoises followed me all day today. Leaping out of the water and almost flying past my ear, flapping their tails, then splashing about in the wake. Grey, like torpedoes. Writing this in my bunk after a meal of dehydrated goulash, followed by five dried apricots. Light swell. Moonlight on the waves. Worse ways to spend an evening.'

The next entry showed him to be in an equally good mood. 'In three days now I've covered close on 200 miles. In the absence of anyone else to do so, gave myself a pat on the back. Weather improving, too. Feeling of great release. It's as if everything that has ever held me up or slowed me down or made me feel miz – I don't usually – is being left behind. Almost like shedding clothes and chucking them overboard.'

After recording his position and appearing to conclude, Kingman resumed. 'Thinking about what I wrote earlier, it struck me that I've never been alone for this long before. All things considered, I reckon I'm doing pretty well. I've only felt really deep-down rotten once or twice, when I couldn't see how things would ever work out. The rest of the time I've been too busy rushing about, repairing leaks and trying to haul this bloody boat back on course.'

Over the course of the next ten days Kingman once again confined himself to the bare details of his voyage, apart from one entry where two words appeared, written in

228

pencil. The first was 'Save'. The second was illegible. On 2 December he failed to note his position, but wrote, 'The generator is down again. Fuses keep blowing and I'm running out of replacements. Haven't used the radio for a week now, thinking it best to stay off air unless absolutely necessary. Nothing quite working out at the moment.'

The next day, 3 December, he did note his position and wrote afterwards, again in pencil, 'Two escapes necessary now. Not one.' At first it seemed as if Kingman had been reluctant to expand on this. The tail on the final 'e' trailed on for almost half a page. Then his feelings came in a burst. 'It's no good,' he wrote. 'I know the sensible thing would be to turn back, but right now I can't bear the shame and the disappointment. For years I've felt that all my life has been leading up to this point, that this voyage is my chance to make something of myself. To put all the disappointments and setbacks that have dogged my life behind me and start afresh. For so long I've felt that I was falling short of what I was capable of. And now, here I am, stuck on board a boat that's barely fit to sail in a river race.'

In the next three entries, two different columns of figures appeared, one alongside the other. It was clear that the figures in the right-hand column had been rubbed out and corrected several times. 'Balance the books,' Kingman had written. 'One in each hand, and another on the end of my nose.'

Up until this point all the entries in the log had been written on the right-hand pages. But now Kingman started to add additional comments on the left-hand page. 'Looked in the mirror this morning and expected to see some sign of change,' he'd written. 'An indication that I was not myself. Not the self I set out to be. As if some terrible mark would have appeared on my countenance. But there was nothing. The same old face stared back, a little more lined and whiskery, otherwise much the same. Amazing how easily everything lies, if only you let it.'

Below it was another list, again of two columns of figures. This time, however, the columns had headings.

229

One had 'Claimed' written above it, and the other 'Real'. The figures beneath the 'Claimed' column were roughly twice those under 'Real'.

After this there were a number of blank pages. On the fourth blank page Hugh saw that Kingman had written something. It was down near the foot of the page, like three speckled footprints, and his writing was smaller than ever.

Oh pray that I may look with scorn
On all the joys of earth
A soul immortal was not born
To stoop to sensual mirth.

When pleasure would my heart allure
I'll lift to heaven my eyes
And bend my studies to secure
A far more noble prize.

Yet while I soar, still let me sink
In penitential shame
From self-dependence ever shrink
And trust the slaughtered lamb!

Hugh put the first logbook aside and turned to the second one. It appeared to have far fewer entries, or rather, the entries themselves were much shorter and more terse. Here, he was relieved to see they were all dated and set out in chronological order. But as he started to read he realized that, to begin with at least, the entries were exactly the same as they were in the first log. The same dates, the same rows of figures, the same comments, all meticulously laid out.

Everything was identical until the entry for 2 December. In the first log, Kingman had started to give way to despair at this point. But here there were only figures, no comments at all. Hugh turned back to the 2 December entry in the first log and compared the two sets of figures. They bore no resemblance to one another.

From now on every entry in the first log came in two parts, with the respective totals being totted up at the foot of each page, one under the heading 'Real' and the other 'Claimed'. These 'Claimed' figures were then transferred into the second log.

Over the next few weeks the gap between the two sets of figures widened steadily. It wasn't clear what, if anything, Kingman was doing. Whether he still had any clear objective in mind, or was just letting himself drift aimlessly about. Meanwhile his Morse messages – all diligently noted in both logs – continued to claim that everything was going well. He'd been able to sustain his burst of speed, he reported, and was heading down the west coast of Africa, with every expectation of rounding the Cape of Good Hope sometime after Christmas. From there he would head out across the Indian Ocean towards Australia.

He'd given up using the radio altogether now, claiming that it had broken down irretrievably. Messages continued coming through, but he dared not reply to them for fear of giving away his true position. People in England continued to hail him on his frequency, unable to tell if their messages were getting through, or if they were simply talking into a void.

It was at this point that Kingman fell ill. He wasn't sure what he'd come down with, only that he 'felt foul' and couldn't eat. In the first log he wrote:

'*December 15*: Been feeling steadily worse all day without wanting to acknowledge it. Tried to eat some food this evening. Heated up a tin of I don't know what – label off – took one look at it and promptly threw up. Assumed at first that it was just a stomach bug, then woke up after a few hours' sleep, covered in sweat and with a raging fever. Temperature 103 degrees. Swallowed antibiotics, but they came up a few moments later. Balance not good either. If the boat lurches one way, I go the other.

'*December 17*: Very weak. Keep thinking I'm getting better, then realize I'm not. Antibiotics don't seem to be helping. Temperature the same. Unable to keep anything down. Nothing left to come up, just dry heaves, but still feel as if there's some poison in me. Contaminated core. Spew it out. Pass it through the system. Won't budge.

'Woke up in the night convinced another boat was in the vicinity, that I'd been spotted. No idea what gave me *that* idea. Strong conviction nonetheless. Couldn't shake it. Crawled on deck. Empty sea. Flat and dark. Gazed all about me. Nothing there.

'*December 19*: Lay on the bunk all morning. Finally got up around noon. Could hardly stand. Everything wobbling and chattering. Temperature the same.

'*December 22*: Over the worst now. Think so anyway. I'm wary of putting this in writing, just in case. Temperature dropping. Less shaky on my feet. Made myself a cup of tea with lots of sugar and managed to drink about half of it. Straightening up in the cabin, I saw my reflection in the glass. Now I do look different. More haggard. Older. Came as a shock. Thought at first there was someone else there. Almost more of a shock to realize there wasn't. Nobody but me. Looked closer. My eyes seem filmy.

'*December 23*: The trouble is, of course, I don't really want to get better. Much easier to stay sick, rolling around twixt bunk and pan. Ministering to myself. But now I have to come back, face things again. It was my mother who always said, When in doubt, do nothing. As if we were all being looked after from on high, and God would get round to us eventually. Sort things out, put us back on course. All right. Come on then. I'm waiting.

'*December 24*: Thoughts turning homeward, to Christmas. I used to think I'd do anything to escape Christmas. Even as a child I couldn't stand it. What bothered me most was the fear of making a fool of myself. Self-consciousness held me back. I felt like an idiot so much of the time anyway. Everything I did was geared towards concealing it. But there was everybody, twitting about, trying to get me to join them. Come and be a silly arse. No, I said. Leave me alone. How ridiculous that I should end up missing it.

'Perhaps if I hadn't felt so self-conscious all the time I might have had more of a sense of belonging, of fitting in. As it is, I never have. It's always seemed to me as if I'm apart from everything, quite separate from the great mass of humanity. Never joining in. Always alone, stuck on some dark road at night.'

Christmas, it seemed, passed uneventfully. Kingman and his wife exchanged cables – Kingman's determinedly upbeat as usual – while she also called him up on the radio, just in case he was able to hear.

'Sat and listened to her voice,' he recorded. 'Did nothing. Didn't move. It came from a very long way away, the words quite empty of meaning by the time they reached me.'

He cooked himself a light meal of what he called Bully Mush, 'washed down with a glass of Collis Brown. Afterwards I went up on deck, daylight fading, and said a prayer, aloud, for all the unhappy people in the world. Felt like a bloody fool, but did it anyway. Asked for a little light to shine on me, too.

'*December 31*: Here I am on the brink of something, God knows what. I know there are things I cannot put off for much longer. It seems to me that there is no way back. That my old life is lost, denied to me now, that I could no more go back to it than get myself out of this mess.

'For the last few days it's been very calm. Sea almost flat. Boat rocking gently away. I feel as though I'm in this enormous bell jar, all on my own, with the air slowly being pumped out. I remember this being done at school with bees. The way the bee would fly frantically around through the thinning atmosphere. The faint drone through the glass. All the children clustered round, peering in. Then the moment when it lost consciousness, or simply gave up. Dropping through the non-air like it had weights on its feet.

'*January 1*: Happy New Year to me in my new world!

More cables and messages – one from Margaret. Much moved. No, genuinely – much moved by all this consideration. But at the same time I find these cables and expressions of goodwill as hard to believe as messages being relayed through a medium. Anyone there? No, no. Wind in the rigging, that's all.

'*January 5*: While two wrongs don't make a right, the second wrong can obliterate the first and so the measure of guilt doesn't actually rise.'

And all this time Kingman had been carefully maintaining the two sets of figures. A good deal of calculation went into ensuring that the 'Claimed' figures were as plausible as possible, hence all the calculations and crossings-out in the first log. These were then entered into the second log and cables sent back expressing appropriate bullishness or frustration. According to his official figures, Kingman was now making his way across the Indian Ocean. In reality, he was still meandering about somewhere near Madeira.

Sometime during January, however, he formulated a plan. If he had been able to get away with his deception so far, he reasoned, then what was to stop him going all the way. His rivals were now far ahead of him. The leading yachts had passed Australia and were heading for Cape Horn. From there they would set off across the Atlantic for home.

Kingman decided to bypass the middle section of the voyage and to pick it up again on the final leg. Accordingly, he set off for the east coast of South America. It took him six weeks, rather quicker than he'd anticipated. But then, as he noted with satisfaction, his boat was now performing better than at any other time since he'd set sail.

Meanwhile, he kept on sending cables – dogged, occasionally jubilant – recording his progress across the Pacific. Officially, he was going one way. In reality, he was heading in the opposite direction. His public self was in one ocean, his private self in another. To begin with, his pleasure in finding a purpose again helped soothe his other fears. But this sense of being divided, of having to switch back and forth from one guise to another, took it out of him.

'Every night I sit down to record the day's deceit,' he wrote. 'What feats will I allow myself today? Shall I put on another bogus spurt, or suffer another simulated setback? When I've finished, I look around me and think, Why shouldn't I be wherever I want to be. Out here it's all the same. Who can say any place is different from another? Not me.'

As he neared the South American coast, Kingman became increasingly reflective. 'Much preoccupied with the subject of happiness of late. Have I ever been truly happy in life? Yes, I believe so. But it seems to me that those moments have only ever come about when I've forgotten myself for a moment. When I've managed to live outside myself and outside time. Otherwise, it's just a scattering of random moments. I'm happy, I go, I'm happy. But by the time I've finished saying it the awareness of being happy has clouded the happiness and turned it into something else. Something less happy. I snatch the air. Streaming through my hands.'

For the next three weeks he sailed up and down the coast of Brazil. It had been almost two months now since he'd communicated with anyone. But on 25 February Kingman decided to break his silence. He sent a cable to the telegraph station in Wellington, New Zealand stating that he expected to be rounding the Horn within ten days and assuring everyone that, despite various, unspecified, difficulties, he was well.

He then disappeared off the air for another nine days. His second message was picked up in Brazil and led to accusations that the local telegraph operator had stupidly failed to make a note of his position. In fact, Kingman had no intention of letting anyone know where he was and phrased the cable in such a way as to suggest that his message had been cut off before he'd finished sending it. In the second cable he claimed to have rounded the Horn and to be heading up the coast of Argentina. He also asked for news of his rivals, in order to work out at what point he should rejoin the race. It would, he'd decided, be prudent to let the first two yachts go by before emerging from cover.

His spirits continued to swing wildly. Sometimes he would allow himself to believe in his deceit, then he'd fall into another bout of self-loathing. There was also the question of how long his nerve could hold. At the same time as he prepared to rejoin the race it was clear that he was being increasingly assailed by doubts.

'I have a fear of ridicule,' he wrote on 8 March. 'Nothing undermines me more. Last night I was lying in my bunk and I heard this burst of sniggering from the other side of the cabin. It appeared to be coming from the radio. Got up and went over to check. Nothing. Turned away, then heard it again. The same low snigger. Knowing and scornful. Couldn't sleep as a result. Sat up, sweating and shaking. Formed this absurd fancy that there was this creature clinging limpetlike to the bottom of the hull. Watching every move I make, and finding the spectacle so amusing that it couldn't contain itself. I even pictured it – like a kind of amphibian koala with suckers instead of paws. What little self-possession I have, and how fragile it is.'

But two days later Kingman began to set sail in earnest once again. As he'd found when crossing the Atlantic before, concerted activity stopped him from becoming too gloomy. By now he'd managed to rig up replacements for almost all those pieces of equipment that had packed up. He'd also become quite used to the way the boat handled. Within a week of rejoining the race Kingman had started to close on his nearest rival.

'*March 17*: Of course one must guard against getting carried away,' he wrote, 'but I don't think I'm being over-optimistic when I say that I now have an excellent chance of winning this race. If not actually winning, then certainly coming a creditable second. Mad to take anything for granted at this stage, I know that, but progress currently exceeding all expectations. Only sleeping sporadically. Appetite almost gone. Odd thing is I don't seem to need either sleep or food at the moment. Sharper without.

'*March 21*: Have been thinking a lot lately about when I was a child. That first holiday on the Kent coast – running from the car, seeing the great sweep of sand before me. And there, in the distance, this little foaming band of grey. So this was it – at last, this was it. Such a disappointment. Yet still I ran down the beach towards the water. Seeing it growing before me, stretching away, further than I had dreamed. My parents chasing after me, calling out in alarm. But I ignored them. I didn't stop. I kept on running, right to the water's edge, ready to cast myself on the waves, as if I might float away, right there and then. My father gathered me up and swung me round. Shouted at me for running away. We walked back up the beach towards the car. I remember seeing the railway go by. The little engine, the carriages, the blowing of the whistle. Steaming around the bay. "Bellamare".

'*March 24*: The faster I go, the leaner I become, or so I feel at any rate. Almost as if I can see all those extra bits of me, all those old anxieties, flying away behind the boat, disappearing in the wake. Mustn't stay in one place for too long, that's the answer. I admit that I had begun to feel rather maudlin. Well, that's the solitary sailor's life for you. Inevitable that one's going to go through all sorts of pitches and swings over the course of almost five months. I'm fortunate in that I've always been pretty good at amusing myself. Comes of being an only child, I suppose. You make your own entertainment. Always rather assumed that referred to masturbation! Now I recognize that it has a much broader application.'

On 31 March Kingman learned that his nearest rival had retired from the race; he'd capsized in a storm and had been unable to right himself. The news left him with mixed feelings. On the one hand he felt understandably pleased, on the other he realized that the risk of his being found out had increased significantly. He began to worry if the calculations in his 'official' logbook were correct, if anyone examining them would become suspicious. Not only would he have to convince any sceptics, but he would never be able to tell anyone about what had really happened.

'This is what worries me the most,' he admitted. 'I may have a talent for textbook duplicity, but to have to keep this up, not just for a week or two. Not a finite time. For the rest of my life?'

By now he was only a few weeks from home. If he continued at his present rate he would sail into Plymouth in early June, less than two months away. Already preparations were being made for his return. On several occasions he resolved to slow down, but it was as if he could no longer stop himself from pressing on. If he kept going flat out he would stand a good chance of winning, and, he suspected, being rumbled. But if he pulled up there was the fear that he would sink back into depression. He had to keep moving. When he did allow himself a few hours' sleep he found that it did him little good; he woke up feeling more unnerved than refreshed.

'*April 10*: Dreamed of my homecoming last night. Sailed into what appeared to be this enormous cleft, with steep banks leading down to the water. Both banks crowded with people, some cheering, others shouting angrily. Before I could land there were certain formalities to be observed. A party came aboard to sort things out, mumbling to one another. Turned out there was a problem and they couldn't let me land without the right documentation. We searched the boat for it, but of course found nothing.

'At one stage it looked as if they might be prepared to waive the rules for me. Then they changed their minds. "I'm sorry," they said. "I'm afraid you can't possibly land here." Something about the risk of contamination. This was duly broadcast to the crowds on both banks, who went very quiet. The officials fell to chattering among themselves once more.

'"But what am I to do?" I asked. The answer was

238

perfectly clear. I had to turn round and head back out to sea, like one of those death ships that can never land, but has to sail the oceans until every last trace of pestilence has disappeared.'

Three days later Kingman heard that the only other yachtsman left in the race had sunk. Desperate to stay ahead, he had pushed his boat so hard that it had started to fall apart. Kingman could hardly believe it. 'How is it that events conspire to unmask me like this?' he wondered. 'All my life I've looked for some evidence that God exists. Now it comes in the shape of divine vengeance. What other explanation is there? Malign fate, I suppose, but you'd need to be a really evil bastard to cook this one up. No, I'm being punished for transgressing. And serve me bloody right.'

It seemed as if Kingman had no alternative but to continue. This was to be his punishment, or so he imagined. Then he found he was becalmed. The wind dropped away, the temperature rose, the sea barely moved. At first he couldn't work out if this was some sort of respite, or just another form of agony. He soon decided it was the latter.

'*April 23*: The boat is surrounded by weed. Long green and brown tendrils with fat berries, the size of gooseberries, attached. If you squeeze one it gives a loud pop and a little puddle of slime shoots out over your fingers. The whole ocean, as far as I can see, is covered with the stuff, trailing over the water. A great, thick carpet of weed. It even clings to the hull. Shades of the amphibious koala. And the heat is worse than anything that's gone before. Both wet and scorching, so that you sweat and itch and fight for breath and feel as if everything inside you is liquefying at the same time. Nothing I can do but wait and hope the wind picks up.

'*April 24*: I can see by my passage through the weed how much distance I've covered. There's a strip of unweeded water about a mile long, at most. The air's so thick it's like breathing through a flannel. Lay on my bunk all day in the shade. This place is unearthly. Made me wonder if there

239

is another world apart from this one. Above, below, alongside – I don't mind where. Somewhere lost souls go when everywhere else is denied them.

'*April 25*: A ripple of wind came by this afternoon. I was on my bunk when I heard something stirring, like a long sigh coming from far off. Went up on deck and saw a wave running through the weed, making it give out a wet rustle. Watched it coming closer – hardly more than six inches in height, but stretching right across the horizon in front of me, like a fold in the weed. As it passed the boat rocked and the sails stiffened for a moment. Nothing more. Then I turned and watched it disappear into the distance.

'*April 26*: What if my punishment is not to die but to live? On and on in this dreadful place. For several hours this morning I sat in the cabin and listened to the blood thicken in my veins and my heart struggle to pump it round. There were times when it threatened to stop altogether and I found myself urging it on like a stubborn horse. On! On! I wonder if this means I want to live, that I still have some instinct to survive. Or that I have no other option. I won't be allowed to die.

'*April 28*: Dreamed of drowning last night. I tried to throw myself overboard, make myself sink, but the weed buoyed me up. It wouldn't let me go under. I bounced as if I was on a trampoline. Those whom the ocean considers unworthy it chucks back.

'*April 29*: I saw a ship today. Couldn't believe it at first and assumed I was hallucinating. But there it was, this small black wedge making its way along the horizon with a plume of smoke hanging out behind. Didn't know whether to signal or to keep quiet. In the end, did nothing. Ship steamed on regardless. Made me realize, though, that the weed doesn't go on for ever. Not for much longer, I suspect.

'*April 30*: I was right. The wind got up overnight. Woke to the sound of the sails cracking. By first light I was already starting to pick up speed, and by midday I'd left the last of the weed behind. As if to compensate, I spent

240

the afternoon and evening rattling along. More miles covered in six hours than in the last week.'

But Kingman's mood did not improve as he had hoped. Try as he did, he found he was no longer able to lose himself in activity. It didn't work any more. Nor had he seen the last of the weed. Two days later he hit it again, and although there was more wind this time the boat still wouldn't budge. Whichever way he turned he was stuck.

'*May 1*: I can't go on. I think I've known this for some time. But here it is, written out in front of me. No homecoming. No heroics. No Margaret. I'm near the end now, not much left. Resources pretty much exhausted. Gave up trying to sail today and simply let the boat drift. Can't go forward. Can't turn back.

'What have I learned from all this? Only that we live in a crueller, more complicated world than I thought possible. Not much of a conclusion, but I wish there was more. I do wish there was more. What lies ahead of me? Enter the Land of Nothingness – that much at least is certain.

'*May 2*: Bellamare! Bellamare! Bellamare!

'*May 3*: Had intended to do some tidying up, but when it came to it I thought, Why bother? Lay out on deck instead. And a strange thing happened. For once time didn't hurry by and I made no effort to catch it. Rather it seemed to envelop me, hugging me, squeezing out all my fears. Time passed, but I passed with it. Neither lagging behind, nor running ahead. Rolled up together in perfect step.

'Sitting here now, having watched the sun go down, dropping into the sea. When I've finished I'll put down my pen and have one last look around. That will be enough. One last look. Then slip away like a thief in the night.'

It was the final entry in the log.

Part 3

'Ratcliff Highway, which leads to Limehouse, is the Regent Street of London sailors, who in many instances, never extend their walks in the metropolis beyond this semi-marine region . . . In about 1745 a mineral spring, known as Shadwell Spa, was discovered by Walter Berry Esq., when sinking a well in Sun Tavern Fields. It was said to be impregnated with sulphur, vitriol, steel and antimony. A pamphlet was written by Dr Linden in 1749 to prove it could cure every disease.'

WALTER THORNBURY, *OLD AND NEW LONDON*, 1881

Chapter Twenty-Five

'Dead? Are you sure?'

'So they say.'

'Where was he found?'

'Southern Spain. Some hikers came across him on a hill-side, lying by some rocks, miles from anywhere. He was in a bit of a mess, I understand. The birds . . . You know . . . They've still got to do a positive identification, but they seem pretty certain it was him.'

Everyone sat in silence and tried to digest this news.

'The poor fucker,' said Julian and shook his head. 'It makes you think, doesn't it?'

'Does it, Julian? What about?'

'You know. About death and stuff.'

Cliff looked surprised. 'It doesn't make me think about death. Retribution maybe. Just deserts.'

'Come on, Cliff,' said Hugh. 'Not now. This is a sad day, for Christ's sake.'

'Oh, it's a sad day, all right. I wouldn't want to argue with that.'

Apparently nobody else wanted to argue with it either.

'I wondered if we should think about a memorial of some kind.'

'That's an idea. We could have a whip-round. See what we come up with.'

'A whip-round?'

'That's right, Cliff. You know, each of us stick in something.'

'Yes. What sort of figure did you have in mind?'

'I hadn't really thought, Cliff. It would depend, wouldn't it? We'd have to think of something appropriate.'

'Mmm. Hard to know what that could be.'

'A statue maybe?'

'A statue? It would have to be a very small statue, I'd have thought.'

'A statuette then.'

'Or a little bust.'

'I'm not sure we could even stretch to that.'

'What then? A fucking glove puppet?'

'No, you know, something . . . well, cheaper. Perhaps Julian could utilize some of his famous woodwork skills.'

But Julian shook his head and wouldn't consider it.

'A plaque perhaps. He wouldn't have wanted anything elaborate.'

'He would have done, you know.'

'Well, he's not in any position to complain.'

'The poor fucker,' muttered Julian again.

'Yes, yes, we've done that bit,' said Cliff.

'You never liked him.'

'I did,' said Cliff. 'I liked him well enough.'

'You said he was a silly cunt.'

'I wasn't the only one. Besides, in many respects he was a silly cunt.'

'Well, we can't put that on a memorial, can we? Be a bit self-defeating.'

'You never liked him,' said Julian again, bitterly.

'What about a cairn?'

'A cairn. What's that, Bobbie?'

'It's a pile of stones, Cliff.'

'A pile of stones, eh? That sounds pretty good to me.'

'But where are we going to put it? Those things are supposed to go on the top of mountains. I mean, Scaife was hardly an outdoors type. He didn't even much like daylight.'

'He was found outside, wasn't he?'

'Well . . . yes.'

'There you are, then,' said Cliff. 'Excellent. I think one of those cairns would be very handsome.'

When Hugh had arrived at work that morning, there had been a great crowd of people standing about outside the newspaper office. As he came closer, he heard the sound of shouting. It grew louder and more angry. The commissionaires were trying to keep order, but it was proving hard to control such a large crowd. When Hugh pushed his way through the revolving doors, several people began to shout at him. He wanted to ask what was going on. But the only people inside were some commissionaires, crouched in formation beneath the mural portraying *The Triumph of Truth over Falsehood*, preparing to go outside.

He started to climb the stairs. The wall lights, shaped like scallop shells, had now been removed. Wires stuck out in their place. The long, silver banister in the shape of a snake had been wrapped in corrugated paper, prior to being removed.

The lawyer was coming down towards him. He was carrying a large bag. Hugh thought he had never seen him looking so pale.

'Are you all right?' he asked.

'No,' said the lawyer. 'I wouldn't say that.'

'What have you got there?' Hugh asked, indicating the bag.

'It's money.'

'What are you going to do with it?'

'I'm going to give it away.'

There was a strange empty sound to the lawyer's voice.

'That's not like you.'

'It's not like me,' agreed the lawyer. 'But I don't have any choice. Some bastard inserted a couple of noughts in the crossword prize and changed it from £5 to £500. No-one seems to have spotted the error before it was

247

printed. All those people outside want their money. If I don't give it to them, there's going to be a riot. This has never happened before. Not in all the time I've been here.'

He cradled the bag in his hands. From downstairs came fresh cries of annoyance. It sounded as if the crowd had now broken into the building. The lawyer began walking down the marble steps. 'What a shambles,' he said.

Some time later, Hugh saw him come back into the office. Now he was no longer carrying the bag. His clothes were dishevelled, his hair ruffled and he appeared to be walking with a slight limp.

When they got back from lunch there were still a few people left outside, complaining they'd been cheated. But they sounded much more half-hearted than before and only one commissionaire was needed to keep the peace.

Almost all the surrounding offices had either been demolished, or were in the process of being knocked down. From street level everything looked much the same as it had always done – the same long line of frontages running down to Ludgate Circus. But that was all that was left. They'd lost everything else; their guts had been scooped out and carted off. As the light flooded in, it reminded Hugh of walking along a high ridge, with the ground falling away on either side.

He had finished answering one box of readers' letters; there were still another three to go. But when he went to collect another box, he was surprised to find a small brown dog in the room, standing on top of one of the fondue sets. The dog yapped uncertainly at him. In that brief moment, as they surveyed one another, Hugh noticed that the dog's coat appeared to be a good deal longer on one side of its body than the other. Then it jumped down from the fondue set and darted between his legs, out into the corridor.

Hugh followed, watching it run around the corner into the office, its back legs spinning away. The effect of the dog on the journalists was unlike anything he could have expected. Something close to panic swept through the office. People began calling out in high, anxious voices. Of all of them, Cliff appeared to be the worst affected. He was all jittery, standing almost on tip-toe, grey thumbs drawn together, looking anxiously left and right to see where the dog had got to. He had, Hugh saw, fallen victim to his own scaremongering.

Meanwhile, the dog scuttled about between the desks, this strange, half-shorn creature. The commotion spread through the office like a weather front; it swung about this way and that, depending on where the dog was. By now, according to the squall of alarm, it appeared to be somewhere by the door to the Gents. When Hugh got there, he found it under a table, scratching away at one of the carpet tiles and sniffing inquisitively. He picked it up. As he did so, he saw Darren standing opposite him with his arms outstretched. Darren looked very embarrassed. His face was red and his thin pelt of a moustache seemed almost to bristle.

'He's mine,' he said.

The dog was licking Hugh's hand.

'What's his name?'

'Brad.'

'That's an unusual name for a dog.'

'He's not actually *mine*,' said Darren. 'I'm just looking after him.'

Hugh handed him the dog. It sat on Darren's elbow. Slowly, the office settled back down. Hugh walked along the aisle to the room where the letters were kept.

'Well done,' said Cliff as he went by.

'What for?'

'For subduing that dog, of course.'

'It didn't take much subduing.'

Cliff shook his head.

'Some of these dogs are very dangerous indeed,' he said.

'Are you sure?'

'Oh yes. You shouldn't be so trusting, Hughie.'

'Are you feeling all right, Cliff?'

'Why do you ask?'

'You don't look very well.'

'Nothing wrong with me,' said Cliff. 'I'm as strong as an ox.'

Chapter Twenty-Six

Hugh sat at his desk and felt his gut tie itself in knots. He shut his eyes and found he was almost able to visualize the soft tubes of his intestine, like blind sea creatures, folding themselves over one another, then drawing tighter. He tried to unearth some initiative he could pursue, some fresh idea that might carry him on. But there was nothing – at least nothing he could come up with. So he just sat and raged fruitlessly at himself while his insides snaked steadily together.

He picked up a letter from the pile in front of him. It was written in crayon and underlined across the top.

'Isn't it about time the Jews started wandering again?' he read.

He dropped the letter in the bin.

He took out Field's Seaman's Discharge Book from his case and stared at it once again. He looked at the section marked 'Next of Kin', trying to work out what words lay hidden behind these crossings-out. As he'd done before, he held it up to the light. It made no difference. All he could see was a thick smear of black ink across the page.

To his surprise he found an image of Vivien in his mind, so clear it was like a memory. She was standing showering, her hair full of shampoo, reaching up blindly to adjust the shower nozzle, eyes tight closed, water streaming down her shoulders. Then the image began to crinkle at the edges, like a photograph burning. And despite his efforts to keep it intact, it soon faded away to nothing.

For want of anything more constructive to do, he watched Johnny Todd preening himself. He was wearing a three-piece suit in a jagged houndstooth material, and was standing with his chest puffed out and his elbows bent, like a fencer admiring his handiwork after running someone through. People walked tactfully around him, so as not to interrupt his reverie of self-regard. After a while, he walked back over to his desk, sat down and began typing away at great speed.

Julian lay sprawled over his chair, his long limbs dangling round him. People tapped away at their type-writers. At the far end of the aisle Hugh could see Darren making his rounds, steering his trolley one-handed across the carpet tiles, not paying much attention to where it went. Beyond him, Battersby sat in his glass booth talking on the phone. He was hunched forward, holding the receiver with both hands.

Hugh shifted about in his chair and his feet banged against the waste-paper basket. Gripping it between his feet, he pulled it out from under his desk. The bin was full of discarded sheets of copy paper. None of them, as far as he could see, were his. The cleaners, it seemed, had given up emptying the bins. Now they simply redistributed them round the office.

He took out one of the sheets. It contained the single sentence, 'I decided to come clean, as delicately as possible.' There was no indication who had written it. Hugh was about to chuck it back in the bin when some memory from childhood came to him unbidden, of producing pale, powdery versions of other people's signatures.

He smoothed out the paper. There was still a sheet of carbon attached to the back. Tearing off the carbon, he opened up Field's Seaman's Discharge Book and laid it flat on the desk. On the back of the page with the crossing-out on it, he placed the carbon paper, matt side down, and rubbed at it lightly with a pencil. Then he put a fresh sheet

252

of paper between the two pages, turned back and rubbed at it again from the other side.

When he'd finished, he turned over the page. A faint blue scrawl had been imprinted on the fresh sheet of paper. There was a name, Joyce Field, and beneath it an address: 37 Abbeville Road, London E15.

He was on his way out of the office when Joy stopped him.

'Hold on,' she said. 'Where do you think you're going?'

'Busy,' said Hugh. 'Can't stop.'

'Oh yes you can,' said Joy. She wagged an ochre-tipped finger at him, then picked up a list from her desk. 'I thought so. You're supposed to be at computer training today.'

'I never had any notification about it.'

'It must have gone astray. Everyone's got to do it. I've done mine. I quite enjoyed it actually. Anyway, what are you in such a hurry about?'

'It's . . . Never mind,' he said.

'You'll just have to go later. And you'd better get a move on. It starts in a minute.'

One of the rooms that was normally used for storing cleaning materials had been cleared out and turned into a makeshift training centre. There were two rows of tables. On them were a number of word processors – grey bulbous screens resting on grey plastic bases, with detachable keyboards in the same grey plastic. In the windowless room the screens gave out a thin phosphorescent glow.

The woman who was to take their class sat at the front with a manual clipped into a loose-leaf binder open in front of her. There were two other people there, already gazing at their screens: Stanley and another journalist who Hugh didn't know. Stanley had brought along a special attachment that enabled his magnifying glass to fit onto his head, like a welder's visor.

The woman began to speak. Her voice was flat, her words dulled by frequent repetition. This, Hugh assumed, was one of the last training sessions, to mop up those embarrassments and afterthoughts who hadn't been included before. She'd already been going a few minutes when the door opened.

'Come in,' she said to the newcomer. 'You haven't missed much.'

Vivien sat down in the row behind Hugh. She had a bag over her shoulder with a magazine sticking out of it. If she noticed his presence she gave no sign of it.

To begin with they were told how to operate their cursors, and then they were given a number of simple tasks to do, such as writing a sentence and then changing the words around. They set to in silence. There was no sound except for the soft clack of the keys.

Hugh found it oddly soothing. They copied out lines that had clearly been chosen for testing their punctuation. After which they were taught how to file a story and call it up again. He managed all these things without difficulty. Vivien sat breathing through her curtain of hair and jabbed away at the keys until the instructress told her there was no need to apply such pressure.

The star of the class was Stanley. As soon as he'd finished each allotted task he pushed back his visor, cried out, 'Done,' and waited for the others to finish. Behind the magnifying glass his head had blurred out of recognition. But his fingers darted around the keyboard with extraordinary agility and the characters sped out across his screen in long, flowing lines.

Soon after midday they were told that they should now type out a passage of their own, and then punctuate and paragraph it. Everyone set to, except Hugh, who sat staring at the blank screen. When he glanced up, he saw the instructress looking at him, wondering why he hadn't started. He was toying with the idea of writing gibberish. Then, quite unexpectedly, some words came into his mind and he began to type away. When he'd finished, he looked in astonishment at what he had written.

On his screen he read, 'All but blind behind his heavy iron visor, Sir Percival cantered into the arena. It was

254

almost time for the tournament to begin. But just as the two knights took their places on either side of the jousting rail, there was a murmur of surprise and the crowd parted. Slowly, commandingly, a third knight, his helmet dented, his armour battered and black, rode right up to the royal dais.'

Hugh couldn't be sure what had got into him. He felt shocked, appalled, by this unconscious Arthurian outburst. He'd always known himself to be troubled by romantic impulses, but had always assumed they were more or less under control. Now it seemed as if they might be seeping out of their own accord. These ludicrous dreams of chivalry, of courtly love. He would have to keep an even tighter grip on himself in future.

At one o'clock they broke for lunch. The instructress left first, followed by Vivien and Stanley and the other journalist. Hugh sat alone amid the screens' phosphorescent glow. For a while he did nothing, then he got up and moved down the table to where Stanley had been sitting. Stanley had written, 'The circles under the Foreign Secretary's eyes were etched vividly into his skin. I expressed my gratitude to him for sparing the time to see me and decided to come clean, as delicately as possible, about the purpose of my visit. When the Foreign Secretary heard what I had to say, he nodded approvingly. Once again, I was able to identify the enormous strain he was under. Using my first name with an ease and familiarity that delighted me, he told me, "Do you know, Stanley, I've never told anyone what I'm about to tell you now."'

Behind him was Vivien's place. Hugh found himself oddly unwilling to look at what she had written, yet unable to stop himself. But when he got to her screen, he saw that only these words were visible – 'lights go out. Lost in self-reproach.'

As they'd been taught, Hugh pressed the arrow on the left-hand side of the screen to see the preceding lines. In his eagerness, however, he hit two keys at once. Instead of scrolling back as it should have done, the screen went blank. Vivien's words had disappeared. Hugh pressed frantically away at the keys to try to retrieve them, but it was no good. They had gone.

When Vivien came back from lunch she sat down, then peered with surprise at her screen. Then she called over the instructress and asked her to have a look. Hugh lowered his head to his screen. Meanwhile the instructress, increasingly baffled, made various efforts to find Vivien's words. In the end she had to admit defeat. Briefly, Hugh felt Vivien's eyes settle on him, then move away.

Stanley put his visor back on. They were given new exercises to do. The rest of the afternoon passed without incident. Partly because he was concentrating on blanking out the memory of what had happened earlier, Hugh found himself doing better than he'd expected. At half-past five they were told they could go.

Hugh caught a bus heading east. It crossed the City, then headed through the evening mist towards Bethnal Green. The bus ground its way between stops, the chassis rattling and trembling whenever it reached any speed. They passed a man driving a column of children along the pavement. The children were in fancy dress. Several were dressed as cats, with long cardboard tails that stuck out behind them and turned up at the ends. Others were dressed as horses, with shoe boxes over their heads. The bus was going so slowly that it kept pace with them for a while.

Something – Hugh couldn't tell what – prompted the children to break into a run. First the ones in front started, and then everyone else, all of them sprinting along, their tails swinging about, threatening to swerve out into the road, while from the back the man cried anxiously to them to slow down.

When Hugh got off the bus, he checked his map and turned left off the main road into a street full of identical late-Victorian houses. At the top of the street was a large stone building, clearly derelict. Above the door was a relief of a bearded figure, propped up on one elbow as if he was reading in bed, his beard draped over the portico. Several bare saplings were growing out of the roof.

Hugh took the right-hand fork. Here the houses were much shabbier than they'd been closer to the main road. The street lamps were a long way apart, and most of the light came from the surrounding houses, spilling onto the pavement in little yellow pools. He found the house he was looking for and rang the bell. Shapes could be seen moving about inside. When the door was pulled open a man stood in front of him with a baby on his shoulder.

'Sorry to bother you,' said Hugh. 'I'm trying to trace a Joyce Field. I believe she lives here.'

The man shook his head. 'No she doesn't,' he said.

'Not any more?' asked Hugh.

From the man's shoulder, the baby stared at him. It looked like an older, infinitely wearier version of its father.

'Dead,' said the man.

'Ah, I see. When did she die?'

'About four years ago now.'

'And did you know a Malcolm Field – her brother perhaps?'

'No,' said the man. 'Why, who wants to know?'

'Thank you,' said Hugh. 'I'm sorry to have troubled you.'

He walked back the way he'd come. When he reached the main road he caught a bus going west and got off at Holborn before it turned north. He collected his things from the office, then went back down the stairs and out into the street. He crossed over the road, heading down St Bride's Passage. After he'd gone a few yards he began to retrace his steps. On one of the benches near the entrance to the church he saw the glowing end of a cigarette. He climbed up the steps into the graveyard. The bench was some way from where Vivien normally sat.

Feeling increasingly awkward, Hugh made his way across the graves to where she was sitting. There was even less light in this part of the churchyard than elsewhere and he found he had to pay more attention to his footing than he might otherwise have done. Ahead of him he could see the figure on the bench start to take shape. Head back, dressed in a long coat, the glow of the cigarette – or joint – swinging up and down.

When he sat down the figure didn't move. For some reason Hugh decided that he wanted to come clean. He had too many unresolved things swirling about in his head as it was.

'It was me,' he said simply. 'I wanted to see what you'd written on the screen and I deleted your words by mistake.'

There was no reaction at first. Hugh thought that perhaps she was going to take it badly, that some further apology might be required. However, he didn't have anything else to say so he stayed quiet.

After a while a low voice – soft, steady, but unmistakably male – came to him from the other end of the bench.

'I don't know what you're talking about.'

The figure turned towards him. When he took a drag of his cigarette his features were lit up in the glow.

'What are you doing here?' asked Hugh.

'I drop by occasionally,' said Darren, 'if I'm going out later. I find it very peaceful.'

He jerked his head. 'Not like over there. How about you?'

'Yes,' said Hugh. 'I come here occasionally, too.'

'I haven't seen you here before.'

'No, well, it's been rather cold lately.'

Darren nodded understandingly. He closed his eyes and pursed his lips to take another drag of his cigarette. His moustache rested on his upper lip like a third eyelash. There was something unnerving about Darren, Hugh decided; he had an exaggerated sense of his own allure.

'I always like to sit and collect my thoughts before I go to my evening class,' said Darren.

'What are you studying?'

'Tonight I'm doing pattern-cutting.'

Darren held out his lapel towards him.

'See this coat. I made it. And these trousers.'

'Really? Do you make all your own clothes?'

Darren laughed. 'I'd like to, but I don't have the time. I do pattern-cutting on Tuesdays and dog-grooming on Thursdays.'

'That must keep you busy.'

'Well, it helps keep me out of mischief at any rate.'

He laughed. 'I'm glad we bumped into one another.'

'Are you?'

'Yes,' said Darren. 'I felt there had been a bit of a misunderstanding between us recently.'

'Really?'

'I did, yes. I thought you needed to be taught a lesson.'

'What about?'

'About consideration,' said Darren. 'You can be very high-handed at times. Perhaps you don't mean to be, I don't know. People mustn't be allowed to get away with behaviour like that, though. They've got to be made to suffer for it. No-one likes to be taken for granted, to feel they don't count. I like to be friendly with people. Not over-familiar, of course, but cordial. You expect that to be reciprocated.'

'Yes,' said Hugh. 'Quite.'

'You just expected me to serve you,' said Darren.

'I beg your pardon?'

'You just expected me to serve you – to get you tea, or whatever.'

Hugh had the feeling that this conversation was running away from him. 'You are a tea boy,' he said.

Darren shook his head. 'You treated me like a skivvy. I won't have that.'

Still Hugh had no idea what Darren was talking about, or which perceived slight he had taken exception to. Under the circumstances, however, he thought it best to apologize.

'I'm sorry.'

They sat in silence for several minutes.

Hugh was wondering if some further abasement was

expected of him when Darren said, 'I'm not a bad person, you know.'

'I'm sure you're not.'

'I'm a nice person at heart. At least, I try to be.'

'I never doubted it.'

'But when someone treats me like that I lose all sense of proportion.'

'Do you?'

'Yes. I was so angry that I went home and wrote down how I felt. You know, just letting everything out. All my anger poured out onto the page. I'll show it to you if you like.'

'Thank you,' said Hugh. 'I should like that.'

'And when it was over, I felt much better. It was like lancing a boil. Now I'm quite calm. We can be friends again, if you like.'

'Good,' said Hugh.

'I don't like to be on bad terms with people. There are enough nasty things going on in this world already without making them worse, don't you agree?'

'Yes.'

'That's settled then. Most of the time I don't find it easy to forgive and forget. But Walter said you were all right, that you'd been kind to him, so I was forced to reconsider. I value kindness more than anything else in life. Apart from consideration, of course.'

'Is there something going on downstairs?' asked Hugh.

'What do you mean?'

'Something odd?'

'Maybe,' said Darren.

'Could you be more specific?'

'No.'

Then, presumably aware that this coyness did not reflect well on their reforged friendship, Darren said, 'It's not easy for me to talk about.'

'Is it anything to do with Hollis?'

'Not necessarily,' said Darren.

'But it might be?'

Darren didn't answer.

'Do you know someone called Malcolm Field?'

'I don't think so. Who is he?'

'Just . . . someone.'

After a while Darren said, 'They know everything.'

'The green-carders?'

He nodded. 'Everything that goes on at the paper. It all passes through them: the internal mail, everything. They're the only ones who know their way around, how everything works, how it all fits together. Everyone else just stays in their little boxes. People treat them like idiots – worse than idiots. Well, they'll see.'

'See what?'

Darren giggled.

'Please tell me.'

'Why should you care?'

'I do care,' said Hugh. 'I didn't used to, but I do now.'

'Perhaps you're changing.'

'Yes,' he agreed, 'perhaps I am.'

'Becoming a better person.'

'I wouldn't say that.'

'What then?'

'More active,' said Hugh.

Darren nodded approvingly. 'It's good to try and stay active.' After a pause he went on, 'Those poor men have worked for the paper for years. Decades. And now they're going to be thrown out on their ears. Well, you can't just treat people like that. It's not kind, or fair.'

'So they've got something planned?'

'They might have.'

Something struck Hugh. 'Did they have anything to do with changing the prize money on the crossword the other day?'

In the darkness he could see Darren grin.

'Is Walter in charge of them?'

Again Darren didn't answer but buttoned his coat. 'Anyway,' he said, 'it's time I got off to my class. Speaking for myself, I'll be glad to go. I've only ever thought of the paper as a stepping stone.'

'Really? A stepping stone to what?'

'Oh, there are all sorts of opportunities out there for someone like me.'

'Well, I'm sure you'll be successful in whatever you choose.'

'Do you really believe that?'

'Almost certainly,' said Hugh.

Darren appeared touched by this expression of faith.

'There is something I'm planning to do,' he said.

'What's that?'

'You know that dog yesterday?'

'Brad?'

'Yes, Brad. I was clipping him for some friends. I'd only got halfway through when I had to take the teas round. When I get out of here I'd like to set up my own dog-grooming parlour.'

'Won't you need quite a bit of capital for that?'

'I've thought of that already,' said Darren, but didn't elaborate.

He stood up and held out his hand.

'Friends again?' he said.

Hugh shook Darren's hand.

'Friends again.'

Chapter Twenty-Seven

The corridor stretched out ahead of him, dimly lit and painted in the same old parchment colour as every other corridor in the building. At times he felt as though the whole geography of the building was liable to change; as though it were made of rubber and might twist and bend itself into new shapes at will. Yet nothing appeared different, at least not as far as he could tell. The corridor hadn't sprung any unexpected forks, the library doors were exactly where they had been before. Although no daylight ever reached the inside of the building, the atmosphere seemed quite different at night. There was a softer quality to the darkness and the air felt somehow heavier.

He opened the library doors and turned on the lights. The shelves sprang into view, crammed with brown envelopes, stacked up from floor to ceiling. There was the same smell of old, fingered paper. Walking down the length of the room, Hugh had the impression that he was scoring a furrow through all these stale layers of air. They parted resentfully before him, then closed up again behind.

He walked through the passageway at the end which separated the library of the living from the library of the dead. He turned on the light switches at the far end of the passage and moved on briskly, almost keeping pace with the lights as they flickered into life overhead. At the far end of the room there were piles of unfiled cuttings, some still in their envelopes, others spilling out over the floor. These grey, rustling mounds of paper were two or three feet high, like piles of ash from old bonfires.

Somewhere around here, according to Walter, was Hollis's room. He could see no sign of where it might be. Beyond the mounds of paper was what appeared to be a blank wall. Bare bricks rose up before him and stretched away on either side. Then he saw that, just to the right of the furthest mound, there was a small door set into the wall. He stopped for a while and listened. There was no sound, except for the rustling of the paper.

The door opened quite easily, swinging away from him. He felt about on the inside wall and found a switch. A single light came on above the door. This room was no bigger than Walter's; another little chamber set into the fabric of the building. There was a desk against the far wall with a chair in front of it. Above the desk, shelves ran round three sides of the room. The shelves were stacked with old printing blocks, metal letters nailed onto pieces of wood. Some of the letters were as big as his fist. Newspaper cuttings hung from hooks screwed into the shelves – twisted yellow strips of paper. Hugh looked at each one carefully. None of them meant anything.

Hanging on one of the hooks was a single key. Hugh lifted the key off the hook and tried it in the door. It didn't fit. He was about to put it back when he saw there was a number printed in the metal. He looked at the number. Then he took Field's Seaman's Discharge Book out of his pocket and turned over the pages. He didn't find what he was looking for the first time, and he had to go back, more slowly this time, holding the book up to the light as he did so. The numbers were written down at the bottom of one of the last pages: 1785. They'd been written at a slant, cutting across one of the corners, the familiar curls and dashes almost seeming to disappear into little spirals. He compared them. The numbers were the same. He stared at them for a few moments to make sure, then put the key in his pocket.

He pulled out the desk drawers. They were empty. Then he started to search the shelves again. He climbed onto the desk and started at the top, working his way down. But he found nothing. Nothing of any interest. There were a few memos to do with work, some pens, a pair of scissors, an old gas bill with Hollis's home address on it and a bottle of ink, but that was all. When he'd finished he sat in the chair and looked about, trying to work out if there was anything that he could have missed.

He found himself oddly reluctant to stir, to get down on his hands and knees to look under the desk, rooting around in more dirt. But eventually, with an air of weariness, he crawled into the well below the middle of the desk. What light there was in the room scarcely penetrated down here. He had to sweep about with his hands to see if they came into contact with anything unusual. The desk rested on four narrow, rectangular legs, with a gap of about six inches between the bottom drawer and the floor.

He could get his hand into the gap easily enough, but once there he couldn't move it very far. The only way to make sure that he was being thorough was to crawl in as far as he could, tucking his head down onto his chest and then pushing the back of his neck against the back panel of the desk. By resting first on one shoulder, then the other, he was able to run his hands under both sets of drawers.

There was nothing under the left-hand side of the desk apart from an old-fashioned typing rubber. It was round and almost flat, the size of a coat button. The rubber had hardened and roughened with age. When he tried the other side, his hand didn't come into contact with anything at all. In order to get out of the gap he had to twist round and push himself out, holding on to the legs of the desk.

As he did so, he felt one of the legs move. His first thought was that the desk was about to come crashing down on top of him. Still holding on to the desk leg, he tried to pull it back towards him, to stabilize it, but he found he was unable to get a proper grip. Again, the leg slid away from him.

By twisting about some more, he managed to get both hands under the same side of the desk. He had hold of one corner of the desk leg and felt about for another. It was only at this point that he realized that what he was trying to get hold of wasn't the desk leg at all. It was a good deal bigger. Nor was it attached to the desk, but simply wedged underneath. Pressing both hands together, he managed to pull it across the floor towards him.

Backing out from under the desk, he saw that he had hold of a box. It was a long, flattish cardboard box, the sort that shirts used to be sold in. He picked it up and put it on the desk. When he opened the lid he saw that there were only two things inside. The first was a membership card from the National Union of Seamen in a laminated envelope. The membership card was made out in the name of Malcolm Field. But the man in the photograph alongside looked nothing like the man in Field's Seaman's Discharge Book. He had thin hair brushed straight across the top of his head, and a bored, disengaged expression on his face. Beneath the union card was a brown envelope. Hugh took it out. Written along the top in capital letters were the words, 'Tom Kingman. Yachtsman. (5 of 5).'

Inside the cuttings envelope there were two pieces of paper. The first was dated 12 March 1978 and headlined RENDEZVOUS WITH A DEAD MAN. An old friend of Tom Kingman's, a West-Country builder called Martin Drew, claimed he had seen Kingman one night while walking along Romney Sands in Kent. Drew had been on holiday with his wife and had gone out for some air before he went to bed, his wife having stayed behind to have a bath. He had seen a man coming towards him at twilight across the shingle.

At first he'd paid little attention, being more preoccupied with where he was going. There were boats pulled out of the water, their bows attached to wire hawsers that stretched to winches higher up the beach. In the darkness the hawsers were all but invisible. There was also a narrow-gauge railway running around the bay, the tracks laid on top of the sand. You had to watch your step.

As they passed one another, Drew had wished the other man good evening. The man had lifted his head to acknowledge Drew's greeting. As he did so, Drew had recognized Kingman. He was a good deal thinner, more stooped, but, Drew insisted, he was the same man he had known when they were neighbours in Devon almost twenty years earlier. Too astonished to speak at first, he had simply stood and watched Kingman go by. Then, collecting himself, he'd set off in pursuit, calling out his name.

At this, Kingman quickened his pace. Drew had to struggle to get level with him. He had almost managed to do so and was, as he put it, close enough to reach out and touch him, when he must have tripped on one of the hawsers and fallen. Drew himself wasn't clear what had happened next. He thought that he must have winded himself when he landed. It took him a while to get his breath back. By the time he'd done so, there was no sign of Kingman. Drew had made a cursory search of the boats and beach huts round about, but in the darkness it was impossible to be thorough. In the end he had given up and gone back to tell his wife what had happened.

The other cutting was dated ten days later. In it Drew admitted that he might have made a mistake. Asked if he could be absolutely certain that he had seen Kingman, Drew said that he couldn't. At the time he had been quite sure it was him. Now, however, he wondered if his imagination hadn't run away with him. 'Things haven't been going too well for me lately,' he said. 'I didn't mean any harm by it and I hope I haven't caused Mrs Kingman any distress.' The article concluded by stating that Kingman had also been sighted in France, Italy, Iceland, South America and the Seychelles.

Hugh folded up the two cuttings and put them back in the envelope. He put the envelope and the union card in his pocket. Then he got back down on his hands and knees, crawled under the desk and put the cardboard box back where he'd found it. He pushed it back in, until it was wedged beneath the underside of the drawers.

When he'd finished, he reached up and took Hollis's gas bill before turning out the light and making his way back down the library of the dead, through the passageway at the end and into the library of the living. At the doorway, he turned off the bank of switches and pulled the door shut behind him.

Turning round, he saw Walter standing in front of him. His skin looked more raw than usual tonight, his frame more stretched. He appeared to have been put together by someone with only a vague grasp of human anatomy. It was as if his joints hadn't been tightened up properly and were in danger of coming apart at any moment.

'What are you doing here?' he asked.

Hugh explained that he'd been checking one or two things in the library.

'At this time of night?'

Hugh mumbled about having a deadline. It didn't sound remotely convincing. Walter continued to regard him suspiciously with his cornflower-blue eyes.

'Did you find what you were looking for?' he asked.

'I did, yes. Thank you,' said Hugh.

Still they stayed facing one another, hanging there, so it seemed to Hugh, in this suspended stand-off. He was aware of Hollis's papers in his jacket, as if they were fireworks leaping and fizzing away in his pocket. It seemed to him that Walter was aware of them, too. It wasn't as if Hugh had any talent for concealment. Nor, he suspected, for dissembling.

Walter's head bobbed about in front of him. Then he straightened up and shrank back into his clothes. He moved aside without saying anything.

As he walked away down the corridor, Hugh felt Walter's eyes upon him, a thin, wavering gaze playing about between his shoulders. He was so preoccupied that he found himself walking aimlessly, paying no attention to where he was going. It was as if he'd given himself up to the shifting geography of the building.

By the time he became aware of his surroundings, he realized he was lost once more. He tried to work out if any of this looked familiar – the piping overhead, the curve in the wall, the occasional doors with their little panels of frosted glass – but there was no way of telling. It was all the same. After a while, whenever he came to a fork, he took whichever turning he felt like without any idea of his direction.

Eventually he came to the room where the type was cut and set. The same men he'd seen before sat crouched at the same machines, pounding away at their keyboards as if they'd never moved. From the back of each machine a stream of shrapnel shot into wire baskets, to be gathered up and carted away. There were shards of metal all over the floor. Overhead, the belts and pulleys flapped and whirred. But this time no-one stopped him to ask what he was doing. They were all too busy to pay him any attention. He made his way down the length of the room, while men in leather aprons carrying galleys of type swerved around him and hurried by. He passed the tables where men with mallets beat the type into shape, driving wedges into any gaps to ensure it wouldn't shift about under the weight of the inking rollers.

Instead of being shoved through a hatch into another stairwell, as he'd been last time, Hugh walked through the typesetting room and out into another corridor at the other end. This corridor was just as featureless as all the others. But now he could hear a muffled thumping that appeared to be coming from under his feet. The soles of his feet tingled with the vibration.

At the next stairwell he came to, he descended another floor. The noise became steadily louder. But now, along with the thumping, he could hear something else – a wet, slurping sound, as if a giant tongue was busily licking away, back and forth, back and forth. At the next landing he went through another set of double doors. Several men carrying galleys of type ran by, shouting, and Hugh had to flatten himself against the wall to allow them past.

He watched them running away from him, before turning round and backing through yet more swing doors. All the time the noise grew louder. The thumping, the slurping and, alongside it, a dry, swishing noise – wind rushing through autumn trees.

He pushed open the swing doors. Immediately, some-thing made him look up. It was as if his attention had been snagged and hoisted into the air. There, far above his head, were taut ribbons of white paper, hurtling along on rollers and seeming to swoop down at him, then veering away towards the presses. He'd been here before. He could see the metal balcony where he'd followed the green-carder in search of directions and the narrow trapdoor he had disap-peared through. But then the presses had been idle, the ribbons of paper hanging limp from the roof.

Now everything was hectic. Everyone was busy. The paper was fed into vast black rollers, and then on through more rollers, with wire cages around them to stop anyone falling in. There were hundreds of rollers all packed together, spinning away, as pistons pumped and men stood on gantries above, peering down through the wire cages into the mass of frenzied machinery. Through huge slits in the floor he could see down to where the paper fed through onto the presses.

The whole building seemed to be throbbing with the sound of a giant heartbeat, and all the corridors, all the passageways that threaded their way through the building, were the arteries that emanated from here. All spreading out wildly, twisting, flailing, knotting themselves into different shapes, but all driven by these thundering black machines.

Rising up the walls at the far end of the presses and spreading out in a fan formation, like flocks of ascending birds, were the finished papers – printed, cut and held in place by spindly metal arms, being swept away on yet

270

more belts. Hugh could see the stream of blurred type, a long black stain speeding by as the papers were whisked away to be packed and loaded downstairs. The printing ink spattered everywhere. There was a dark slick on the floor and a cloud of tiny, inky particles hung dancing in the air above the rollers.

At the far end of the room, a section of floor had been cordoned off with a series of interlocked barriers. 'Keep Out' signs had been hung from the barriers. In the middle of the cordoned-off section the floor appeared to have collapsed. There was a small crater and a shallow depression running down to it on all sides. Several of the presses here were not in use, some looked as if they hadn't been used for a long time and were covered in crusted ink. Set into the far wall was a row of doorways. They looked like the entrances to monks' cells. Hugh could see a number of green-carders. Some were standing by the ink vats, talking, others were pushing trolleys full of neatly trussed papers.

As he watched, he realized the presses were coming to the end of their run. The last few ribbons of paper were being fed into the rollers. The thumping was less frantic now, but as it slowed down it sounded even more thunderous, more belligerent, than it had done before. The finished papers soaring overhead on their belts were slowing down, too. They looked as if only their momentum was keeping them aloft and they might all tumble back to earth at any moment.

Hugh closed his eyes and listened to these great booms resounding through him, rattling his ribs, shaking his flesh from his bones. When the last thump had died away, he returned the way he'd come – up the stairs, down the corridor, then through a set of doors into what he was confident would be the typesetting room. But it wasn't. This was somewhere he'd never been before.

He was in another enormous room. There were tables and chairs and a stainless-steel counter running down one side of the room. People were sitting at the tables and

271

queuing up along the counter, holding trays. Many of them appeared to be wearing rags.

On the other side of the counter women in white coats ladled food onto plates. The smell was so bad Hugh thought he might be sick. It took him a few moments to realize that he had finally found the canteen.

Chapter Twenty-Eight

The next morning the heating failed. There was no indication what had gone wrong. No-one seemed sure whose responsibility it was to look after the boiler, or indeed where it was. In the middle of the morning word came through that the boiler was now being repaired, but that it would be some hours before heat was restored. In the meantime, everyone sat at their desks and shivered. The cold reminded Hugh of railway stations, with the wind blowing down the platforms and cutting through your clothes. When he exhaled, clouds of condensation hung about in front of his face.

The newsroom was busy, everyone bashing away at their typewriters, as much out of a desire to keep warm as anything else. Battersby continued to patrol the aisles, head lowered, hands clasped behind his back. Hugh listened to the roll and clatter of keys around him. He imagined these thousands of words raining down on him, all jumbled and shredded and quite meaningless in their profusion. This great cascade of the literal world.

Opposite him, he could see Stanley's eye, vast and green behind his magnifying visor. It seemed to be looking at him, although he couldn't be sure. Vivien walked by as he was trying to concentrate. Her eyes were bright and her whole manner seemed to bristle with a kind of electric scorn. As she went past his desk their eyes met. Nothing more than that, yet Hugh found himself feeling oddly hopeful. He couldn't be sure why. It wasn't as if there had been any expression of encouragement in Vivien's face, even warmth come to that. Nonetheless, he was aware of something. He wasn't sure what. In the end he decided it was simply an absence of malice. This in itself didn't seem much to build on. But given the state of their relations lately it seemed to signal some sort of improvement, and for that at least he was grateful.

He swung round and watched her make her way to the Ladies, striding out with that new purposeful air of hers. Hair bouncing on her shoulders. She was wearing a tighter skirt than usual and Hugh noticed that as she walked her thighs brushed against one another. There was a heftiness about her that lent momentum to her move-ments, gave them a certain loping unstoppability. He thought of Scaife materializing out of one of the cubicles in the Ladies, out of the milky light and the eye-smarting stink of disinfectant, acting as if nothing untoward was going on, and once again he couldn't help feel a twinge of admiration.

Watching her go through the door into the Ladies, he noticed Industrial Gavin and Bobbie standing together near by. Bobbie was talking animatedly with much pointing of fingers and jabbing of elbows, craning upwards for additional emphasis. Gavin appeared characterist-ically impassive, stooping slightly to hear what was being said, but otherwise offering no reaction. Yet his whole manner seemed to Hugh to be heavy with disapproval. He guessed that Bobbie was telling another joke – presumably filthy – and had cornered Gavin, who felt that he had no choice but to listen.

It wasn't hard to imagine the effect this would have on Gavin, whose stern, low-church sensibilities were under-stood to be easily offended. He watched as Bobbie continued to talk, doubtless labouring to some foul crescendo, while Gavin stood unhappily alongside. Hugh thought he could detect various reactions passing in spasm across Gavin's face – disgust as well as disbelief.

At that moment, Darren came by with the tea trolley. As well as a cup of tea and a bun, he put some folded papers down on Hugh's desk. Hugh picked them up.

'What are these?'

'You know last night I told you I'd written down how I felt,' he said.

'Yes?'

'You said you'd like to have a look at it.'

'Of course,' said Hugh. 'Thank you.'

As Darren moved off, he opened the papers. There were several handwritten sheets. The top sheet was headlined, 'ON BEING TAKEN FOR GRANTED by Darren Dickinson'. Hugh immediately folded up the papers again and put them in his jacket pocket.

Then he turned back to see what was happening between Bobbie and Gavin. Bobbie was still talking. Gavin, meanwhile, reared back, as if loath to share the same air.

Hugh was quite unprepared for what happened next. Bobbie stopped talking. After a moment or two's pause Gavin began to laugh. Slowly, somewhat hesitantly at first, as if some long-rusted mechanism was turning again after years of neglect. Then with greater gusto, as he straightened up and threw his head back.

Bobbie, he saw, appeared almost as taken aback by this as he was, looking on with surprise and delight at having provoked such a reaction. That wasn't all. When Gavin had finished laughing he leant forward, bringing himself back down to the same level as Bobbie, and began to talk.

Hugh tried to remember if he'd ever seen Industrial Gavin talking before – except in the most cursory, reluctant way, as if there was something improper in the whole idea of conversation, let alone laughter. But here he was, apparently happily chattering away.

For some reason it was this more than anything else that made him realize just how quickly everything was changing around him. How things that had once appeared so fixed and immutable could no longer be taken for granted and were liable to the most unexpected transformations.

Gavin still appeared to be chattering away when Cliff walked past. Hugh expected Cliff to react in some way. Some measure of jealousy might be in order; if Gavin was going to talk to anyone, then by rights it ought to have been Cliff. He, after all, had been the one who'd nurtured him, who'd taken him under his wing.

Cliff, however, walked straight past without paying either of them any attention. At the time Hugh assumed that Cliff must be preoccupied with the editorial succession. At lunch, however, he learned that Cliff had something else on his mind.

'I don't know why you're making such a fuss,' Cliff was saying. 'I should never have brought it up.'

'Naturally, we're concerned,' said Johnny Todd; he had a ministering air to him as he went about his business of extracting information. 'Let me get this straight, you woke up and found Pauline gone.'

'I've already told you this once. What do you want to go through it again for?' Cliff sounded uncharacteristically flustered. He sat astride his stool, with his knees bent and his trousers broken into little ridges down his thighs. 'I woke up in the middle of the night and Pauline wasn't there. At first I assumed she'd just gone downstairs – I've often been troubled by night starvation myself, and I thought she'd probably gone to make herself a sandwich. When I got downstairs there was no sign of her. So I searched the house. But she wasn't there either.

'Next thing I did was look in the garden. By this time I was getting concerned. I mean, it was two thirty in the morning. I looked out the back. Then I thought I'd better check the front. I opened the front door and stuck my nose out. Then I put on my dressing gown and some slippers and walked down the street.

'It was a very cold night. There was frost on the ground. I got to the end of the road and I saw . . . nothing really at first. Just this pale shape by the side of a hedge. Standing there. When I got closer I saw it was Pauline. She was still in her nightdress, standing by the hedge, half hidden. I called out to her again, but she didn't seem to recognize me. It wasn't until I reached out and put my hand on her shoulder that she reacted at all.'

'Do you think she might have been sleepwalking, Cliff?'

'That's what I thought at first. But – I don't know – she didn't act as if she was asleep. She knew who I was, all right. But she wouldn't talk. I managed to persuade her to come with me, and we went back to the house. I got her into bed, and that was it. Then, this morning, she acted as if nothing unusual had happened.'

'Did you ask her what she'd been doing?'

'She just said she'd felt like a walk.'

'You don't think . . .'

'What?'

'Well, Cliff. You don't think these eye-exercises might have, you know, got her down?'

'She hasn't said anything. I'm sure she'd tell me. But Pauline's not a quitter. Never has been.'

'You haven't thought about seeing a psychiatrist, Cliff?'

Cliff shifted his buttocks in a half rotation round his stool.

'What do I want to see a psychiatrist for?'

'Not you. Pauline.'

'Pauline doesn't need to see a psychiatrist,' said Cliff. 'She just went for a stroll to clear her head, or whatever. My God, that's no reason to send her to some shrink. I daresay she's got things on her mind. Womanly things. Things that you and I can't have any conception of.' He laughed. 'It's not as if she's gone mental or anything.'

The silence that followed was broken by Johnny Todd, who said, 'No, Cliff. Of course not.'

It was five o'clock before the heating started working again. When it did, however, the building warmed up so quickly that people were soon shedding layers of clothing.

277

After that they began complaining they couldn't breathe. Hugh took off his jacket and hung it over his chair. As the office grew steadily hotter, the familiar smell of burned gravy began to seep out of the carpet tiles and rise once more into the atmosphere.

Chapter Twenty-Nine

Rain was falling. It spattered on the river and enveloped everything in a fine Scotch mist. Hugh walked along the highway, heading east towards Limehouse. It was the same road he'd driven down with Long to the morgue. Past the rust-coloured fortress of the News International building with its swirls of razor wire; past the estate agents' boards offering warehouse conversions; past the Hawksmoor church and the azure window of the car show-room opposite.

Back in the early eighteenth century, he'd read recently, there was a 'Wild Beast' shop along here where almost any animal could be purchased, however commonplace or exotic. Apes and elephants had been sold there, as well as mice. But the shop had disappeared long ago and it was hard to imagine anything less exotic than the stretch of road before him now.

On his left were tower blocks, irregularly dotted about. Between the tower blocks were strips of wasteground with clumps of muddy grass and streets truncated by wartime bombs. Over the last few years a lot of Asian families had moved into this area. Cowed-looking women darted silently about, swathed in long strips of material. A smell of curry lingered in the damp air.

Consulting Hollis's old gas bill, Hugh discovered that he had lived in one of these blocks. It turned out to be the furthest from the road and was set some way apart from the others, as if it had been quarantined off. Hugh circled the building looking for a way in. The entrance was hidden by a large white van that had been parked up on the pavement outside.

The lift was a tin box, refashioned by generations of amateur panel beaters. Hugh rode up to the sixth floor. The doors opened to reveal that it had stopped several inches short of its destination. He stepped up onto floor level. There was a concrete walkway ahead of him, a long grey gulch, open to the elements on one side with doorways into flats on the other. It was like walking along a jetty. Some of these doorways had been customized, turned into mock baronial entrances with brass knobs and carriage lamps hanging above. Others had metal grilles across them, to protect the occupants from unwelcome visitors.

Hollis's door was the last but one along the walkway. Before he took out the key, Hugh stood for a while looking out over London. Through the drizzle he could only see for a few hundred yards. Then everything merged into the same orange blur, with only dim silhouetted shapes beyond. Cars moved noiselessly through the rain. Below him were stooped figures scurrying for shelter, their heads sunk down into their shoulders.

The key from Hollis's box slid easily enough into the lock. Through the window of the next-door flat Hugh had seen the bright pink square of a television screen. He tried to be as quiet as possible. When he turned on the light switch nothing happened. He moved further into the flat. On the opposite wall, a little further along, was another switch. He pressed it. This didn't work either. He realized the power must have been turned off and cursed his stupidity for not bringing a torch.

He was standing in a hallway that led into a living room. One wall was covered with shelves, another had a large mirror fixed to it. He could see the outline of an easy chair and a trestle-table laden with piles of books. It was even colder than it had been in the office.

The curtains were drawn. He made his way over to the

window and pulled them open. It didn't make much difference; the flat was too high up to catch the glow from the street lights. There was a kitchen leading off the living room. White formica-fronted cupboards stood out in the gloom, as did a stainless-steel sink. He could make out an upturned mug on the draining board and a single saucepan on the cooker. He picked up the mug and felt that it was dry. He'd expected something else, he wasn't sure what, but the flat appeared unremarkable in every way. He went back into the living room and sat on the sofa. If he stayed there until it got light at least he'd be able to see more clearly. Even then, he suspected, he'd find nothing.

His eyes had become accustomed to the darkness. He saw that there was an additional door leading off the living room, which was closed. Opening it, he found himself in another curtained room. This one was smaller than next door. He was about to pull back the curtains when he heard something: a faint rustling sound, like pieces of material brushing against one another. He stopped and waited by the window, but the sound didn't come again. At the far end of the room he could see what he took to be a rug – a black rectangle on the floor, like a trapdoor. Beyond it was the low rumpled bulk of a bed against the wall.

As he stood there, a figure sat up in the bed and turned towards him. Hugh's first reaction was to cry out. But only a little moan of disbelief drifted out of his mouth. The figure in the bed stayed motionless. It seemed to be staring back at him. Then it swung itself up and got to its feet.

Still Hugh could see nothing except a dim outline before him. It began to come towards him. This looming shape, making its way across the room, growing in size all the time, yet somehow remaining as indistinct, as lacking in substance, as before. When the figure was about six feet away from him it stopped. Hugh could hear its tremulous breaths and make out two moist specks of light at around head height. Although he couldn't be sure – he couldn't be sure of anything – he had the impression of a grizzled countenance before him. As if the contours of its face were somehow smudged.

Momentarily, the figure seemed to rear back. Then it rocked forward, lunging for the door. Afterwards Hugh wondered what had possessed him to get in the way. He wanted to believe it might have been courage. He suspected, though, it was simply clumsiness. The two of them collided with one another and fell to the floor.

It was only at this point that Hugh could be sure the figure he lay entangled with was a man. He got to his feet first, but the man seemed to slither past him. One papery foot went into Hugh's face, the other paddled about on the floor. The man half-climbed to his feet, then tripped and fell again.

Hugh grabbed onto what he took to be his shirt-tails. As the man struggled to get away, Hugh could feel the material slipping through his fingers. With his other hand he managed to take hold of the man's calf. It was naked. He could feel the narrow shank of bone and the thin, dry skin. The shock of touching someone else's skin made him slacken his grip. Once again, the man tried to stand up. This time he managed to get to his feet, but, impeded by Hugh's grasp, he began twisting this way and that.

Together they tumbled through the doorway into the living room. All the time Hugh had the sense that he was wrestling not so much with a man as with a shadow. One who might vanish at any moment and leave him there feeling foolish, like the victim of some practical joke. But still they carried on, fumbling and flailing, furniture going over. The man struggling to get away, Hugh endeavouring to hold him. Hanging on as much through fright as anything else.

Now they were beneath the window. Hugh could feel the ridges of a radiator against his back. He lifted his head. As he did so, a cloud moved aside in the night sky. A sudden rush of moonlight filled the room. The shadow above him hardened and inflated. It became at once less sinuous, more bulky. He saw the features coalesce, as if they'd been rounded up and hurriedly pressed back into shape. Now the sense of disbelief hit him harder than ever. He rose to get a closer look at the man. For a few moments they stared at one another in the moonlight, clasped together.

Then Hugh was aware of toppling backwards. Sinking through the air in a long arc, like a diver. He felt a sharp blow on the back of his head, jolting his neck, throwing his head forward. And a flat, metallic note resounding in his ears, spreading all round. Then he fell into unconsciousness, like someone plunging into a pond.

When Hugh opened his eyes, the room had lightened. It had also become smaller and strangely distorted, tilted over to the left. He felt if he was to try and walk down the steeply canted floor he was sure to lose his footing and slide away, out of the picture. His first thought was that he must be on board a ship. A ship pitching heavily from one side to the other. He braced himself for it to slew the other way, flattening his hands on the floor. But it didn't. It stayed where it was. Stuck fast.

He looked up again and tried to work out what had happened. He could see a strip of carpet climbing away up the side of a narrow incline, and a chair skewed round so that only the front legs were visible. And over everything lay a sort of wash, like cloud drift, that swept slowly across the frame, from left to right. It took him some time to realize that he was gazing up into a large mirror. Not only was it reflecting the room in which he lay, but also a much fainter image of the sky outside, caught in the window above his head. Their two reflections were banging weakly against each other, back and forth, while he lay sandwiched between these planes of light and glass. Everything was twisted about, turned on its head. And, if he concentrated hard enough, he could stare into a long run of rooms and clouds. One overlaid on top of the other, flopping left upon right, right upon left, stretching off into infinity.

Hanging up in the left-hand corner was a picture. He

couldn't be sure what sort of picture it was at first, or how it was fixed to the wall. But there was a frame and he could make out what appeared to be some figures standing together, a cluster of blotched, silvery faces. He found that by narrowing his eyes he was able to bring them into focus. But the moment he widened them they once again blurred back into one another.

When he stood up everything swayed, then steadied itself. He stayed there for a while, not moving, waiting to make sure his legs didn't buckle. As they struggled, they must have knocked one of the trestles away from the table. It had collapsed. The books that were on it had slid to the floor in a small avalanche. He picked his way across them to the mirror and inspected his face. As he looked at his reflection – his face was unmarked, although his shirt collar was spotted with blood, like dabs from a shaving cut – he noticed the same framed picture that he'd seen from the floor. Once again it jutted into his eyeline, this time from a different angle.

He turned to his right. The picture was hanging on the wall above the fireplace. It was a framed page of the paper, specially made up to mark someone's farewell. Whenever anyone retired, their colleagues would print an imitation front page of the paper, complete with spoof articles and photographs. This would then be signed by everyone and presented as a leaving present, along with the metal plate from which the page had been struck.

It was one of these metal plates that had been framed and hung on the wall. There was a photograph in the middle of the page, or rather the negative of a photograph. He saw the same cluster of faces that he'd spotted from the floor. Except that now they looked quite different. He stared at them more closely, then took the frame off the wall and held it up in front of the mirror.

The faces switched from left to right. Hugh didn't recognize the man whose leaving party it was. Small and earnest-looking, with his feet planted wide apart, he was holding up what appeared to be two small saucepans.

People were gathered all around him. Scored into the surface of the metal he saw a younger Walter, more thick-set and with bushier hair.

Two places away from Walter, Hugh recognized the man whose photograph was on Field's union card, which he'd found in Hollis's room. He was standing facing the camera, the same rather bored, languid expression on his face. Hugh leaned towards the mirror to see if there was anyone else he could recognize. One or two of the other green-carders looked vaguely familiar, but nobody stood out. After a while their features started to disappear in the same blur as before and he felt his legs start to sway.

In the bedroom, he sat down on the bed. This room was quite undisturbed. Apart from the slept-in bed, there was a chest of drawers and a bedside table and chair. He looked about hoping to see some clothes, even a bag perhaps. But his assailant must have collected everything before he'd fled. He looked again, more carefully this time. There must be something here, he told himself.

He got up and stripped the blankets off the bed, then the undersheet. There were no pillowcases on the two pillows. He even turned over the mattress and examined the bed springs. Nothing. Then he opened the chest of drawers. It too was empty. He took out the drawers and felt about in the recesses. He pulled back the rug from the floor; he even shook out the curtains, although he had no idea what he expected to find.

In the living room he went through Hollis's belongings, flicking through the books, searching the shelves. This too proved fruitless. He righted the table and gathered the books into some semblance of a pile.

Chapter Thirty

The first person Hugh saw in the office was Julian. He was standing in the shadows by the vending machine with his hands in his pockets looking preoccupied.

'There you are, Hughie. I've been looking all over for you.'

'What's the matter?'

'I don't know,' said Julian. He twisted about unhappily and pushed his dark hair out of his eyes. 'I've been getting such a bad feeling recently. It's one of the worst feelings I've ever had. I keep waking up with this sense of dread, as if everything is falling apart.'

'Perhaps it is,' said Hugh.

Julian considered this. 'You don't think it's me?'

'Not necessarily.'

The idea that there might be some justification for Julian's sense of unease was a novel one, and he obviously needed time to mull it over. 'It's not just here, though, Hughie,' he said. 'I've been having problems at home, too.'

'Have you?' said Hugh.

A group of green-carders were walking slowly down the corridor towards them. They moved in a kind of fragile tandem, almost as though they were bound together; as if each was in some way helping the other along. Their dun-coloured cardigans hung by their sides.

'Did I tell you that I've been building this porch?' said Julian.

'Yes,' said Hugh, 'you did.'

'Did I?'

His manner suggested he had no recollection of ever having done so, and suspected this information may have been extracted from him by underhand means. 'Well, it's almost done now. But my neighbour has complained about it to the council. Says it's an eyesore. I've tried to reason with him, but he just won't see sense. He's complained to the council and says he wants it pulled down.'

From the other direction, a group of journalists were coming towards them. Moving more briskly, strung out across the width of the corridor, talking to one another. As they grew nearer, they made no effort to bunch up or to check their pace. Instead, they simply kept right on going, walking straight through the middle of the green-carders, who scattered before them, quite losing whatever semblance of co-ordination they had mustered. Meanwhile, the journalists swept on regardless, still talking, while the green-carders silently regrouped in their wake.

A sense of great tiredness overcame Hugh.

'Not now, please,' he said.

'What do you mean, not now?' said Julian.

'I've just got some problems of my own at the moment.'

Julian struggled to put this into some kind of context. 'Like my problems?'

'No,' said Hugh. 'Different problems.'

Julian looked at Hugh more closely.

'What's that brown stuff on your head?'

'Blood.'

He moved closer.

'My God, it is blood. What's it doing there?'

'I had an accident.'

'What sort of accident?'

'It doesn't matter.'

'Why won't you tell me what's going on?'

'Not now, all right,' said Hugh. 'Some other time.'

287

He moved away, hearing Julian's voice arch upwards behind him. 'No-one tells me anything. Why is everybody so secretive? There's something going on, isn't there?'

His voice trailed away. Hugh walked towards the office, then down the main aisle to the Gents. Great shafts of light from outside lit his way and almost dazzled him. Inside the Gents, the smell of disinfectant made his eyes smart; it seemed even stronger today than usual. He ran some water and dabbed at his head with a wad of damp lavatory paper. From the farthest cubicle he could hear the sound of loud, tuneless whistling. Not so much a tune, more a series of blasts, like a ship's foghorn. Whoever was in there was trying to alert everyone else to their presence. The whistling continued, only stopping when the chain was pulled.

Battersby came out of the cubicle. When he saw Hugh, he tugged as surreptitiously as possible at his clothing, then made his way over to another of the basins. Hugh continued to dab at his head. The damp lavatory paper turned a watery pink colour. Battersby didn't say anything and gave no other sign that he had registered his presence.

Instead of sitting at his desk, Hugh went downstairs. Along the corridor, past the vending machine, through the doors to the stairwell and down one flight of steps. Then along the corridor, as if he was going to the library. The air smelled dry and churchy. He pushed open the door. Walter was sitting at his desk, a single lamp shining above him, going through some papers.

When he saw Hugh he came to with a shudder.

'Ah,' he said. 'You gave me a shock.'

Hugh moved into the room. 'Can I ask you something?'

Walter readied himself beneath the hard cowl of light. He looked even more frail and brittle than usual.

'If you like.'

'Who is Malcolm Field?'

'What makes you think I know?'

'I came across a photograph of the two of you together.'

288

'Did you? Where was that?'

When Hugh didn't answer, Walter shrugged and said, 'He used to work here. Some time ago.'

'What happened to him?'

'I really can't remember. As I say, it's a good while ago now.'

'Is he still alive?'

'Again, I really can't say.'

'I think he died,' said Hugh.

'Did he?' said Walter. 'Well, I'm very sorry to hear it.'

'I think he used to work here and he died, and for some reason his death was concealed.'

'Why would anyone want to do that?'

'I don't know. That's what I want you to tell me.'

Hugh took out the Seaman's Discharge Book and the union card from the inside pocket of his jacket and put them on the desk. He tapped the photograph in the Seaman's Discharge Book. 'This man was staying at a Seaman's Mission until five weeks ago.' He tapped the photograph on the union card. 'In theory, this is the same man. Yet, as you can see, they look nothing like one another.'

Walter's hand reached out and touched the Discharge Book. His long fingers rested lightly on it but he didn't pick it up.

'What are you getting at?'

'Well, it would appear that, at some stage, Field died and another man took on his identity. That, at least, is how it appears to me. One of those men worked here. I don't know about the other.'

'And you think I do?'

'Do you?' said Hugh.

'Don't you think you're rather letting your imagination run away with you?'

'I wouldn't have thought so.'

'Why not?'

'I don't have an imagination. That's why I'm a journalist.'

Walter bent his head forward. 'I know rather less than you seem to imagine. As I said before, Hollis was a very remote man. Most of the time he stayed in the library and hardly saw anyone.'

He picked up the Seaman's Discharge Book.

'This man was a friend of Hollis's,' he said, pointing at the photograph. 'He'd come in and see him sometimes. I never spoke to him and we were never introduced. Hollis kept him out of the way. Now you'll want to know how his picture ended up in here, but I can't answer that. I don't know.'

The light in the room was the colour of old blankets. Hugh felt suddenly exhausted and his head had begun to throb again. Abruptly, and quite unexpectedly, the image of Vivien showering came back to him, as clear as it had been before. She was reaching up blindly to adjust the shower nozzle, her hair full of shampoo, water streaming down her shoulders. All the time now she seemed to be in his mind. However hard he tried to push her out, it was useless; she just came flooding back.

He took another step towards Walter's desk, thinking he might need to hold on to it. Then he looked at the papers sitting there. He swivelled round so that he could see them better; they appeared to be internal memos, sent from one department to another, laid out in a series of small piles.

'What's going on down here?'

Walter followed his glance. He slid the papers together beneath his hands.

'What makes you think there's anything going on?'

Again Hugh found he couldn't answer. His legs felt weaker than ever. He thought how odd it would be if he was to faint and Walter had to help him back to his feet.

'Why don't you give it a rest,' said Walter; his cornflower eyes looked concerned. 'You certainly look as if you could do with one.'

'I don't feel too good,' he admitted.

'Why don't you go home and have a lie-down?'

There were, thought Hugh, few things that he would rather have done.

'Sadly I can't,' he said.

290

*   *   *

'Julian's moping,' said Cliff. 'Look at him.'

Julian sat in the pub at lunchtime, his shoulders sagging, his head turned away.

'Something on your mind, Jules?' asked Johnny Todd. He spoke more loudly than usual, but Julian didn't answer.

Cliff looked on delightedly. He loved to see Julian like this and to pass inappropriate comments.

'Well,' he said, 'something's got him down. Could be something specific. On the other hand, could be a more general thing. What do you call it when you're sick of life? There's some German word.'

'*Weltschmerz.*'

'That's it, Hughie. Well done. *Weltschmerz.*'

'No,' said Hugh, 'the W is pronounced as a V – it's "*Veltschmerz*".'

'Never mind about that. You know who Julian reminds me of when he's in this state?'

Cliff gazed about, waiting for someone to make a guess. No-one answered.

'The drug woman!' he said triumphantly.

'Who's that?'

'Joy's friend. The one who sits and takes drugs in the churchyard. She's like that – walking around as if she's carrying a sack of coal the whole time.'

Abruptly Julian came to. 'What are you fucking saying?'

'See,' said Cliff, 'that got him.'

'I'm nothing like her.' Julian sounded very aggrieved. 'Nothing at all. If you must know – not that it's any of your business – I have some extremely awkward domestic problems.'

'Poor Julian,' said Cliff, and winked at the others.

'Anyway, she's not like that either,' said Hugh.

Cliff twisted in his seat and turned to him.

'Who isn't, Hughie?'

'Vivien.'

'What about her?'

'She's not like that,' he said again.

291

'Not like what?'

'Like you said.'

'How would you know?'

'I don't know,' said Hugh. 'I guessed.'

Cliff was looking at him more attentively. 'Did you now?'

'Yes.'

'What made you do that?'

Hugh shrugged. 'One just notices these things.'

'One does, does one?' said Cliff.

'If you keep your eyes open, you do. She's changed. I don't know why, but she's not the same as she used to be. That's all.'

Hugh took another sip of his drink, then stared back at Cliff. 'She's a much deeper, more complex person than you'd ever imagine,' he added.

Cliff continued to peer at him in an uncomprehending sort of way; his lips moving aimlessly.

'I'm in the funny farm,' he said at last. 'Eh? I must be. I can't hang about here. It's bad for my head.'

'Talking of heads,' said Julian. 'How's Pauline?'

'Very much better,' said Cliff, twisting the other way. 'She doesn't know what got into her the other night. Something must have disagreed with her. No, she's right as rain now. But thank you for your concern, Julian.'

'Battersby wants to see you,' said Darren.

It was late afternoon. Hugh's head had begun to pound in a thick, irregular way, as if there was something flailing around in there, a weighted sock being swung this way and that.

He got to his feet. As he did so, Darren asked, 'Did you read what I'd written?'

He remembered the pages of notepaper that Darren had given him the day before. He had forgotten all about them. The pages had stayed folded in his jacket pocket.

'Not yet,' he said. 'I'm sorry. But I will do.'

In preparation for the move, several of the desks had

already been taken away. As a result, the aisles were a good deal wider; it looked as if some road-widening scheme had swept through the office. There were gaps between the desks, with nothing there except patches of pale, liverish-green carpet tiles, uncovered and exposed to the light for the first time in generations.

Battersby was sitting in his glass-sided box, looking out at the flattened landscape all around. Hugh found he could hardly remember what buildings had been where. Only a few days before they had been standing, solid and familiar, yet now they seemed as distant and ghostly as Bridewell Palace. Hugh felt disorientated in these new surroundings, less certain than ever where he belonged.

Battersby sat with his hands resting flat on the top of his head, his glasses on the end of his nose. As he'd done in the lavatory, he ignored Hugh at first, only turning to him after a while, and looking at him with a dry sort of distaste.

'I've been trying to work out what to do with you,' he said.

'What have you decided?'

'Your presence here is becoming an embarrassment.'

'I'm sorry you feel that way.'

'I do feel that way,' said Battersby. 'When the editor . . . If the editor doesn't recover – which I'm afraid now looks inevitable – then I want to be sure that everyone here is working to their highest possible potential.'

'I see.'

It was as if he'd been allotted a length of string inside Battersby's head; that length of string was now coming to an end.

'Yes,' he went on. 'So if you don't come up with a decent story, then that's it. You understand what I'm saying? We can't be carrying passengers.'

'You're telling me this is my last chance.'

'This is your last chance. Exactly right. Spot on.'

Hugh gazed back at Battersby. He was filled with a sudden swell of loathing for him. He hated his scratchy,

293

clattering manner, his relish for humiliating people, his blinkered little mind, his ridiculous hair. It struck him that he knew nothing about his private life – if he was married, had children, where he lived. He wondered if there was a softer, more humane side to Battersby. Some vast senti-mental streak that only came out on family occasions. Almost inevitably, he thought, and this only made him hate him the more.

'I think I have got a story,' he said.

'You have?' Battersby couldn't conceal his surprise. 'What's that?'

Once again, Hugh began to tell him about Field and the Seaman's Discharge Book. Battersby shifted about irritably in his chair and took his hands off his head.

'Not again. Can't you leave that bloody thing alone?'

'I've found out more, though.'

'More? Who wants more of it?'

'Please,' said Hugh, 'just listen to me. A man jumps off Hungerford Bridge and drowns. Behind him, he leaves a coat with a Seaman's Discharge Book in it in the name of Field. It turns out that this man Field has disappeared from the Seaman's Mission where he's been staying; he's been missing for about three weeks. It therefore looks as though Field and the drowned man might be one and the same.'

'I'm with you so far,' said Battersby reluctantly.

'There's a photograph of Field in the Seaman's Discharge Book. Now, Field proves to look remarkably like an older version of the round-the-world yachtsman Tom Kingman, who disappeared and was declared dead almost twenty years ago. Not only that, Field is in possession of Kingman's logbooks from his yacht, and their handwriting is the same. So, it's beginning to look more and more like Kingman and Field are the same person.'

Battersby didn't say anything.

'But then it turns out that the drowned man wasn't Kingman or Field at all. He was a man called Hollis, one of the green-carders who worked downstairs.'

'Downstairs?' said Battersby. 'I had no idea.'

'Hollis, then, had drowned himself, leaving behind Field's Discharge Book.'

'Yes . . . why would he do that?'

'Possibly so that people would assume it was Field who had died. But there's a further complication.'

'Oh God,' said Battersby. 'Is there?'

'I think that, at some stage, Kingman took over Field's identity. Either to enable him to get work, or to have somewhere to live.'

Battersby's eyes began to flicker back and forth; he was wrestling with his gullibility, attempting to subdue it.

'There was a man,' said Hugh, 'an old friend of Kingman's from Devon, who reported seeing him, alive, ten years ago, walking along the beach at Romney Sands. At the time he was quite sure it was him, but then he changed his mind. The envelope with this story in it was missing from the library. I found it hidden in Hollis's room.'

'Why would he want to conceal it?'

'Perhaps he was trying to protect Kingman.'

Outside, Battersby's secretary had started to tap on the glass. Battersby ignored it. 'So what you're saying is that you think Kingman is still alive – after all this time?'

'I don't know. It's possible.'

'And where is he now then?'

'I have no idea,' Hugh admitted.

Battersby shook his head.

Again his secretary tapped on the partition wall.

'Go away,' he shouted.

'I have the Home Secretary's office on the line,' she said.

'Do you? What do they want?'

'He wants more time for his dog piece.'

'How much more time?'

'That's what they want to talk to you about.'

Battersby muttered exasperatedly to himself, then called out, 'You'd better keep them on the line.'

He turned back to Hugh.

'All right, I'll tell you what I'll do. You've got two days to find Kingman and write the story. Otherwise you're out. Is that clear?'

'Quite clear.'

'Good,' said Battersby. 'Now leave me alone.'

Chapter Thirty-One

When Hugh reached the restaurant where he and Noel had
arranged to meet there was no sign of him. He asked the
waiter if a reservation had been made for two in the name
of Chivers. The waiter looked down his list.

'The reservation is for three,' he said.

'Are you sure?'

The waiter wasn't sure; he hadn't taken the reservation
himself. Nonetheless, he sat Hugh down at a table with
three places. The restaurant was rather smarter than the
ones they were used to. There were even other people
there. Hugh waited. Noel was late. This too was unheard
of. Hugh had grown so used to keeping Noel waiting that
he couldn't help but feel offended by such behaviour. He
also found himself troubled by a faint sense of dread; he
suspected it must have rubbed off from Julian. It grew
steadily over the next few minutes.

When Noel came in he had his head back and was
laughing. His hair had been combed down. There was a
girl with him. She too was laughing, but in a more
restrained, more appreciative way. The girl was tall and
blonde and wore some sort of jerkin.

Hugh lowered his head to the wine list, as if to shut
himself inside it.

'This is Monica,' said Noel.

'Hello,' said the girl.

Hugh lifted his head. 'Hello,' he said.

There was an air of glassy good humour about Noel, a kind of unfocused sheen of pride. So much so that, having performed the introductions, he plainly had difficulty either talking or moving. The girl helped him into a chair. But once there he did little except play with his cutlery. The waiter came to take their orders, which seemed to take even longer than usual. After several minutes of indecision, Monica took hold of Noel's forearm by way of encouragement. He turned to her, grinning. She had to guide his attention back to the menu.

Eventually he made his choice. As soon as he'd done so, Monica excused herself and went to the lavatory. It was in the nature of their friendship that Hugh should have prepared himself for an eventuality such as this. He knew that. However, he had not, and now that it was here he found it took him a while before he could ask the question the occasion demanded.

'What happened?'

Noel looked at him from out of his glassy haze and blinked.

'She answered my call,' he said.

'What call?'

'I broadcast my message on the radio, just like I told you I was going to do.' His face clouded over. 'You said I was mad, that it would never work. But it did. You were wrong. Three days later – when I'd almost given up hope – I got this call from one of the radio stations saying someone had called them and giving me a number. So I phoned up and it was her.'

'And that was it?'

'Yes,' said Noel, 'that was it.'

They sat in silence until Noel said, 'Are you all right, Hughie? You look terrible.'

'I'm all right,' said Hugh.

As Monica sat down again he said, 'I was just telling Hugh how we met.' She smiled, apparently finding nothing unusual about the circumstances. In one sense, of course, she was right. People meet like that the whole time

298

– chance encounters that determine the course of their lives. But there was an awkward equation here: the more you spent your life waiting for such an encounter, the less likely it was to happen. He was reminded of the West Indian woman in Harlesden, sitting in her living room with her children chopped up in rubbish bags around her, patiently waiting to be hoovered up into the sky. After a while doubts must have begun to set in. What was happening? Something had gone wrong. They weren't coming – she'd been overlooked, had dropped through the net.

Monica was a slightly bossy, talkative girl with inward-sloping teeth, who worked in a legal firm and went riding at weekends. They could only have spent a few days together, but already, Hugh saw, a pattern to their behaviour had established itself. The change in Noel was more pronounced than anything he would have believed possible. That mirthless little flicker of a smile had gone. So too had that dulled, wounded look Hugh had grown used either to provoking, or seeing stamped already on his features.

Not only that. All the deluded optimism – those alternating bursts of doggedness and hesitancy, that unbroken line of failure stretching back for as long as either of them could remember – all those things, in fact, that Hugh had come to rely on in Noel, to regard as the cornerstones of their friendship, had disappeared.

In their place was this terrible eagerness that he'd never actually seen directed at anyone before. A rapt, puppyish expression that came over Noel's face whenever Monica said anything. Far from being put off by this, she seemed to take enormous pleasure in it.

Hugh found he could only watch and make the most cursory contributions to the conversation. That and drink. He drank with an increasing sense of abandon, slopping wine into his glass and throwing it back in an effort to improve his mood. But nothing happened. Nothing, except that the evening slid by like a raft, with Hugh wanting to throw himself overboard, yet dreading being left behind.

There was, he had noticed before, a look that came over certain people when they were happy. A joyous yet apologetic look, as if they knew they were doing something untoward and naturally felt awkward about being so exposed, but couldn't help themselves. All their normal safeguards were down.

'Stop me,' they seemed to be saying, but in fact they weren't saying that at all. They'd cast away all those things they'd worked so hard to maintain – poise, self-preservation, a sense of proportion. Instead, big, idiotic grins spread over their features and stayed there. You tried to reach out to them, to offer guidance, but they were gone, lost in this fug of enchanted disbelief.

'You should see Monica riding,' Noel was saying. 'She looks completely at home in the saddle.'

'But you did very well yourself,' she said.

Hugh roused himself.

'You rode a horse?'

'I did actually,' said Noel. 'Very good fun. Of course, my horse wasn't anything like Monica's. I found out afterwards they normally use it to give rides to backward children.'

'But it was a start,' said Monica.

'Exactly,' he agreed. 'It was a start.'

It was around about then that Monica dug Noel gently in the ribs. At first Hugh wondered if he'd triggered some private joke between them. Then he realized it was just an intimate thing. There was nothing overt or self-conscious about her behaviour. Indeed, Noel didn't even react to it. Nonetheless, Hugh didn't think he could have felt any worse if they'd climbed on the table and torn one another's clothes off.

'Do you ride?' she asked him.

'Not the type,' he said.

'That's just what Noel said. But it's amazing what you

can do if you're only willing to try. I could easily get you a mount if you like.'

Soon afterwards Hugh knocked over a glass of wine. But there wasn't much in it and what there was went mainly over him. The waiter helped mop him up and poured another glass.

When they got up to go, Noel and Monica offered him a lift. Hugh refused. Noel asked how he was going to get home. Hugh said that he'd walk to a tube. He stuck to his story when he was reminded they were some way from a station.

'It was very enjoyable meeting you,' said Monica.

They were standing outside. She held out her hand. Hugh took hold of it, rather more firmly than she'd been expecting. She winced and tried to pull her hand away.

'I'm sure we'll all meet again soon,' she said.

Further concern was expressed by Noel about how Hugh was going to get home.

'Are you sure you're all right?' he said in a low voice. 'You were chucking it back in there.'

'I'm absolutely fine. One hundred per cent.'

'I don't like to just leave you here.'

'Please don't worry about me.'

In the end they had little choice but to leave him by the side of the road. They waved and hooted as they went by.

After they'd gone Hugh began to walk. He wasn't so drunk that he couldn't keep his footing and walk in a straight line, but he still found that everything streamed past surprisingly fast – buildings as well as cars – so that soon he had only a dim notion of where he was.

At one stage he sat down on a bench by a canal. It was only after he'd been there a while that he realized he was holding his head in his hands. There'd always seemed something absurdly theatrical about such a gesture. Before he'd felt blindly miserable, now he found himself doubting his misery, as if it was as affected as his posture. Even so, he stayed where he was for some time longer. He looked at the flat black surface of the canal with the surrounding houses reflected on it. Big white houses behind high white walls, all neatly inverted, balanced on their chimneys. There were a few willow branches trailing in the water, and a waving thicket of darker subterranean branches reaching up from below.

Only a few weeks earlier the canal had been frozen over. There had been pictures of it in the paper, with children sliding about on trays and dogs losing their footing. But now, although it was still cold, there was no ice, no dusting of frost, to be seen. Perhaps spring was coming, he wondered.

Hugh had no idea how long he stayed there. But then he didn't know what made him start walking again. The rest had sobered him up a bit, and after a while he found himself paying closer attention to where he was. There were mansion blocks on either side of the street. It was like walking down a huge red-brick canyon. The moon hung above in a cloudless sky. It seemed to be full, or somewhere near it, fat and bulging and speckled with grey.

Although he couldn't be sure, there was something familiar about his surroundings. Most of the mansion blocks had been done up. He could see the carpeted hallways within and the polished brass on the lift gates. But as he went on they grew shabbier, more neglected. The brick looked as if it was somehow dustier, the hallways were unlit.

He walked on for a while. Then he stopped outside one of the front doors and rang the bell. There was no reply. He rang again, leaning on the buzzer. This time he heard a voice through the intercom. It sounded thick with sleep and annoyance.

'Yes?'

He spoke slowly, in order to make sure he was understood.

'I want to come in,' he said.

'Who is it?'

'Please let me in.'

He imagined his voice disappearing off up the stairwell inside.

'What do you want?'

'I want to come in.'

'What for?'

'I want to see you.'

'What's the matter?'

'I want to see you,' he said again.

There was a pause.

'It's too late.'

'Help me,' said Hugh.

'What's the matter?'

'Help me.'

'Are you hurt?'

He didn't answer.

He heard a sigh through the intercom.

'You'd better come in.'

Chapter Thirty-Two

A thin yellow light shone through the glass above the front
door. It lit up the hallway and the stairs. Hugh stopped at
each of the landings and looked up. At first he saw
nothing. Then he began to make out a figure above him,
slowly taking shape. She seemed to be wearing a white
dressing gown, or nightdress, that made her stand out like
a pale spectre in the darkness. She stood and watched him
climb towards her without saying anything.

When he got to where she was standing she didn't say
anything, but turned and let him follow her into the flat.
Now that he was here, it was less familiar than he'd
expected. He thought that he'd imprinted the layout on his
mind, but somehow the place was smaller than he remembered. Smaller and less densely furnished. He sat on the
edge of the sofa while Vivien sat in an armchair opposite
and tucked her feet beneath her thighs.

She regarded him through her curtain of tangled hair.
As he'd learned before, there could be something oddly
soothing about Vivien's presence. Not necessarily that
often. Sometimes she gave the impression of just biding
her time before another burst of hostility. But it was
enough. Sometimes it could be enough.

'Why have you come here?'

Hugh found he couldn't speak. He tried once or twice,
but he felt choked and didn't want to carry on. Besides, he
found that he had no wish to say anything. Not for the time

being anyway. He just wanted to stay sitting where he was and not think at all. So he shook his head, leant back and closed his eyes instead.

It seemed to him that he had held himself back for longer than he could remember. Parcelled himself up and held himself back. It was as if he was laden with all these unexpressed feelings, like a bursting sack. The more he tried to purge himself of these longings, these liabilities, the more they seemed to swell inside him and weigh him down. Still he kept it tied as tight as he could, fearful of letting anyone see him unravelling. Now he realized he didn't much care any more what happened.

'I wanted to see you,' he said.

She turned her head away.

'Why?'

'I don't know. I just did.'

'That's because you're drunk.'

'Probably,' he agreed. 'Although I'm not as drunk as I was.'

'You stink of wine.'

'Yes, but that's because I spilled it. I was unhappy,' he said. 'And I thought I'd be less unhappy if I came here.'

'Are you?'

'Yes.'

'Why?'

Hugh found he was unable to answer this.

'Are you expecting to stay here?'

'I don't know,' he said. 'It doesn't matter.'

Then Vivien got up and came over to the sofa. Hugh thought that she was going to sit beside him. But she simply stood over him, looking down, as if to inspect him more closely. The bottom of her nightdress was trimmed with lace. Hugh could see the white cotton folds falling away in front of his eyes. Without thinking, he took hold of the back of her knees and embraced them.

'What are you doing?'

She put her hands on his shoulders to steady herself, but toppled over onto the sofa. She lay there with her knees across his and her hair spread out over the cushions.

'What did you do that for?'

'I felt like it,' he said.

She sat up and pushed her hair back. Her feet stuck out of the bottom of her nightdress. They swung about from side to side. He watched them, fascinated. Then she put them down on the floor and stood up.

'It's late. I'm going back to bed. You can sleep on the sofa if you want. There are blankets in the cupboard.'

'I'm not sorry I came here, you know,' said Hugh.

'It's all right,' she said. 'Good night.'

'Good night.'

When she had gone he made himself as comfortable as he could on the sofa. He lay back, thinking he might review the events of the evening, replay them in his mind. But before he could properly begin he fell asleep.

When he woke up his head was spinning. He looked at his watch. It was just after ten past three. There was a faint glow from the street lights outside, which seemed to roll beneath the curtains like a mist, and a thin, regular creaking noise, as if the house were swaying in the wind. He got up and crept along the corridor to Vivien's room and listened at the door. He thought he could hear the sound of her breathing. Then he wondered if it wasn't his own breathing he was listening to.

As quietly as he could, he turned the doorknob. The bedroom was darker than the living room, but he could still see Vivien lying in bed, her head turned towards him. Her face was very pale and her mouth was open. One arm was flung out across the pillows. He stood there. Then he went and sat on the edge of the bed. Asleep, she looked quite different. Untroubled. Calmer. As if all her cares and woes had fallen away.

He reached out and put his fingertip in the hollow at the crook of her arm, just where her skin was at its whitest. A tremor ran through her, but she didn't pull her arm away. A sound came out of her mouth, a long, swooping sort of sigh. He knew he had no business being in her bedroom, but neither could he bring himself to leave. He stayed there looking at her until it began to get light.

When he got up to go, Vivien said, 'What are you doing?'

'I thought you were asleep,' he said.

'I was asleep.'

'I'm going now.'

'What were you doing?'

'Just watching you.'

'How long for?'

'An hour or so. Maybe longer.'

She looked down the front of her nightdress, as if checking for signs of interference.

'Why were you watching me?'

'I wanted to.'

'God, you're a strange man,' she said.

'Am I?'

'Yes,' said Vivien, 'you are.'

Hugh felt enormously pleased. He couldn't think of anything anyone had ever said to him that had delighted him more.

'I couldn't sleep,' he said, pointlessly. He didn't want this ebb and flow of conversation between them to subside.

'Why not?'

'I was thinking.'

'What about?'

'Do you really want to know?'

'I'm awake now,' said Vivien.

And so he told her. He told her what he'd told Battersby earlier – about Field and Kingman and the logbooks – but this time with rather more confidence than before. And he told her he would be sacked if he didn't find Kingman in two days. Once again he had the impression that he was unloosing this heavy sack and shaking out its contents on the floor.

'You think the man in Hollis's flat was Kingman?' Vivien asked.

Hugh remembered the features hanging over him in the

307

moonlight, bunching together, hardening for an instant.

'I think so. I can't be sure, though.'

'If it was him, where is he now?'

Hugh shook his head. 'There are so many things I don't understand. This name, for instance, "Bellamare". It crops up in one of the logbooks when Kingman is feeling really desperate. Presumably it refers to something in his past, but I've no idea what.'

He looked over at Vivien. She lay there with her head back, not saying anything. She remained that way for some time. Hugh wondered if she'd gone back to sleep. But when he looked more closely he saw that her eyes were open and she was staring up at the ceiling. He fell to pondering once more. After a while he became aware that the light which had been spreading under the curtains seemed to have come to a halt.

At around the same time, the quality of the silence between them changed from being restful to something else. To begin with, Hugh assumed this was simply his imagination. He wondered what could have brought it on. He looked over at Vivien, but she hadn't moved. Nonetheless, something had changed, he felt sure of it. There was a tightening around his chest. Not unpleasant, but a general sense of constriction, as if the air was less plentiful than it had been before.

He got to his feet. His head felt light and he thought he might topple over.

'Where are you going?' said Vivien.

'I thought I might go out into the corridor.'

'What would you want to do that for?'

Hugh wasn't sure he could answer this. He might have said that he wanted to breathe more easily. But in the event he said nothing. What did he want? Only to be alone for a moment and to relish this sense of uncertainty, of being sandwiched between one thing and another.

So he left the bedroom and stood outside in the cold corridor, and he felt eagerness, gladness and tranquillity descend on him in roughly equal measure, falling through the air. There was also something else he wanted to check. He opened the bathroom door. On the right was a basin and beyond that a bath. He looked at the bath. There was a shower coiled around the tap and a hook on the wall to hang it from.

Then he came back in and got into bed beside Vivien. She didn't move, just as he'd hoped she wouldn't. What delight he took in this indifference, or acceptance, or whatever it was. He didn't know. He didn't want to know. And when he reached across and touched her, still she didn't react. It was marvellous, he thought, to be lying in the half-light, dark enough to be concealed from one another. This brittle divide between them where anything might happen, with the world spreading out all round like a mill pond.

But when he moved his hand she flinched, and he heard her catch her breath.

'What is it?'

'Nothing,' she said.

He moved his hand again.

Once more he felt her flinch.

'I'm a bit sore,' she said.

'Sore? Why is that?'

Sounding unusually embarrassed, Vivien said, 'It's that liquid from the vending machine. It scalded me. You'll have to be careful.'

He had never imagined that sex between them could ever be anything other than the angry, flailing, upright sort of sex they'd had before, like monkeys scrambling to the uppermost branches of a tree. He held himself above her, trying to make sure he wasn't chafing her skin, doing all he could to be gentle. Slowly, cautiously, they moved together. As they did so, Hugh was struck by a thought. He didn't care to be distracted, but it came to him anyway. It seemed to him that what they were giving one another in terms of enjoyment was matched by what each of them was holding back. Even at the moment of their greatest intimacy, it was as if some small sphere of secrecy stayed intact. A measure of impenetrability was retained. Yet, far from diminishing that intimacy, it seemed instead to enhance it.

Afterwards they lay together in bed. The day had leap-frogged forward. The room was now light. The curtains hung ineffectually in front of the windows, merely softening the light rather than shutting it out. Hugh looked at the pink patches on Vivien's thighs, lightly tracing their outline with his finger. They were like continents set on the white of her skin. Great uncharted lands. A world seemed to be taking shape before him; it drifted up from the bedclothes and sat hovering there, within reach. They could be its only inhabitants, could do whatever they wished, lose themselves completely.

'Bella mare,' said Vivien from somewhere above his head.

He was so engrossed that he didn't pay much attention. 'What about it?'

'It means beautiful sea in Italian.'

'Are you sure?'

'Of course I'm sure,' said Vivien. 'Bella, beautiful. Mare, sea.'

Still he carried on tracing with his finger on her skin, careful not to stray onto any inflamed areas.

'But in the logbook Kingman spelled it as one word. What do you think that means?'

'Perhaps it's the name of something.'

'Of what, though?'

Vivien didn't reply.

He heard the sounds of day starting up outside: the rumble of traffic, shouts in the street.

'Could be a guest house,' she said. 'Or a bed and breakfast. When I was a child we used to go and stay by the sea. All the guest houses had names like that.'

Hugh stopped what he was doing.

He raised himself up to face Vivien. As he did so, he saw that edge of defensiveness come back into her eyes. It was the first time he'd noticed it in a while.

'I don't know,' she said, shrugging. 'It's only an idea.'

Chapter Thirty-Three

Hugh couldn't remember when he'd last driven out of London into the country. He didn't count the two journeys to the Seaman's Mission. On both occasions it had been dusk, and there'd only been the briefest glimpse of sparsely covered fields before the buildings closed in again. But now, as he finally left the suburbs behind and saw green fields around him, he felt his heart lifting. He was almost tempted to stop the car, jump over the hedge and roll about in the long grass, just for the pleasure of feeling the dampness on his skin.

He didn't, of course. He kept on going. But he wound down the window and breathed in deeply, smelling the exhaust fumes and the fresher air that blew across the tarmac and buffeted round the inside of the car. A flock of birds swooped down on the traffic coming towards him, then wheeled away, as if they too were casting off the stiffness of confinement, stretching their wings.

The journey took longer than he expected. The road was busy, with lorries heading to Dover and families off on winter breaks. But he was in no hurry. He stayed in the middle lane and watched as the land flattened out around him and the fields gave way to larger, scrubbier patches of grass, dotted about with hunched fruit trees. The frost had melted and the ground looked soft and boggy, with pools of water lying in the hollows.

After almost an hour and a half he turned off the

motorway and made his way down narrower, deeper lanes with muddy banks rising up on either side of him. There was no sign that he was near the coast. Then, coming out of a long left-hand bend, he caught sight of what might have have been sand, a smudge of khaki, in the gap between two wooden chalets. He couldn't be sure. Almost immediately, a concrete wall, much thicker at the bottom than the top, cut him off from any further views. He followed the signs for Romney Sands. After two or three miles, the wall abruptly tailed off, as if it had plunged underground, and there at last was the sea.

The tide was out. There was a wide horseshoe bay spreading out in front of him, and far, far away in the distance, a ruffled band of white where the waves began. And now he did stop, pulling over onto a patch of gravel by the side of the road. The ground in front of the car shelved down onto the beach. The tufts of gorse and dry spiky grass had scraps of litter impaled on them. On the other side of the road he saw a narrow railway track laid on top of the sand and scrub, the rough brown rails heading off around the bay.

Something of the mingled exhilaration and disappointment he remembered from childhood visits to the seaside swept over him. The anticipation of arrival, and then, after all the build-up, the disbelief, the refusal to believe that this could be it, that they had arrived. To his dismay he felt his eyes brim with tears and he had to force himself to concentrate on the view.

The sky too seemed to shelve down into the water. They were both the same shade of grey, but, if anything, the sky looked slightly darker, as if it was bearing down on the sea, soaking it up. People were walking on the beach, striding out, their movements oddly exaggerated, leaving lines of footprints behind them that soon faded and disappeared in the sand. Dogs ran about wildly, their feet churning, kicking up clouds of sand behind them.

Now that he was here he had little or no idea what he was going to do. He didn't want to think about it, at least not for a while, and so he stayed put, sitting in the car with his head back, gazing out of the windscreen. In the end it was hunger that made him move. When he opened the door, the smell of salt and seaweed was so strong it reminded him of the tang of disinfectant in the lavatory at work.

He walked to the nearest pub, but they'd stopped serving food, so he just had several packets of nuts and a pint and a half of gassy cider. There were only three other people in the pub; none of them were talking, but they stood watching the racing on television, their faces obediently lifted to where the set was fixed on a bracket above the bar.

Afterwards Hugh went for a walk on the beach. He hoped that the breeze, the exercise and the cider might dislodge the things that were on his mind. It didn't; they slewed about and bumped into one another, but otherwise showed no sign of budging. When he got back to the car he drove until he reached a cluster of shops. Despite the weather, all of them had buckets and flippers strung from the awnings and rubber rings stacked up in teetering columns outside.

In the first four shops no-one knew what he was talking about, and the sense of relief almost made him turn round and head home. But he kept on going, driving on to the next cluster of shops. The railway tracks ran parallel to the road. The railway itself wasn't running – it was only open during the summer, he was told. But every so often there were miniature stations with thin strips of platform and their names hanging on chains.

He tried again at the next group of shops. Here were the same beach toys and bottles of sun cream. Once again, everyone looked at him blankly. Slowly he made his way round the bay. In this manner the afternoon went by. He never had a glimmer of success, no tiny twitches of recognition. Some people rolled the name around in their mouths, trying it out for familiarity. Others simply shook their heads and waited for him to go away. Either way the result was the same.

The tide came in. The long, pale strand of sand grew steadily narrower. The walkers on the beach began to go home, calling for their dogs in exasperated voices. The sun sank swiftly and undramatically into the sea. The light faded. The temperature fell. Again, Hugh trudged back to his car and drove on. By now he was almost at the far end of the bay. He looked at his map and saw that the road soon turned inland.

By now it was dark. The wind had got up and there were half-hearted gusts that buffeted the side of the car. He passed a number of old railway carriages that had been converted into homes by the fishermen, their wheels buried in the shingle at the top of the beach. Ahead of him, on his right, there was a fish-and-chip shop next to a deserted car park. He stopped again. There were photographs in the window of pieces of fish and other food that was on sale. The photographs had faded so that the fish were all but invisible and the gherkins alongside were almost turquoise-coloured.

There was a woman inside. Hugh bought some chips then asked if she'd heard of a guest house called Bellamare. The woman thought she recognized the name. She repeated it several times, but couldn't be sure. Nevertheless, she directed him to where she thought it might be. He should carry on for another mile or so, until the road forked, with the main road bearing inland and another, smaller road continuing to follow the shore.

Hugh drove to where the road forked. The left-hand road was covered in places by drifts of sand and marked out on either side with lines of rusted railings. His wheels made a soft, shushing sound as they rolled over the sand drifts.

The road led out onto a spit of land that jutted out into the sea like an extended tongue. Towards the tip were several houses. Maybe it was the light, the dusk, or just his mood, but instead of getting bigger as he drove towards them, the houses seemed to stay where they were, hanging suspended before him, so that it wasn't until he'd pulled up outside the nearest one that he could be sure he'd really arrived.

But once here they seemed normal enough. Much like the other houses along this stretch of coast, the same dream homes and hideaways. Pebble-dashed bungalows with glassed-in porches, and then larger, steep-gabled, Edwardian buildings, blotched by the sea air, with spongy-looking woodwork, hung with tiles, and with faded signs outside offering rooms.

Again he got out of the car. Outside the air had turned colder and damper. He could taste the salt on his lips and feel it crystallizing on his exposed skin. He could hear the waves breaking close by, flopping over and over. A slow, constant churning almost under his feet. Some of the houses appeared deserted, even derelict. It was hard to tell. Others had lights on behind curtains with stretched, wavering shapes beamed across the folds of material. It was still possible to make out the shape of boats beached on the shingle, along with the wire hawsers that had pulled them out of the water. They formed a criss-cross of hard black lines against the gloom.

He began to walk down the line of houses, looking at the names. Most had no names or numbers. Near the end of the spit there was a house standing on its own. He climbed the steps. There was a wooden sign nailed to the brickwork, with the letters scored into the wood. He read them quite easily, familiarly – 'Bellamare'. And, beneath it, 'Vacancies'.

He pressed the bell. There was no sound from within, so he pushed against the door. It was unlocked. There was a light on inside. The hallway was deserted. He'd expected a reception desk of some kind, or a landlady who would emerge bustling from a back room. But there was no desk, no landlady. Nothing.

He stood and waited for a while. No-one came. On the left-hand side of the door was a small table for the post. Hugh looked through it. Most of the letters had been there for some time. The envelopes felt as if they'd been stiffened by the salt. None of the names on them meant anything. For the first time he realized he wasn't even sure who to ask for. He was standing there wondering what to do when he heard a movement from upstairs. The sound of a tread on bare boards, and then a door closing.

He began to climb the stairs. There was carpet on the first flight, covering the full width of the stairs. But on the next flight it shrank to a thin strip that meandered about like a trail of spilt paint. He stopped to see if he could hear anything. The sound of footfalls came to him again, louder this time. It seemed to be coming from the door to his left. He knocked and waited.

When the door opened he saw an old woman standing before him.

'Excuse me,' Hugh began. 'I'm looking for someone I believe lives here.'

'Who's that?'

'A man. His name is Field, or perhaps Kingman.'

'Not here,' she said, much more loudly than necessary. Her voice echoed round the stairwell. Hugh assumed she was deaf. Then something about the way she was standing made him suspect she was drunk.

'Not here,' she repeated.

'Yes,' said Hugh. 'I'm sorry.'

She reached for the door knob and Hugh saw how the skin had bunched like loose cuffs around her wrists. Holding on with one hand, she shook herself about until she was more comfortable.

'There's only the three of us,' she said. 'I'm the only woman. There's Mr Hobbs and Mr Pine, that's all. Mr Hobbs doesn't get out much any more, not since his wife died. He stays in his room.'

'I see,' said Hugh. 'And Mr Pine?'

'Mr Pine. Mr Pine I don't see much either.'

'How long has he been here?'

'Why do you want to know?' she asked.

'There's something I need to talk to him about,' said Hugh. 'It's important,' he added.

She smiled at him without saying anything. He couldn't tell what was going on, if he was being mocked, or if she was just collecting her thoughts.

'He came here about a week ago,' she said. 'I introduced myself to him on the stairs. That's all. I've hardly seen him since.'

'Which room is he in?'

'Next flight up,' she said. 'Number seven.'

'Thank you.'

He continued up the stairs and knocked on the door of number seven, but there was no reply. He tried again. Still nothing. After a while, he went back downstairs and out of the front door. He leant on the railings outside and watched the sky turn from mottled cream to black. Afterwards he wondered how long he'd stayed there, facing out to sea. It must have been at least an hour, he decided. Possibly longer. But time seemed to have grown baggy, to have stretched obligingly around him, so that he couldn't be sure what was going on. He had a sense of inevitability, yet also of boundless possibility.

He wasn't sure what made time snap shut again and resume its natural course. He wasn't aware of hearing anyone coming. Nor did he see anything; he wasn't even facing in the right direction. Besides, he'd been staring out to sea for so long that his eyes seemed almost coated with the darkness. But awareness came back to him abruptly, reluctantly.

He turned and saw the shape of a man making his way up the steps to the front door. The man held on to the rail, then paused on the top step to open the door. There was a momentary pale flush of light from within, and then the door closed behind him.

Hugh didn't move. He waited for time to billow out, to accommodate him once more. But it was too late. Now, it seemed, he had no choice but to follow. He pushed open the front door. A light was on in the hallway. Again he listened for footsteps. This time, though, he heard nothing. He might have been quite alone. He climbed the stairs, passing the door to the old woman's room, and stopped outside number seven. When he knocked there was a pause.

Hugh felt as if he was lobbing a stone into a well.

Then a voice called out, 'Come in.'

Hugh twisted the handle and pushed open the door.

Chapter Thirty-Four

Hugh's first impression was that there was no-one in the room. He looked left, over a bed and a wardrobe, a suitcase on the floor and a single bedside lamp. The bed was unmade, a crumple of sheets and blankets with the pillow twisted round lengthways. He looked right. There was a bay window with the curtains open and two chairs facing one another. Through the window he could see patches of cloud hanging over the sea with the moon behind.

Jutting above the wing of the left-hand chair was the top of a man's head.

'Who is it?'

Hugh didn't answer.

'Who is it?' said the man again.

Hugh heard the note of alarm in his voice. When he said who he was, the man half lifted himself out of the chair. The top of his head twisted round, then fell back.

'What do you want?'

'I've been looking for you.'

Hugh came closer and looked down. The man in the chair was much smaller than he'd expected. He didn't know why he should have envisaged him as being especially large. Perhaps he had just elongated him in what passed for his imagination, bulked him out with a few seemingly appropriate additions. But this man wasn't large at all. His feet hardly reached the floor. He looked as if he'd shrunk into the innermost recesses of the chair.

His head, though, was different. It reminded Hugh of one of those portraits that tourists pose for in the street; those drawings in coloured chalks, where the features are all roughly in the right place, but look oddly burnished and distended. Pumped up too hard. Almost boyish in a ruined sort of way. The eyes that seem somehow evacuated, never quite there. Blind people sometimes had eyes like this – sunk so deep in their sockets they appeared to be looking inward rather than out. His white hair might have been cut with shears.

Hugh realized he was staring, but he couldn't help himself.

The man stared back at him.

'So,' he said, 'you've found me.'

'Yes.'

Kingman swallowed. 'I always thought someone would come eventually. But I hadn't expected you to be alone,' he said. 'I assumed there would be . . . others.'

'No-one else would believe me,' said Hugh.

Unexpectedly, Kingman laughed. It was a sharp, dry sound, like fire running through kindling. When he had finished, he touched the corners of his lips uncertainly with his fingertips.

'How did you find me?'

'The logbooks,' said Hugh. 'Bellamare. You came here as a child, didn't you?'

'Oh yes, every year. Of course, it was very different then. It's where I first saw the sea. Where everything started for me. And ended too, in a way.'

He paused, then went on, gathering pace as he did so.

'I've often imagined this moment. Not so much at first. For years I imagined I was invisible. I couldn't believe that anyone would ever notice me. They all seemed far too preoccupied, too busy with one another. I felt like a wraith. Neither of this world, nor of anywhere else. As if I'd passed into a realm where life and death had ceased to exist.

'There is a song I remember hearing a long time ago. A

folk song about a sinful mariner who sinks to the bottom of the sea. There, on the sea-floor, he finds the skeletons of men who had died long ago. They reach out their bony hands to him and warn him that, if he doesn't change his ways, then his fate will be the same as theirs. He floats back up to the surface, but by the time he gets back to dry land he has been so changed by the experience that no-one recognizes him. So he passes among all his old friends, a stranger in their midst.'

'What happened to you?' asked Hugh.

Kingman looked up. 'You're curious to know how I got here?'

Hugh nodded.

Again he paused, shifting himself in his chair, raising himself up very briefly on his hands and settling down again. 'When I climbed into the dinghy I didn't care what happened to me, whether I lived or died. I didn't take any food or water. I just . . . abandoned myself. I decided that I would do nothing to save myself, at the same time I didn't want to be the instrument of my own death. For two days I drifted in the weed. If anything, it grew even thicker than it had been before. The dinghy hardly seemed to be floating at all, but hanging, suspended, above the tops of the waves. As far as I could tell I wasn't moving at all. I suppose I must have been, though, or else the weed itself was moving, because I soon lost sight of the yacht.

'On the third day, I noticed that the weed had thinned out around me. By this time I was very weak and I didn't think I'd last much longer. There was no shade in the dinghy. I could feel my skin drawing tighter and tighter, and my eyes were so dry I could hardly blink. I lay back and waited to die.

'And then I saw a boat. At first I assumed I was imagining it. I watched as it came closer, and all the time I thought to myself, This is not real, this is death coming for me. I could hear voices, but I didn't pay them any attention. The boat drew up alongside, and a man climbed into the dinghy. Even then I was sure it was all a hallucination. I felt myself being lifted and carried onto the other boat. I wasn't able to eat, but they gave me some water to drink, and after that I don't remember anything for a while. It turned out they were fishermen from Bermuda. By the time we reached port I had almost recovered. Of course they wanted to tell the authorities about me, but I persuaded them not to and they were very decent about it.

'I rested up in Bermuda for a couple of months. One day I got into a conversation with some Venezuelans who were working on a container ship bound for Spain. There had been an outbreak of food poisoning on board and they'd had to put into Bermuda to take some crew members off. As a result they were short of hands. They asked if I had any sailing experience and when I said I did, they asked if I'd like to join them.

'I stayed in Spain for a while, and then I was offered another crewing job, this time on a boat bound for Harwich. I'd always known I would come back to Britain eventually. I had to. I . . . needed to. And for a while I seemed to be quite invisible, secure in people's indifference and forgetfulness. I felt I could lose myself among them for ever.

'But then doubts set in – I don't know why. At least I do, but it was such a minor matter. I saw someone I'd known a long time ago. Not far from here. A former acquaintance. Not a friend, nothing like that, just one of those faces that stick in your mind and bob up again. I walked past him and his eyes caught mine. I saw this look of confusion come over his face. But I hurried by and lost him easily enough.

'I'd seen people I'd recognized before, once or twice. Passed among them and left no trace. But all of a sudden I felt exposed, visible. Without ever wanting to, I'd become someone again. Just when it seemed as if I might fade away for good.

'I grew used to scanning faces and wondering, Is it you? Or you? Can this really be the one? All these figures looming towards me. Bearing down.

'And I seemed to hear my name being mentioned everywhere. As if it had stuck to people's conversations and they had to keep repeating it to try to shake it off. All the time, they couldn't help themselves. But nothing happened. That was the strange thing. I became more and more suspicious. Yet nothing had altered. Nothing. No-one but me.'

'What did you do?'

'What could I do? Except watch and wait.'

'How did you meet Hollis?' asked Hugh.

'Hollis? He was very kind to me. I had no money and I needed work. I'd heard from people that he might be able to help. I don't think he knew who I was. Not straightaway. But it didn't take him long to work it out. I knew I was apt to imagine these things. In his case, though, I was quite sure. He never said anything, though. Never. In all the time we knew each other.

'But he helped get me some work. Then after a couple of months, he came up to me and handed me this envelope. Still he didn't say anything, he just handed it to me as if I'd dropped it. One of the casual workers had died in an accident at work. A man called Field, a former sailor. They hushed it up. He had no dependants left alive. Hollis had his Seaman's Discharge Book. Really, the whole thing couldn't have been easier. I was able to stay in Seaman's Missions for as long as I wanted. Still Hollis never let on, never treated me any differently. He never tried to intrude. But then, latterly, something changed.'

'What do you mean?'

Kingman turned towards him. 'I don't know what,' he said. 'He had something on his mind. It seemed to be weighing him down. I asked him what the matter was, but of course he wouldn't say. He just got more and more bowed with worry, as if it were crushing him. Then one day he came and said he had something to tell me. He said that he was worried for me. That there was some scheme afoot – he wouldn't tell me what it was – and that he was worried it might lead to my being exposed.

'He gave me a key to his flat and told me that I should

323

treat it as if it were my own. Then, finally, he asked me for Field's Discharge Book back. That was the last time I saw him.'

'Hollis is dead.'

Kingman, he saw, was trembling. Soon afterwards he began to cry. Hugh took a handkerchief out of his pocket and handed it to him. Kingman wiped his eyes, then looked up at him.

'What happened?'

'He drowned himself.'

'Why?'

'They're kicking all the green-carders out of the paper. Perhaps he couldn't face life outside. He had Field's Discharge Book with him,' Hugh added. 'I think he was worried that someone would track you down and he wanted to throw them off the scent.'

'So even then he was looking to help.'

Kingman took the handkerchief and held it in front of his face, bunched it into a ball. 'I assumed something must have happened,' he said. 'I kept waiting for him to come back to the flat. But he never did. Then, the other night, someone else turned up.'

'That was me,' said Hugh.

'Ah.'

Downstairs, the front door opened and closed. Footsteps climbed the stairs. They waited as the footsteps climbed towards them and went past.

'I saw your wife,' said Hugh.

When Kingman spoke again his voice sounded smaller, as if it were coming from some hidden cavity in his chest. 'Tell me, have you ever felt wanting, as if there was some absence in you where things – vital things – ought to be?'

Hugh found his own voice had shrunk.

'Yes.'

Again Kingman twisted himself round, like someone with bedsores. 'When I first met my wife, I couldn't believe that she seemed . . . that she seemed to care for me. The idea that she might love me for myself was laughable. I was sure that sooner or later she'd see how unworthy I was, what a mistake she'd made. It was like a terrible accident. A case of mistaken identity. It couldn't last for ever. Somewhere out there was this certainty, like a tiny light on the horizon that never went away.

'I wanted to be able to match her feelings. But always there was this gap. I couldn't make the leap. I tried and tried, but every time I found I couldn't. The more I tried to extend myself, the more I withdrew. Further and further into myself. All the time being borne backwards—'

Kingman broke off. 'I dare say none of this makes any sense to you.'

'It does make sense,' said Hugh quietly.

'I decided to try to make myself worthy of her. But it was beyond me. I couldn't even make a decent job of faking it. When I came back, how could I face her? I was dead. It was better for her that I should be dead. Much better. And this, I thought, could be my punishment: to be in the world, but not of the world. Knowing that she was out there, yet not able to reach her.

'You see, most people, when they love one another, they wonder, What happens when it ends, when just one of them is left? They try not to think about it and most of the time they manage it, they do a decent job, but then they can't help themselves. Sooner or later one of them will be alone. And when that day comes they'll be as lost to each other as if they had never met.

'What's left then? Memories, mementos. You can't live on those. You look at photographs. You peer at them as if you're peering into the eyes of the dead, trying to imagine that something, some channel – something – might be opening up between you. But there's nothing. No union of souls. Nothing. All gone.

'I used to think that I'd been spared that,' said Kingman. 'I seemed incapable of feeling love. So instead I settled down in my isolation. But slowly I began to yearn for it. This longing rose up in me. But it was too late. I'd denied

325

myself the chance. It was out there, but I couldn't get at it. Not any more.'

Hugh thought of his own yearning for love, and his desire for escape – his sense of being borne steadily backwards, into this disengaged seclusion. Withdrawing, withdrawing. Struggling to come forward, but all the time feeling as if the floor was moving beneath him. Scanning the faces on the tube every night to see who he could fasten on to. And his own feelings of yearning. At times they were so strong they threatened to engulf him. He had to try to beat them back, to get himself under control. But still they flailed angrily about inside him.

'What are you going to do with me?'

Hugh didn't answer.

'I'm not going anywhere,' Kingman said. 'Not any more. It's up to you.'

Through the window came the sound of the waves, rushing and receding. With it came a memory from Hugh's childhood; he must have been about six at the time and was sitting on the floor at his father's feet. They were playing, pretending to fight. It wasn't the sort of thing they normally did – perhaps this was why Hugh had become overexcited and had failed to observe the rules.

At some stage he'd kicked his father in the knee. He remembered his foot connecting with his father's leg and the peculiar twangy resistance it encountered. Then his father cried out in pain. Hugh remembered his astonishment at hearing this; his father crying out, clutching his knee and shouting angrily, 'What did you do that for?' He hadn't intended to hurt him. Indeed, it had never occurred to him before that he might be able to, and the surprise, the shock of having done so, had always stayed with him.

Hugh wanted to explain himself. He wanted to explain how he really didn't have any choice, how his livelihood depended on this, his future. Everything, in fact. He wished their roles were reversed and that all he had to do was sit and wait for the inevitable. And then he thought how life so often brought about the one thing you most sought to avoid. Laid it there patiently before you, like a dog that won't stop fetching a stick, however far you hurl it away.

But this urge to justify his behaviour was soon succeeded by a sense of great weariness. He felt that if he closed his eyes for an instant, he'd fall into a deep, engulfing sleep, with the waves beating back and forth in the background and the darkness outside. Not waking for hours, even days.

In the end he neither spoke nor slept, but swatted away at his mouth with his hand, as if this might coax some words out into the open. Then he gave up and let his arm fall into his lap.

'What is it?'

Hugh shook his head.

'Nothing,' he said. 'I'm sorry.'

'About what?'

'About everything. About finding you.'

When he got up to go the room seemed to swim with dark ripples of light, as if the sea had swept into the house and pulled it into the water.

Kingman looked up at him. 'You're not what I expected,' he said.

'No,' said Hugh. 'Nor are you.'

He was halfway towards the door when Kingman said from his chair, 'When will you be back?'

'Not long, I expect.'

'Where are you going now?'

'I'm going home,' said Hugh.

'Ah,' said Kingman. 'Home. Goodbye then.'

'Goodbye.'

Hugh made his way out, down the stairs and through the empty hallway. He stood on the top step outside, where he'd seen Kingman holding on to the rail scarcely more than an hour before, and listened for the sea. But already it was growing fainter, drawing away.

He got back into his car and drove back to London. The traffic had tailed off and for much of the journey he almost

327

had the road to himself. He was hardly conscious of driving, still less of following road signs. When he finally pulled up outside his house he found himself looking round before he tried the front door, checking that he had the right address.

The sloping street with its rows of narrow houses looked both familiar and unfamiliar. Everything was where he expected it to be – his neighbours' houses and his own. But at the same time it seemed suddenly inconceivable that he'd spent a substantial portion of his life here, so absurd that it almost made him laugh out loud. He felt as if he'd been away for a long time, and that things had changed irrevocably in his absence.

Part 4

'Known as Water Lane previous to 1844,
Whitefriars Street was named after the
monastery of the White Friars. The monastery
was founded here in about 1241 and enjoyed the
privilege of sanctuary, covering practically
the whole district at this point from Fleet Street
to the Thames. The precincts of the monastery
were eventually built up into houses, many of
which were occupied by noblemen and people
of importance. There seems, however, even at
that early date, to have been another portion of
the precincts occupied by residents of doubtful
character. This portion was afterwards known
as Alsatia, and in time the elements in it overran
the other portions of the area, and the district,
as a whole, acquired a very bad reputation.

'Whitefriars Street was the main entrance
into Alsatia, which eventually extended from
Bouverie Street to New Bridge Street and from
Fleet Street to the river. The privilege of sanctuary attracted a choice collection of scoundrels
and vagabonds, who lived here in security until
the privilege was abolished in 1697, but the evil
reputation of Alsatia lasted long after that time.'

GEORGE H. CUNNINGHAM, *LONDON*, 1924

Chapter Thirty-Five

In the reception area several of the commissionaires were struggling to remove *The Triumph of Truth over Falsehood* from the wall. It was proving difficult. They were standing on stepladders, pulling at the metal panels to try to dislodge them. Other commissionaires were kneeling down hanging on to their ankles. Little jets of dust fell on their uniforms.

Hugh climbed the stairs to the office. The banister had now been removed. Several more desks had also gone. They'd been piled on top of one another near one of the exits, along with various pieces of discarded office furniture. First one pile had appeared overnight, then another alongside it. In order to get in and out now you had to squeeze your way between the two jagged piles. More carpet tiles had been exposed. Now there were broad, liverish-green avenues sweeping through the office.

For a moment Hugh was sure that his desk had disappeared. Then he saw it and realized that he'd lost his bearings again. Cliff was standing in the middle of the floor, his portable phone at his feet beside him. His big thumbs were hooked over his jacket pockets and he was jabbing his foot against one of the carpet tiles. His face looked greyer than ever – it had a damp sheen to it, like putty – and he wore an expression of intense annoyance.

Hugh realized that Cliff must be thinking – or what passed for it in his case. Anything that detained Cliff for long, that couldn't be sorted out with the minimum of fuss or contemplation, was apt to cause him almost physical discomfort, irresolution passing through him in a series of small spasms. Here, instead of appearing to be engaged in any form of reflection, he seemed to be willing himself to make an impression in the floor, daring the ground not to give way beneath his feet. Calling into play the great weight of certainties that made up his life to lend him additional bulk.

'Hughie,' he said flatly.

Hugh stopped and greeted him.

'How's Pauline?'

'Pauline? She's not too bad. Why shouldn't she be?'

'No particular reason. How are you, Cliff?'

Cliff drew an arc with the toe of his shoe across the floor. 'There's something funny going on,' he said.

'You're getting as bad as Julian.'

'What's that supposed to mean?'

'He was saying much the same thing the other day.'

Cliff straightened up and the twin saddles of fat rode up his chest to sit alongside the certainties on his shoulders. 'I think it's very unlikely we are referring to the same thing,' he said.

He gazed around the office, looking for something upon which to turn the massive force of his indignation. As solid, as brutish as usual. Nonetheless, some small tremor of doubt seemed to have taken hold of him. Hugh saw Battersby emerge from his office, looking much smarter than he had ever seen him look before. Battersby wore a jacket, and his tie was pulled up to the top button of his shirt. His hair was brushed back and wedged in place under the arms of his spectacles. He headed for the lifts, head down, pushing up his spectacles as he went.

'Where the fuck's he off to then?' Cliff muttered.

Hugh sat at his desk and stretched his legs out in front of him. His foot hit something on the floor, but instead of withdrawing his leg, he swung a kick at whatever was in his way. From the other side of the desk Stanley cried out in pain. 'What are you doing?'

'Sorry.'

Again, Hugh stretched himself out and tried to think what to do. He'd always thought of his life as this wavering, insubstantial thing, snaking its way out in front of him. It wasn't necessarily what he wanted, or had hoped for. He'd expected something a good deal more substantial, more certain than this. Some squat edifice with doors and windows and voices within. But there it was, this faint path in the darkness, and for that at least he knew he should feel grateful. So he kept on going, unsure of what he was doing. And now it had run out. If he closed his eyes, he imagined he could see it just dwindle away before him.

He thought how easy it was to be notionally in touch with the world through journalism, with its accidents, disasters and occasional triumphs, yet at the same time to be utterly cut off from it. Journalism invited this notion of being in touch. For a time it sustained it. But then, abruptly, this too gave out.

The sunlight flooded in all around him. It seemed to sit on top of the carpet tiles, swaying and lapping and stretching off in every direction. He felt quite disorientated, as if he'd been pushed out into the middle of a vast green pond. All morning he tried to work out what he was going to do. It was on moral decisions such as this, he thought, that people's lives had once been based, even judged. Perhaps they still were, although he found it hard to believe. It seemed such a quaint notion, yet somehow admirable for all that. Still admirable – whatever the circumstances.

At lunchtime he decided that he wanted to be on his own. He walked down the stairs, out of the building and went to a bar he'd never been to before. He bought himself a pint of beer and a sandwich and sat on a stool with a copy of the paper. But he wasn't hungry and could only manage a couple of bites of his sandwich. He set it back down on the plate and tried to read the paper. But the noise of chatter all around him was too loud and the news too dull, and after a while he gave up.

He left the pub, crossed over Fleet Street and went down into Alsatia, the abode of the rogues. These streets leading down to the river were always deserted – he had no idea why. But even at lunchtimes you hardly ever saw anyone there. There was no sign of 'the bad characters of every description' who once congregated here. This 'rake-hell', full of 'shaggy, uncombed ruffians with greasy shoulder-belts, discoloured scarves, enormous moustaches and torn hats – when the dregs of an age that was indeed full of dregs were vatted in that disreputable sanctuary east of the Temple'.

As he walked down the streets of dull, red-brick offices with listless-looking commissionaires behind plate-glass doors, Hugh wondered just how low he could bear to sink. He wondered too if he had it in him to match the spirit of recklessness that had once imbued the place.

He headed for Blackfriars Bridge. Standing there, gazing out over the river, he could see the Thames stretching away beyond Hungerford Bridge and Westminster. A swathe of grey sliding by. There was a tug coming towards him pulling a line of barges. The wash from the barges scored a long white furrow on the surface of the water behind. Otherwise the river was deserted.

It seemed to him as though his world was coming to an end, and that all this – everything he was used to – would soon be swept away. He gripped the balustrade to reassure himself that, for the time being at least, he remained anchored to the ground. But this feeling of being somehow untethered, of walking on sponge, persisted all the way back to the office.

He only came back down to earth when he saw Vivien. They hadn't spoken since he'd spent the night at her flat. It seemed like a long time ago to Hugh, so much so that he found himself doubting if it had happened at all; these moments of intimacy were so rare for each of them that they tended to be succeeded by feelings of disbelief.

Now he saw her coming towards him, heading for the gap between the two jagged piles of desks. He quickened his pace, thinking he would be able to get through before she did. Possibly she did the same thing. Or else he had simply miscalculated, failed to take into account that Vivien now moved a good deal faster than she'd done before. The result was that each saw their way blocked by the other. They both came to a halt. Hugh stood to one side and waited for Vivien to come through. She didn't emerge. After a reasonable interval he peered round one of the piles of desks, only to see Vivien doing the same. There was a stand-off.

'Please come through,' called Hugh.

He felt appalled by his nerves, his stiltedness. Reluctantly, she did so. They regarded one another. Vivien had done something to her hair, brushed it back off her forehead. There was no telling if this was deliberate or accidental. Either way, he wasn't sure if he cared for it.

'So what's been going on?' she asked.

'It's not easy to explain.'

'Try me. Did you find Kingman?'

Hugh nodded.

'So what are you going to do?'

'I don't know.'

'What do you mean you don't know?'

'I mean I don't know.'

Vivien didn't say anything.

'I don't know, all right?' said Hugh again, more angrily this time.

Battersby advanced on them through the gap between the desks, twisting himself sideways and half skipping from foot to foot. He stopped when he saw them.

'Why are you two standing around gossiping?' he asked.

Without waiting for an answer, he strode off down the aisle back to his office. He hadn't gone far, though, when he turned round and called out to Hugh, 'I'm still waiting.'

Vivien continued to look at him. Once again Hugh had the sense that his internal workings were there dangling before her. He had already learned that she didn't care for people who equivocated. She took it personally, like a door being slammed in her face. In this, he reflected, they were not dissimilar. Both were so fearful of being stung that they withdrew immediately and shrank back into their shells. In her case, however, this involved a good deal more hostility than in his.

Before he could think of anything else to say, she too had turned and walked away. He stood and watched the faint sway of her thighs with a familiar sinking feeling in his stomach.

Later that afternoon Darren came by with the teas. He seemed in an unusually good mood. 'How are you then?' he asked.

'Not too bad,' lied Hugh.

Darren was manoeuvring his trolley across the floor, as well as carrying a large brown envelope. Owing to the wrinkled state of the carpet tiles, this was proving difficult. The tea in the urn threatened to slop over. He needed both hands to control the trolley. The envelope had been tucked under his arm, from where it was about to fall.

'What's that?' said Hugh.

He pointed at the envelope. It had 'From the office of the Home Secretary' printed on the front and a large red seal on the back.

'This? Just something for Battersby. It came by bike from Westminster.'

'I'll take it to him if you like.'

'Would you?' said Darren. 'That would be very kind.'

He looked warmly at Hugh, who reflected that at last he seemed to have earned Darren's approbation.

Hugh took the envelope and put it in his desk drawer. Not long afterwards he saw Julian. There were dark-blue rings beneath his eyes and his hand was bandaged.

'What's the matter with you?'

'I've been having a terrible time,' said Julian. 'Really terrible.'

'What happened?'

'I don't want to talk about it here. Why don't we go for a drink?'

'I'm not sure I can,' said Hugh.

'Please, Hughie,' said Julian.

They got up and went round the corner to the pub. It was only just opening time and there was hardly anyone there. Julian sat down and Hugh bought them both drinks.

Julian picked up his glass with his unbandaged hand.

'I don't know if I've told you that I do certain home improvements,' he said.

'Yes.'

'I may have mentioned that our neighbour had complained about the porch I've been building.'

'Yes.'

'Well, I was lying in bed last night,' Julian went on. 'About eleven thirty or so, not much later. I'd already heard this noise coming from downstairs, but I hadn't paid it any attention. Anyway, I was lying there . . .'

'Yes?'

'And this axe came through the wall.'

'What?'

Julian's dark eyes seemed to glitter momentarily.

'An axe,' he repeated. 'An axe came through the fucking wall.'

'What did you do?'

'Well, I screamed – shouted, to raise the alarm. But there was no-one to hear me. Next thing I knew, it came through again. This time in a different place, just above my bed. And this noise, like an animal, bellowing away. I'd never heard anything like it.

'I ran to the phone and dialled nine nine nine. But the operator told me to hang on. All the lines to the police were busy. By now there were pieces of plasterboard all over my bed. And I could see my next-door neighbour through the

337

hole in the wall, surrounded by dust, swinging this axe round his head and shouting that he was going to sort me out. I'd never seen anything like it.'

Julian paused, breathless. 'Finally, the police answered the phone. They said they'd be right over. But by now the hole was almost big enough for him to get through. I ran into the bathroom and barricaded myself in. Everything went quiet for a while. Very quiet. I didn't know what was happening. Then I heard this rattling on the bathroom door. And this voice – quite calm-sounding – asking if I was in there. At first I assumed it must be the police. I was about to open up when the door—'

Julian held his bandaged hand in front of him. It stuck out of the end of his sleeve like a great white club.

'What about the door?'

'It disintegrated, just flew apart in front of me. And there he was, standing there. This fucking ape. I can't tell you, Hughie. I thought I was going to die.

'I climbed onto the lavatory seat and opened the window. But it was too small for me to fit through. So I tried to shield myself behind the fittings. But that wasn't any good either. There wasn't room. Then I heard these footsteps running up the stairs, and all these policemen rushed in. They must have knocked the front door down. Anyway, they jumped on him. One on top of another. A great pile of them. Eventually they got him handcuffed and led him away.'

'Jesus. How terrible for you.'

'Yes. Unfortunately that wasn't the end of it, Hughie.'

'What do you mean?'

'The police told me it was safe to come down. But it turned out . . . it turned out that I'd got stuck behind the cistern. I couldn't move. In the end they had to turn the water off, fetch a hacksaw and cut the cistern off the wall. The policeman with the saw didn't have a clue what he was doing and caught my hand with the blade. Made quite a mess of it, too.'

'What about the house?'

'The house is in a terrible state. There's an enormous hole in the wall. Mess everywhere. The only thing that isn't in a mess is the porch. It turned out he'd already tried to demolish it, but he hadn't been able to. It was too well built, you see,' said Julian, with satisfaction. 'That was what had driven him mad.

'But I'm not properly insured or anything. I've never been very good at sorting out that side of things. I don't know how I'll ever pay for the repairs.'

Julian shut his eyes. 'How am I going to cope?'

Hugh didn't answer.

'That porch meant a lot to me.'

'I know it did.'

'I don't know how much longer I can stand it here. I feel so frustrated. I keep wondering which would be worse, Battersby as editor, or Cliff. Either one . . . it's just too terrible to contemplate.'

'I would have thought you'd prefer Cliff,' said Hugh.

'What on earth makes you say that?'

'I don't know. I always thought you quite respected him, despite everything. Didn't you once call him a pro?'

'A pro?' said Julian in astonishment. 'I never said Cliff was a pro. I said he was a prole, that's hardly the same thing. I don't respect him at all, he's an awful man. Walking around dragging that stupid fucking portable phone the whole time. Serve him right if he ruptured himself. No, there's nothing for me here any more. I suppose I'll just have to find something else to occupy my hands – or my mind at any rate. Perhaps I'll follow in your footsteps, Hughie.'

'I'm sorry?'

'Didn't you say you once wanted to be a writer?'

'Oh, that was a long time ago. I've forgotten all about it now.'

Julian took a drink and wiped his mouth with his bandaged hand. 'Don't you need to be interested in other people if you're a writer?' he asked.

'I wouldn't have thought so.'

'No?'

'Not if you're sufficiently interested in yourself.'

'Mmm,' said Julian thoughtfully. 'Maybe I'll give it a go then.'

The pub was starting to fill up with people leaving work.

'Julian . . .' said Hugh.

'Yes.'

'Do you remember when we had a drink before, a few weeks ago, we talked about how far you'd go for a story.'

'No,' said Julian.

'We talked about whether you'd betray a friendship for a story.'

'Did we? What did I say?'

'You said your life was made up of betrayals.'

'Well, that's true enough,' Julian reflected glumly.

'Could you live with yourself afterwards, though?'

'What, if I betrayed someone for a story?'

'Yes.'

Again, Julian gave this some thought. The pub was now quite full. There were people standing in ranks at the bar, waving banknotes, trying to attract the barman's attention.

'I don't see why not,' he said.

'Really?'

'Of course. You'd soon forget all about it.'

That evening Hugh waited in the emptying office. As he'd been when it was light, he was aware of this vast acreage of empty space, fanning out all around. After a while he took a folded bundle of handwritten pages from his pocket and propped them against his typewriter. Then he took one of the sheets of copy paper from the box beside his desk, threaded it into his typewriter and began to type away.

He didn't stop to think about the sense of what he was writing. He just set to, almost as if he was taking dictation. He felt nothing, neither shame nor embarrassment, only this crisp sort of efficiency. He'd finished the first page almost before he realized he'd started.

Before long – he had to check his watch to make sure it hadn't stopped – there was a small stack of typed sheets on the desk beside his typewriter. The next time he looked it had grown to twice the size. When he broke off for a third time – this time to fetch some more paper – he realized the office was deserted. Yet all the time, as he typed away, he seemed to feel Vivien's eyes on him, hanging over the back of his head. He struggled to blank them out, to escape her scrutiny.

Once he had finished, he detached the top pieces of paper from the carbons beneath, clipped them together and walked over to Battersby's glass box. He left them on his desk, in the tray marked 'Articles Pending'. Then he put another copy of the piece in the tray on the news desk, so that it would be sent straight downstairs to the type-setters. And when he'd done this he couldn't help but feel a sense of relief, as if he'd at last unburdened himself.

On the tube all the seats were taken, and so he stood, strap-hanging, swaying and rocking along with everyone else as the train wound its way through the tunnels. At the station he fed his ticket into the slot at the barrier. The boys on their bicycles were riding up and down the road past his flat. As he got closer, he expected to hear the familiar cries of annoyance from his neighbours as their televisions hopped from channel to channel. But the boys, it seemed, had outgrown this trick. Now they cycled back and forth, practising their turns, not saying anything. Everything was quiet.

There was a postcard on the doormat from his mother. The picture on the front was of a girl lying in a canoe, one foot dangling over the side. The postmark was impossible to make out.

'Trip to volcano a great success,' she had written. 'Mr Glim such amusing company – I know you'd like him. We trekked up to the crater and looked over. Clouds of sulphur and sparks everywhere. Most exciting thing I've ever seen. We've decided to postpone rejoining the cruise in Port Moresby and will pick it up sometime later. There's another volcano not far away that Mr Glim is keen to show me. Will keep you posted on whereabouts. Much love, Mum.'

Chapter Thirty-Six

As Hugh gazed around the office, it seemed to him as though everything was more sharply defined, more glossy than usual. All these familiar things giving off one last unlikely burst of lustre. As if they were made out of some hard, polished material – bakelite or malachite, or something like that. They were real enough, he knew that, but not quite there any more. Not in the way they had been before. Different – although he would have been pushed to say exactly how.

People were still making their way into the office. He watched them stepping forth on cue, all conforming blindly to some grand design. They took their places and waited to spring obediently into action. But this morning he found he had no desire to be any part of this. So instead he went downstairs, not with any particular purpose in mind, just to get away.

He tried the door to Walter's room but it was locked. Then he walked through into the library. Already some of the cuttings files had been taken down from the shelves ready to be transported to the new office. There was a line of trolleys running down the middle of the room, all linked together, each of them fully laden with files.

In the passageway between the library of the living and the library of the dead there was no milky gleam in the gloom before him. When his eyes cleared he saw that the bound volumes of back issues had also been removed.

As far as he could tell, the library of the dead had not been touched. There was the same smell as before, the same shelves crammed with brown envelopes.

At the far end of the room Hugh tried the door to Hollis's office, again, with no particular purpose in mind, just out of idle curiosity. He twisted the handle and the door swung open before him, as it had done before. He felt around inside for the light switch. When the light came on he saw that the room was empty. Everything had gone. He looked around in surprise. There was no sign of Hollis's occupancy. Nothing at all, save the outlines of books and boxes and other bits and pieces left in dust on the shelves. The desk too had disappeared. So had the box that he'd found beneath it.

He stayed there for some time. As he walked back through the two libraries for the last time and closed the doors behind him, he felt an odd sort of exhilaration, a lightness in his head and veins.

Walter was back in his room. He was sitting at his table with the lamp on and the internal mail spread out around him. He stopped reading and beckoned him in.

'Hugh,' he said.

Hugh couldn't remember Walter ever using his name before.

'Yes.'

'There's something I think you should see.'

He took an envelope off the table and held it out. Hugh took the envelope and opened it. The flap wasn't stuck down. There were two sheets of paper inside, stapled together. The top sheet was marked for the attention of the managing editor. He read, 'Further to our discussions this afternoon, I enclose a list of proposed redundancies for your consideration.' Below it was Battersby's signature.

He turned to the second sheet. There was a list of six names on it. He found his own near the top. Several names further down was Julian's. He turned back to the top sheet. He saw that it was dated the day before Battersby had agreed to give him one last chance. At the bottom of the page were the managing editor's initials and the single handwritten word, 'Approved.'

Hugh put the sheets of paper back in the envelope.

'I'm sorry,' said Walter. 'Looks as if you'll be joining us, after all.'

'Looks that way.'

'Must be quite a shock.'

'In a way,' said Hugh.

'You don't seem too bothered. Made any plans?'

'No,' he said. 'Not really. How about you?'

'Well, we've had longer to think about it than you, of course. I'm sure you'll think of something.'

Walter continued looking through the pieces of paper, picking them up with his long fingers and reading them, then putting them carefully back on top of their envelopes. Hugh stood and watched. He found himself oddly loath to leave.

'Found anything else?' he asked.

'Just bits and pieces.'

Walter handed him another sheet of paper. It was from the managing editor to the proprietor and concerned the editorial succession. In the event of the editor's death, only two internal candidates were to be interviewed for the job. As expected, Battersby's name followed. Beneath it was Cliff's. Beneath that was a space, and then the managing editor had once again added his initials.

Hugh looked at the piece of paper. As he did so, something stirred within him. It seemed such a little thing. Hardly even a favour, more like an experiment. A futile gesture – there could be little doubt about that – but all he could do in the circumstances. Besides, there was nothing left to lose. He laid the piece of paper on the table and took out his pen.

'What are you doing?' asked Walter.

It only took him a moment. When he handed the paper back, Walter looked at him, eyebrows raised.

'It's nothing you need worry about,' said Hugh.

345

Walter shrugged and put the piece of paper back in its envelope. Then, to Hugh's surprise, he got to his feet and held out his hand.

'I wanted to say goodbye. Just in case we don't get the chance later.'

'But surely you're not going now,' said Hugh.

'Not immediately,' said Walter. 'But just in case.'

They shook hands.

Once again, Hugh felt as if he was sliding his hand into a long, dry glove.

Upstairs, Darren was making his rounds with the first edition of the paper. There was already a copy on Hugh's desk. He picked it up, then set it down. He looked around for Vivien, but couldn't see her anywhere. Not far away, Joy was flicking envelopes into wire trays. As usual, he found himself distracted by the long tendons in Joy's calves. There was a taut ridge of muscle that ran up from above each ankle to just below her knees. Despite the weather, her legs were bare and she wore sandals. When he craned forward he saw that her toenails were painted a light peach colour.

Once again he picked up the paper. He found what he was looking for on the leader page. A photograph of the Home Secretary was prominently displayed. Alongside it the headline ON BEING TAKEN FOR GRANTED was printed in large letters.

Hugh ran his eyes over the page. As far as he could tell, there'd been no changes made to the piece he had placed in Battersby's articles pending tray the night before. The article was just as Darren had written it, and as he'd transcribed it. There were the same resentful references to being treated without a shred of consideration, as well as a number of references to pattern-cutting and to Darren's ambitions to own a pet-grooming salon. It was strange, reflected Hugh, how in print his words seemed to possess a gravitas they had lacked before.

In order to quell his nerves he went to the lavatory. To his surprise he saw that the cubicle doors had all been replaced on their hinges; there was no sign that they had ever been removed. He shut himself in one of the cubicles and sat down. As he had done the day before when he'd walked down to the river, he felt as if he was floating in a strange state of suspension. Not really tethered to the ground, but hanging there in the air, swaying about.

He became aware of two journalists talking as they stood at the urinals. The reappearance of the cubicle doors hadn't passed unnoticed by them either.

'Seems a bit late now,' said one to the other. 'I can't think who could have taken them, or why.'

'Probably a practical joke,' suggested his colleague.

'Not a very funny one, though.'

'They never are.'

'What?'

'Practical jokes.'

'Quite. I never liked the idea of going when there were no doors. Always made me feel rather tense.'

'Did it?' said the second journalist. 'Never bothered me.'

Their conversation moved on companionably.

'Extraordinary article on the leader page,' said the first journalist.

'Yes, I don't think I've ever read anything like it.'

'Must have been boiling up for quite a while.'

'Do you think that accounts for the tone?'

'The tone is unusual, isn't it? How would you describe it?'

'Peevish?'

'Quite. It's more peevish than I would have expected.'

'Just goes to show how fed up he is, I suppose. All this dog business must have been getting him down. The meaning's clear enough, though.'

'Oh, perfectly clear.'

They went off to the basins. Hugh couldn't hear what they were saying over the noise of water running. He got up and pulled the chain. Outside the door to the Gents, the

347

two journalists were still standing and talking. As Hugh started to walk back to his desk, a figure brushed roughly past him. He saw that it was Battersby. He was heading for the exit at great speed. Halfway down the aisle there was a chair blocking his path. Rather than walk round it, Battersby took hold of the chair and hurled it against one of the desks with such force that it almost rebounded in front of him. The noise of the chair hitting the desk produced a loud metallic boom, like a gong being beaten. Battersby, meanwhile, kept going, looking neither left nor right, but with his eyes fixed in front of him. Slowly the noise died away.

'I wonder what's got into him,' said the first journalist.

'Nerves,' said the second one confidently.

Battersby did not reappear for the rest of the afternoon. Without anyone to supervise them people began to take advantage and drift home early. By then there had been a number of developments. No-one seemed to know what had happened, or who had written the article that appeared under the Home Secretary's name, but everyone agreed that the responsibility for such a mistake lay ultimately with Battersby. The Home Secretary's lawyers had already been in touch, threatening legal action and demanding an apology. The Prime Minister's office had issued a statement. Other journalists on other papers had lost no time picking up on the story. Everyone was understandably keen to share in the general embarrassment.

Once again Hugh looked around for Vivien. Still there was no sign of her. On his way out he was joined by the lawyer. Together they walked down the corridor.

'What a day,' said the lawyer. Hugh hadn't seen him so shaken since the day he'd had to give cash away to the crowd outside.

Coming towards them down the corridor was a figure carrying two cardboard boxes. At first Hugh thought it was one of the green-carders. Only when he got closer did he see it was Battersby. When he drew level with them Battersby stopped. He stared at Hugh. There was a hectic, uncomprehending sort of look in his eyes. Once or twice he seemed about to say something, but nothing came out. After a while he kept on walking.

The lawyer cleared his throat.

'Not much hope left for him, I'm afraid,' he said.

They walked out onto the marble staircase.

'Let's hope things get back to normal tomorrow,' said the lawyer.

'Do you think they might?'

'It's possible. Have you heard about the editor?'

'No. Is he . . . ?'

The lawyer shook his head.

'Not dead, no. Quite the reverse. He's better. The doctors are astounded. So much better that he's coming back to work in the morning. There's a surprise, eh?'

'Yes,' said Hugh. 'That is a surprise.'

'From what I hear he's a changed man.'

'In what way changed?'

'Apparently he feels out of touch with those things that most concern our readers. He wants to get a feel for their preoccupations. So in future he's going to come to work on public transport.'

'I've never heard of that happening before.'

'No,' said the lawyer. He pursed his lips disapprovingly. 'Let's hope it doesn't catch on.'

They reached the bottom of the stairs. Hugh held open the main door.

'Good night to you then, Hughie.' The lawyer raised his hand as if he were holding a glass. 'Here's to normality,' he said.

Owing to the editor's extended absence and his intention of returning to work by public transport, no-one was unduly alarmed by his non-appearance the following morning. It wasn't until after eleven o'clock that rumours

349

began to circulate that he had been involved in an accident. But after the excitement of the day before no-one showed much eagerness to take them seriously.

Shortly before twelve came the news that he had had a stroke. Later this turned out to be a misunderstanding. The editor had not had a stroke, he had been run over crossing the road to get to a bus stop. In the absence of any hard evidence, people embroidered what little they had as best they could. Hugh got up and went over to Cliff's desk. Julian was standing there, along with Bobbie and Gavin.

'It was a hit-and-run driver,' said Julian.

'Are you sure?'

'Positive.'

Strangely enough, he proved to be right. As the morning wore on, more information emerged.

'The driver took no notice at all,' said Julian. 'Drove on as if nothing had happened. Never stopped or anything. Weaving all over the place. Drunk, I suppose. A witness got the number, though.'

'What a fucker, eh?' said Bobbie. 'Who would do a thing like that?'

No-one could answer this.

'So how is the editor?' asked Cliff.

'Not at all good, I gather. They say it's only a matter of time.'

The telephone on his desk began to ring. Cliff ignored it.

'That's what they've been saying for months,' he said.

'This time at least there's the chance of a more accurate diagnosis. The car went right over him.'

Cliff struggled to compose his features into an appropriate expression of sorrow.

It was just before they went to lunch that they heard the editor had died. They sat in the pub in silence. At the next-door table a group of tourists were raking through the filling of their Pepys pies, forking the gristly lumps to one side.

'Still, it's an ill wind, eh, Cliff?' said Bobbie at last.

'What do you mean?'

'Well, there's no doubt who'll become editor now.'

'I don't know about that, Bobbie,' said Cliff. He endeavoured to convey an air of humility, as if he had never sought such a position but couldn't harden his heart against any tide of opinion in his favour. In this, thought Hugh, he wasn't entirely successful. But already his bearing had begun to change. His flesh appeared less mobile, more securely anchored to his frame, and he held his head higher than usual, as if posing for his portrait. His portable phone began to ring. Cliff heaved it onto his lap. He began twisting his head about and saying, 'I can't hear you.' He said it several times and with increasing irritation. Eventually he put the phone back down on the floor.

'Bad signal,' he explained. 'I just kept getting this wailing sound. Probably feedback.'

'I don't know why you bother with that stupid thing,' said Julian.

'You wait,' said Cliff. 'They're just teething problems, that's all.'

Only a few minutes later the same thing happened again. This time he shouted into the phone, 'I can't hear you, understand? Try later.'

Soon afterwards he began musing on the force of destiny.

'I've never been much of what you'd call a believer,' he said. 'But it does make you wonder, you know. If there isn't maybe . . .'

'What?' said Julian.

'A grand plan,' said Cliff simply. 'A natural process of adjustment. Whereby everything works out for the best in the end.'

In the absence of any reply, he went on, 'Circumstances, you see. Conspiring to bring about the most favourable possible outcome.'

'You're going a bit far for me there, Cliffy,' said Bobbie.

'Oh well,' said Cliff. 'Suit yourself.'

When they got back to the office Hugh cleared his desk. There wasn't much in his drawers and it didn't take him long. When he'd first joined the paper he'd opened his desk drawers to find that they were both completely full of cigarette ends – there must have been thousands of them in there. His predecessor had used the drawers as giant ashtrays. Before he'd started work he had to first empty them into rubbish bags. The ash rose in his face and settled on his clothes. Even now, the smell still stuck to the contents.

Cliff, meanwhile, was doing his best to be unruffled and statesmanlike. Various people came up to him, either to offer congratulations or to curry favour. As Hugh looked, he saw Industrial Gavin come into the office and walk towards Cliff, then stop some feet away.

Cliff had seen him, too. He beckoned him forward.

'Gavin,' he said. 'I was just saying how much I've come to rely on your good sense and guidance.'

Gavin, however, stayed where he was.

'He may not say much, but he's absolute gold dust,' said Cliff.

Gavin's face was as immobile as ever. But it seemed peculiarly stretched, as though two sets of people had taken hold of his ears and were pulling in opposite directions.

Cliff, however, hadn't noticed anything unusual. Again he beckoned him forward. 'Come and join us, Gavin. It's at times like these that you want your friends around you.'

But still Gavin didn't move.

'I wonder if I might have a word, Cliff,' he said.

Hugh tried to remember if he'd ever heard Gavin speak before. He supposed there must have been one or two occasions when Gavin had said something within his hearing. Nonetheless, the shock was considerable. All the more so, as Gavin's voice was nothing like Hugh had imagined. He'd always assumed it would have a dry, flinty sort of quality. Instead, it was soft and rather halting, though this might have been due to lack of use.

Everyone turned to look at Gavin.

Cliff hitched himself up. 'Whatever you have to say you can say it in front of these good people here,' he said.

Only now did Gavin come forward. Slowly, reluctantly, as if under extreme duress – less intent on making an announcement, so it seemed, than on reasoning with Cliff at closer quarters.

'They've found the driver,' he said.

'What driver?' said Cliff.

'The hit-and-run driver who killed the editor.'

'Have they?' said Cliff. 'Well, I'm delighted to hear it.'

'No,' said Gavin. 'No.'

'No?' said Cliff. He never liked anyone disagreeing with him. 'What do you mean, no?'

'It's Pauline,' said Gavin quietly.

'Pauline who?'

'Pauline your wife, Cliff.'

A strained sound came from Cliff's throat. It started like a laugh, then got caught and died away.

'Pauline ran over the editor?' he said.

'I'm afraid so.'

Everyone stood there, almost frozen. Cliff had tilted his head back, as if he were gazing at a flock of birds passing just above, skimming along under the ceiling. When he'd finished, he turned again to Gavin and said, 'Where is Pauline now?'

'They've arrested her. She's been trying to get in touch with you.'

Everyone parted before Cliff. He made his way to the exit – hands in his pockets, shoulders lowered – and squeezed his way between the two piles of desks. Once he had gone people began to speculate on what would happen now. On one point at least they could all agree: it would be inappropriate for Cliff to take charge of the paper when his wife had killed the previous editor.

Julian was standing by Hugh's chair. His arms hung limp by his side.

'I always told Cliff those eye exercises were a waste of time,' he said.

Chapter Thirty-Seven

At two o'clock on the following afternoon, as soon as the last edition of the paper had been printed, everyone filed out of the building and across the road to St Bride's Church. The sun was shining and there was a smell in the air that Hugh couldn't recognize. He realized it must be the smell of spring. The trees were even coming into bud. Little purple flowers bloomed between the graves.

By the time Hugh stepped inside the doors, the church was already filling up. He found himself being shown into a pew next to people he didn't recognize. He closed his eyes and listened to the sound of the traffic and the birdsong coming in through the open doors of the church. After a while they seemed to merge together.

He opened his eyes and looked around for familiar faces. On the other side of the aisle, three rows back, he saw Joy and Vivien sitting together. Joy was wearing a black pillbox hat with a piece of gauze hanging over her face. She was leaning forward and appeared to be praying. Vivien sat impassively alongside, her hair loose. Julian was further along the same pew.

Hugh could see no sign of Cliff. Up in the gallery the organ was playing. When the church was full, the priest got to his feet and announced that they were there to honour the memory of the late editor. First there were prayers, then 'Jerusalem' and then the choir sang an anthem. Their voices seemed to blur and thicken, rolling through the church and filling it with noise. And when the anthem was over, it was as if the sound of their voices hung like moisture in the air, slowly dispersing.

Through this mist came the figure of Stanley, holding a sheaf of papers in one hand and his green magnifying visor in the other. He walked without difficulty up to the lectern, arranging his papers in front of him before he started to speak.

When he did so, a murmur of surprise spread through the congregation. To begin with, Hugh couldn't work out what was going on. Meanwhile, Stanley kept talking, unaware that anything was amiss, his head stretched and flattened behind the visor, his voice growing in confidence as he went on.

He was, Hugh realized, speaking as if he were dictating a piece over the phone, complete with punctuation marks and any proper names or awkward words spelled out in full. Years of doing so had ingrained the practice in his mind so that it lay there like a template, hidden for the most part, but only showing through in times of stress.

'New par, cap T,' continued Stanley. 'Those qualities that had stood him in such good stead in cap B Barnsley, comma, were to prove especially valuable when he and cap J Janice moved down to cap L London, stop. Here, comma, amid the clatter and bustle of life on cap F Fleet cap S Street, comma, he found himself in his element, semi-colon, throwing himself with characteristic gusto, no e, into this new m–e–t–r–o–p–o–l–i–t–a–n world, stop.'

Hugh buried his face in his hands. Several people around him did the same. Eventually Stanley finished and made his way back to his seat. He was walking more slowly now and Hugh noticed that his bottom lip was turned over, showing more gum than usual. Once again the vicar got to his feet. There were prayers and responses, with the vicar's entreaties – 'O Lord hear our prayer' – being answered by a rumble of indistinct voices.

After this the proprietor got to his feet – a man whom Hugh had never seen before, except on television. Boxlike

356

in his double-breasted suit, holding both hands flat over his chest, almost as if he were being laid out himself, he gave a speech laying great emphasis on how the editor's life had been spent toiling in his service, thus ensuring financial stability as well as an unusually high degree of personal fulfilment.

Towards the end of his address, Hugh's attention was caught by the sight of figures moving about in the gallery above. As he watched, they advanced to the front of the gallery and stood there in a line, looking down. They all held something in their hands – long tubes of metal. Sudden flashes of golden light bounced about the church from hand to hand.

'To end our funeral service today, the congregation will rise and sing "The Battle Hymn of the Republic",' announced the vicar.

Everybody stood. A few introductory chords sounded on the organ.

'"Mine eyes have seen the glory of the coming of the Lord,"' they sang, '"He is trampling out the vintage where the grapes of wrath are stored."'

The trumpeters lifted their instruments to their lips and blew. The blare of brass made the air shudder and spread like a shelf across the church.

'"Glory, glory! Alleluia! Glory, glory! Alleluia! Glory, glory! Alleluia! His Truth is marching on."'

As he sang, Hugh let himself be carried along by the rhythm of the music. He found himself more moved than he had been for many years. But he couldn't help himself. All these emotions coursed through him, charging through his veins. Yet he didn't try to push them away, or dread them being there. Rather than engulf him as he'd always feared, they seemed instead to enrich him, to swell him out.

He had a chance for happiness. It wouldn't be there for long, and if he didn't try to take it soon it might be too late. Perhaps he was wrong, perhaps this was just another delusion, but it was all he had. And to squander it now would be the biggest mistake he'd ever made. For so long this spectre of self-consciousness had been at his heels, holding him back. It never left off. He'd given up trusting his reactions, even believing in them. They always struck him as either underpowered, or laid on too thick, or inappropriate in some way or other.

He thought of being with Vivien and that sense of being flopped over, freed of all those things that normally held him back. It was like a mirror world. Somewhere he'd given up thinking could really exist. But there it was, opening, however briefly, before him. He only had to slide through and there he'd be – turned on his head, his circuits reversed.

'"Glory, glory! Alleluia!"' they sang.

Their voices rose, the trumpets blared. '"Glory, glory! Alleluia! Glory, glory! Alleluia! His Truth is marching on."'

At the end of the hymn there was a period of silence, and then a final prayer. Afterwards, people began to leave the church. Hugh stayed where he was for a while. He felt awash with feelings. At the same time the great hum of life resounded around him. When he opened his eyes he saw that the church was empty, except for the priest and a group of people standing uncertainly by some flowers. He walked past them, through the door and out into the churchyard.

He'd hoped he might find Vivien sitting on her bench, but there was no sign of her. He walked back through the loading bay to the main entrance to the office. Now the bay was empty. No lorries, no rolls of paper, nothing there except a thin slick of oil on the ground. In the hallway people were still milling about, the usual busy knots of petitioners and complainers. *The Triumph of Truth over Falsehood* had finally been removed. In the space where it had been, instructions, presumably to do with its installation, had been chalked on the wall – figures and angles and lines of smudged scrawl. Whoever had written them, thought Hugh, must be long dead by now.

In the office those journalists that hadn't yet packed up were busy doing so. The piles of discarded furniture had grown bigger; they almost reached the ceiling. On top of the left-hand one Hugh was surprised to see Darren's tea trolley. It looked as though it had been thrown up there. The thin metal legs and black castors were sticking in the air.

He found Joy shovelling the contents of one of her desk drawers into a polythene bag.

'Have you seen Vivien?' he asked.

'Vivien? What do you want her for?'

'Just tell me if you've seen her.'

Joy stopped and looked up. She blinked at him in surprise. 'I have actually. You've just missed her.'

'Where did she go?'

'I think she was heading downstairs.'

'Downstairs? What did she go down there for?'

'I don't know,' said Joy. 'She just wandered off. You know what she's like. Perhaps she just wanted a last look round.'

Hugh headed down the stairs to the floor below. Unsure of where to look, he headed first towards the library. The library was locked, but Walter's room next door was open. The room was empty. There was no sign of Walter, nor any of the green-carders. Nor of the piles of paper that were usually on his table. Nor of the keys that hung behind his head. The room was as bare as Hollis's office had been.

He walked down the empty corridors. A couple of times he called out Vivien's name, but there was no reply. He pushed open a set of double doors and found himself in the typesetting room. He remembered the first time he'd come in here – seeing the typesetters at work, sitting on their saddles like charioteers urging their machines on. The air full of shards of lead and noise. Men in brown aprons shouldering him aside.

Now this room was deserted. The machines were standing idle, the long tables bare. He walked on, expecting to feel the great thump of the presses beneath his feet at any moment, steadily growing louder. But there was nothing. He walked through to the other end of the room and down a flight of stairs. Still he'd seen no-one.

The canteen too was empty. Chairs piled on top of tables. Nothing on the shelves, or in the glass hatches behind the self-service counter. He came out of the canteen and went down another flight of stairs, along a length of corridor and through two sets of swing doors. The room ahead of him was in darkness. He had no idea where the switches were. Something – it was more the scale of the darkness around him than anything else – made him realize he was in the room with the presses. He could smell printing ink, that familiar rich black tang. As his eyes grew used to the darkness, he was able to make out the huge gleaming bulk of the printing presses ahead of him, like half-submerged submarines.

There was no sound apart from his footsteps on the asphalt floor. He made his way forward until he came to the safety mesh that surrounded the press. Keeping one hand on the mesh, he walked along the length of the press, shuffling his feet forward so that he didn't trip over anything. Slowly another press took shape before him. Again he shuffled forward until he felt the wire cage around it. If anything, the light seemed to diminish as he made his way along the second printing press. Several times he thought of turning round, but it was no easier finding his way back than it was carrying on.

When he got to the far end of the second press, he stopped, trying to remember the layout of the room. He'd only been here once before. He remembered the little open doorways and the rooms beyond, like monks' cells.

But between the end of the second press and the row of doorways he encountered an unforeseen obstacle. He banged into something. Not hard, but the shock made him gasp and step back. He put out his hands, feeling about. There appeared to be a line of pillars in front of him, rising up above his head, each pillar pressed tight against its

360

neighbour. He realized they must be drums of ink, stacked on top of one another.

When he got to the end of the ink drums, he realized he no longer had any idea where he was in relation to the row of doorways. All the while he kept expecting the gloom to lighten. He stayed still, trying to get his bearings. The longer he stayed there, the less certain he was. For a while he thought he could see these blacker rectangles laid out before him in the darkness, like the entrances to tombs. But when he started towards them they melted away, losing what faint definition they had. So he retraced his steps. As soon as he was back where he'd been before, they took shape before him again.

He kept still, listening, hoping he'd hear something he could aim for. After a few minutes of this he launched himself once more into the darkness. The rectangles disappeared, then seemed to hover uncertainly before him. He kept going. His hand touched something. A length of wall. He moved his hand across it and came to an edge. He ran his hand up the edge. Just above his head there was a right angle. The edge ran up, then along. He realized he was standing in the entrance of one of the cells. As he moved forward, he stepped on pages of paper, scattered about the floor.

He put his hand down, below his knee, and touched a bench. He patted the top of the bench, then turned himself round and sat down. The darkness pressed upon him, crowding in like a cloud of noiseless insects, wings flattened against his face. When he got up to go he had difficulty finding the door. He thought he'd reached it, but his hands only touched another expanse of wall. He'd just located the opening once more when he heard a noise coming from the next-door cell.

He stopped. The noise seemed to stop with him. When he started again, the noise did too, like a ragged echo of his own footsteps. This time, though, it continued briefly after he had stopped. He wondered if it could be rats. But there was something more solid, more weighty about it than that. He got to the doorway and felt his way around the wall until he found the next entrance.

The noise had stopped. He stayed waiting in the doorway. When the noise came again, he realized that it wasn't coming from this cell, but the next one along. There was a dim light too, a worn patch in the darkness, like a child's night light.

As he started towards it, the light went out and the darkness swept back in. He waited for a while, listening. Although he heard nothing, he had the sense that there was someone close by, holding their breath. Staying as quiet as he was.

Keeping his back against the wall, he started to make his way into the next-door cell. There were more papers on the floor in here. He could see these misty white shapes down by his feet and feel them rustling whenever he moved. He tried to work out if there was anyone else in there with him. He peered into the gloom, expecting to see some human form take shape before him at any moment. But there was nothing. Then he heard the noise again. The sound of someone clearing their throat.

'Hello,' he called out. 'Vivien, is that you?'

There seemed something disapproving about the silence that followed.

'What are you doing down here?'

He'd emerged from the second cell and was standing outside, unsure what to do next, when he saw the light go on. Not inside one of the cells, but outside, only a matter of yards away from where he was standing. The light was dimmer this time. He couldn't be sure if it was a candle or a torch.

This time he saw that there was a figure holding the light, with its back turned towards him. He caught a glimpse of sloping shoulders, a baggy coat of some kind, sleeves hanging down. Hugh moved towards the light. As he got closer the figure turned towards him. This thin, wavering beam of light pointed in his direction. So dim it barely reached him, but still enough to conceal the identity of whoever was behind.

He kept on walking. Then the beam of light jerked sharply across his path. He stopped.

'Have you brought it?' came a voice.

'Brought what?' said Hugh.

'Who's that?'

'It's . . . My name is Hugh Byrne,' he said.

There was a pause.

The beam of light swung towards the floor.

'Well, well, well. Hello, Hughie.'

Chapter Thirty-Eight

Hugh moved towards the torch beam. It stayed pointing at the floor, then climbed up his legs towards his face.

'Who's there?' he said.

'Don't you know, Hughie?'

'I – I can't see. Your voice is familiar though.'

'I should hope so.'

The torch beam turned again. This time pointed straight upwards. The figure before him looked as if it had stepped from a painting, some thickly varnished nocturnal landscape. Travellers seeking rest, seeing a half-open doorway with a figure inside, holding a lamp to illuminate a darkened hallway. A thinner, much more ragged figure than he remembered. But recognizable for all that.

Hugh stopped.

'Bit of a surprise, eh?'

'Yes,' Hugh admitted. 'Yes, you could say that.'

Again Scaife laughed. 'It's been a while, hasn't it? And I dare say I'm not looking my best. But you wouldn't be, either. Not if you'd been down here for as long as I have.'

Hugh saw that Scaife's hair had turned grey, and his skin seemed to be the same colour, like old bed linen. He'd also lost a lot of weight and his clothes hung off him in long pleats. Hugh realized he was wearing one of the green-carders' dun-coloured cardigans.

'I thought you were dead,' he said. 'There was a body

matching your description found on a hillside in southern Spain.'

'Was there?' said Scaife. 'That's news to me. Still . . . it could be useful.'

'And all the time you've been down here.'

'You don't know what it's been like for me, Hughie. All alone with no-one to talk to. Just my food once a day. And then even that stopped coming. I thought I was going to die. I haven't seen anyone for almost two days now. Where's everybody gone?'

'I'm not sure,' said Hugh.

'They left me here. Oh, Hughie, it's been terrible. You can't imagine.'

'You've been here all this time?'

The torch beam swung up towards him again. Hugh could see the filament in the bulb burning weakly; it looked more brown than yellow.

'I'll show you,' he said. He led the way past several more doorways, then ducked down slightly – the light bobbed with him – disappearing into another sloping black rectangle. Hugh followed him. He found himself in a cell, just like the others, but with an inflatable mattress on the floor, and a jug and a pile of dirty plates stacked up at one end.

'This my home,' said Scaife. 'Sit down, if you like.'

'I'm all right standing up.'

'Bit squeamish, eh? Can't say I blame you.'

Scaife sat down on the mattress. Both ends rose off the floor and jutted out on either side of him like wings.

'At first I was out there,' said Scaife; he pointed towards the entrance. 'Underneath the printing presses. There's this great pit where they load the rolls of paper onto the machines. They built me this makeshift cell from panels of wood.'

'Ah, yes,' said Hugh. 'The lavatory doors.'

'I was there for weeks,' Scaife went on. 'Walled up in this black hut. In the early days they let me out once in a while to stretch my legs, but then they said it was getting

365

too dangerous. Then, about ten days ago, they moved me up here. Said someone was bound to spot me down there, what with everybody moving out. Not much of an improvement, as you can see.'

'But what happened?'

There was a candle in a saucer beside the plates. Scaife lit the candle and turned off the torch.

'Ever since . . . ever since my difficulties at home? I suppose you know all about that. Well, I didn't know what to do, where to go. I knew the police were going to come looking for me, but I didn't have enough money to get away. And then I thought of here. I'd found out some things about the green-carders, you see.'

'What sort of things?'

'When my wife and I first began to get on badly, I slept in the office for a while, under my desk. I wasn't the only one, there was a whole group of us. I couldn't sleep too well. Hardly surprising, I suppose. So I started wandering about. One night I went down to the canteen – it had just reopened after another botulism scare – and I saw these down-and-outs there. Some of them were dressed almost in rags, all eating away as if they hadn't had a decent meal in ages.

'I can't say I paid much attention at first. Then, a few days later, I was having a look round one of the cubby holes where the green-carders sit and I came across these ledger books. There were two of them, both the same size. I started having a look through. Idle curiosity really. But after a while it became clear that there was something funny going on.

'I've always been pretty good with figures – probably better with figures than with words, if the truth be told. One book contained the official figures that had been prepared in the bought ledger office. All perfectly above board. The other one was the same in a lot of respects, but not entirely. There were additions, amendments and so on. The figures had been altered, and so had the names.

'I realized the green-carders were intercepting one set of

books when they came down from bought ledger, then preparing their own figures, which they sent on to accounts. Once I'd got that far, it didn't take me long to work out what they must be doing: putting their friends on the payroll, all sorts of wastrels and God knows what. Anyone who took their fancy. Running the place like a bloody charity shop. They must have been doing it for years. Quite clever really. No-one would ever have suspected them because they thought they were all a bunch of half-wits.

'I put the books back, as if nothing had happened. The next day I went to see one of the green-carders – a very twitchy type who worked in the library.'

'Hollis.'

'That's the one. I told him what I'd found and asked him what was going on. I thought he was going to pass out there and then. He got into a terrible state, said it was nothing to do with him, and he didn't know what I was talking about, although it was perfectly clear he did.'

'Hollis killed himself,' said Hugh.

'I can't say I'm surprised,' said Scaife. 'He obviously lived on his nerves. But before I could find out anything else, my wife phoned up. She told me she'd fallen for the man who ran the local off-licence and wanted a divorce. Came as a hell of a blow, I don't mind telling you, Hughie. I looked upon this man as a friend of mine. God knows, I'd given him enough custom.

'So I went back home to reason with her. But by the time I got there she'd already moved out. I went round to his place, and that's where things turned a bit nasty. It's all been blown up out of all proportion, though. Attempted murder and all that. Actually, I'm hoping the police might drop the charges now that the dust has settled.'

'I wouldn't have thought so.'

'Why not?'

'The man's still in a coma, as far as I know.'

'I never hit him that hard, you know, Hughie. Only a little tap.'

'You hit him with a shovel.'

'Don't get all pious on me. You were always like that. Anyway, afterwards, I didn't know what to do. I was all in a spin. Then I thought of the green-carders and a little scheme began to hatch in my mind. So I came back here and went to see the head man.'

'Walter.'

'Yes,' said Scaife bitterly. 'That's right, Walter. I told him what I'd found out about them and I persuaded him to look after me for a while.'

'So you blackmailed him.'

'Blackmail!' cried Scaife. 'You see, you're doing it again. Don't be so melodramatic. We reached an accommodation whereby they'd protect me in return for my keeping quiet. I thought, under the circumstances, it was quite a good arrangement. They gave me clothes and brought me food, and for a time it all seemed all right. Then the meals started getting less regular. One day they didn't bring me anything at all. When I asked what was going on they told me to mind my own business. Very brusque and uncaring, not pleasant at all. It occurred to me then that maybe this wasn't such a good arrangement. In fact, they could do anything they liked with me, and there wasn't much I could do about it.

'Then I realized they'd got this other scheme going,' said Scaife.

'What other scheme?'

'I overheard these two green-carders talking one night, outside my cell. They must have forgotten I was there. They were discussing how they were going to distribute the money. It didn't make any sense to me at first. They were walking about, so it was difficult for me to follow their conversation. But then, as they went on, I realized what they were up to. They weren't just putting their friends on the payroll. It was much bigger than that. Much bigger. They were bleeding the entire paper dry. Syphoning off all the money into offshore tax havens.'

'No!'

'Yes! Same scheme as before: intercepting one lot of books and substituting them with another. Making up their own figures and sending them on to accounts. Never too much at any one time, but every month, without fail, they'd cream off some more. The management never guessed. I suppose they'd got so used to losing money on the paper that they assumed it was nothing out of the ordinary.

'They've got the lot. Everything. All those old cripples in their cardigans. Even that nasty little shit who used to bring round the teas.'

'Darren?'

'Yes, Darren; he was in on it, too.'

'So what's happened to them now?'

'That's what I'm trying to tell you. You're not much of a listener, are you, Hughie? I thought you were supposed to be a journalist. Yesterday I didn't get my food again. I thought maybe there'd been another mistake – at least that's what I told myself. They'd be along soon. They wouldn't just leave me. I mean, it's not humane.

'Then today, the same thing – no food, nothing. I went looking for them and they've gone, the bastards. Cleared out.'

'Where to?'

'I don't know. Somewhere they can't be traced in a hurry, that's for sure.'

Hugh began to laugh. The sound resounded round the small cell.

Scaife was shocked. 'I must say I'm surprised at you, Hughie. Taking that sort of attitude. They've ruined the paper, don't you realize? There's nothing left. And what's going to happen to me? I haven't eaten for days. I need food.'

'I suppose I could go out and get some.'

'Would you, Hughie? Be a pal. And some batteries for my torch, if you don't mind.'

Hugh took the torch so that he could find his way out. He walked through the deserted printing hall, up the stairs, then through the typesetting room. There was a sandwich bar on the other side of Fleet Street which was just closing up for the day. He bought two packets of sandwiches and some biscuits, and some batteries from the newsagent. When he got back Scaife was still sitting on his mattress, the candle burning alongside.

'There you are,' he said. 'I was beginning to think you'd cleared off, too. Mind the bucket.'

Scaife crammed the food into his mouth, hardly bothering to chew it. When he'd finished he took several swigs from the jug, then toppled over onto his side, clutching his stomach.

'Are you all right?'

'Argh,' he groaned.

'What's the matter?'

Scaife sat up. 'You must help me, Hughie. I've got to get away from here. How much money have you got?'

Hugh took out his wallet. He had ten pounds and some loose change. He held out the money to Scaife, who didn't attempt to hide his disappointment.

'Is that it? That's not going to get me very far. Haven't you got anything else?'

'I'm afraid not.'

'What, nothing at all?'

Then Hugh remembered that he did have something else. He reached into the inside pocket of his jacket, took it out and gave it to him.

Scaife held it towards the candle flame.

'What the fuck's this?'

'It's a Seaman's Discharge Book.'

'A what? It sounds disgusting. What use is that to me?'

Hugh explained how it would enable him to stay in Seaman's Missions, and might even help him to get a job. Scaife was still unimpressed. He turned it over in his hands and put it in his cardigan; there were two pockets sewn into the sides, like little string bags. Then he got to his feet.

'What are you going to do?' Hugh asked.

'What can I do? I'm lighting out for the territory. Isn't that what they used to say in the olden days?'

'Something like that.'

'Strange that it should end like this. I can't really say I'll miss anyone. What's happened to old Joy? She wasn't too bad.'

'Joy's OK.'

'And that friend of hers she always hangs around with.'

'Vivien.'

'Vivien, that's right. I could never stand her. Stroppy bitch.'

'She never liked you, either.'

'Didn't she?' said Scaife. He sounded more pitying than surprised.

'She said you tried to pick her up once. In the Ladies.'

'Did I? I don't remember. Maybe I did. It all seems such a long time ago now.'

They stood in silence for a while. The candlelight flickered around them.

'Think of me once in a while, won't you, Hughie.'

'I will,' he promised.

Together, they walked through the printing room to the double doors. When Hugh pulled open the door, Scaife shrank back into the shadows. Hugh's last sight of him was turning and walking away, his cardigan trailing behind him, until this too was swallowed up in the darkness.

Chapter Thirty-Nine

Upstairs, Hugh saw Cliff standing by himself in the middle of the floor. Bobbie and Industrial Gavin were walking over to join him. All around the desks had been cleared. There was nothing left, only a huge expanse of wrinkled carpet tiles and a coat-stand propped against the wall. He was reminded of one of those films in which the Earth has been devastated by a mysterious cataclysm and the survivors gather to survey the ruins of their world. They beckoned him over.

'How's Pauline?' Hugh asked.

'Not too bad considering,' said Cliff. 'Obviously, the conditions of bail don't make it easy.'

Gavin cleared his throat and said, 'I've got an announcement to make.'

He put his arm around Bobbie's shoulders. Bobbie was looking much tidier than usual, Hugh noticed – hair straightened, a new royal-blue outfit.

'We're getting married,' said Gavin.

'Married?' said Cliff.

'That's right.'

Cliff looked from one to the other.

'You must have guessed,' said Bobbie.

'No,' said Cliff. 'Never.'

'It must be quite a shock then.'

'It is a shock,' Cliff admitted.

'That's not all,' said Gavin. 'We're leaving, too. We're going to buy a little cake shop. Somewhere in the Highlands if we can. Our families are both up there. You'll both be very welcome to stay.'

'Although it might get a bit crowded,' warned Bobbie.

'It might get a bit crowded,' Gavin agreed. 'Bobbie's pregnant, you see.'

'Are you sure?' said Cliff hoarsely.

'Oh yes. Almost two months gone now.'

'What are you going to do, Cliff?' Hugh asked.

'Christ knows,' he said. He flicked up one of the carpet tiles with his foot. 'I suppose I might have to go into television.'

Hugh became aware of a figure in a red coat moving towards the coat-stand, picking up something, then heading for the exit. He realized it was Vivien.

'I've got to go,' he said.

'Why? Where to?' said Cliff.

But Hugh had already begun to move away. He lifted his hand. 'Goodbye,' he said to them. 'Goodbye.'

He turned and walked swiftly towards the lifts, past the recess where the vending machine had been. He could see Vivien at the end of the corridor, pushing open the doors that led out onto the main stairwell. He hurried after her. But when he reached the lifts she'd gone. He leaned over the marble parapet, and heard, rather than saw, her make her way down the stairs, heels clicking on the steps.

He followed, running after her footsteps. As he rounded each new bend he expected to see her, but all he ever saw was this flash of red, less like a definite sighting, more like a stain left in the air. He was almost at the bottom when he saw Julian coming towards him. Julian was wearing a new suit. Whereas his clothes usually served only to accentuate the angular, jagged shape of his body, this suit smoothed down any such awkward contours, making him look almost plump, or at least cushioned. Sleek. He moved in a quite different way too, each step measured and molten.

'Where are you going?' he asked.

Behind Julian's shoulder Hugh could see Vivien pushing open the main doors.

'I can't stop now,' said Hugh.

But Julian had moved in front of him and was barring his path.

'What do you mean?' he said.

'I'll explain later.'

'You can't just run off like this,' said Julian. 'It's still office hours, you know.'

Half turning around, Vivien held open the door for someone to follow behind her.

'Later,' said Hugh.

He endeavoured to push past, but ran into one of Julian's outstretched arms.

'Wouldn't you like to hear my ideas?'

'I don't care about your fucking ideas,' said Hugh. 'I'm not interested.'

Julian stiffened. A little of Cliff's affront had already transferred itself to him. 'I think you will be. They're very radical, just like I promised.'

Hugh could see Vivien through the glass door – the top of her head, the same dim flash of red – as she joined the dark mass of people outside and disappeared, swallowed up among them.

'You haven't even congratulated me,' said Julian.

'Congratulations,' said Hugh.

'Thank you. Of course, it was quite an enlightened gesture on their part even to consider me. But the interview went better than I could have dreamed of. I think it was the calibre of my ideas that so impressed the board. I've never been so fluent or persuasive. I don't mind telling you, Hughie, I was a revelation to myself.'

Again Hugh tried to push past Julian. Again Julian held him back. Lazily, almost absent-mindedly.

'What are you in such a hurry about?' he asked.

'Get out of my way!'

'I beg your pardon.'

'Get out of my way!' shouted Hugh. 'Haven't I done enough for you already?'

'For me?' said Julian. 'For me? What have you ever done for me?'

But the shock of Hugh shouting had unsettled him. He drew his arm back in surprise. Hugh pushed past, spinning him round. But by the time he got through the door and out onto the street, Vivien had long gone. He stood there on the pavement as people surged around him like water round a rock.

It was dusk. The street lights had already been turned on. Hugh crossed the street, squeezing between the stacked-up cars, then found himself temporarily swept along by the crowd. It was as if he had to anchor himself to the pavement to stop them carrying him any further. He ducked down the alleyway by the side of the church and looked in the churchyard, but the benches were all empty. He ran down past the second-hand bookshops and the sandwich bars, through the narrow gap between the buildings and out onto the main road.

Now he ran down the road towards the tube station, turning round, looking for another red stain in the air. Once or twice he thought he saw her. Each time he realized he was wrong, but only after he'd almost succeeded in moulding the person's features into roughly the right shape, refashioning them with his eyes, giving them some semblance of Vivien – of the way she held her chin, or the slope of her nose. Then he saw that it wasn't her and the remoulded features seemed to disintegrate before him and become suddenly quite unrecognizable.

He hurried on. Craning upwards, stretching to see. There was a thin, almost feathery feel to the air. It blew against the sweat on his face and past him, across the tops of other people's heads. When he got to the entrance to the tube he stopped and spun round, thinking that perhaps she might have taken some roundabout route and had ended up behind him. But she wasn't there. She didn't come.

He bought a ticket at the machine and went down the

escalator. He looked on both platforms, running from one to the other. But there were only the usual lines of commuters, standing at the edge of the platforms, staring out across the dark trench beyond, waiting for the trains to come.

It was only now that he acknowledged he had lost her. She had gone. Standing there in the passageway between the platforms as the trains came and went, back and forth on either side. The shush of the doors, the twang of the rails as another train approached. Hugh thought of getting on one – he didn't mind where to – but he couldn't face it. Instead, he went back up the escalator, handing in his unused ticket and going out onto the street.

The rush of people was thinning. The sluice had opened and out they all rushed, but eventually the flow died away. He waited by the station entrance. No longer with any hope of seeing Vivien. No longer even bothering to look for her. Just idly loafing. He began to walk towards the river. The road rose up slightly as it approached the bridge. The air turned colder as he got closer. Before he reached the middle of the bridge he stopped. There was a bench set back from the balustrade, and he sat there for a while, gazing up to Tower Bridge. There were no boats to be seen and the surface of the water looked quite unruffled. The lights in the office blocks were reflected perfectly within. Each building, each street light, appeared to have its own perfectly inverted double.

It was only when he got up from the bench and went over to the balustrade that he saw how they all shimmered slightly in the water. He wondered where he belonged – in the harsh, bright world above, or in this brittle, quivering illusion below. He put his hands flat on top of the balustrade. When he looked down, he saw that the water was moving faster than he would have believed. It rushed by, under his feet, hurrying towards the sea, as if it couldn't wait to get away from this hard mass of concrete stacked up on both sides. He saw how the water swept around the foot of the piles. It frothed and churned and gave out long rending sucking noises. And he thought of that scooped basin of mud below the water, the soft clay bed with bodies rolled up there like sleepers.

Things had changed for him, he realized. Everything had been shaken up, thrown in the air. He'd always thought of the future unfolding before him like some length of rush matting, dry and neatly trimmed. He'd clung to certainties, battened on to any beliefs he could find, whoever they might have belonged to. Now the future flapped about before him, wild and untethered, and he had no idea where it led.

When he turned away, he became aware of another figure standing several yards away, also looking out over the river. And there was something else, a kind of ruddy blur at the corner of his eye. He saw the figure lean forward, hunched over the balustrade, head bent. As he looked, it straightened up and turned.

Now quite the opposite thing happened to him. Before, he had tried to convince himself that one of the faces in the crowd might belong to Vivien, only to find it disintegrating before him. Now he had a job convincing himself that this could be her. As if she too might fly apart at any moment and leave him feeling more bereft than ever.

He moved towards her. But someone hurried between them and he had to hang back and check his step to allow them through. The closer he got, the more convinced he was that Vivien would crack or crumble before him, or stage some other kind of disappearing act. But she didn't. She stayed where she was and watched him approach.

'I thought I'd lost you,' he said.

She didn't speak. Again he had the sense that he might be addressing an illusion.

'I saw you go,' he said. 'I saw you go through the doors, but when I got out you'd gone. I looked everywhere – the churchyard, the tube station, on the street. You weren't there. I thought I'd lost you.'

'You're here now,' said Vivien.

'I am here now,' confirmed Hugh. Nonetheless, it was all rather too arbitrary for his taste.

There was a breeze coming off the river; it buffeted around them in chilly gusts. Vivien had her coat buttoned to the neck, her collar turned up and her arms wrapped across her chest. The cold didn't agree with her; it made her more withdrawn, harder to penetrate than ever. Her face appeared unusually pale.

'I can't stop thinking about you,' he said. 'Every time I close my eyes it's as if your face seems to rise up in front of me. Even when I'm asleep it feels as if it's there, underneath my eyelids. I feel as if you're all around. And then, when I wake up, you're there too – never far away. That's never happened to me before.'

'You might get over it,' said Vivien.

'No I won't,' he said vehemently. 'Don't think that, because it's not true. I'll never get over it. I don't want to get over it.'

Vivien gripped the top of her coat under her chin with her gloved hand.

'You never even told me what happened with Kingman.'

So he told her about going to the coast, about finding Kingman, and putting Darren's article in the paper. And then, by way of a last flourish, he told her about adding Julian's name to the list of editorial candidates.

'I had you wrong,' she said when he'd finished. 'I never realized you were so devious.'

'No,' said Hugh. 'Well, nor did I.'

They were only standing a couple of feet apart. He wanted to reach out and touch her; to make some movement, however fractional.

'Meeting you changed me,' he said.

'In what way?'

'Well, I wanted to be worthy of you.'

She laughed, shortly. 'Don't be ridiculous.'

'No. It's true.'

'What are you going to do?' asked Vivien.

'I'm not going back. Not any more.'

'No,' she said. 'I'm not going back either.'

They looked out over the water, watching the buildings shimmering all around.

'What do you want?'

'I want to be with you,' said Hugh.

She looked at him and said something, but a gust of wind took her words and carried them away.

'What did you say?'

'I said good. I'm glad.'

'Really?'

'Yes.'

'You mean it?'

'Don't push me,' said Vivien.

There seemed to be a clamour in the air, although he couldn't be sure where it was coming from, whether from inside him, or outside. It swelled around them both like the tramping of feet and died away. Afterwards, they stood there for a few moments, not saying anything. Over Vivien's shoulder Hugh could see the far end of the bridge, bright and orange under the lights.

'Shall we go then?' he said.

THE END

Acknowledgements

I would like to thank the following for their help: Revd David Hodgson of Missions to Seamen, Tilbury; Reg Hulbert, Former Production Manager of the *Daily Telegraph*; PC Nigel Selby, Divisional Identification Officer at Wapping police station and Terry Simco of the Queen Victoria Seaman's Rest in Poplar.

I am indebted to *The Strange Voyage of Donald Crowhurst* by Nicholas Tomalin and Ron Hall, Hodder & Stoughton, 1970.

Above all, I would like to thank Bill Scott-Kerr for his patience and encouragement.

GHOSTING
John Preston

Dickie's one asset, it seems, is a smooth and seductive voice.
His career, at first distinguished only by its indistinction –
as a stagehand at a provincial theatre, then a filing clerk at
the BBC – is unexpectedly propelled into orbit when the
usual late-night radio announcer swallows a locust.
Dickie steps into the breach and knows for the first
time the meaning of success.

From gentle midnight intonations to TV quiz show presenter
and so-called 'personality', Dickie's rise through the fledgling
media world of the 1950s is meteoric, his indistinction the
perfect vehicle for the requisite BBC accent and brilliantined
charm. But as his success grows, so does the likelihood that
his darker past will reveal itself, especially when he begins
to see the bleak spectre of his father who he had spurned
many years before . . .

Beautifully-written and original, chilling and bitingly
funny, *Ghosting* is at once a revealing portrait of radio and
television's first faltering steps, and one man's battle to
reconcile past failures with present triumphs.

0 552 99667 X

BLACK SWAN

HUMAN CROQUET
Kate Atkinson

'VIVID AND INTRIGUING . . . FIZZLES AND CRACKLES
ALONG . . . A COMPELLING STORY WITH EXCURSIONS
INTO FANTASY, EXPERIMENT AND OUTRAGEOUS
GRAND GUIGNOL . . . A *TOUR DE FORCE*'
Penelope Lively, *Independent*

Once it had been the great forest of Lythe – a vast and impen-
etrable thicket of green with a mystery in the very heart of the
trees. And here, in the beginning, lived the Fairfaxes, grandly,
at Fairfax Manor, visited once by the great Gloriana herself.

But over the centuries the forest had been destroyed, replaced
by Streets of Trees. The Fairfaxes had dwindled too; now
they lived in 'Arden' at the end of Hawthorne Close and
were hardly a family at all.

There was Vinny (the Aunt from Hell) – with her cats and her
crab-apple face. And Gordon, who had forgotten them for
seven years and, when he remembered, came back with fat
Debbie, who shared her one brain cell with a poodle. And
then there were Charles and Isobel, the children. Charles, the
acne-scarred Lost Boy, passed his life awaiting visits from
aliens and the return of his mother. But it is Isobel to whom
the story belongs – Isobel, born on the Streets of Trees, who
drops into pockets of time and out again. Isobel is sixteen
and she too is waiting for the return of her mother – the
thin, dangerous Eliza with her scent of nicotine, Arpège
and sex, whose disappearance is part of the mystery
that still remains at the heart of the forest.

'READS LIKE A DARKER SHENA MACKAY OR A FUNNIER,
MORE LITERARY BARBARA VINE. VIVID, RICHLY
IMAGINATIVE, HILARIOUS AND FRIGHTENING BY TURNS'
Cressida Connolly, *Observer*

0 552 99619 X

BLACK SWAN

A SELECTED LIST OF FINE WRITING
AVAILABLE FROM BLACK SWAN

THE PRICES SHOWN BELOW WERE CORRECT AT THE TIME OF GOING TO PRESS. HOWEVER
TRANSWORLD PUBLISHERS RESERVE THE RIGHT TO SHOW NEW RETAIL PRICES ON COVERS
WHICH MAY DIFFER FROM THOSE PREVIOUSLY ADVERTISED IN THE TEXT OR ELSEWHERE.

99619	X	HUMAN CROQUET	*Kate Atkinson*	£6.99
99674	2	ACTS OF REVISION	*Martyn Bedford*	£6.99
99832	X	SNAKE IN THE GRASS	*Georgia Blain*	£6.99
99532	0	SOPHIE	*Guy Burt*	£5.99
99686	6	BEACH MUSIC	*Pat Conroy*	£7.99
99833	8	BLAST FROM THE PAST	*Ben Elton*	£6.99
99827	3	IN COLD DOMAIN	*Anne Fine*	£6.99
99721	8	BEFORE WOMEN HAD WINGS	*Connie May Fowler*	£6.99
99731	5	BLUEPRINT FOR A PROPHET	*Carl Gibeily*	£6.99
99679	3	SAP RISING	*A.A. Gill*	£6.99
99760	9	THE DRESS CIRCLE	*Laurie Graham*	£6.99
99677	7	THE INFLUENCING ENGINE	*Richard Hayden*	£6.99
99796	X	A WIDOW FOR ONE YEAR	*John Irving*	£7.99
99037	X	BEING THERE	*Jerzy Kosinski*	£5.99
99748	X	THE BEAR WENT OVER THE MOUNTAIN		
			William Kotzwinkle	£6.99
99807	9	MONTENEGRO	*Starling Lawrence*	£6.99
99569	X	MAYBE THE MOON	*Armistead Maupin*	£6.99
99762	5	THE LACK BROTHERS	*Malcolm McKay*	£6.99
99785	4	GOODNIGHT, NEBRASKA	*Tom McNeal*	£6.99
99718	8	IN A LAND OF PLENTY	*Tim Pears*	£6.99
99667	X	GHOSTING	*John Preston*	£6.99
99783	8	DAY OF ATONEMENT	*Jay Rayner*	£6.99
99810	9	THE JUKEBOX QUEEN OF MALTA		
			Nicholas Rinaldi	£6.99
99122	8	THE HOUSE OF GOD	*Samuel Shem*	£7.99
99846	X	THE WAR ZONE	*Alexander Stuart*	£6.99
99809	5	KICKING AROUND	*Terry Taylor*	£6.99

Transworld titles are available by post from:

Book Service By Post, PO Box 29, Douglas, Isle of Man, IM99 1BQ

Credit cards accepted. Please telephone 01624 675137
fax 01624 670923, Internet http://www.bookpost.co.uk
or e-mail: bookshop@enterprise.net for details

Free postage and packing in the UK. Overseas customers: allow £1 per
book (paperbacks) and £3 per book (hardbacks).